MY
SAVAGE
MUSE

MY
SAVAGE
MUSE

The Story of My Life

EDGAR ALLAN POE

——————

An Imaginative Work by

BERNHARDT J. HURWOOD

EVEREST HOUSE   HOUSE
Publishers   New York

To
Laura, Ann, Moira,
Ritva, and Vir

ACKNOWLEDGMENTS

THIS BOOK COULD NEVER HAVE BEEN written without the support and encouragement of family, friends, and colleagues. Their contributions, from inception to completion, were invaluable. I am indebted, too, to the scholars whose previously published works provided the sources from which all my research was gathered, and to the staffs at libraries from which these works were obtained: The New York Public Library, The New York Historical Society, The Bronx Historical Society, and The New York Society Library, where Poe once lectured. Deserving also of special thanks is my friend Vladimir R. Piskacek who took time from his crowded psychiatric practice to devote hours and days instructing me in psychodynamics and arcana of literature, mythology, and European history germane to *My Savage Muse*. To mention the names of all those who contributed in some measure to this book would require something on the order of a small telephone directory. I would be most remiss, however, if I did not mention my editor, Jerry Gross, whose enthusiasm did not interfere with his objectivity and, finally, my agent, Jane W. Wilson, who kept the candle burning during some of the darkest days.

MY
SAVAGE
MUSE

1

I could not love except where Death
Was mingling his with Beauty's breath.

I AM THE MOST abject sinner in the eyes of Almighty God—an object of scorn, of horror, of detestation in the eyes of my fellow men. To read my work is to decipher my shame.

It was never my need or intent to embody in a written record the unspeakable misery that it has been my wretched fate to endure since the earliest days of my life: a life spent in the darkling umbra of the raven's wing. Yet surely as I know that my candle flickers and sputters into its own oblivion as dawn draws nigh, so do I know that, in this year of 1847,* my death approaches. The shadow that foreruns it, however, has thrown a softening influence over my spirit. I long, before passing through life's last dim valley, to leave a testament which will in some small way disencumber my poor soul of the terrible guilt which has burdened it with a weight ponderous as a paving stone from the fiery streets of hell. I would fain have posterity believe that I have been, in some measure, the slave of circumstances beyond human control. I would have them allow that, although temptation as great may have existed before, no man was ever so cruelly tempted—certainly, no man ever *thus* fell. Have I not indeed been living in a dream? And am I not now dying, a victim of the horror and mystery of the wildest sublunary visions?

The principal reason for my never before having entertained the conceit of setting to paper a detailed account of my own life

---

*He died in Baltimore on October 7, 1849.

was ever the gaunt spectre of poverty. What time was ever granted me by an unkind Providence wherein to unburden my soul for the edification of future generations? There is no doubt that after I am laid to my final repose in the cool recesses of the sepulchre, enemies and friends alike will cast oral and written images that will be presented to the world as true likenesses of the poet Edgar Poe. Yet who of them could ever know the dread content of the nightmares that haunted my mind and lacerated my spirit? Which of them could ever suspect the nature of those long-imprisoned secrets that might have rendered me—were they known—an outcast, a leper among all men of healthy mind and spirit? Therefore, how could I dare risk the revelation of such knowledge during my lifetime? For this reason, should I survive long enough to complete my narrative, I shall make certain it is hidden from the eyes of all men until long after I have returned to dust.

The subject of such a personal narrative was first broached to me by Professor Longfellow in a brief note in the year 1841. In deploring the mythic distortions that arise and undergo metamorphosis from legend to fact, he singled out the lives of the literary immortals and opined what a blessing it would have been had they preserved in their own hand the simple truths of their own existences. I was overcome with emotion at his suggestion that I purloin the precious time to pursue this course of action myself, but my heart chilled in contemplation of what pursuit of the truth might uncover were I to embark on such an undertaking.

The subject of autobiography arose again during the following year, in the spring to be exact, when I had the great pleasure of meeting with Mr. Dickens. I found him to be a jovial gentleman, possessed of a fine sense of humour. We enjoyed a hearty laugh together when we recalled how he had said of me the year previous—"The man must be the devil!" upon learning that I had predicted, in the columns of *Graham's Magazine*, the outcome of his new novel, *Barnaby Rudge*, before publication of its final installment. It was after our discussion of the deplorable state of the copyright laws that he expressed a hope to one day read the history of my life, written by me to a point after which he might have the pleasure of predicting the ending. I am certain that he meant me no offence, but as I recall the expression which over-

4

came him at the time, he must have fancied that I betrayed some displeasure, for he immediately changed the subject.

These were my sole communications with any of my acquaintances on the matter of my undertaking any manner of personal narrative. No more did I afterward give even the most fleeting thought to such an endeavour. My life—my very soul—was dedicated to poetry, and had not my melancholy existence been perpetually dogged by the fearful apparition of poverty I would, so disencumbered, have scaled the lofty heights and become at very least the Byron of the New World. But alas! Such was not my destiny. Even as I pen these very words in the chill and lonely silence of my chamber I recognise—to my everlasting mortification—that I must humble myself at the feet of intellectual inferiors to sustain life. My tortured soul cries out in agony. My neglected muse weeps rueful tears, but deserts me not. Without her I am undone. Yet, as the ultimate dissolution which awaits all mortal men threatens to engulf me, as my eyes grow dim, as my fingers tremble, and the black frost of eternity seeps relentlessly into my marrow, I know that my days are finite and few.[1]

Five years ago, a wife whom I loved as no man ever loved before, ruptured a blood vessel in singing. Her life was despaired of. I took leave of her forever, and underwent all the agonies of her death. She recovered partially, and I again hoped. At the end of a year the vessel broke again. I went through precisely the same scene over and over again at varying intervals as it became clear that she was suffering from the dreadful scourge of consumption. Each time I felt the agonies of her death, and at each reappearance of the disorder I loved her more dearly and clung to her with greater desperation. But I am constitutionally extremely sensitive, nervous in a very unusual degree. I became insane, with long intervals of horrible sanity. During these fits of absolute unconsciousness, I drank—God only knows how often or how much. As a matter of course, my enemies referred the insanity to the drink, rather than the drink to the insanity. I had, indeed, nearly abandoned all hope of a permanent cure, when I found one in the *death* of my wife early in this year in which I am writing. The death I can endure as becomes a man. It was the horrible, never-ending oscillations between hope and despair which I could

5

not longer have endured without total loss of reason. In the death of what was my life, then, I received a new—but O God! how melancholy—an existence.

Ere long I shall join my beloved in the dreamless slumber of the tomb. But today I would unburden my soul and place before those who will come afterwards—plainly and succinctly—the circumstances, events, and consequences of my life. These events have terrified, have tortured, have in great measure undone my health and sanity.

I was never to know the gentle love and affection of natural parents. My father, a poor player, vanished mysteriously from the face of the earth during the first months of my life, never to be seen again. My unfortunate mother, also a member of that despised theatrical calling, languished, dying poverty-stricken in a squalid, mosquito-infested room above a shop near the banks of the James River in the city of Richmond, Virginia. I, a scant two years and eleven months of age, lay wailing from hunger in a wretched trundle bed upon a straw pallet.

If any true recollections of that dim and dismal time remained in my memory, they were transformed by passing years to the spectral mist of horrid nightmares. My sole inheritance consisted of a painting depicting my place of birth, the port of Boston, and a pocketbook containing locks of hair from the heads of my deceased parents. There was as well a bundle of letters, one in particular containing the shocking truth of my sister's paternity. Abject confession of guilt though it was, it proved my unfortunate mother to have been cruelly victimised by a wretch she regarded as a friend. Oh, wine! how thou dost betray those who trust thee.[2] The rest of the letters were of so private and trivial a nature as to be of no interest to posterity, and I have left instructions that they be consigned to the flames upon my death.

The last item remaining of that pitiful legacy was a small locket with a miniature portrait of the unhappy woman who had given me life. O God! What a curse not to have known the tender love of this delicate and ethereal creature. How often in the solitude of my chamber did I gaze at this fragile likeness of her whom I was destined never to cherish save in the fevered fantasy of a poor orphan's imagination. Though without question on the fanciful and romantic side, the small portrait must have reflected the soul of this tragic young sprite—for that is indeed what she resembled. Her lineaments were decidedly childish, her gown and bonnet of a fashion most favoured after the turn of the century. What rendered this likeness remarkable lay in her elfin face, most especially in her great, luminous, mysterious eyes, from which effused a near supernatural radiance. Under intense scrutiny they appeared to shimmer and expand, gradually assuming the proportions of twin maelstroms that beckoned to the spirit with the invisible force of lodestones upon compass needles. Surrounding her porcelain features were abundant raven tresses that fell in profuse ringlets about her head and shoulders. Perhaps the gods in their wisdom chose to favour me by providing me with a mother whose beauty would never fade, who would never be ravaged by sickness or by age. She would repose always by my side in the direst of adversities as well as in the loftiest of triumphs, never to suffer the pangs of loneliness on my behalf.

It was not my destiny, however, to know the miseries of deprivation or poverty in my early years. Though it is not my intention in this narrative to relate the entire chronology of my existence— I shall leave that onerous task to others—certain details are germane to my personal history, and must be included. Even as my natural mother, Elizabeth Arnold Poe, lay dying in her dreary chamber, the hand of fate intervened in the person of an angelic being, heaven sent, to rescue me from oblivion. She was Mrs. Frances Allan, of blessed memory, and wife of the wretch whose infidelities were to shatter her tender heart, hastening her own untimely end.

This gentle and loving soul took me to her heart and her home, and lavished upon me, the orphan child of two penniless actors, the tenderness and affection it might never otherwise have been my lot to receive. The merchant to whom she was bound by ties of matrimony did not take kindly to the intrusion into his house of a child whose lineage he despised. Indeed, though John Allan tolerated the presence of this boy, whose nemesis he would one day become, he arrogantly counterfeited the role of loving father, biding his time until the day dawned when serpentlike he could strike down this stranger, who might well have proven his only link with true immortality. Oh! If my inkwell were filled with reeking black venom, and my pen a quill from the wing of hell's most foul demon, even then would it be quite beyond my powers to adequately describe this fiend incarnate, this stone-hearted scoundrel, whose implacable maleficence undoubtedly earned him an eternity in the pits of Gehenna.

Fortunately, for a few short years my beloved "Ma" and her dear sister, whom I loved with near equal fervor as "Aunt Nancy," lavished upon me every tenderness, every manifestation of love and affection that could emanate from their great hearts. To grant the devil his due portion, even my guardian, John Allan, treated me with a certain degree of kindness at that time, but it was an easy pretence to behave thus toward a guileless child only five years of age.

I mention the age of five because to the best of my recollection it was the year that the nightmares began to assail my youthful slumbers. I know that I am correct in this assumption because it was in the bleak autumn they began, the year before we sailed for England. Even now, in the twilight of my life, my blood turns icy in my veins at the thought of these hideous dreams, for they plague me still. Only the soothing balm of gentle opium has the power to still the terrors they inspire in my trembling bosom.

The nature of these ghastly dreams has remained unchanged since the first terrible day they arose from the depths to torment my soul. In the beginning of the dream I imagine that I am gradually awakened, though I pray that I am still locked in the embrace of Morpheus. A nameless, unknown terror envelops me. Swirling, spectral mists churn ominously about on all sides, their hideous, poisonous vapours rolling ever nearer. I gasp for breath, recoiling in fear that their touch will inflict pain so agonising as to render the rack of the Inquisition a mere plaything by comparison. I struggle to rise, to flee, to seek the familiar reassurance of my own bed and reality. The only reality, however, is *here* and *now*. I am, like Prometheus, bound, but by strangling, invisible fetters. I know that if I can close my burning eyes the horrors will vanish, but alas! they are held wide open as though iron rings had been thrust beneath the lids by some fiendish torturer.

My heart now pounds a mounting tattoo like the beat of some

far Afric drum. A fetid, suffocating stench assails my nostrils, and a ululating chorus of unearthly voices pierces the air— shrieking, wailing, groaning, sobbing till every fibre of my body and soul trembles in agony. The mists recede and I perceive demoniac eyes of a wild and ghastly vivacity. They belong to a giantess of marble pallor. She clutches me to her bosom in a crushing, icy embrace. I struggle to free myself, but cannot. I yearn to cry out, but I cannot. A trickle of crimson blood drips from her immense lips, and for a brief moment of exquisite terror I fear she will devour me, tearing my flesh with her gleaming teeth. Then a gleam of light bathes me and the giantess in its glow. My fear departs and I am overwhelmed with an ineffable grief.

Suddenly I am released from her embrace and begin tumbling backwards. I am being drawn away by powerful unseen hands. My sadness becomes unbearably intense and I find myself hud- dled in the corner of a great, bare, sepulchral chamber, dark as the night save for a shaft of yellow light that pierces the gloom. As I lie there motionless, a procession of hooded figures rises from the dust. Giants all, attired in dark cerements, they solemn- ly raise the corpse of the giantess and bear her away. A single, gruesome, blood-chilling shriek now rends the air. It is from far away; yet it seems to issue from the depths of my own soul. I am now fully awake, sitting upright in my bed. My nightclothes are drenched, my eyes wet with tears, and my breath escapes in convulsive gasps. An overwhelming melancholy holds me in its oppressive thrall, I know not why, only that I will sleep no more that night.

Upon many an occasion I have pondered the origin of these dreadful nocturnal visitations. Perhaps they issued from a taint in the blood of my forebears, for they began to plague my slumbers long before my lips were to taste the juices of the poppy or the grape. I daresay, however, there may still be another explanation, and I offer it here for the bearing, howsoever indirect, it may have on the further revelations I am about to make of the terrible secrets I have so long and efficaciously concealed from the world.

My guardian, being a successful Richmond merchant, kept the

usual complement of servants, and from my earliest childhood
the greater responsibility for the more mundane aspects of my
daily care lay in the hands of a Negro "mammy." Often after
dusk, most especially during the long, fragrant summer evenings,
I whiled away the hours in the humble Negro cabins of the slave
quarters, listening as these sons and daughters of Africa spun
weird and terrifying tales of graveyard ghosts, walking corpses,
and frightful spirits with strange and foreign names. As a child,
though white of skin, I was admitted to the secret conclaves
where the servants, obsequious by day, cast off their yoke of slavery and harkened back to the dim African past in story, legend,
song, and dance. Thus was I transported to worlds of terror and
the grotesque which stirred in me romantic fancies and de-
lights.

Indeed, so firm an impression did the melancholy harmonies
and haunting rhythms of these gentle black folk have upon me
that for a time I truly believed in talking beasts, malefic apparitions, and deadly perils lurking in the vicinity of graves.

I recall most clearly an incident that befell me in the early part
of my sixth year. I was occasionally taken by my foster parents to
Staunton, where resided the Valentines, relatives of my dear
"Ma." I was particularly fond of her cousin Edward for he
always displayed a distinct partiality towards me. During the
course of our visits he often took me for a ride in the neighbouring
countryside. It was his custom when we embarked on these brief
but pleasurable jaunts to seat me behind him on the horse so that
for support I could encircle his waist with my arms.

On the occasion to which I now refer, we chanced to ride past a
humble log cabin in late afternoon as the shadows of darkness
descended. Adjoining the cabin was a sere patch of earth from
which there protruded, some at precarious angles, several mossy
graves. For a brief, wild moment, the icy chill of terror overcame
me and I cried out in shrill alarm. My childish imagination,
inflamed by tales I had heard in the servants' quarters of "hants
and spooks" had conjured up the frightful image of malignant
corpses, or spectres of the dead, rising up from their mouldy
coffins to seize and drag me, helpless in their bony clutches, to
the dank earth from whence they had arisen. "They will run after

us and drag us down!" I cried in frozen terror. Only after the good man had taken me from the seat behind him and placed me securely between himself and the neck of his steed did my fears leave me.

It was later the same year—1815—that an event of immense bearing upon the darker side of my future came to pass. Following news that hostilities between America and Great Britain had ended, and that the Treaty of Ghent had been concluded, my foster father made preparations to fulfill his long-standing desire to effect a reunion with his relations in Scotland. The idea of being thus rudely uprooted pleased me not, the principal reason for my displeasure being that my youthful heart, barely past its sixth year, had been pierced by Cupid's arrows: I was desperately in love with my dear "Ma's" goddaughter, the pretty Catherine Elizabeth Potiaux.

My vociferous protestations notwithstanding, we embarked on the good ship *Lothair* on the seventeenth day of June, 1815. Not wishing to let my elders know that my attitude had gradually undergone a reversal, I took pains to display an external air of melancholy. In truth, however, this sea voyage soon took on the aspect of a glorious adventure, most probably because I had previously read portions of Richard Hakluyt's *The Principall Navigations and Discoveries of the English Nation.*[3] Seizing the advantage offered by what was called my "childish tempers," I took every opportunity to post myself in solitary vigil by the rail. There, gazing with eager anticipation into the foamy turbulence of the sea, I vainly sought to obtain a fleeting glimpse of the terrible kraken, the fanged sea serpent, or, at very least, a romping school of merfolk. My fondest desire had been to encounter King Neptune himself, the substance of my childish dream being to capture the attention of this mythic regent of the deep, and so arouse his compassion as to be adopted into his briny court, therein to dwell until the final judgement day. How simple are the unfettered fantasies of the young!

After a crossing of thirty-six days we disembarked at Liverpool no worse for the experience save for a lingering touch of mal de mer. Proceeding thence by coach we terminated our journey at Irvine, in Ayleshire, Scotland. A beautiful country, to be sure, but it made no favourable first impression on me, for the grey mists, heavy rains, and penetrating cold made me long desperately for the warm and sunny clime of Virginia.

I will not take the trouble to describe every impression or event of that time, for despite the cold and frequent gloomy weather, there was much about the countryside to recommend it. These were the environs of Robert Burns, and during my brief stay there I came to absorb much beauty that was to etch itself upon my brain and serve me well in times to come.

Most distasteful to me was the school to which I was sent when the autumn mists rolled in from the sea, bringing with them a brooding kind of gloom I was to remember for the rest of my life. Austere and dreary beyond anything I had known in Richmond, the classroom was devoid of refinements. In a place of bare necessities, we young scholars attended to our lessons there with a fearful assiduousness lest we feel the sting of the master's birch, which was frequently and liberally applied to all he suspected of shirking their required lessons.

It was here in Irvine I first learned to overcome the terror of graveyards which had been inspired by the Negro servants with whom I had spent so much of my time in Richmond. As part of our curriculum we were required to take our slates and chalk to the chill burial ground adjoining the wee kirk nearby. There, under the supervision of the scowling, black-clad master it was our duty to scrutinise the ancient tombstones and copy their epitaphs, and after the task was completed, to return and transcribe these grim, necrologues into our copybooks. On my initial excursion to this Celtic Golgotha I was convinced that if I did not stumble and fall into an open grave, it was my certain doom to be snatched by the clutching hands of a mouldering corpse and dragged to some darkened sepulchre, there to be devoured by ravenous ghouls. My breath came forth in tortured gasps and my entire body trembled with every footstep. All that kept me from fleeing for my life was a more mundane fear, namely that of the schoolmaster. By maintaining vigil between the kirkyard's iron gate and the graves he effectively deprived me of any means of egress. I knew that were I to make even the slightest move contrary to his will I would be subject to the immediate and painful consequences of his wrath. Somehow, facing the unknown seemed preferable. The dead, after all, lay beneath the ground, and the dour Mr. Duncan stood within arm's length, ominously swinging a stout, gnarled stick of oak.

Upon quickly discovering that tenants of the venerable graves had no dark designs upon my person, I soon developed a feeling of kinship for them. After reading the dates of birth and death, and finding in certain instances the resting places of persons no older than myself, my imagination turned to thoughts of what they must have been like in life, and upon many a solitary evening after returning to my bed, I held imaginary conversations with the dead, not a few of which were continued in my dreams. Some of the night creatures, alas, had the most evil of intentions, and more than once caused me to wake up screaming in the cold and dreary midnight hours.

It was most likely that my sojourn in the precincts of Irvine and Kilmarnock influenced the binding unto my soul of the dark and savage muse ordained to follow me forever. Though beauty I did ever seek and hold more dear than Midas his gold, her sombre beckoning became in time a force enduring as chains of iron. Thus, though fond memories of times and places, blithesome and serene, still linger, it was predestined that the night side of nature affix itself to my spirit for all time to follow.

So it came to pass that where once the shadowy regions of gravestones and tombs had inspired my heart with suffocating terror, they now held a strange attraction for me that would one day inspire many a necrological tale and verse. Upon more than one occasion I trod with pounding heart the haunted walk in the park of Lord Kilmarnock where, it was whispered, the ghost of its one-time mistress still stalked during the midnight hours.

It was here in the land of strange valleys, misty terrains, fiery golden sunsets, and lingering twilight that I listened to lilting Scottish voices reciting awesome legends of mythic heroes, unrequited loves, monsters of the lochs, blood-sucking vampires—even man-eating fiends. How similar they were to tales of Africa that had made my blood run cold whilst huddling in the corner of some Negro cabin in Virginia, yet in curious ways how vastly different.

Of all such fanciful legends to befall my tender ears, one alone gripped my imagination and remained ever more. It was the tale of a dreadful curse, uttered by the apparition of a ghastly figure clad in armour. So powerful was this malediction that a mighty castle crumbled to dust, and the two lovers, conspirators in a most heinous assassination, met terrible fates as befitted criminals of such bloody culpability. So indelible a mark did this legend leave upon me that to this moment I can close my eyes and summon forth the image of that hideous spectre.

There is a ball of gala and voluptuous proportions. Gaily clad revelers dance to the melodious tune of richly garbed musicians. Suddenly the murderer and she for whom he struck his treacherous blow touch hands to dance. The music stops and turns to such a cacophony that the very blood congeals. Laughter and merriment are transformed to pitiful cries and ululations of terror and dread. Now silence, save for the rustling of silks as a solitary figure stalks noiselessly across the ballroom floor. With purposeful stride the armoured spectre, enshrouded in a torn and bloody cloak, approaches the dais and leaves in its wake a trail of crimson, moist footprints. The onlookers shudder convulsively and gasps of horror escape their lips as the grisly figure slowly turns to face the assemblage. Fresh blood drips from the armour as the hideous being raises its visor to reveal the reeking features of a corpse in the advanced stages of putrefaction. Then, pointing an accusing finger at the treacherous pair, it pronounces its sentence of death in hollow syllables that strike terror into every heart.

So potent an influence did this ancient Scottish legend have upon me that in time, it, too, became a recurrent theme in my pantheon of uneasy dreams. At last, a scant five years ago, not long after my dearest Virginia suffered the first of her horrible and bloody hemorrhages, I composed my tale *The Masque of the Red Death*, combining the lore of antiquity with an expression of my own despair upon witnessing the effusion of gore from the lips of my doomed beloved.

In retrospect I cannot but admit that my early years in the British Isles had a salubrious effect upon my future, yet, at the time, except for short terms of youthful pleasure, this time for me was one of trial and loneliness. Indeed, at one early juncture I formulated a childish scheme to flee either to London or America, a scheme which was fortunately thwarted.

Unfortunately the damp, chilly climate of the British Isles ravaged the already delicate health of my gentle and loving foster mother. When she suffered, my melancholy was boundless; when the rose returned to her alabaster cheek, my spirits soared. My greatest delight was experienced when, freed from the confining restrictions of the schoolroom, I accompanied her and dear Aunt Nancy on adventuresome excursions about the environs of London. I trod with awe midst the tombs and cenotaphs of Westminster Abbey; I thrilled with excitement in the bleak Tower of London with its ghosts and mementoes of foul murder, crown conspiracies, and other evil deeds too grisly for the ears of one so young as myself.

One event providing great illumination in that gloomy year of 1816 was an excursion to the British Museum where the celebrated Elgin Marbles were first exhibited to the public. Oh, what flights of lofty fancy swept me on viewing the magnificence of their design. Standing in their presence for the first time, dazzled and astounded, my eyes wandered from object to object, and rested on none as I trembled in the presence of the glory that was Greece.

As always since acquiring the skill to read, my greatest solace was taken from the pages of books. Eagerly I awaited publication of the poems and tales that so inflamed my fancy. I devoured Byron's *Siege of Corinth* with the voracity of a drunkard with a flagon of fine wine. His *Manfred* had a special meaning for me, most especially the lines:

> *I linger yet with nature, for the night*
> *Hath been to me a more familiar face*
> *Than that of man; and in her starry shade*
> *I learned the language of another world.*

Moore's *Lalla Rookh* transported me in ecstasies to the romantic splendours of the Orient, and many a dreary day was made gloriously radiant by the shining presence of the fabled poet-king who so captured and spurred my romantic fantasies.

Though by far my favourite reading matter, poetry did not occupy my every hour. When Sir Walter Scott's *Rob Roy* and *The Heart of Midlothian* appeared I read them with the intensity of a critic, searching for flaws. I found nothing but delight in his words.

The year before my guardian took us back to America, I read a book which moved me profoundly for many reasons. It was Mary Shelly's *Frankenstein*. It had first appeared a year or more before, but I had not been able to obtain a copy earlier. Though told with more passion than skill its theme held me captive, and as I followed the narrative of the unhappy Swiss inventor, I wept tears of pity for the hapless monster he had so cruelly endowed with life. What man or beast could endure to live bereft of friend or love, or soul? Even now, in poverty and failing health, my body racked by cold and pain, my brain ever menaced by the spectre of insanity, I would not change places with the pitiable, misshappen creature born of Mrs. Shelley's pen.[4]

The happiest day I ever knew in England was the one on which my foster father announced his decision to return to Richmond. Unlike my first ocean voyage, I anticipated my second with boundless enthusiasm. I was nearly twelve, possessing in my own mind all the assets of man's estate save size and authority.

2

Helen, thy beauty is to me
Like those Nicean barks of yore,
That gently, o'er a perfumed sea,
The weary, wayworn wanderer bore
To his own native shore.

THE RICHMOND to which I returned that summer provided a welcome change from England with its chill winds and leaden skies. Though I was beyond doubt fortunate indeed to have experienced the advantages of English schooling and exposure to the rich heritage of antiquity, my heart rejoiced at the prospect of returning once again to the familiar and beloved scenes of my early childhood. Furthermore, having now added to my accomplishments some schoolboy French, a little Latin, and the beginnings of mathematics, I fairly burst with self-confidence and, I must confess, the early flowerings of arrogance.

After all, had I not heard Shakespeare recited in the mother tongue itself, a different language by far from that to which I had grown accustomed as it issued from the mouths of Virginians, well bred and of low degree alike? And what of the wonder I had seen of modern science and industry, still unknown in provincial America: factories from whose chimneys great clouds of black smoke billowed heavenward, and carriages run by steam engines that roared like dragons of yore as they were drawn, clattering discordantly, across gleaming double rails of iron.

Yes, my horizons had been widened, and never again could I be the same lad who had sailed from Hampton Roads five years before. There now burned within my heart a romantic hope to voyage abroad again, to the farthest reaches of the earth: Dante's Italy, the mysterious East, and even dark Africa.

Behind me forever were the Scottish lochs and craggy peaks,

17

the quiet English tarns and ancient dwelling places in misty villages. Even now, I can evoke the refreshing chilliness of Stoke Newington, where I read the poetry of Byron and Shelley in secret. I recall with fond melancholy the fragrance of its thousand shrubberies, and thrill anew to the deep hollow note of the churchbell in the fretted Gothic steeple breaking each hour with sullen and sudden roar upon the stillness of the dusky atmosphere. Yes, there was much of England that I would carry in my heart and that I carry still.

As I settled back into the life of a Virginia schoolboy, my inclinations alternated between ordinary activities and the pursuit of my dreams. While one side of my nature led me to join my fellows in raids on turnip patches, swimming, and pranks, another drew me aside to the solitude of my room where I wove rich tapestries of daydreams and wrote verses on romantic subjects. I found as well that I possessed a fair talent for sketching, and for a time I even entertained thoughts of one day becoming a painter. But poetry was my first love and I was loath to desert it.

Though I enjoyed passable relations with the youths of my own age there were those times when I could not bear to be in the company of others, and for these voluntary flights into exile I was frequently the object of unkind abuse. But such disapprobation troubled me not. What encouragement I required was proffered amply and profusely by my dear foster mother and her sister. Indeed, even upon those occasions when I aroused the ire of my guardian—who, by degrees, the older I grew, commenced nurturing in his breast an increasing animosity towards me—these saintly females shielded me. More than once they rescued me from a sound beating.

Such was the case on the occasion of a late evening card party attended by no less a dignitary than General Winfield Scott. Abetted by several playfellows, I wrapped myself in a sheet, and howling like a hound baying at the moon, burst into the parlour in hopes of convincing the guests that the house had been invaded by a ghost.

The general, in a bad humour, no doubt from losing at cards, leapt to his feet, spilling a carafe of red wine on the gentleman seated at his left. The ruby liquid cascaded down the table onto the lap of the victim, splashing his yellow waistcoat and rendering his trousers soggy and purple. Paper money flew in the air and jingling coins slid to the floor and rolled in all directions as the disconcerted players added to the chaos by their cries and shouts of dismay.

"Och!" ejaculated my guardian, reverting as he often did to the accents of his native Scotland. "Tha whelp o' Satan! I'll grind his bones and feed them to the pigs o'Byrd* when I get my hands on him!"

The tumult brought several servants running, followed by my foster mother and her sister. Luckily for me and for my friends, "Ma" succeeded in calming my guardian by speaking soothing words, and making light of my boyish prank. No doubt for the sake of appearances, he permitted his wrath to subside and allowed me to escape. I was not, however, always so fortunate.

To the casual observer, I appeared to enjoy many advantages. But this was illusion. In reality a pervasive disquietude overtook me. Though he refrained from any overt and substantial expressions of enmity towards my person in the presence of others, most especially his wife, John Allan never hesitated to remind me of my origins, and that I was, in the eyes of the world, an orphan, destitute save for his charity, and subject, therefore, to the most exiguous manifestation of his will, howsoever tyrannical or whimsical. Even the most innocent of my boyish peccadilloes inspired his wrath. On such occasions, when we were alone, he would narrow his keen, small eyes and glare, his craggy eyebrows bristling, and his long, hooked nose protruding like the sharp beak of some grim bird of prey. Then shaking a finger whilst pronouncing his menacing words, he would threaten to turn me out, a friendless beggar in a world of strangers. I knew not that during these several years following our return from England the fortunes of his business were perilously austere, thereby raising to unhappy prominence the most disagreeable side of his parsimonious nature.

To escape his scorn and loathing I pursued the illusive aura of

---

*The Lower Byrd, a 6,000-acre plantation belonging to Allan's uncle, which he subsequently inherited.

beauty, scribbling verses in the solitude of the woods or in my room after darkness. I was now becoming a sturdy lad, but unlike my schoolfellows I perceived within myself a bittersweet vulnerability to Cupid's rosy darts. Not a day passed without my heart being smitten with love for one of the deliciously sweet naiads, those beribboned virgins, rosy of cheek, and sparkling of eye, who fluttered like innocent birds across the path of my daily pursuits.

In the mind of my hawkish nemesis, however, every expression of love, every verse, indeed every flowery phrase from my ardent imagination was looked upon as a transgression. By the strange intervention of fate and stranger juxtaposition of circumstances, I came to experience the first, the purest, and perhaps the most glorious love of my life. O God! I close my eyes and see her before me even now, an ocean of time having passed: her hyacinth hair, her classic beauty, her gentle airs that were and will remain forever perfection in my heart; the divine Helen, who brought with her fragrant presence the first tranquillity ever to settle upon my soul.

Our first introduction occurred under circumstances so commonplace I shudder and pale in contemplation of how easily the Fates could have conspired to prevent that precious moment from coming to pass. But it was a meeting predestined in heaven, where one day our souls will meet and touch in the joy of ecstatic purity.

It was in the month of May. The flowers of spring, bursting forth in their sweet profusion, perfumed the air with their honeyed fragrances. The earth rejoiced, having banished to the realm of darkness the chill winds and frosts of winter. Due in part to my prowess as a swimmer I had formulated a friendship with an amiable lad some three or four years my junior named Robert Stanard. He sought my acquaintance after observing me swim one day some six miles from Ludlow's Wharf to Warwick. Our friendship blossomed quickly. Though barely out of early childhood, young Rob had a keen mind, a sweet disposition, and a sensitive nature uncommon among my contemporaries. As the older and wiser of the two I became his mentor and protector.

On that day that was destined to live forever in my heart, he extended to me an invitation to his home that he might show me his pet pigeons and rabbits. The house—which stands to this day—faced the Capitol Square on Ninth Street. There was a broad portico of gleaming white, access to which was gained by means of a flawless marble stoop protected by brightly polished brass railings. Rob's gentle pets were housed in the garden, an Eden of verdant shrubs and scented blossoms.

It was midafternoon when my young friend suggested that we repair to the house and take tea with his mother. The interior was light and cheerful, but the heat of the day had rendered the atmosphere moist and oppressive. This condition being rather the natural state of affairs in Richmond at this time of the year, it is a detail that might have vanished from my recollections had it not been for the significance of the occasion in my life, one which has prompted me over the passing years to ransack my memory in order that I might always remember every blessed moment as it was lived. Shortly after crossing the threshold we were informed by an aged Negro that tea was to be served in Mrs. Stanard's sitting room. Rob insisted upon leading the way himself and bade me follow at his heels.

The room in which his mother awaited us was furnished with a refined simplicity in the Queen Anne style. She stood half smiling alongside a recessed window niche through which the golden rays of the sun spilt upon her like the treasure of the Danaë. Suddenly my heart began to pound and such a lightness assailed my head that for a moment I feared I would collapse in a swoon. I could not move. Her beauty was so glorious as to render all other women inferior who dared enter near the aureole of her radiance. Then, as I stood there, dazzled by her presence, I swear I could hear the tinkling bell-like tones of an unearthly voice murmuring in my ears, "Behold, the divine Helen!"

I could have stood there for eternity drinking in her beauty. Bathed as she was by the light, she gave the appearance of being its very source. Her hair was half loosened, perhaps to grant her some relief from the oppressive heat. A snowy-white and gauze-like net obscured a portion of her ebony hair, and the folds of her flowing white gown covered her delicate form as heavy marble hangs around the Niobe. Her dark and limpid eyes sparkled as

21

she smiled, and in a voice that sang like an angel's laughter, thanked me for my kindness to her boy, and bade me welcome to her home.

"So you are Edgar Poe," said she. "My Robbie has told me so much about you. I do declare, for a time I thought he would never bring you here."

Though it was not my wont to be at a loss for words, they failed me now. Stammering like some foolish oaf I barely succeeded in thanking her for her gracious hospitality, whereupon she said, "I trust that I shall have the opportunity to extend it more often." She paused, smiled in a way that caused my heart to leap for joy, then placed her hand on my arm and said, "I know we shall become great friends. But now I must fly. Adieu, dear Edgar."

Jane Stith Stanard was her name, and though she was more than twice my age, I worshipped her with a pure, devoted love that would find nurture in my soul and remain a part of it forever. Could she have known how my heart cried out to hers? Perhaps not in her waking hours, but such was the pervasive intensity of my love that I knew from the very depths of my psyche it reached into her heart and mind on the winged flight of dreams.

From the moment I first set eyes on my adored Helen she became the centre of the universe in which I dwelt; all objects revolved around her warm and radiant presence. Ere long I was spending every possible fleeting hour by her side. How I thrilled at the touch of her soft hand, how my heart leapt with exhilaration at the musical sound of her voice. No pleasure filled me with greater joy than that I felt on those blissful occasions when permitted to sit by her side in the garden beneath the fragrant blossoms reading my verses and gazing into her lustrous eyes. How I dreaded the lengthening shadows which presaged the onset of evening, thus ordaining my return to the Allan household, which seemed threatened by darkening clouds of desperation.

My foster father, still beset by financial woes, appeared more grim of visage and disposition than before. Often my dear "Ma" could be found weeping copiously in the privacy of her chamber, for reasons I believed at the time to issue from her delicacy of health but which I came to learn were caused by the distressing intelligence that her husband was having secret liaisons with other women which, indeed, had resulted in his siring more than one bastard.

Had it not been for the heavenly mantle of bliss cast upon my entire being by the gentle and beauteous Helen during that fateful year I might never have succeeded in withstanding the thousand insidious schemes and plots hatched against me by my wretched guardian.[1] So cunning was he in his efforts that none in the household save I ever detected any evidence of his designs against my person. Only by exercising the utmost restraint and caution in my every word and deed did I succeed in parrying his thrusts. Though at best there eventually emerged a stalemate between us, I was temporarily safe from the expulsion he would so gladly have imposed upon me. Much of my success in this endeavour was due to Helen's kindly ministrations. She tendered me both sympathy and guidance when I confessed to her in the guise of romantic parables the burdens of my own tortured soul.

It was in the bleak month of November that the Fates first conspired to destroy my happiness. At the close of my first school day I ventured with a sheaf of new verses to the Stanard home only to be denied entrance by a solemn-faced Negro in whose eyes I detected the haunted look of fear. No explanation was tendered; even my entreaties to converse with Master Rob were denied. With a certain anxiety commingled with annoyance, I turned to leave when, in the final instant before the door was closed, I fancied that I heard a scream so unearthly as to freeze the very blood in my veins. Instead of proceeding down the marble steps, I paused, then tiptoed back to the door, and placed my ear upon it. The thudding of my heartbeat seemed to grow so loud that I feared its clamour would betray me to the inmates of the house. Not a sound could I hear save the twittering of the birds and the distant clatter of hoofbeats on cobblestones. Recognising then what the consequences might be were I to be discovered in so compromising a situation on the portico of Judge Stanard's residence, I drew back, turned, and proceeded with aching heart toward home.

That something was strangely and terribly wrong I knew within a fortnight. Young Rob was rarely seen, and at the mere mention of the Stanard name my elders lowered their voices and spoke in hushed tones. The sweet dream in which I had been dwelling was shattered, for without the presence of dear Helen, my daily existence became again an empty ordeal. In a fit of depression one day I burned all the verses I had written for her so that they would never be profaned by the eyes of others. That the gentle creature was ill I soon ascertained, but for reasons that I could not fathom it was impossible for me to penetrate the mysterious curtain of silence that had been flung around the circumstances of her malaise.

Even when my young friend returned to school and play he would not speak of the affliction that kept his mother in seclusion. I was frantic. I could not sleep or partake of food. I could not even read one line after another. My thoughts, my heart, my soul were filled with nothing but longing for her. Then, two days before the new year, I received a note in Helen's hand inviting me to take tea with her and her son on the following afternoon. I was so overjoyed that it was all but impossible for me to restrain myself from running to her side that very moment.

My impatience was so great that each of the intervening twenty-four hours felt to me like a century. As the appointed hour drew near I took my leave and proceeded in joyful anticipation to her house. The leaden sky was unbroken by blue and a chill wind blew steadily from the north. By the time I was across the square from Helen's abode I found myself running as though propelled by a supernatural force, and when I had climbed the marble steps and crossed the portico to the front door my breath came forth in veritable gusts. I did not want anyone to see me thus, so before taking the brass knocker in hand to announce my presence, I impatiently waited to regain my composure.

The house was silent as I entered. A young Negro woman I had never seen before ushered me inside and without speaking conducted me to the adored lady's sitting room. To my astonishment she was alone. I had fully expected to meet Rob and perhaps several of his cousins there. It was not that their absence displeased me, the thought of being alone in her presence for even a few moments was a joyful prospect. But the moment I entered her presence I knew within my heart that something was dreadfully wrong. Dark circles ringed the once luminous eyes that now appeared lifeless. Her cheeks and forehead were very pale, and her sable tresses now tumbled loosely about her shoulders in an unfamiliar *déshabille*. Involuntarily I shrank from the glassy stare of her eyes and focused my attention on the thin and shrunken lips. They parted a wan smile that appeared to form with some effort on her part. I knew at once that some dread disease had fallen like the simoom* upon her delicate frame. And, even while I gazed upon her, a fearful change swept over her, affecting her mind, her gestures, and her temperament. Worse still, in a manner most subtle and terrible, it disturbed even her identity so that she seemed a strange and altogether different person from the Helen I had come to worship.

Yet when she beckoned to me and called me by name, the sweet sound of her voice reassured me and I approached the sofa upon which she was seated. At that moment I was seized with a terrible apprehension. With all my heart and soul I wished to take her in my arms and press her to my breast. But what a presumptuous and rash act this would have been had I abandoned propriety and acted on this sudden, deep desire. The very thought of such an impulsive deed inspired me at once with painful feelings of shame and guilt, and blushing I halted before her. Whether she mistook this to mean that I spurned her gesture of affection or not I shall never know, for at that instant she burst into tears and began weeping so copiously I rushed to her side in hopes of providing some consolation. But my efforts were in vain and instead of giving succour to her piteous lamentations I soon found myself as lachrymose as she. The sound of our mingled sobs attracted the attention of several servants and family members, who rushed into the room and conducted us away, each in a separate direction. The last glimpse I had of my adored one was on the arm of a female servant, who was leading her up the stairs half swooning and stumbling until she disappeared from sight. It was the last I was ever to see of her in this life.

No explanation was given me other than that the poor lady was

---

*Sometimes called *Simoon*, a hot, sand-laden desert wind that blows in the Middle East. Archaic, rarely used today. Poe liked the sound of it. He used it often.

ill and distracted, nor was any given as to how or why she had
sent me the invitation. I was treated with sympathy and courtesy,
but with the obvious intention to dispatch me from the Stanard
home with all due haste.

I was disconsolate. I told no one but my foster mother and Aunt
Nancy what had happened, and swore them both to secrecy. I was
not told directly what tragedy had befallen sweet Helen, but,
though barely fifteen years of age, I knew. She had gone insane[2],
and wandered now aimless as a disembodied spirit in the shadowy
darkness between heaven and hell. Sickened by the final dismal
stages of that lingering illness called "living," it would soon be her
good fortune to recover in the cool embrace of Death.

The unhappy creature took leave of life on the 28th day of
April in the year 1824. Though I had come to expect the dread
news daily since I last saw her on that dreary December day, the
grim knowledge that she no longer lived assailed me with an
overwhelming melancholy. The prospect of gazing upon her lifeless form as she lay in the coffin both thrilled and repelled me.

But alas! I was denied a last glimpse of her. The judge, her
husband, decreed that her funeral was to be a family affair, and
none save her kinsmen were to be permitted a final farewell. I
was overwhelmed with grief at the prospect of never seeing her
again, and flung myself onto the bed in the loneliness of my room
where I wept torrents of tears until nightfall, refusing admittance
to all who knocked on my chamber door.

My foster parents along with Aunt Nancy were absent from
Richmond, visiting cousins some distance away, and I was under
no constraint to take my regular evening meal. This I could not
have done under any circumstances now, for neither food nor
drink could offer me any degree of consolation. Indeed, the very
suggestion of eating at this time would have been sufficient to
render me deathly ill. By the time I had exhausted my tears it
was darkest night. I lay on my back gazing into the gloom and
imagined that I, too, was dead, reclining in the stygian recesses of
my own sepulchre. Somehow this brought a measure of tranquillity to me. Then rising from my bed I harkened to the distant
sound of a mournful bell tolling. Was it sounding a knell for my
lost Helen I wondered?

It was at that moment I knew that neither the angels of heaven nor the demons of hell could restrain me. It was the first stroke of insanity ever to insinuate its cruel touch upon my fevered brain, for the plan that began to take shape in my mind was beyond question one that could only be thus adjudged. I would wait until midnight when all of the city slept save owls, cats, and scurrying rats, those living creatures of darkness and restless spirits of the dead. Then enveloping myself in a dark cloak I would venture out, taking pains to hide my egress from the house, and steal through the streets to the Stanard home, making certain to muffle my face lest I encounter anyone who might recognise my features.

Summoning all the stealth and cunning at my command, I proceeded to put my plan into execution and succeeded in departing from the house without arousing any of the sleeping servants. The streets of Richmond were deserted and dark as the grave for the weather was exceptionally cold. Had I not been favoured with the faint illumination provided by a gibbous moon that faded and waned amid dark sliding clouds, I would have been lost, for at that hour the city was totally bereft of artificial illumination.

Instead of crossing the square directly to the front entrance of the Stanard house, I took a circuitous route in order that no one might see me. Then, trembling with emotion, I traversed the final distance that lay between me and my sombre destination.

Once there I circumnavigated the entire perimeter of the house to make certain that no light burned within, signaling the presence of some sleepless member of the household. At first glance I could detect nothing. But then, glancing upward, upon what mysterious inner prompting I do not know, I saw a dim flickering of yellow light emanating from a window on one of the upper floors. For one terrible moment I froze where I stood, my gaze fixed upon the source of the light for what seemed to be an eternity.

It was then that the truth of what I beheld dawned upon me with irrefutable logic. The pale glow above me could only be emanating from burning candles, and what manner of candles would be burning in this house in the dismal midnight hours save those providing grim illumination for a bier? I knew that beyond

27

that window pane lay the cold, silent form of my dear Helen, awaiting the final passage to her tomb.

My longing to see her and whisper a final farewell strengthened my resolve. Gathering my courage, fearing not the consequences should I be discovered, I climbed into the spreading branches of a shade tree alongside the house. I recognised it well, having often sat with the dear lady in the room where now she lay, watching the birds as they came to light upon the very branch which now I prayed would provide me access to her side.

Though a cold night wind blew, rustling the early spring leaves, my brow was hot and my heart beat wildly. Up, up I went, driven by a determination stronger than any I had known before. Suddenly something seized me by the throat. Clutching the branch to which I clung, it took all of the strength I possessed to keep from crying out in alarm, and I could not prevent a hoarse gasp from escaping my lips. For a moment I lay still, listening. There was no sound but the gentle rustling of the leaves and the low moan of the wind. Cautiously I raised one hand to my neck while carefully maintaining my grip on the branch with the other. At that instant waves of relief overcame me and I sighed with the deep gratitude of a man saved from the gallows as the trap was about to open. There was nothing more monstrous about my neck than the cord securing my cloak, which at its outer extremity had become entangled in a broken branch.

Extricating myself and cautiously wriggling into close proximity to the window, I raised my head and peered within. The sight I beheld filled my heart with strange stirrings of sweet melancholy. There in the centre of the room, resting upon two plain trestles of wood, was an open black coffin. In it, reposing on cushions of white satin was the fair Helen, tranquil and more beautiful in death than she had been even in the full bloom of life. At the head and at the foot of her coffin stood tall, black candles, sable sentinels of mourning, their flickering flames casting dark shadows in all directions.

Fighting back tears, I gathered my cloak about me to avoid a second mishap, then kept moving steadily forward until I was able to reach the windowsill. A dreadful thought crossed my mind. What would I do if I could not open the window? Were I to break the pane, surely the sound would attract someone. But rather than succumb to fears of obstacles as yet present only in my mind, I manoeuvered myself into such a position that it was now possible for me to attempt to push the window open. It was difficult, for I had to support myself and coax the fingers of my free hand into precisely the proper place. Nothing happened and my heart began to sink. O, God! I thought, it is locked. Then I felt a slight movement and my hopes rose. Gradually the lower window began to slide upwards. Let it make no noise, I prayed wordlessly, and I applied the necessary force ever so cautiously in order to accomplish my purpose in silence. Finally—the process took so long I half believed I would momentarily be overtaken by dawn—I succeeded in providing an aperture of sufficient size to allow me passage into the room.

After closing the window behind me I stood still and appraised my surroundings. Except for the coffin in the middle of the room everything was exactly as it had been when I was last present: the simple writing desk with its polished brass inkstand and crystal vase of flowers, the green velvet sofa with its matching footstool, and bookcases lining the walls, save for where a single framed painting of a pastoral scene hung above the desk.

Fixing my attention now on the pale figure lying in the coffin, strange stirrings arose within me. Although somewhere deep within my tormented soul a small voice soundlessly encouraged me to weep, I found no tears. The pounding of my heart grew so intense I feared that its dull thudding would be heard echoing from the walls. I advanced upon the coffin and stood at its edge staring at the lifeless form of my dearly beloved. Oh, how strange was her pallor! So waxen were her lovely features that they almost seemed at one with the white satin cushions upon which she reposed, and the soft linen of her shroud. Yet the ebony tresses arranged so carefully about her dear face glistened with life in the pale glow of the flickering candlelight. Her lips were slightly parted, providing a glimpse of her pearl-like teeth.

The blood now coursed through my veins like a raging flood, and the beating of my heart thudded in my ears. My breath issued from my lungs in heavy, tortured gasps and I trembled as if I had suddenly been afflicted with the ague. I had to touch Helen's pale white cheek, her dainty hand, to kiss those soft lips that had never touched mine in life. Like one in a trance I reached down into the coffin and caressed her icy cheek. Oh, what a fearful thrill passed through me!

No longer able to contain myself I bent down and gently pressed my lips to hers. Such exquisite pleasure I had never known. Now, as if driven by some demoniac external force far beyond my power to resist, I reached down and encircled her with my arms, drawing her to me as I covered her alabaster face and bosom with my kisses. The world stopped turning. I knew then an ecstasy the world would damn me for experiencing. I knew then, at that moment, that I had met my secret self, and was transfixed between terror and delight at that special knowledge. Where before I had merely trembled, I now was taken with a seizure, a paroxysm of such strange intensity I could neither see, nor hear, nor sense anything save the presence of the beloved corpse I held in my arms.[3] For that one brief ecstatic moment all the pleasures of paradise were mine, and I knew joy supreme as I had never known it could exist. Was this a passion known only to lovers, madmen, saints, and other doomed creatures of the earth?

Abruptly my sanity returned and the enormity of what I had done filled my heart with terror and remorse. In my madness I had half lifted the poor dead creature from her coffin, disturbing her coif and gown, nearly causing the coffin itself to tumble from its trestle to the floor. I feared I made some sound in that instant of abandon that might arouse the household. Knowing that I must leave quickly I hastily returned my immortal beloved to a situation of repose in her coffin. But no longer did she wear upon her face the expression of tranquillity moulded there by the fingers of death. Her eyes, now half open, regarded me in a baleful glare of reproach—or so it appeared at the moment—and her mouth was now hideously agape, her lips drawn over the teeth in a sneer that destroyed her gentleness and beauty.

I could not leave her like that. I wanted to remember her as she was in life: smiling, gracious, a vision of tender loveliness. Fighting the terror that inspired me to flee blindly into the night, I closed her once luminous eyes for the last time, restored her ebony hair to its beauteous symmetry, and closed her mouth, restoring the lips to their former wan smile. Now my love slept in solemn silence, her countenance again serene. I paused for one final, melancholy moment to gaze upon her features, then with a saddened heart, turned to the window and departed as I had come.

3

And thus thy memory is to me
Like some enchanted far-off isle
In some tumultuous sea—

THE NIGHT THAT FOLLOWED the terrible farewell to my
first love was one of such horror that I shall carry its memory to the grave. Although by means of stealth and caution I took
leave of the Stanard house undetected, and returned to the
benign shelter of my room, the agitation in my heart did not cease
to trouble me. Oh! what a bewildering tangle of anguished
emotions assailed my consciousness. In the eyes of the law, were
my acts ever to become known, I was a criminal. Illegal trespass
was a serious matter. The burden of my guilt grew heavier. To
have laid profane hands upon the helpless form of a corpse was
surely so unspeakable a transgression, a crime of such evil, that
never, even were I to attain immortality, would I find means of
absolution. O God, what naïveté! How simple was my boyish
belief that in my uncontrolled expression of grief and love I had
reached the very nadir of human depravity.

For seemingly endless hours I tossed about in agitation beneath the covers of my bed, reliving the events of the night. A
hundred times I must have traversed the darkened streets of the
city to the sepulchral chamber where the lifeless body of dear
Helen lay. Over and over again I disturbed her solemn sleep, and
in the secret, dark recesses of my grief-maddened brain I visual-
ised myself committing acts so unspeakable that even in this most
intimate of confessions I dare not pen the words.

In time I fell into a fitful sleep, whereupon I descended into a
maelstrom of horrors unlike any nightmares I had ever experi-

enced. Even now, my hand trembles as I write. Fragments of these hideous dreams have remained to haunt me ever afterwards. That they corrupted my soul and branded my flesh are facts immutable as the mountains, sombre as the tomb.

In time, these frightful *ephialtes** were to overwhelm, by their capacity to inspire me with horror, the earlier nightmares of childhood, dreadful and persistent though these were. I need not describe in gruesome phrases here every detail of these hideous nocturnal afflictions. They found egress from the shadow world of unreality via the medium of verse, tale, and deed—of which only the last has been hidden from the world until now. I will confess, however, that the night's memory marked a crossroads that would determine with utter finality the course of my life's voyage.

In the haunted regions of darkness where my soul remained trapped that night I met with horrors which would have driven a lesser man into the yawning pits of eternal madness. I encountered worm-infested graves, where reeking putrescent corpses tore at my clothes and flesh in malefic attempts to drag me under the earth into their stinking abode of perpetual darkness. Sulphurous fumes arose from blazing fissures in the earth that threatened to engulf me as I fled, stumbling, gasping, choking, my eyes burning from hot cinders and ashes.

These and other terrors tormented my brain. Their culmination came upon me in the cool, dark, recesses of a tomb. I lay motionless on a cold slab of marble, suffocating for lack of breath. There then appeared by my sides the cerement-clad figures of dark-haired women with great luminous eyes, yet wearing on their pale countenances the hideous, expressionless mask of death. Moaning piteously, they bent over me and laid their icy corpse hands on my face. The emotions within me were so terrible I wanted to scream aloud, but could not. When I awakened I was trembling, barely able to breathe, and so overwhelmed by terror that I crawled beneath the blankets in a desperate effort to escape the demons of my anguished imagination.

Is it any wonder then, that in time I took refuge in the cup that

---

*Archaic: originally, a lewd, nightmare demon, akin to the incubus or succubus.

brought dreamless oblivion, or in that other draught which summoned the tranquillity of ethereal trances and images from which
reality's sting had been mercifully plucked?[1]

The great and full significance of the events which transpired
that night was not to become apparent in my own mind for some
time to come. Yet, the next day, when I had regained some
composure, I was aware to a certain abstract degree that I had
been touched by the hand of fate. Though I knew it not at the
time, I awakened that morning no longer a boy, but a man, with a
man's aspirations and dreams. I had for a fleeting moment felt a
love so profound that I knew it was my destiny to sing of it and
inscribe it upon the indelible pages of eternity so that all who
might read my words could gaze into my soul and learn of my
ephemeral joys and burdensome pains.

I would not succumb to defeat at the hands of my rival, Death,
but would enlist him as an ally so that I might steal from the folds
of his dark and sombre cloak those precious shards of beauty that
neither he, nor time, could destroy. I would not languish in solitude, nurturing my melancholy by devouring the words of other
poets. I would join their ranks and, with my own pen, fashion the
laurel that one day would rest upon my head alone. And indeed,
though misery and poverty have hounded me through all the days
of my years, and no doubt will follow me to the grave, I know that
my words will survive.

Thus I recall with utter certainty that April day so long ago when
I first took pen in hand determined to extract verses from the depths
of my soul. I *knew* that from that day forth, no matter what obstacles might hinder my path, I had begun a quest for immortality.
Neither battle, nor poverty, storm nor plague—indeed, not death
itself—would deter me from my life's purpose.

On the unhappy day of Helen's interment in the Stanard family plot I was unable to attend school, so enormous was my grief.
Having received no invitation to the funeral, and having been
sternly warned by John Allan to refrain from intruding upon the
burial rites, I was on the verge of distraction. Had I been older I
would no doubt have gone forth to a tavern and drunk myself
senseless. Instead I took a solitary walk along the banks of the
James River and took my solace in the penning of a few paltry

lines of verse. However, their rereading so displeased me that I tore them to shreds and let the wind carry them to oblivion.

The family meal was a solemn affair that evening, for pervading the atmosphere was a pall of gloom, inspired no doubt by the rites that day at Shockoe Cemetery. Even the lord and master of the domicile appeared subdued by the intrusion of death into our daily affairs, and judging by the expressions on the faces of my foster mother and her sister, even the slightest untoward word would have brought on a profuse effusion of tears.

Entertaining no desire for the company of others, I excused myself at the earliest opportunity afforded me without violating the limitations of good manners, and retired to my room. But sleep evaded me. Only a few days had elapsed since the terrible night of my rash and final farewell to Helen. Thus, as I lay abed, gazing into the darkness, fighting the torment that threatened to drive me mad with grief, I fell without knowing into that half sleeping state midway between deep slumber and wakefulness. It was then I fancied that I saw Helen's face at the window. Tears rolled down her pallid cheeks and her lips moved silently, forming my name.

I leapt from bed and flung open the window, hoping with all the desperation of a distraught lover to catch one last glimpse of her disembodied spirit, if indeed this was the nature of the apparition I had seen. But all was darkness and reason told me that what I had beheld was but an image arising from the oppression of a wishful, anguished heart. I could endure it no longer. Nothing could keep me from her side. Hastily dressing, I donned my cloak and stealthily left my room, tiptoeing down the staircase in precisely the same manner I had on my previous excursion. Ever so slowly I avoided one midway step that creaked when trod upon and, exercising the utmost caution, succeeded in making my exit from the house undetected. Gaining entrance to the stable presented no obstacles, and even the saddling of a horse proceeded without incident. The greatest difficulty I encountered was the muffling of the horse's hooves. This I finally accomplished by slashing a portion of material from the edge of a filthy old blanket and cutting it into four square patches of equal size. These I then tied to the hooves with cord before leading the animal out

into the street. Once I was well away from the house I removed
the patches, folded them carefully, and placed them in my pockets. Then mounting my steed I rode in the direction of Shockoe
Cemetery.

The moon provided barely enough illumination for my midnight ride, but I knew the way to my destination. As I rode up to
the cemetery gate I felt an involuntary chill. By now my eyes had
become quite accustomed to the dark; nevertheless, the tombstones beyond assumed the hideous shapes of voracious ghouls,
lurking in the shadows to pounce upon me when I entered their
midst. I felt all the horrors of the damned. I truly have not the
words to describe all of my fearful sensations. Yet I would not be
deterred.

I dismounted and tied my horse to the cemetery gate. It was
closed and locked, which circumstance required me to scale the
fence. This I accomplished with no difficulty for I was an
extremely agile lad. My only dilemma now was where to proceed.
I knew not the exact location of the Stanard family plot. From
the moment my feet touched the ground on the far side of the
graveyard fence, the entire world around me became a scene
from hell, a nightmare come to life. Though my intellect told me
that the rustling of leaves was but an ordinary sound, the trees
assumed a menacing, primeval nature, their branches rocking
hither and thither with a crashing and mighty sound. No longer
did I walk amid gentle grasses and flowers of the spring, but in a
morass of poisonous vines and blossoms, writhing at my feet. The
gentle breeze became a sobbing, moaning wind ridden by restless
spirits of the dead.

I wrapped my cloak about my trembling shoulders as I stumbled along on my dread and lonely quest, cursing myself for not
having thought to bring along a lantern to dispel the darkness.
Suddenly, at long last, after having wandered among the graves
in fruitless search, the scent of freshly turned earth mingled with
that of violets aroused my senses. My heart thudded with excitement and I redoubled my efforts, which were soon rewarded.
Beyond a little gate leading to a plot of fair dimensions was a bed
of flowers, violets predominating. Her freshly tenanted grave, as
yet unmarked by a permanent monument, lay before me.

My efforts were rewarded. Once beyond the gate I knelt among the flowers and peered at the temporary wooden marker. "Jane Stith Stanard," it read. "Departed this life on the 28th of April, in the year 1824, in the 31st year of her age." I was on hallowed earth, close enough to her that, given the implements, I might descend to her coffin and touch her cold cheek; yet I was separated from her by the invisible frontier between the living and the dead. My desperation maddened me and, bursting into tears, I wept until overtaken by exhaustion.[2]

Though this clandestine excursion to the tomb unquestionably meant that I had taken partial leave of my senses, I recognised the very real dangers that might face me were I to be discovered in this act, which would be adjudged by my elders as thoroughly insane. I therefore rose to my feet, muttered a silent *adieu*, and plucking a single violet from the grave as a cherished memento, vowed that I would return.

My sleep was less troubled that night and I discovered on the following day that I was better able to engage in those activities which comprised the normal routine of my life. I felt compelled later, as the shadows of night descended upon the earth, to scribble a few lines, which afterwards I destroyed for the childish imperfections they contained. And though time has erased the full body of that poem from my memory, the first two lines remain with me, for they symbolise the intense preoccupation of my mind during that unhappy time:

The dead lay in the graveyards, the living in their beds
With horrors of the ghostly night flying about their heads.

Springtime that year was sorrowful for me without the presence of Helen in my life. No doubt my behaviour was a trial to those around me. My foster father, with his absence of sensitivity and growing aversion to my presence, behaved with his accustomed sullen demeanour. My "Ma" and Aunt Nancy, both being women of deep sensibilities, unquestionably entertained private suspicions of the nature and quality of my melancholy, and treated me with the utmost kindness. I in turn spent as many of my waking hours in their company as possible, not only for the sweet consolation their nearness offered, but because of my foster mother's delicate health. There was now a distinct aura of sadness about her, for she could no longer ignore her wretched husband's infidelities, and this recognition had a most insalubrious effect upon her. Yet, as such a matter was an unthinkable topic of conversation in my presence, the time I spent with her was employed in the pursuit of subjects more suitable to our mutual tranquillity and efforts to infuse our spirits with good cheer.

Slowly the pain of having lost my beloved friend eased, though I often stole from the house during the dark hours between midnight and dawn to commune with her spirit by the violet-covered patch of earth beneath which she slumbered. The sweet, sad memory of her inspired in me thoughts of such lofty beauty and love sublime that, more than ever before, the poet's white-hot flame of creation burned brightly in my soul. Yet the terrible dreams I had endured since early childhood commingled with those of more recent vintage and more hideous aspect. They inflamed my fantasies and strengthened the darker side of my muse. Beauty, Love, and Death became the sombre trinity of my inspiration. Though I was not possessed of sufficient maturity to comprehend the exact nature of my spiritual metamorphosis, melancholy itself was now my great passion, exacting of me a loyalty greater than any mortal mistress demanded of her most ardent lover.

The summer to come was for me an end of childhood. The game of the Fates at that juncture in time was one of heavy portent in my young life. My beloved foster mother's health was growing ever more delicate. Through no great desire of my own, but rather arising from a sense of obligation, I found myself spending more time in the company of my guardian. Although he hardly became what society regarded as a rich man at that time, his affairs had improved to a noticeable degree. This I was able to ascertain by means of personal observation, for upon many an occasion I served without pay as a clerk behind the counters and in the warehouse of the establishment in which he was a partner, the mercantile firm of Ellis & Allan.

Whenever my serving from time to time as a reluctant employee of my foster father allowed, I stole whatever precious moments I could to pursue those solitary interests so dear to my heart. I spent little time in the company of my schoolfellows, although on the hottest days I occasionally joined a group of them to swim in the James River. It was on the second day of June that year I chanced to strengthen a friendship which had begun to blossom a year earlier, but which had not previously occupied a place of great importance in my scheme of things.

News arrived by packet that morning announcing the tragic death of Lord Byron on the nineteenth day of April past. A bright, hot sun warmed the earth and the fragrant scent of honeysuckle, roses, jasmine, and myrtle wafted on the breeze. On such a day even the gloom of the mossy tomb was dispelled by nature's radiance. There was nothing, alas, to offer me cheer, however, for I felt as though I had lost a boon companion upon learning that Byron, for whom I had borne such deep admiration, was no more.

I commenced wandering aimless as a mayfly through the streets of the city and without thinking soon found myself drawn to a spot that had always been dear to me, that enchanted garden across from the house of Charles Ellis, my guardian's partner. It was a leafy retreat from the world of reality, a place of peaceful solitude where one could retire to indulge in quiet reveries and nurture hopes or memories. Barely had I entered the garden and begun to drink in the peaceful beauty of its tranquil seclusion when I heard a familiar female voice calling my name.

Turning to face in the direction from whence it had come I beheld, seated upon a low stone bench surrounded by bowers of honeysuckles, a young neighbor and friend with whom I had been acquainted for about a year. Her name was Sarah Elmira Royster ("Myra" to those who knew her), and her age was approximately the same as mine. Possessing lineaments of slender grace, her charming face was surrounded by an abundance of glossy, chestnut locks, that tumbled about her shoulders in delightful profusion. Her pink lips, both childlike and sensual, were upturned in a warm smile of greeting, and her large black eyes were luminously intimate as she addressed me.

We had often engaged in the youthful caprice of waving to one another with fluttering handkerchiefs from the windows of our respective domiciles—I from my bedroom, she from a casement directly across the way. During the unhappy months when I was denied the company of my lost Helen, Myra accompanied me on occasional walks where we discussed the romantic poetry of Byron and Shelley without fear of reprimand from our elders, who held these poets in ill-repute as authors of florid, indeed scandalous, verse.

When I related to her the melancholy news that Lord Byron had died in Greece, her eyes filled with tears and I consoled her by offering my handkerchief. As my hand brushed against her pale, wet cheek, an unexpected thrill of dormant passion quickened my heart, along with a peculiar, almost frightening sensation of apprehension.[3] We conversed until the sun began sinking in the western sky, at which time Myra, suddenly realising the lateness of the hour, and concerned lest she arouse the apprehension or ire of her parents, insised that she must take her leave.

I was somewhat puzzled by this. We did, after all, dwell in adjoining houses. Would it not be foolish for us to return separately to our families? She agreed with me and consented to my escorting her all the way to her front door, declining, however, to take my proffered arm as we walked. As we paused to exchange our goodnights, we agreed to meet secretly in the garden on the morrow. She would bring some cheese and bread, I would bring a book of Byron's verses, and we would pass a few pleasant hours together. Perhaps we might have tarried a moment longer, but the appearance of her mother at the window brought a blush to Myra's cheek and she hastily bid me *adieu*.

As she took the brass door knocker in hand, her mother remained at her post in the window, and I fancied that she stared at me with an expression of disapproval. I pretended not to notice her and proceeded at once in the direction of my own house. For what reason, I asked myself, should Mrs. Royster object to such harmless, neighbourly conversation? I learned the answer, to my consternation, much later, when I discovered the nature of the many vile and slanderous statements made to Myra's father by my guardian.[4] Upon those occasions he maligned my character to such a degree that in similar circumstances a grown man would have demanded satisfaction on the field of honour. The full import of this matter was to have tragic implications for me and, indeed, for poor Myra as well. But how, in our youthful innocence, were we to suspect what malignity the Fates were weaving into our respective lives?

4

And so, being young and dipt in folly
I fell in love with melancholy

I SHALL PASS superficially over the circumstances of my life for the balance of the years 1824 and 1825. They comprised what must remain forever in my memory as among the more blissful times of my youth, despite occasional shadows that hovered at the periphery of my happiness.

Though in my youthful naïveté I believed after the loss of Helen that I should never love again, I soon became enamoured a second time with the gentle and adoring Myra. I now came to understand the true nature of affection for the dear departed one: it was a love of beauty, a love of purest and most noble character. With lesser frequency, I still made secret pilgrimages to her grave under the protective cover of darkness. For I knew in the secret recesses of my soul that no matter where the Fates would lead me later in life, I would always carry her sweet memory in a special alcove of my heart.

Had I not been chosen by destiny to live my life as a poet, how easily I might have become like the others of my age and station. Indeed, it was during these times that my guardian commenced entertaining thoughts as to how best he might rid his household of my presence. I was still of sufficiently tender years to ensure my continued shelter beneath his roof for another two years or more. Being a man who was greatly desirous that others hold him in the highest esteem, he had no intention of ejecting me precipitously from his house, and by so doing garner the disapprobation of his friends and neighbours. Instead he began formulating a scheme[1] that would not only serve his own ends, but do so in such a way as to create in the minds of others the impression that he had acted only with the noblest of intentions.

He was not unaware of my early efforts to compose verses. As a merchant who dealt in periodicals and books as well as the more mundane articles of common usage, he recognised the commercial value of the printed word. A year earlier, in response to my suggestion that a volume of my poems be published, he grudgingly concluded that the possibility existed of his realising a financial profit from their sale. Unfortunately, his confidence in my literary efforts was of mininal degree and he made the mistake of consulting Mr. Joseph Clarke, the pompous headmaster of my school. Though a classical scholar who taught the purest Augustan Latin, this fiery son of Ireland had little patience for poetry in the English language, especially that composed by one of his students. He was notably scandalised by the fact that most of the verses were love poems addressed to certain young ladies who had aroused my juvenile affections, and were inmates of the boarding school of Miss Jane Mackenzie, in whose care my young sister, Rosalie, had been entrusted. Thus, the volume was never published, and John Allan, unable to ignore my obvious intellectual accomplishments, gradually came to the conclusion that his purposes (and only incidentally my future) might be better served if I were prepared for a career in law.

In the privacy of the home, when none were present save the two of us, he would cast the usual aspersions upon my true lineage. As a rule his tirades commenced after I had made some innocent comment on a poem or novel that I had recently read.

"Och!" he would exclaim, using expressions of his native Scotland whenever he wished to convey his displeasure. "Must ye forever be squanderin' yer precious time on worthless drivel scorned by men of means and affairs?"

Though I might endeavour to offer a defensive protest, I was rarely able to best him in debate, my histrionic talents notwithstanding. Barely might the words, "But Pa," escape my lips than he would whirl about, his beady eyes narrowed, the nostrils of his hawk nose flaring, and his square jaw set in indignation. Shaking his index finger at me as though it were a weapon, he would aim his words and fire them like projectiles.

"What am I tae do with ye?" he would demand. "I've ta'en ye in an' gie'en ye shelter. From a feckless orphan ye've grown to a bonnie lad. Ye've had th' best a mon could offer. Ye've been led down th' path o'righteousness, yet, yer tainted blude keeps risin' tae the fore. D'ye want tae die lak yer ain faither?"

On and on like this he would go, eventually holding forth the hope that if this "tainted blood" of mine were to be overcome and I diligently pursued proper studies I might one day become a member of the bar. Then, said he, it was not inconceivable that one day I might find myself in the legislature, if not in the halls of Congress at Washington. Only by following such a course, he declared, would I eventually succeed in demonstrating the proper gratitude to him for having provided me with shelter, food, and education.

Knowing the man for the wretch he actually was, I recognised that these conversations did not bode well for me, though I knew not exactly in what direction the future lay. I determined nonetheless to follow my muse and perfect my art regardless of what John Allan or any other person might say or think of me. I will freely admit to having been on occasion a trial to those closest to me, for I was given to fits of melancholy and rage. Being blessed with a more than handy command of the language along with my histrionic gifts, I had no compunctions about calling them into play when I deemed it necessary.

When I chose to be alone, anyone attempting to force his companionship upon me tried my patience. I was not infrequently rude and abrupt, and many times I regretted having subjected persons around me to the rapier slashes of my tongue, but such was my nature. In the company of youths my own age I was able to maintain an even greater air of arrogance. I excelled in swimming, boxing, running, and jumping. I was better read in the classics as well as in the more contemporary works, and I surpassed most of my fellows in languages. For reasons of utmost clarity then, save for a very few boon companions, I was not regarded by my peers as an object of affection, though I had the admiration of all. The opinions of others meant little to me, for I was rich in the greatest treasures bestowed by heaven on the young—robust health and a comely appearance. How sorely I mourned their loss when they were taken from me, and how often I pondered over the perversity of youth that permits the irretrievable squandering of these priceless gifts.

These were times of great consequence for me. The frequent acrimonious exchanges between my guardian and myself notwithstanding, there still remained between us a thread of affection that might have been strengthened had either of us been prepared to give ground.[2] The closer I came to man's estate, the stronger I became, thus giving rise to greater disharmony between John Allan and me. Our domestic discord, a trial on its own account, was overshadowed by an all-pervading atmosphere of gloom. My foster mother's delicate health was the subject of perpetual concern, and often I pondered whether my foster father was in some mysterious way responsible for her sufferings. These dark musings on my part gave rise to an even deeper antipathy for my guardian, which, as a passionate youth, I was unable to conceal.

Thus, on those occasions when she was confined to her bed, and an altercation arose between John Allan and myself, I invariably experienced dreadful pangs of guilt afterwards. The very thought of being the cause of additional pain to her was more than I could bear. Though she and I never exchanged words on the subject, so powerful were my convictions that I had transgressed against her that my sleep for several nights thereafter was plagued by those recurring nightmares which filled me with such horror.

My days were pleasant enough because of the unquestionable pleasure of having attained the reputation for academic achievement. The romantic attachment that had grown between Myra and myself provided both of us with many blissful hours together. Many an idyllic afternoon was passed, our youthful voices mingled in song as she played accompaniment on the piano. What rapturous joy I experienced in those stolen moments when, beyond the profane view of others, we exchanged warm kisses, our two hearts beating in harmonious contentment. Yet beautiful as was this romantic love that kept growing between us, a gnawing disquietude crept uninvited into my soul whenever I departed from Myra's presence.[3]

Was it apprehension? If so, apprehension of what? Was it guilt? If so, for having committed what misdemeanor? Certainly there was nothing in our love deserving of reproach. Why then should I be haunted nightly by my dreaded nocturnal terrors? What had I done to deserve such relentless punishment? I believe that had this regular nightly visitation continued indefinitely I should either have been forced to renounce Myra or to face the prospect of insanity. However, a curious incident befell me after which I was able to obtain a modicum of peace.

While visiting the home of my cousin James Galt one afternoon, I told him of the affliction that was depriving me of all but an hour or two of nightly sleep. I might never have mentioned the matter to him had he not made the observation that there were ominous dark circles beneath my eyes, and that they were most unbecoming to a person of my age. No sooner had I revealed to him the probable cause of my unsightly discoloration but he took me by the arm and led me into the kitchen. There before the stove, stirring a steaming cauldron of broth, stood an aged Negress, who, had it not been for the pigmentation of her skin, might well have served as a living incarnation of a witch from *Macbeth*. Indeed, she well might have been a practitioner of some ancient sorcery handed down over the ages from her remote ancestors in Africa. Upon hearing from my cousin that I was experiencing difficulty in sleeping she smiled, emitted a deep, musical chuckle, and told me that I need worry no more.

She next crossed the room and opened a cupboard with a key that she carried in her apron pocket. From the cupboard she took a mortar and pestle and an ancient wooden casket bound with brass bands. Then, turning and fixing us with a piercing look, she instructed us to go to the garden and fetch her some fresh mint and columbines.

Upon our return she took the mint, ground it in the mortar, and added it to a brown liquid in a small earthenware pot. She then extracted the nectar of the columbines and added it as well. After stirring the mixture thoroughly, she strained it through a cloth, poured it into a vial, and presented it to me with instructions to drink five drops in a cup of camomile tea before bedtime. This, she solemnly assured me, would make me sleep like a *jumbee*. A look of fright must have crossed my countenance, for I knew that a *jumbee* was a dreaded human monster, neither living nor dead, that dwelt in the dark jungles of Negro superstition. Again she laughed her deep, rumbling, musical laugh and reassured me that I would not become a *jumbee*, only sleep like one. Thank heaven she was right, for on that night, and on many others while the potion lasted, I slept like a dead man.

Now having recaptured the blessed ability to drift into sweet slumber without fear of molestation by those hideous apparitions that lurked in some dark corner of my fantasies, I took advantage of every opportunity to spend time in Myra's company.

Some weeks after receiving the mysterious sleeping draught from the aged Negress, I determined one night to remain awake and compose some lines of poetry. I took my customary cup of tea before bedtime, but with nothing added to it save a quantity of honey. I then retired to my chamber, lit the lamp on my desk, prepared paper and pens, and made ready to write. But no words would come to me.[4] A feeling akin to panic fluttered in my breast. As I sat in silence watching the gentle glow of the lamp flicker occasionally, no inspiration came, though my soul cried out from within to express my feelings of love, my praises of beauty, my awe of death. Still I could form no words on paper. This had never happened to me before. Surely my well had not run dry! But why could I not write? I felt in reasonable health. I had not quarreled with my guardian for nearly a fortnight and my dearest "Ma" had been in reasonably good spirits for some days. What was wrong?

I arose from the writing desk and went to the window. Myra's house was dark, not a ray of light shone from it, and as I stood there quietly gazing, my thoughts, unbidden, drifted back to that terrible night upon which I bade my last farewell to the dear, dead Helen. My heart began to pound wildly and strange, disturbing emotions assailed me. Suddenly I felt a horrid sense of suffocation and I knew that even were I to throw the window open to its fullest aperture I would obtain no relief. As if driven by a supernatural force beyond my capacity to resist, I moved like a somnambulist to the armoire, removed my cloak and hat, donned them, and slipped from the room.

As I descended the staircase I knew not where I was going, only that I had to venture forth into the darkest night and walk in the company of its denizens, with whom I now felt an overwhelming and compelling kinship. I had no desire to take a horse, only to walk wherever the Fates were to lead me; and as the distance between myself and the house lengthened a mysterious calm overcame me, impelling me to quicken my pace.

How long I continued thus I cannot say, and though I know that the city was virtually deserted save for an occasional drunkard or clattering carriage, I somehow fancied that I had been transported to another place and was surrounded by teeming swarms of humanity indescribably alien in quality. Their habiliments consisted of various modes. The men wore every variety of dress from that of the desperate thimble-rig,* with velvet waistcoat, fancy neckerchief, gilt chains, and filigreed buttons, to that of the austerely attired clergyman.

All were distinguished by a certain swarthiness of complexion, a filmy dimness of eye, and pallor and compression of lip. In their midst were street beggars whom despair had driven forth into the night for charity; feeble and ghastly invalids, upon whom death had placed a sure hand, and who sidled and tottererd through the mob, looking everyone beseechingly in the face, as if in search of some chance consolation, some lost hope; modest young girls, shrinking more tearfully than indignantly from the glances of ruffians, whose direct contact could not be avoided; women of the town of all kinds and of all ages: the perfect beauty in the prime of her womanhood, putting one in mind of the statue in Lucian, with the surface of Parian marble, and the interior filled with filth; the loathsome and utterly lost leper in rags; the wrinkled, bejewelled, and paint-begrimed beldame, making a last effort at youth; the mere child of immature form, from long practice an adept in the dreadful coquetries of her trade, and burning with rabid ambition to be ranked the equal of her elders in vice. There

---

*The practitioner of an old confidence gimmick, better known today as "the shell game."

48

were drunkards innumerable and indescribable, some in shreds and patches, reeling, inarticulate, with bruised visage and lacklustre eyes; some in whole though filthy garments, with a slightly unsteady swagger, thick sensual lips, and hearty-looking rubicund faces. Others were clothed in materials which had once been fine, and which even now were scrupulously well brushed. These were men who walked with a more than naturally firm and springy step, but whose countenances were fearfully pale, and whose eyes were hideously wild and red. These sodden wretches clutched with quivering fingers at every object which came into reach as they strode through the crowd.

Was this some frightful, waking hallucination that presaged my own future? Did I behold in the midst of the spectral figures who paraded before me in preternatural silence a fateful vision of myself at some far off time to come.

How long I had been immersed in this limbo of unreality I know not; however, with the suddenness of a summer storm I regained my senses. The frigid night air sent a shiver coursing through my body, and trembling, I drew my cloak more tightly about my shoulders. In the distance I heard a churchbell toll a single note, announcing that dreary time of morning proclaimed millennia past by the sages of Cathay to be the hour of the rat.

Looking about me and peering into the gloom I perceived that I had wandered into one of the shabbiest districts of Richmond. It was a noisome quarter of the city that by day was given over primarily to the commerce of tradesmen and pedlars, tinkers and thieves. By night it became the haunt of scavenging dogs, slinking, yellow-eyed cats, and loathsome, creeping vermin. Here and there, however, interspersed among the more decrepit commercial structures, were antique, wormeaten tenements, tottering slowly to their fall. The semblance of a passage between them was barely discernible. The paving stones about me lay at random, displaced from their beds by the rank grass. Horrible filth festered in oily, dammed-up gutters and the noxious effluvia assailing my nostrils served to strengthen the melancholy umbra of desolation that hung so heavy about me.

None but the most wretched poor dwelt in the vicinity and it was my intention to hasten away from this dismal place at once until something curious arrested my attention. A peculiar sound, halfway between a laugh and a sob issued from a nearby doorway. Drawing back into the shadows I observed a faint nimbus of light forming a thin yellow outline around the door. The sounds grew louder. There were several voices, and accompanying them was the creaking of footsteps upon ancient, rotting boards.

Suddenly the door burst open and out staggered four tattered, miserable inebriates, who had in all probability been worshipping at the shrine of the fiend gin in some pestilential temple of intemperance. Two of the wretches were women, and though it was too dark to discern the details of their features, they passed in sufficient proximity to where I stood huddled in the shadows for me to ascertain that they were in the throes of the most distressful grief. Scarcely had they disappeared into the night beyond when a gust of wind blew open the door to the hovel from which they had emerged.

The abruptness of it caused me to start in alarm and a gasp escaped my lips. The door rattled several times, its rusty hinges creaking a raucous accompaniment. Then the wind died down, whereupon the door sagged but failed to close. Not daring to emerge from my place of concealment, yet moved by a certain curiosity concerning the specific nature of what lay beyond that gloomy portal, I fixed my attention upon it.

The light beyond flickered and waned as though cast by a candle or an oil lamp approaching its final moments. Emboldened by the deathlike silence I withdrew from the shadows and strode boldly to the open doorway. The rank odour of decay assaulted my senses as I peered inside. Before my eyes there was a bare passageway, empty save for a broken bannister to the left, leading to a grimy staircase, and a narrow archway to the right from which issued the dim and flickering light.

My heart pounding wildly, I entered the filthy passage, determined not to take my leave until I had slaked my curiosity as to what lay beyond the archway. Scarcely had I crossed the threshold when a beady-eyed rat scurried across my path. In an instant it was gone, leaving behind only a tiny swirling cloud of dust. I shuddered, yet proceeded undaunted towards the archway.

The reckless foolhardiness of this youthful trespass still evokes a chill of terror even after these many years. At the moment of its commission, however, I was driven only by the thrill of the forbidden unknown, blissfully unaware that had I encountered a gang of criminals, whose wont it was to frequent this district, I might well have paid for my indiscretion by having my throat cut for the boots on my feet alone. But the murderer's blade was not to be my fate.

Upon reaching the archway and peering beyond I beheld a sight for which I was utterly unprepared, and which so unnerved me as to nearly deprive me of my senses. There, upon a crude, bare table of rough-hewn pine, lay the corpse of a young woman, my senior by at most five years. My mind reeled. I had eyes for nothing else in the chamber save this still figure. Her head was cushioned upon a block of wood and she was clad in a coarse, drab dress of unbleached, hand-sewn muslin. Clasped in the pale hands, which rested on her bosom, was a pitiful bouquet of dead and wilted wildflowers.

Save for the table upon which the pale corpse lay there was no furniture in the room. However, against the far wall leaned a freshly made coffin lid and on the floor below a stack of rough boards clearly destined to be fashioned into that funereal receptacle.

The pale yellow light casting its melancholy glow upon her came from a single candle thrust into a bottle and standing beyond the head of the deceased. Her burial raiments were stiff and new, though of humble cloth.

What morbid fascination drew me to her I cannot say, but I was incapable of flight. Had I been bound to the spot by chains of iron, no more a prisoner would I have been than I was at that moment. Then, as if drawn by some invisible magnetism, I approached her. Oh! what a ghastly pallor coloured those features. Though wearing an expression of placid repose, that marble countenance bore the mark of deep suffering and as I gazed at it tears began to cloud my eyes. The translucent white skin was drawn taut over her skull, long golden tresses tumbled about her shoulders, and below her pale cheeks were deep hollows. The eyes, only partially closed, stared horribly into the air above, dark circles below, and the lips, half parted, were slack and bloodless.

The palpitations of my heart grew unbearable. Indeed, it felt as though that pounding organ were about to leap from my bosom. Suddenly, inexplicably, I became aware of the strange, familiar emotions which both thrilled and terrified me. The disturbing ferment that now suffused my whole being was identical to what I experienced on the fateful night I last gazed upon the lifeless form of the lost Helen. How could this be? I asked myself. Why should the corpse of a strange woman, lying alone in this deplorable ruin, inspire in me feelings akin to those I had known only in the presence of one for whom I had felt such a pure and lofty love? Was I going mad? Was the "tainted blood" of my forebears—so often mentioned by my guardian—rising in my veins to destroy me before I attained my majority?

Such was the nature of the questions which rose up in my troubled brain. Yet I could not stop myself. How could I caress that ghastly, clammy cheek? How could I press those icy lips to mine? How could I clutch this nameless, reeking clay to my breast with all the ardour of a young swain in the tender embrace of his loved one? Oh, that I should sink to such depths of depravity! Yet, I did these unspeakable things, and knew one brief moment of unutterable ecstasy, followed by an overwhelming rush of remorse and despair so deep I might have flung the gauntlet across Death's own cheek had the challenge been proffered that moment.

The temporary insanity that had afflicted me having now departed, my own desire was to return as expeditiously as possible to the protective seclusion of my own bed, and to that end I set my feet in motion.

I slept badly that night, as I was to sleep badly on many an occasion thereafter. For some days to follow I was in the blackest of moods, and quarreled frequently with my foster father. But my melancholy notwithstanding, I found consolation in the solitude of my own company during which time I found the words to flow quite freely when I set pen to paper.

I look back now upon that frightful nocturnal fugue with emotions of painful distress. This was the beginning of a pattern, a dark design which was to be graven upon my soul like the mark of Satan on some necromancer of old. Invariably when I thought back to the horrid events into which I was impelled by the dark side of my soul I swore mighty oaths that never again would I permit myself to succumb, no matter how powerful the temptation. Yet again and again, when intoxicated by the vapours of the night, the spell of the moon, the call of the grave, that hellish influence enslaved me! This curse lay hidden, waiting in that body of secrets to which I never dared so much as to allude until I commenced work on this narrative.

I could no longer be like those simple men who die in their beds, wringing the hands of confessors, and looking them piteously in the eye. These men die with despair of heart and stricture of throat because of the hideous mysteries they will not suffer to reveal. Now and then, alas, the conscience of man takes up a burden so heavy with horror that it can be set down only into the grave. Thus the enormity of the crime remains undivulged and the sinner unreleased. My own transgressions, therefore, I knew had to be revealed somehow before I sipped that final cup with the Dark Angel. But I digress, and I must not allow my philosophical peripatetics to interfere with the proper telling of my personal history.

5

Oh, outcast of all outcasts most abandoned!—
to the earth art thou not forever dead? to its
honors, to its flowers, to its golden aspirations?—and a cloud, dense, dismal, and limit-
less, does it not hang eternally between thy
hopes and heaven?

THOUGH THE PASSAGE OF TIME has mercifully soothed the sting suffered from the lashes inflicted upon me by an unkind fate during that time of my life, I shall nonetheless carry painful memories with me to the grave. To be sure, in the twilight of my days as a member of a prominent Richmond family there were fleeting times of tranquillity, even pleasure: the warm days upon which my beloved "Ma" was free from pain; the blissful moments with dear Myra, when, between stolen kisses and embraces, she pledged her heart to me; the happy days, whether grey or bright, when my guardian's dour presence did not darken the premises. Indeed, there was that triumphant moment when, as a lieutenant in the Richmond Junior Volunteers, I had the honour of meeting that most noble of Frenchmen, Lafayette.

Yet none of these faint rays of light in my otherwise sombre existence could compensate me. My beloved foster mother's health continued to wane and the shadow of death hovered ominously about her. Had she been blessed, as she deserved, with a true and loving husband, her declining days might have been spent in the congenial aura of tenderness and affection. But such, alas, was not her fate. This parsimonious wretch lived only for one purpose—the accumulation of wealth—and when it became apparent to him that ere long he would come into a fortune he became obsessed with the determination to undo me.

Never did a day pass without the exchange of acrimonious words between us.[1] Whereas not long before he had grudgingly accepted my literary aspirations, and in some small measure had given them his blessing, he now declared his utter contempt for such "idleness." Upon occasion I observed him regarding me with glances of such burning enmity that a stranger looking upon us might well have mistaken me for his rival.

What I did not know in my youthful naïveté was that he had devised a scheme of diabolical cunning to rid himself of my presence once and for all, to cast me penniless and friendless into a hostile world. And, furthermore, he schemed to execute his plan in such a manner as to place upon my shoulders the entire burden of guilt for my downfall. In all likelihood he first formulated his despicable plot during the early spring of 1825. With the death of his uncle William Galt, John Allan inherited the prodigious sum of $750,000, propelling him upon that auspicious occasion into the ranks of Virginia's richest men.

In June of that year he purchased a fine house on the corner of Fifth and Main streets, a mansion of grace and beauty with a magnificent vista affording views of the James River valley. Within, splendid paneled rooms, richly furnished in the Empire style bespoke his wealth. Etruscan vases and Canova casts graced the chambers, providing intimate proximity with artistic renditions of Dante, Helen, and the Medici Venus. On the walls were hand-painted reproductions of del Sarto, Perugino, and Cimabue. My own room lay at the end of a hall that terminated in an alcove beyond a turn in the stairs on the second floor.

Initially upon moving into such opulent surroundings my spirits were lifted and my imagination took frequent flights of fancy. For a while, my guardian, too busy with the details of his newly acquired wealth, left me alone, and during that summer I was afforded ample opportunity to dream as I wandered in the fertile double gardens lying to the south and east of the house. Had I but known what lay in store for me at the hands of that blackguard, who knows what course I might have followed? But blissful in my ignorance, I drank in the beauty of the flowers and shrubs, ate sweet figs and grapes, and lost myself in the reading I so loved— Coleridge, Byron, Burns, and Cervantes. Best of all I loved the evenings, for on the upper portico of the house was a splendid swing and, mounted on a tripod, a fine brass telescope through which I gazed on many a fragrant summer's night to behold the moon and the constellations in all their sparkling glory.

Not long after we had settled into our new home my foster father implemented the first phase of his nefarious scheme to destroy me, though none in the household save he had an inkling of that dark design fermenting in his brain. Having declared that the time had come to prepare me for a proper niche in the world, he announced one evening that he had taken steps to settle my future. My heart sank, but I betrayed no emotion as he wove his treacherous web of deceit. He began with the declared conclusion that my superior scholarship precluded any ordinary career, such as that of a merchant like himself. Oh, the hypocrisy! Never had I observed this pompous shopkeeper utter a single word of self-deprecation, yet such was his pretense that evening. He continued his sanctimonious proposal by suggesting that my brilliance would be wasted on such foolishness as the composition of poetry. At this juncture I was unable to control myself and told him with some sarcasm that all he needed to do was supply me with a garret, paper, pen, and ink, and one day I would make him the father of a genius.

How cleverly he dealt with this outburst. Instead of flying into a rage—as was his wont when I defied him—he feigned a benign smile and said that he would be happy one day to have that distinction bestowed on him, but at the moment, through the exercise of his superior judgement, he had concluded that the only means open to my attainment of eminence was through a career in law. The first step for me to take, said he, was to matriculate as a student at the university. And in order to attain that status my immediate educational needs were to be attended to by private tutors until the propitious moment arrived for me to enter that institution of higher learning.

What rendered my guardian's proposal concerning my future education so monstrous was that its apparent generosity concealed means to banish me forever from the Allan household. The mendacity of the scheme lay in its simplicity. Having attained his position of affluence and power, John Allan was now a man to be reckoned with by all who crossed his path. None save members of the immediate family knew of his smouldering animosity toward me, and even they were ignorant of its vehement malignancy. It was considered, by virtue of there being no issue from his marriage, that I would one day be named as his heir, and it is remotely possible that had I subjugated myself to his will in all matters, I might one day have shared in his estate.

Whatever virtues were lacking in the man, he was no fool, and I am convinced that his perspicuity of intellect was not entirely lacking insofar as I was concerned. True, he had no patience or understanding for beauty save in conjunction with objects that might be bought and sold for profit. To him poetry and novels were but a waste of valuable time, and despite his outward pretenses that he might dissuade me from a career in the world of letters, he knew that never would I abandon my chosen destiny.

By enrolling me in the university he would accomplish the first step of his grand design, namely to remove my person from his house without arousing the concern or suspicion of his wife, whose love for me was unselfish and pure as that of any natural mother. Once I was settled at the university I was more thoroughly under his absolute domination than ever I had been while residing under his roof. There I was protected by dearest "Ma" and Aunt Nancy. In Richmond I enjoyed a modicum of freedom denied me at the university in Charlottesville. Yet before I departed and indeed for some time after joining the body of students, I was light of heart and filled with great hopes for a splendid future.

The remaining months before my departure were happy and free from travail. The new mansion became the cynosure for Richmond society. Scarcely did a week pass without its share of gaiety, song, and laughter. The tutors were delighted with the progress of my studies, and upon those joyous occasions when I could be alone with the lovely Myra, our mutual love and affection blossomed to the point where we solemnly pledged to marry when I returned from the university.

The date for my departure was set for Monday, February 13, 1826. Towards dusk on the previous day Myra and I exchanged tearful farewells along with small tokens of our love. Her black eyes glistened and she ardently covered my face with tender kisses, promising faithfully never to betray our love. Later that night, however, after all the household had retired and the hour of midnight had passed, donning muffler and cloak, I slipped from my room to steal down the staircase, past the dimly glowing agate lamp beyond my door, and out into the chill darkness of the night. I could not leave for the university on the morrow without paying a visit to the tomb of another love, one who would remain for all eternity the essence of perfection.

Little need be said of the journey from Richmond to Charlottesville, for it was a melancholy affair. I was accompanied by the saintly woman who had sheltered and loved me from the day I had been orphaned. Despite the presence of a bright sun and cloudless sky above, our mutual cheerlessness was not to be overcome, and by the time we had reached our destination there settled over us both a resignation to the fact that we must part for an indeterminate interval of time.

Poor gentle creature! Had she possessed but the slightest measure of the termagant in her nature she might have had the strength to survive. I firmly believe that the frailty of her constitution was the result of an oppression of the mind, a melancholia resulting from the cruel persecution she suffered at the hands of her husband, an illness whose precise nature was so aptly described long ago by Cicero in the *Tusculan Disputations.*[2] Though there was room in her ample heart for husband and son, she was deprived by a cruel fate of the fulfillment she so desperately craved. If in her joylessness and despair she lavished too affectionate a disposition upon me it was because she was denied love by the very one who was most obliged to give it.

But if the stony-hearted Creon[3] was penurious in both lucre and love alike, he would of necessity be deemed the most lavish of all men if he were to be judged by the quantity of venom and gall he showered upon me. That it was his premeditated determination to drive me to absolute ruin should I not submit to his will, I believe to this day, and will continue to believe until I sink into the grave.

When I matriculated in the schools of ancient and modern language, on St. Valentine's Day of 1826, I entertained no immediate ambitions save those of becoming an outstanding scholar.

In my youthful innocence I truly believed that were I to prove by my intellectual accomplishments the logic, the *necessity* of a future in the world of letters, my guardian would eventually relent and give me his blessing. The anticipation of becoming conversant with the classics in their original tongues filled my bosom with such excitement I gave little thought to the more mundane aspects of my situation. I gave no thought whatever to the trap that was being treacherously set for me, and by behaving precisely in the manner to which I presumed I had been brought up, I sealed my own fate.[4]

It must be understood that the university, situated though it was in the wild and primeval heart of the Alleghenies, represented a dream come true to its principal architect, Thomas Jefferson. Though still under construction, by virtue of its sessions having commenced this "Oxford of the New World," as the old gentleman was wont to call it, attracted the sons of Virginia's most prominent families. Attendance amid its colonnades and halls was prestigious and offered future distinction to those who survived the rigours of its curricula and the discipline of its professors. Falling short of that high purpose, life at the university held forth the promise of ample debauchery and dissipation for those possessing both the inclination and the means.

Indeed, there were those among the one hundred and sixty-seven matriculated scholars who had come for the express purpose of attaining a sound and liberal education. But there was among them an ample contingent of high-spirited young bloods, whose principal intentions were to avail themselves of unlimited entertainments. The acquisition of higher learning fell low in their inventory of aspirations. Those who came to study the varieties of pleasure came amply prepared for the pursuit of their interests with equipages of the most elegant and prodigious quality, including carriages drawn by blooded horses, servants, hounds, and arsenals of weaponry affording the owners opportunities ranging from fashionable hunts to duels to settle affairs of honour.

In the company of such as these I was cast adrift with exactly one hundred dollars to provide for all my needs, and considering that the barest essentials—board, lodging, furniture, and lectures under two professors—came to a total of one hundred forty-nine dollars, I found myself in debt from the very first day I set foot upon the campus, and for this, which was due to no fault of mine, I was subjected to the mortification of being looked upon in no better light than a beggar. Upon appealing to my guardian for sufficient funds to survive in a dignified and gentlemanly manner, he reproached me as if I were the vilest wretch on earth for attending two instead of three lectures. He further humiliated me by demanding an itemised accounting of my expenses, and upon receipt of them he grudgingly dispatched the sum of fifty dollars—forty-nine to discharge my public debts, and a princely dollar extra for spending money.[5]

Was it any wonder then, that I should soon commence my descent in a downward spiral that would lead to my eventual undoing? It was, however, a slow decline. In the beginning, flushed with the excitement of my daily acquisition of knowledge, I was light-hearted, and succeeded in banishing the ever lurking spectre of pecuniary insolvency. At the urging of certain of my more reckless and affluent fellow students, I took advantage of the general knowledge that my guardian was among the richest men in Virginia. Drawing upon the ample credit extended to me by merchants, I was able, by means of certain rather elementary machinations, to transform goods into cash.

After the lapse of some months, having heard nothing from my beloved Myra, I was given to fits of sullen melancholy, despite my continued excellence in the classroom. Worst of all, I fell into the vile clutches of a fiend more hideous, more baneful and injurious to body, mind, and soul than all other diabolic evils known to contaminate the human race: strong drink. The vortex of thoughtless folly, into which I soon so rashly plunged, left a mark upon me which will never be washed away.

Briefly I shall trace the course of my miserable profligacy here—a profligacy which defied the laws, while it eluded the vigilance of the university. My insolvency led to gambling. My drinking led to recklessness, which in turn led to substantial debt. The passing months served to give me rooted habits of vice and instilled in me a firm habituation of soulless dissipation. Thus by strange alchemy of brain my pleasures always turned to pain.

I should explain at this juncture that though I gave myself up with wholehearted enthusiasm to the evils of drunkenness, I must confess that my passion for strong drink was quite unlike that of my companions and remained so throughout my life. Never did I care for the flavour or aroma of spirits. In fact I have often commented that I found their reeking sweetness distasteful. Alas, it was not the taste of the beverages that influenced me, but the effect. For this very reason I was rarely given to sipping, as the French do their cognac. Although I have now forsworn the cup, and have not permitted spirituous liquors to touch my lips for a significant period of time, I will admit that when it was my wont, I preferred seizing the glass and sending it home with a single gulp after the fashion of the Muscovites.

How often in those bygone days, which now in retrospect seem not unlike paradise compared to what I have endured, I knew that death was preferable to the agonies I suffered for my nights of drunken debauchery. One chill April day while a thousand raging demons stabbed my throbbing brain with fiery swords, I sank with despair in a corner of the library, a copy of Tasso before me, which I knew I could not read until my suffering abated. Suddenly a shadow fell across my book. It was the aged Jefferson, his eyes blazing, his countenance fixed in an expression of stern disapprobation. How long he had been observing me I do not know, but it was obvious that he was fully conversant with the nature of my affliction. He was, usually, exceedingly tolerant of our peccadilloes; in fact, there were few disciplinary measures for breaches in deportment by students at the university. On this day, however, his sentiments on the matter must have wavered, for after regarding me with undisguised disapproval, he seized me by the ear and led me to a bookshelf, extracted from it a venerable volume of Seneca, bade me open it to a page of his choosing, then letting go of my ear, he pointed to a single line and ordered me to translate it and read aloud. Trembling with embarrassment, I hastened to obey the revered author of the Declaration of Independence. "Drunkenness," I muttered hoarsely, trying desperately to focus my eyes on the well-thumbed page, "drunkenness is nothing else but temporary madness." "Aye, lad," quoth the old gentleman, "and remember it most especially the next time you encounter a brimming cup of peach and honey." He was referring to the favourite potation of the student body, and upon satisfying himself that the full import of his words had penetrated my skull, he turned and strode off.

Would that I had taken greater heed of his advice. Unfortunately, the exigencies of my circumstances drove me into periodic states of nervous excitation. I despaired at having received no communication from Elmira Royster. The fear that she had forsaken me gnawed at my vitals like a rat at a mouldering corpse. But even more painful was the perpetual awareness of my miserable state of poverty, wherein I was expected to maintain an outward air of affluence. How could I not fall into the pits of despair, or give myself up to the excesses of drink? Whenever I looked around me I saw among my peers—wealthy fellows all— those whose riches enabled them to vie with the heirs to the wealthiest earldoms of Great Britain.

Only by means of the most devious machinations was I able to avail myself of funds, knowing full well that in time the full burden of my crimes would fall heavily on my shoulders. I did not relish the thought of that future day of reckoning which I thoroughly expected would precipitate a tempestuous eruption on the part of my guardian. In my naïveté I still nurtured the hope that when he learned of my superior scholarship he would relent and open his heart to me. My principal error lay in the belief that within that frigid breast there beat a heart rather than an icy lump of Scottish granite.

Thus I continued my extravagant ways. Often I invited small parties of the most dissolute students to secret carousals in my chambers. We would meet at late hours of the night, for our debaucheries were to be protracted until morning. The wine flowed freely, and there were not wanting other and perhaps more dangerous seductions;[6] so that when the grey dawn had already faintly appeared in the east our revels were usually at their height.

Excited by such a dedication to vice, I spurned even the common restraints of decency in the frenzied enjoyment of my carousals. But it is too far removed in time for me to recount the details of my youthful excesses. Let it suffice, that among spendthrifts I out-Heroded Herod, and that in giving name to a multitude of follies, I added a lengthy appendix to the already extensive catalogue of vices common in this dissolute university.

Having become an adept in the gambler's despicable science, I practised it habitually in a futile hope of supplementing my all but nonexistent income. But alas, these pitiful attempts to stave off the inevitable came to naught. The recklessness of my nature knew no restraints and at last it led me to a loss of caste among the more high-spirited of my associates.

As the end of the university term drew near I had accumulated debts of approximately two thousand dollars, most of which were debts of honour. Upon learning about this unfortunate state of affairs my guardian journeyed to Charlottesville from Richmond for the purpose of a confrontation. It was a meeting I dreaded even as a condemned man shrank at the contemplation of coming before Jack Ketch.* I was fully prepared to be unmercifully upbraided, to be blasted by invectives worthy of a Poggius.[7]

John Allan entered my room, closed the door behind him, and stood there contemplating me, his arms folded across his chest, his face almost expressionless. Growing uneasy at his silence I assumed as cheerful a countenance as possible and offered him my hand. "Pa," said I, "how good to see you here."

Finally he deigned to speak. "Is it now, laddie?" he said softly.

"Why should it not be?" I rejoined, beginning now to feel the coldness of his words. He spoke deliberately, measuring each phrase, barely a trace of Scotland in his pronunciation.

"Why?" he repeated, a mirthless smile coming over his lips. "Because, laddie, I do not think you will be pleased to hear what I have to say."

There was something about the way he pronounced the word "laddie" that made me feel like trembling. But I fought the impulse and, mustering all the fortitude I could summon, said, "Then pray tell me, sir, and I shall do my best to judge honestly."

Though his eyes remained cold as sapphires, his mouth curled slightly upwards. Said he, "I can see that your fine silken tongue has gained its share of polish at the university."

---

*British slang of the time for the hangman.

I was puzzled by this observation. "I fear I do not follow the meaning of your words, sir," I replied, the expression on my face becoming the mirror of my words.

"You shall," he said. "You shall. Have you ever, by chance, overheard the old proverb, 'He that hasna silver in his purse should hae silk on his tongue'?"

He uttered the quotation in rolling syllables of the Highland and before I was able to answer continued speaking. "If you haven't, I recommend that you commit it to memory, because from this day on, Edgar my lad, you will need it. You are leaving the university and you are not coming back. You have abused my generosity! You have dishonoured my house! You have proved to be a wretched ingrate and a spendthrift! You have tried my patience and have exhausted every scrap of it. As for your future, we shall discuss it in Richmond."

Had he raised his voice, had he showered me with angry imprecations I would have been prepared. I would have traded him insult for insult. But this chill, deliberate, and passionless declamation left me with the conviction that he was planning to cast me adrift forthwith. Panicstricken I flung myself on his mercy.

Of my total debt a mere three hundred dollars would have saved me from ruin, for that was the amount, or an approximation thereof, owed to certain merchants in Charlottesville. My appeals were for naught, however, and when my guardian swept resolutely from the chamber, my hopes and aspirations for a university education dissolved like mists in the wind.

I was disconsolate. My return to Charlottesville the following term was barred as effectively as if I were to be chained. Without his financial support I could not rematriculate. Furthermore, were the debts I had accrued among the tradesmen of the village not satisfied, warrants would be issued against me, which would prevent my return to the county. Although the contemplation was hardly any cause for cheer, I clung to the belief that even the miserly John Allan would eventually settle these obligations. Were warrants eventually issued in Richmond I would be forced to leave the state or face debtors' prison, and surely, I thought, he would not abandon me to such a fate and permit the shadow of my disgrace to fall upon his own hearth.

Thus, on a cold December night, less than one week before Christmas, though filled with despair and remorse, as I prepared to make final disposition of my meagre possessions, one spark of hope still burned in my bosom. Perhaps after I had returned to Richmond, the all-pervading warmth and sentiments of the season might yet melt his heart.

My chamber, Number Thirteen, West Range,* was cold and gloomy. The fire was reduced to a few glowing embers, emitting an occasional thin finger of flame. With the assistance of a friend, one Will Wertenbaker, I collected what rubbish it was my intention to burn and consigned it to the fire, which flared up sufficiently to give forth a warm and cheerful glow. I then took a hatchet and chopped into firewood the writing table upon which I had composed lines and written letters during my term as a student. The crackling of the fire helped measurably to dispel the cheerlessness of my plight, and we conversed until well after midnight, until the fire began to wane and the chill once more crept in from the darkling night.

On the following day, along with my small trunk, which contained all my worldly possessions, including the manuscripts of several poems in need of revision, I boarded the coach in the company of some classmates from Richmond. The trip was arduous and cheerless for me, although my travelling companions appeared to be in the best of spirits. And why should they not have been? They were returning to the bosom of their blood relations in anticipation of merrymaking and revelry. There was no question in any of their minds that they would be welcomed with love and warmth. What had I in store for me save the bitter reproaches of a man who gladly would have seen me dead? The love and tenderness extended to me by my beloved Frances Allan and her dear sister notwithstanding, I was in the eyes of the world an orphan with neither standing nor heritage—an interloper, an outsider—and though I knew it not at the time, soon to be a fugitive from the law.

---

*Now enshrined by a bronze plaque, inscribed
EDGAR ALLAN POE
MDCCCXXVI
Domus parva magni poetae [the tiny dwelling place of a great poet].

6

From childhood's hour I have not been
As others were—I have not seen
As others saw—I could not bring
My passions from a common spring.

T HE GENTLE, healing hands of time soothe all past travail
and I can now look back upon that melancholy winter
season without reviving the anguish that overcame me upon my
return to the house of my foster parents. Certainly I was the
unhappiest of all youths. Not only did the umbra of disgrace over
the matter of my debts darken my path wherever I ventured, but
I quickly discovered that the stony-hearted John Allan had
cunningly erected an impenetrable wall behind the adored Myra
and myself. I did not deduce the facts until many years later, but
clearly it was he who turned her parents against me, thereby
prompting them to intercept my letters from Charlottesville.[1]
Knowing nothing of this cruel interference with the natural
course of our love, the unhappy maiden assumed that her place in
my heart had been eclipsed by another, and when her hand was
offered to a stranger in marriage, she obeyed the dictum of
parental decree.

Being thus disquieted and beset with emotions of grief and
misery, I was hardly consoled by the news that my dear foster
mother and her sister had planned a gala soiree in my honour on
the Eve of Christmas. Undoubtedly, in all sweet innocence, they
had hoped to assuage my discomfiture by means of this festive
gathering. It would, they reasoned, convey to all of Richmond
society that harmony reigned in the Allan household. How could
they possibly have known that every fibre of my being cried out
against attendance? Far from desiring the company of others, my

deepest craving at this time was for solitude. I truly believe that had I the means I would have taken flight forthwith. Indeed, had I anticipated the suffering it would be my lot to endure in the immediate future there is no doubt now as to which course I would have chosen. But the fearful mystery that has ever darkened my soul impelled me down the path upon which I trod and will forever be hidden from me.

Now, with the crystalline clarity of hindsight, I comprehend the Iago-like malevolence with which my guardian subverted that occasion. By placing on the list of invited guests virtually every Richmond classmate from the university to whom I was bound by a debt of honour, he flaunted my disgrace as subtlely as he concealed his marital infidelities and debaucheries.

As a tender youth, yet to see the eighteenth anniversary of my birth, I had not yet developed such power of reasoning and deduction which only attend maturity. Thus, I could not fully comprehend why John Allan felt such hatred for me. I was fully cognizant of the fact that I had gambled recklessly and accrued debts of considerable magnitude, but what choice had I been given? Had he provided me with means sufficient to deport myself at the university in keeping with the station in life to which I had been reared, I would never have succumbed to the lure of the gaming table. My interests were of a far loftier nature. Certainly my scholarly attainments, which by their nature brought honour to the house of Allan, gave ample testimony to my ultimate purpose in life.

How I cudgeled my brain and pondered as to the cause of the ever-growing chasm between us. Indeed, although the simplest path of logic would be to attribute his animosity essentially to my extravagance, it being a natural affront to his Scottish frugality, I cannot in honesty say that this was truly the case. Far from being the penurious Scotsman of caricature, John Allan spent lavishly on those things he deemed important. It is ironic indeed that he himself was responsible for inculcating in me a spirit of unreserved dependence upon him.

I recall as a boy, whilst enrolled in the academy of the Reverend John Bransby, in Stoke Newington, arousing the approbation of that austere gentleman by very virtue of my relative affluence. On one occasion, as a result of some boyish peccadillo, immediately prior to his vigorous application of the birch to my tender fundament, he delivered a stern lecture in which he asserted that my misdemeanors were due to my having been thoroughly spoilt by my parents. Their chief error, said he, was in their ill-advised insistence upon providing me with an extravagant amount of pocket money.

It is my considered opinion, in retrospect, that John Allan did not *hate* me upon my return from Charlottesville, but rather that his affection for me had diminished almost to a point of neutrality.[2] I was now a commodity, a species of merchandise in which he had a monetary investment of long standing. It was his intention to enhance the value of that investment as best he could, but by the most economical means at his disposal. Having concluded that I was not properly suited to membership in the mercantile firm of Ellis & Allan, he had sent me to the university. It was his hope that after having absorbed the necessary knowledge and erudition afforded by that institution, I might enter politics. Imagine then, his chagrin at my avowed passion for poetry, music, and beauty.

Erroneously concluding that my indefatigable pursuit of the classics would not fill his coffers, he determined to direct his investment along a different path. O God! What fools doth fate make of us all. When I asked him for his blessing, and offered to make him the father of a genius, he mocked me. The harsh ring of his laughter echoes in my ears even to this day. Had he but listened, how different my life would have been! Perhaps if a kindly fate chooses to clothe my memory in a robe of glory my suffering will not have been altogether in vain. However, the monstrous irony—if such is to be the case—is that he will then live in posterity only by virtue of having sheltered me beneath his roof for barely three lustra* of my life. As for his treatment of me, let history be the final judge.

Returning once more to that melancholy December of 1826, I can now state with reasonable assurance that my guardian had no intention of casting me out. Although I was self-willed, addicted

---

*Lustrum: a 5-year period; hence, 15 years. The term was a favorite of Poe's and appears often in his works.

to the wildest caprices, and prey at times to near ungovernable passions, I was, as yet, incapable of independent action. Had it not been for the love of my foster mother I pale at the thought of what might have befallen me. But knowing of her affection for me, and not wishing to cause her further pain, John Allan made up his mind to break my spirit and mould it to his will.[3]

On the morning of the gala party, much to my astonishment, he bade me accompany him to the library after breakfast, and announced that there was to be a truce between us until Twelfth Night. "For the sake of your mother," he said at the end of a long and tiresome declamation. And as he uttered the words, a sudden, fearful chill swept over me, which vanished as swiftly as it had come, leaving in its wake an evanescent wave of sadness which, upon its dissipation, left me in a state of vague uneasiness. Perhaps the impression issued from some momentary disorder of my troubled brain, but for one brief instant, as my guardian addressed me, I fancied that this reference was not to his wife, but to my natural mother, whom I knew only from the medallion which I carried in a locket near my heart.

Undoubtedly taking my taciturnity for acquiescence to his will, Allan announced that our conversation was at an end, and offering me his hand, permitted a smile to spread over his countenance which temporarily caused it to remind me of a falcon that had just devoured its prey. Then, bowing to the call of business matters, he bade me a cordial adieu, and left me alone in the library.

I was justifiably confused. What had thrust the image of that poor, departed soul into my mind with such unheralded abruptness and clarity? I strolled to the window and gazed out upon the vista of the James River valley, sombre and grey beneath the gloomy, December sky. How seldom I thought of her, she who gave me life and love unrequited. Reaching into my waistcoat I took the tiny locket in my hand, opened it, and beheld her doll-like face.[4] As I regarded the portrait, I slowly began to sense a diminution of perception. It was as though some mysterious vapour had enshrouded me in a white mist, obscuring all but the miniature portrait upon which my attention was now focused. Though I had no conscious recollection of her, having been a mere infant when she had so untimely left this earth, I now imagined that I could hear a tinkling laugh, an ethereal and soothing tone, as if her gentle spirit were there, watching over me, consoling her wretched child with sentiments of assurance that all was not lost.

A distant, strident clatter followed by angry Negro voices, heralding some mishap in the kitchen, snatched me out of my sweet melancholic reverie, and returning the locket to its place near my heart, I perceived that my eyes were filled with tears. Hastening to my room, lest someone see me in this lachrymose condition, I took comfort in my solitude and wondered: were these tears for the lost mother whose loving touch I could not remember, or were they nothing more than tears of self-pity? Reflecting on that unhappy occasion I wonder if, indeed, they were not tears of prophetic vision.

For reasons I am unable to fathom even unto this day, I have no recollection of what befell me from the moment I entered my chamber until later that evening when a friend, one Tom Bolling, came to borrow a suit of clothing more appropriate to the revels of the evening than the less formal raiment he wore at the time. Since he was a youth of my approximate age and bodily proportions, that matter was readily attended to, after which he expressed admiration for the books and pictures with which I surrounded myself. I endeavoured to observe the proper social amenities for, as I recall, Bolling was a likeable enough fellow, but my heart was elsewhere, my brain in fearful turmoil.

In order to afford him the privacy of my chamber while he exchanged his clothing for mine, I ventured down to the floor below and crossed to a rear staircase so as to descend to the kitchen unobserved by any guests who might make their appearance before the appointed hour. Having been sequestered in my room since late morning, hunger necessitated my partaking of some light fare sufficient to quiet the offensive sound of my stomach's rumbling. It would never have done for me to attend the evening's soiree in such a condition, and though I would gladly have given virtually anything I possessed to avoid making an appearance, I knew that my presence was required. I was the de facto guest of honour. I could not disappoint my dear foster mother, most especially in view of her fragile health.

How tenderly she embraced me after breakfast, pressing me to her soft bosom, assuring me that the cloud which I perceived as having descended darkly over my future was but an ephemeral mist that would dissipate ere long. I reflected on how gaily she had recounted the myriad preparations that she and her sister had undertaken to ensure the merriment of the occasion. Torn as I was between such powerful, conflicting emotions, I resolved to put aside my inner anguish, strive to mask my true feelings, and perform like a player on the stage.

I was indeed ideally suited to such a course of action. As a child, in happier days, had not my guardian often placed me on the dining table in the presence of guests that I might entertain them by reciting verses I had committed to memory? And upon those darker occasions, had he not flung into my face, like a gauntlet of bitterness, the censorious reminder of my lineage, flawed by the "tainted blood" of despised actors? But alas, my resolve was unable to withstand the unspoken assaults of accusing eyes and mocking whispers of certain guests. Oh, it was a gay and magnificent revel. The fiddlers struck up one joyous reel after another. The golden glow of the candlelight enhanced the finery of the ladies in their silks and velvets of red and gold and purple and green. Laughter rang out, intermingled with the clink of crystal goblets.

More than once in the early part of the evening I nearly succumbed to the merriment of the moment, but each time my spirits were dampened by flashes of accusing eyes, fleeting expressions of disapprobation on the faces of those to whom I was in debt. I had thus far refrained from the freely flowing wine and spirits, but now I was seized with a thirst for a draught of the potation which might lessen the disquietude growing within me. Yet, accompanying this desire, which soon burned fiercely in my bosom, was a nameless terror. If I did not take immediate flight I felt my very sanity to be endangered.

As I peer through the dim curtain of time gone by, the events of that night re-create themselves before by eyes as though I were beholding a silent drama enacted by a cast of dumb players. For reasons unclear to me at this moment, the sounds and the voices seem to have vanished from my recollections, leaving only a panorama of moving images.

71

No longer able to bear the cacophonous melange of emotions welling up within me, I persuaded my friend Tom Bolling to accompany me in my flight. Although reluctant to take his leave at first, for fear of offending his host and hostess, he at length gave in to my blandishments and joined me in what became a debauch of drunken impropriety. Although I was assured upon several occasions thereafter that I committed no act of greater indiscretion than a loss of sobriety, I have no recollection of what transpired from the moment I entered the tavern of Mrs. Richardson until I awoke in a fright on Christmas morning.

In contrast to her habitually ill use of me, Providence has kindly shielded me from the memory of whatever horrors agitated my mind as I slumbered that night. That they must have been hideous beyond measure is attested to by my recollection of having been awakened with a cry of terror on my lips. Something or someone was shaking me violently as a throbbing pain threatened to split my aching skull asunder. The first image to impress itself upon my sleep-fogged brain was that of a black face with bright, piercing eyes, glaring at me above a blood-red mouth filled with gleaming white teeth, gaping open as if to devour me. For a fleeting instant I believed myself to be in the grip of Guede,* dreaded lord of graveyards, spirit of Death. How often as a child I had heard the name of that fearsome deity invoked by the Negroes in whose care I was for so long entrusted. How vividly I still recall their secret conclaves, where away from the disapproving eyes of their white masters, fantastic images of black Africa were conjured up through dance and chant and sonorous tale.[5]

As consciousness restored my reason, emotions of relief flooded over me, for though the stabbing pain continued to reverberate inside my skull, beating a tattoo in time with my heart, I knew that I was securely ensconced in my own bed. The dusky countenance belonged to Dabney Danbridge, a servant who worshipped my foster mother, and with whom I had always enjoyed an uncommon familiarity. He wore an expression of apprehension,

----

*The name "Guede" actually refers to an entire family of spirits of which the "lord of the graveyards" was a member.

and the timbre of his voice conveyed a foreboding that was not inherent in his words. His brow was furrowed, and he bit his lip as he spoke. All he would say to me was that the master had ordered him to fetch me at once, and that he was to act as guarantor of my immediate descent to the library.

I hurriedly bathed my face with icy water from the washbasin on the commode, and hastily dressed, after convincing the fellow that I would not survive long enough to answer my summons unless he first brought me a cup of hot coffee. His initial reluctance, and nervousness of manner, when he finally acceded to my request, gave rise to the suspicion that my foster father was in a state of anger and intended to upbraid me for my misconduct of the previous night.

Not by the wildest of my premonitions could I have imagined the extent of my guardian's rage. His eyes were narrowed and his nostrils flared. His lips were curled in a smouldering sneer. Indeed, his expression was akin to that he wore upon those occasions when he ordered the corporal punishment of a servant who had incurred his wrath. For a moment I believed that he intended to inflict bodily punishment upon me, as he frequently did when I was a mischievous boy, for clutched in one fist was a small riding whip which he rhythmically slapped against the palm of his left hand.

There suddenly flashed before my minds's eye a grim scene I had witnessed some years past, one summer, while at The Lower Byrd, the family plantation in Goochland County. A recently purchased servant, a strapping youth of perhaps sixteen summers, had committed some serious infraction, regarded by my elders to be so scandalous that its very nature was spoken of only in hushed voices on the part of the ladies to the accompaniment of fluttering eyelashes and gasps of horror. Upon learning of it my guardian flew into a rage and ordered the unfortunate, miscreant flogged in the presence of the other servants. This was done as a warning, no doubt, as to what might await any others who dared to commit a similar heinous offence.

My foster mother had most probably been indisposed that day, and her sister, Nancy, no doubt in attendance. As to their activities that summer my memory fails me, for I spent my principal waking hours in the care of my black mammy, Judith. Why the recollection of that particular incident remains so indelible in my brain I cannot say. Yet such are the facts of the matter. The Negroes of the household were solemn and silent on the morning of the punishment; even Judith, of whom I was inordinately fond, spoke few words. I was to be barred from the proceedings, it having been determined in advance that my tender years precluded my presence. Whether the decision was made by my guardian or my mammy, I do not know to this day.

However, sensing the air of melancholy on the part of the servants, I was determined to see for myself what transpired. Since even Judith was required to bear witness when the appointed hour came, I was left to my own devices. Being both nimble and fleet of foot, I ran via a circuitous route to the rectangular courtyard surrounded by the servants' quarters where the flogging was to be carried out. Then, climbing a tree from which vantage point I was able to observe the proceedings unseen, I clung to a branch and awaited the fustigation of the unhappy black.

On one side of the yard the servants were assembled—field hands and "house niggers" together—their faces solemn and impassive. In the eyes of several younger females I fancied I observed a distinct glisten of tears. Across from the blacks, facing them, stood my guardian in the company of several friends. Included were General Scott; a cousin, James Galt; and Edward Valentine, a "cousin-in-law" as John Allan occasionally referred to the gentleman. (This was a pallid attempt at jocularity, his actual relationship being cousin to my foster mother.) They smoked cigars and conversed in a jovial manner as they awaited the arrival of the youth who was to be punished. He soon appeared, naked to the waist, his hands bound behind his back, and was led to a hitching post by the plantation overseer, a sallow-faced octoroon with heavy-lidded eyes, a long drooping moustache, and hollow, pock-marked cheeks.

Without speaking a word he unbound the wrists of his victim and replaced the cords with iron shackles which he fastened to an iron ring on the hitching post. Next, taking the rawhide whip, which he held under one arm, he stood back and cracked it several times in the air. Still without uttering a word, he glanced at the now silent John Allan, who nodded gravely to signal the commencement of the thrashing. Without further ado he raised the whip and commenced flogging the unfortunate miscreant. Having never witnessed such a sight before, I became paralysed with fear, for I, too, had often felt the sting of the lash at the hands of my guardian, although not upon my bare flesh, and only by means of a slender birch rod.

Although I had no way of knowing it, the number of strokes to be applied were predetermined and dependent upon the severity of the offense. The chastisement in this instance consisted of twenty lashes. The entire scene took on a dreamlike quality, for though the recipient of the scourge writhed and twitched, his face contorted in agony with each stroke, not a whimper of complaint escaped his lips. His brethren, watching soberly, began a chant, their voices raised in unison, counting each crack of the whip. "One!" "Two!" "Three!" But most perplexing, and at the same time terrifying to my tender, unworldly mind, was the fact that after the fourth or fifth stroke of the lash, I cannot remember precisely which one, the unhappy wretch began crying out, "More, master, more!"[6] even as the scourge slashed open the flesh of his poor back until it was transformed before the eyes of all to a weltering mass of blood and gore.

My mind snapped back to the present, although the fading image of that long-past incident lingered. It was reinforced, no doubt, by my guardian's rhythmic slapping of the riding whip against the palm of his left hand. He was in a fury.

"Ye miserable, ungrateful cur!" he ejaculated. "An' drunken sot besides! Were it not for tha' puir sweet soul, who lies abed drenchin' her piloow wi tears, I'd drive ye in tae the gutter where the likes o' ye belongs!"

"Why do you hate me so?" I cried out in anguish, unable to answer his accusations, feeling burning pangs of guilt at the thought of my foster mother's unhappiness.

"Hate ye?" he responded. "I dinna hate ye, ye puir bloody fool. I pity ye for the midden* tha'l be yer grave if ye dinna mend yer ways. D'ye deny tha ye rudely stole awa last nicht, abandonin'

*A dunghill

75

yer guests, and guzzlin' yersel in tae a stupor? Wha hae ye tae say for yersel?"

Drawing myself up to my full height, I looked up into his eyes, knowing full well that he would understand nothing I might say in my defence. "With all due respect, sir," said I, "it was impossible for me to stay. I was driven! Had you not . . ."

"D'ye think I'm daft?" he roared, interrupting me, his eyes now blazing with anger. "Listen tae me fer I mayna be sae saft-hearted next time."

He then upbraided me for my moral turpitude, reciting a catalogue of sins so grave as to render me a villain of the most vicious stripe. Then he warned me of the grievous fate awaiting me were I not to mend my ways. Indeed, were some unseen observer to have overheard his accusations that morning, it would have been a simple matter to rank me in the Book of Infamy along with the likes of Sawney Beane and Jonathan Wild.[7]

What consummate irony! Though I was guilty of such minor vices as occasional overindulgence in spirits, gambling, and other extravagances, they were naught compared to the hideous demons still slumbering deep within my youthful breast. I sometimes wonder, did he possess some supernatural prophetic vision, enabling him to penetrate the depths of my soul, or did he by means of his deep antipathy, in some mysterious fashion help to unleash my wild and untamed spirit, like the *loa bossal*[8] of the African, before the baptism of his soul.

As I gaze back through the misty vale of time, I truly believe that the painful and acrimonious exchange between John Allan and myself on that fateful Christmas morning marked my entry onto the path from which there was to be no return. It would soon be my fate to embark alone upon the sea of my life, to navigate the river of my dreams and aspiration,

> *By a route obscure and lonely,*
> *Haunted by ill angels only,*
> *Where an Eidolon, named NIGHT,*
> *On a black throne reigns upright . . .*

7

Oh! that my young life were a lasting dream!
My spirit not awakening, till the beam
Of an Eternity should bring the morrow.

IT HAD ALWAYS been the custom of my beloved Frances
Allan to prepare a celebration on the occasion of my birthday.
I knew, however, that now, at the commencement of my eighteenth year, such an endeavour on her part would be inappropriate. Even she recognised the folly of it, and I still suffer
remorse and regret for having caused her the deep unhappiness
resulting from my rude withdrawal from home on Christmas Eve.
A simple creature, her intellect was dwarfed by the immensity of
her heart and the great beauty of her soul, which was reflected in
her lovely features. Frances Allan nonetheless recognised the icy
chasm which now grew ever wider between her husband and her
"dear Eddy."

Though John Allan made no effort to eject me from his household, he also elicited no warmth.[1] Indeed, his demeanour towards
me was like that unto a stranger only recently met—distant,
proper, and reserved. He rarely addressed me directly, and
responded laconically when I endeavoured to engage him in
conversation. Were it not for the ministrations of my foster mother and her sister, I would not have had even a penny to spend. It
was as though I were no longer a member of the family in his
eyes, but a transient guest soon to depart, and never to return.
Certainly, had even the most infinitesimal sentiment for me
burned within him, he could not have treated me thus. Even the
house servants were aware of my fall from grace; indeed, they
were, in all likelihood, even more cognizant of my abasement

than I myself, for their previous manner of deference now became one of indifference.

Recalling my past arrogance, and fearing the consequences which might arise from a confrontation involving my guardian and myself, my foster mother made arrangements for me to absent myself from Richmond and sojourn for a time at the plantation in Goochland County. Unaware of her true motives I eagerly acceded to the suggestion, having little desire to remain in Richmond under the circumstances into which I had been forced. There was also the manner of the warrants from Charlottesville. My guardian had adamantly refused to pay a single one of my debts and the spectre of debtors' prison haunted my every waking moment. With the exception of my friend Ebenezer Burling, with whom I made occasional nocturnal excursions to the tavern, there was no one I cared to see, even among the fair sex. My poor heart still ached over the loss of Elmira Royster, whose lovely features still haunted my dreams.

With the understanding that comes only with maturity, I comprehend now what was happening to me, but in the callowness of my youthful innocence, I still harboured the dream that one day John Allan would soften towards me and name me his heir. I departed Richmond for the plantation early in January with the full expectation of returning after the passage of a month or more to find myself fully restored to a position of favour in the eyes of my guardian. It was thus, with an erroneous sense of confidence, that I journeyed to Goochland County, determined to take every advantage afforded me by the solitude and beauty of the place.

The only other inmates of the household were servants who busied themselves mostly with the maintenance and repairs in preparation for the coming spring season. My personal needs were at a minimum, for it was my intention to devote my time to reading, composing verses, and to solitary walks in the surrounding countryside. Although the weather was cold, and the sky ofttimes sombre and grey, to trudge for hours along the banks of the James River, where it had narrowed to a modest stream, was a palliative to the distempers which often troubled me after a night of demon-haunted dreams.

78

It was my good fortune that the library at The Lower Byrd was well stocked with classics, despite my foster father's open disdain for literary excellence. His shopkeeper's soul, ever mindful of material values, had instilled in him a canny appreciation for fine, leather-bound volumes. Their worth to him was actually twofold in nature: the aesthetic quality of their presence upon his shelves imparted to guests the false impression that he was a man of taste in the matter of letters. His principal concern for them, however, was rooted in the firm conviction that they had great intrinsic value should he at any time be inclined to dispose of them.

I devoted the principal portion of my reading during this sojourn in the country to dramatic works. On many a night I drifted to sleep with a volume of Shakespeare open on my lap. With the voracity of a ravening beast I devoured the works of the bard, of Beaumont, Dryden, and Marlowe, to mention only a few. I was especially enchanted by Marlowe's *Tamburlaine the Great*. How I thrilled over the *Prometheus* of Goethe, and reveled in the comedies of Molière.

The most curious work I encountered was secreted behind a set of Gibbon's *Decline and Fall of the Roman Empire*. Upon perusing its pages I understood at once why it lay hidden. It was attributed to John Wilmot, Second Earl of Rochester, during the reign of Charles II of England. Entitled *Sodom; or, The Quintessence of Debauchery*, it employed language so vile, so depraved, that had I not such an innate love of books, I would have found it no difficult task to hurl it into the fire. Yet, as I read the lines, all in perfect iambic pentameter, I thought I could detect an imitation of Dryden's style. It became apparent to me after having read the play to its conclusion, that Rochester was not merely depicting such detestable indecency for its own sake, but rather to compose a vicious satire on it. For all the monstrous and disgusting debaucheries he described, often employing words from the most loathsome depths of London's gutters, the final curtain descended only after the entire cast of miscreants was smitten by a heavenly scourge of fire and brimstone.

The impression of this scabrous and scandalous opus on my youthful and sensitive mind was such that for some days afterward I found it necessary to refrain from reading drama. For a change of literary ambience, I read Henry More's *Anti-dote Against Atheism*, with its chilling accounts of vampires, and other fearsome revenants, which brought to mind the Negro tales which had made me shudder as a tender child. I must confess that after such vivid and perturbing fare I once again required a change. Remembering that I had brought with me a selection of recently arrived periodicals from London and Paris, I turned my attention to more modern matters.

Concerned as I had been with both personal affairs and my education in the classics, I had, over the past year, quite neglected the world in which I dwelt. News of London especially interested me, for though I had still been but a child when I returned with my foster parents to America, clear recollections of the city still burnt brightly in my mind. How dearly I had loved strolling along the Strand before dusk, or in Covent Garden early in the morning, listening to street cries, avidly, unabashedly staring at the jiggling, jangling river of humanity that passed before my eyes.

Though I enjoyed many a day of tranquil repose at The Lower Byrd, filling my soul with beauty and knowledge, I also spent many a solitary day and evening brooding over the lost Elmira. My heart still ached with a burning pain of love for her. I cursed with bitter anguish the fate that had plucked her from my life, and then, to soothe the hurt, I began composing verses inspired by the thought of her.

> *O, she was worthy of all love!*
> *Love—as in infancy was mine—*
> *'Twas such as angel minds above*
> *Might envy; her young heart the shrine*
> *On which my every hope and thought*
> *Were incense—then a goodly gift,*
> *For they were childish and upright—*
> *Pure—as her young example taught:*
> *Why did I leave it, and, adrift,*
> *Trust to the fire within, for light?*

A melancholy overcame me as I continued setting pen to paper and I began to feel a longing for the companionship of others, the warmth of my fellows in conviviality, the gentle smile, the modest glance of the fair sex—the latter if only to remind me of my lost love. The thought then occurred to me one moonlit night that if, perchance, I strolled out to the slave quarters after the evening meal, I might tarry a while to listen to a fragment of the weird tales or mesmeric chants which had so entranced me as a child. How I used to thrill with exquisite terror at the invocation of images so starkly drawn by the deep and sonorous Negro voices. How I trembled at each hearing of how shrieking ghosts and howling spirits, risen from the dust of mouldering graves, would rant and wail and tear asunder all who dared defy their murderous purposes.

Only brief images of recollection remain, like frozen figures of motionless basalt, illuminated against a moonless sky by lightning flashes and throbbing drums. Swaying dancers, black skin gleaming in the flickering firelight, rising voices chanting strange, exotic names—voices evoking far-off places by the borders of the rivers Gambia, Congo, Volta, and Zaire. The rumbling, tumbling, grumbling drums accompany the voices, rising, swelling, and chanting unfamiliar names.

Fragments, mysterious fragments of long-forgotten and ancient lore. Broken glass and broken leg, twitching bodies, writhing in the dust, gasping, moaning, crying out in ecstasy. Broken glass and Legba. Agwé, Agwé, where the waters are. Where woods begin. Black Baka[2] barks in the satin of the night. When falls the night the fingers touch. The time of death. The time of birth.

> Agwé ties them all together
> Agwé sleeps over them
> Agwé dances over them
> Agwé rules the dance
> Agwé rules the sleep.

What strange and powerful force gripped me as these distant memories enveloped the shadowy corridors of my brain? Even now, as I write, 'tis as though I were in the power of some unseen agency. Mesmerized[3] by a dim figure, obscured by the mists of time, it eludes me. I cannot distinguish its face; yet it beckons to me and only by exerting the most strenuous concentration can I wrest myself from its fearful influence.

Casting a backward glance upon that melancholy night, a deep sadness envelops me like a shroud. I had barely entertained a single thought of thus evoking the past when an enigmatic oblivion overcame me. When I regained my senses[4] I was no longer in the warm solitude of my lamplit chamber. Still in my trance, I found myself standing at the threshold of a poor cabin in the slave quarters. Barring my way, a lantern held high in one gnarled hand, was a familiar figure. Upon recognising her I was overwhelmed with spontaneous emotions of affection, for it was Judith, the woman who had been my mammy until the sixth year of my life. No woman of my own race could have lavished more affection upon me, so tenderly had she cared for me and ministered to my needs. The harsh changes wrought upon her by time bore grim testimony to the impermanence of that greatest of all heaven-sent gifts: youth. The cherished, rotund countenance of yore was now gaunt, etched with deep wrinkles, and hollow of cheek. The once sable, woolly hair had faded to grey, and the once dancing eyes now contemplated me, lustreless, empty, and reflecting ineffable sadness. Her easy familiarity of manner was no more, and though she still addressed me as "Master Eddy," she made no effort to enfold me in her arms. Indeed, when I impulsively reached out to her, she recoiled from my touch as from some poisonous reptile or loathsome and noxious vermin.

A thousand disconnected thoughts raced through my mind. I knew what inevitable schism had been enforced upon us. No longer a child in the eyes of society, I was excluded by powerful, unspoken rules from recapturing those happy moments of my past when Negroes were not seen as property, to be regarded as little more than animated specimens of merchandise. Then, in my eyes, they were fantastical beings, akin to faeries and elves, giants and sorcerers, within whose dusky breasts were locked secrets of countless mysteries, tales of tragedy and triumph, magic and arcane lore, now barred to me forever.

Gradually comprehending what had occurred, I drew back, muttered some vacuous explanation for my presence, which we both knew to be falsehood, then nodding decorously, I took my leave. But then, when I had put a distance of perhaps twenty yards between myself and the cabin, like Lot's wife, I was impelled to stop and turn back. She still stood there, framed by the shadowy doorway, her lantern in hand, raised as if to illuminate my way, a final act of solicitude. Although the distance was too great for me to ascertain with any degree of accuracy, I will swear until I breathe my last that there were tears in her eyes. Watching me as I stood there in the moon-drenched path leading back to the main house, she shook her head slightly from side to side, turned, and retreated into the cabin. At that moment I knew that it was time for me to return to Richmond.

How quickly the days had flown. Wintry frosts were on the wane. Sunlight's golden warmth pervaded the countryside. The skies above assumed a deeper shade of blue, and tender buds of green began appearing as early harbingers of birth and renewal. Inspired by the primal forces of awakening nature, my heart was filled with hope that upon my homecoming there would be a reconciliation between my guardian and myself.

I had formulated a plan, which in the guilelessness of my youthful inexperience, I was convinced would find favour with John Allan. It had grown out of a suggestion made in a letter[5] to me from my brother, Henry, who, having lately returned from sea, had settled in Baltimore with members of the family to commence his own literary career. Having known only poverty, which was the overwhelming misfortune of the Poes, he had been deeply impressed with the luxurious surroundings in my adopted household.[6] No Grecian busts, rich tapestries, crystal chandeliers, or fine oil paintings graced the modest walls where Henry was domiciled. Only the honour emanating from the illustrious reputation of our late grandfather, "General" Poe, remained. But honour and patriotism, though noble traits which can never be taken away, have never been known to satisfy the omnipresent demands of the landlord, the greengrocer, and the haberdasher.

Knowing all of the details surrounding the misfortunes having befallen me upon my return from Charlottesville, Henry was concerned lest I take some fatal step, arising from my impulsive and passionate nature, which would prompt my guardian to eject me from his house. "You must not forget, dear brother," he wrote, "that Mr. Allan has never formally bestowed his name upon you, or to your knowledge, named you as his heir. That he desires you to pursue a worldly course in life along lines parallel to his own, is understandable. But you are still in possession of your youth and good health; therefore, I beseech you, do not antagonise him or inspire his rath [sic] prematurely. Humour him to the fullest extent of your capability. Your muse will not desert you if, for expediency's sake for a time you endeavour to please your benefactor, who, you must never forget, is one of the richest men in the state of Virginia. . . . "[7]

Henry's suggestion was that I seek employment in another state with a mercantile firm. By so doing, he reasoned, I would accomplish a twofold purpose. I would convince my guardian that I had given in to his wishes for my future by entering the world of commerce and I would gain his respect by making the effort of my own accord. Secondly, I would place myself beyond the reach of any warrants which might be issued against me in the state of Virginia; yet in earning money of my own, I would be in a position to commence repaying my creditors.

O God! How naïve we both were. Late in January John Allan sent me an oral message via the medium of a servant. Why he did not commit himself to paper was a mystery to me at the time, but I believe now that it was done merely to afford himself the means of denial afterwards were he to so choose. It was a brief suggestion that I return at once and consider reading for the law in Richmond. I responded with a short note requesting permission to remain at the plantation a while longer, but adding respectfully that should he desire me to return at once I would do so. Receiving no reply I assumed that he was willing to postpone matters until my return.

By the last week in February, shortly before my resolve to quit The Lower Byrd, and face whatever awaited me in Richmond, I wrote a letter to the Mills Nursery Company in Philadelphia, making a request for employment. I knew it to be a reputable firm which had done business with Ellis & Allan for a number of

years. Having had no reply from them by the time I determined
to leave the plantation, I made arrangements for any reply to be
forwarded, packed what few belongings I had in my possession,
and embarked on the short journey which would bring me back to
the only home I had ever known.

My adored "Ma" greeted me with warm effusions of love as
she clasped me to her bosom. My guardian was not at home when
I arrived. He was no doubt lavishing his attentions upon one of
his mistresses, for he did not return until well after the midnight
hour. This caused me no discomfort, for it gave me the opportunity to be alone for the greater part of the day with my foster
mother. What a joyous occasion it was! I read her my latest
verses and spoke to her of my dreams, while she spoke gaily of all
the doings in Richmond, making an effort to avoid mention of
those topics which she felt might disquiet me. Yet, something
about her troubled me. Her skin was too waxen and too transpar-
ent, the blue veins of her lofty forehead appeared too prominent,
and the hint of dark circles beneath her loving eyes bespoke of
matters I cared not to dwell upon.

The delicacy of her health required that she retire to her bed
shortly after the evening meal, and being somewhat wearied
myself by the journey from Goochland County, I betook myself
to my chamber. I must confess that, though refreshed after a
night of sound sleep, it was impossible to repress the apprehensions I felt on contemplation of seeing John Allan at breakfast.
He greeted me civilly, but with the cool reservation I recalled so
well from that bleak period before I repaired to The Lower Byrd.
Indicating no concern for me over any private matters, he said
nothing about our communication regarding his recommendation
that I read for the law. When I alluded to the subject, he merely
glanced briefly at me, peering down his hawk nose, and muttered
some nonsequitur to the effect that he was not my keeper, but
rather my protector. There was a ring to his words that I did not
like.

For two entire weeks we continued thus, neither engaging in
fruitful conversation nor crossing swords in warlike confrontation. Yet there was an unmistakable air of tension between us
which grew ever more taut until the fateful Sunday, March eigh-

teenth. By that time, what transpired between us was inevitable, manifesting itself in the manner of a loud and fearful skirmish of verbal bellicosity. My nerves by this time had begun to feel the strain of this and other unpleasantnesses. In the precise manner that I had known during the period between Christmas and New Year's Day, I was again subject to the whims and caprices of certain household blacks. The constant humiliation taxed me to the limits of my sensibilities.

Upon my mentioning this to him at the dinner table, he fixed me with a piercing glance and imperiously suggested that we refrain from such conversation until afterwards, at which time we might resume it in the library. My heart began beating wildly in my breast, for I knew full well that whatever bad blood had so long been festering between us would now erupt into the open, either to wash away all past ill-will or break whatever bonds remained between us for all time to come.

I finished my meal in silence and waited for my guardian to signal his readiness to remove himself to the library. He appeared in no great hurry and pointedly lingered over a cordial after his demitasse. After what seemed to me the passage of a veritable eternity he rose from his place at the head of the table and announced to his wife and her sister that he had business to discuss with "Master Poe," pronouncing my name most peculiarly and in a fashion that I felt in my heart did not bode well for me.

A man who was as frugal with his words as he was with cash—at least, insofar as I was concerned—John Allan had little to say that I had not previously heard from his lips on previous occasions. He upbraided me in one breath for "eating the bread of idleness," then contradicted himself by demanding to know by what right I dared to presume that I could slink out of town like a criminal in the night, leaving my debts unpaid. At first I was baffled, and knew not to what he referred. "Sir," said I, "it was never my intention to do anything of the sort!" Whereupon he brandished before me, like Macbeth's bloody dagger, a letter from the Mills Nursery Company in Philadelphia. They had written him to verify my position in his household upon receiving my application for employment.

Though I endeavoured to explain to him my reasons for having written the company, he refused to hear me, instead hurling further reproaches at me, not only for my "sinful and profligate ways," but for insolence and ingratitude. I parried this thrust by volunteering to show him how, by means of my scholarship, I had been naught but a credit to him, reminding him that had he but provided me with the necessary means to support myself in the accepted manner at the university, I would never have accrued so much as ten pennies worth of debt.

An ejaculation of contempt and disbelief escaped his lips followed by a declaration that I knew not whereof I spoke. In the consummate folly of my arrogance and youth (he told me) I had failed to learn the value of money and the importance of frugality. The very thought of accruing debts at my age, he exclaimed, was abhorrent. Then, lapsing into the distinctive burr of his ancestor's speech, he hurled an ancient Scottish proverb at me: "He tha spends afore he thrives will beg afore he thinks!"

Then pausing, no doubt for dramatic effect, he thrust a cigar into his mouth, and after some difficulty with the flint, ignited it from the flame of a candle. Exhaling a thick cloud of smoke, he said, "Ye hae brought naught but tears tae the cheek o' my puir wife an' disgrace tae this house! An' if it were no fer tha dear, bonnie creature's sake, I wad turn ye oot fer th' ingrate ye be." Then, pausing once more, he contemplated me solemnly, shaking a long, bony finger in my face before he spoke. "Ain mair chance an nae mair than tha' I'll gie ye. But mark me weel! Ye'll dance tae th' tune o my piper no yours."

Though burning with apprehension and humiliation, there nonetheless remained within me a spark of hope. Perhaps there was a vestige of kindness left in his heart. I said, "Am I to understand, sir, that if I vow obedience you will satisfy my debts and return me to the university next year?"

Upon hearing this he threw back his head and uttered a mirthless laugh. "D'ye take me fer daft?" he retorted. "Ah, no laddie, my intentions fer yer future run quite a different coorse."

"But, Pa," I repeated, "what of my debts?"

Once again he laughed, but this time his voice assumed a dark, sardonic tone. "He tha has his hand in the lion's mouth maun tak it out as best he can," he quoted. His meaning was all too clear. If I wished to extricate myself from the jeopardy in which I found myself, I had to do as best I could without the expectation of assistance from him. Without giving me the opportunity to further plead my cause, he bade me a curt "goodnight," and said that he would expect to hear my decision in the morning, at which time we would discuss the nature of his plans for me. I slept badly that night, dreaming dreams so fantastic I remember them to this day, perhaps because they differed so from any I had experienced before.

When I awakened, gasping for breath, morning had dawned and I was exhausted, as if I had not slept a single moment during the demon-haunted night.

Soberly I performed my ablutions, dressed, and descended to the dining room. Though I had no inkling at that precise moment, I was embarking on what would be one of the most momentous days of my life.

8

And, pride, what have I now with thee?
Another brow may even inherit
The venom thou has pour'd on me—

W E BROKE OUR FAST together, my guardian and I, alone in the privacy of the library. There was a certain smugness to his expression, for I believe he was convinced that he had finally triumphed in his relentless campaign to break my spirit and mould me into a pale likeness of himself. Would I have acceded to his Draconian demands had he consented to settle my debts? I do not believe it was within my capacity to have done so. I am also convinced that he was, in that respect, as conversant with my true nature as I myself. I believe that he committed an act akin to one of the very offences he so bitterly opposed in me—he gambled.

Knowing too well the nature of my boyish pride, he cunningly goaded me, heaping accusation upon accusation, insult upon insult. First he uttered vile words on the character of my poor dead mother by raising the issue of the paternity of my sister, Rosalie. These cruelties came from the hypocritical lips of this wretched seducer, betrayer of the wife who went to her grave unblemished and pure. Next he defamed the familial blood flowing in my veins—he, whose bastards gave eloquent, living testimony to his duplicity and villainy. And as a final gesture of malice, with a gauntlet of acerbic words flung into my face like a challenge to mortal combat, he declared that had it not been for his generosity, his charitable nature, and his deference to his loving wife, he would have cast me out into the streets "like a dog" long ago.

Had I entertained any doubts, they fled at that moment. That he bore me no affection was confirmed by his words. My hopes, my aspirations were blasted. Were I to retain so much as a fraction of my dignity I had to quit his house forthwith. And so, leaping to my feet, I seized the empty china cup from which I had just drunk and flung it to the floor, smashing it into a thousand fragments. "Scoundrel!" I cried, in a voice husky with rage, while every syllable I uttered seemed as new fuel to my fury. "Scoundrel, accursed villain, you *shall not* use me thus until my spirit is broken!"

His face turned livid, for never before had I addressed him in tones and words of such defiance. Raising himself to his full height, he turned, and with outstretched arm, pointed to the door; then he shouted: "Get out ye foisonless, cankered gileynour,* and dinna let me ever see yer gloomy face again! Yer faither I'm not and n'er will be!" And with that I fled from the house with naught but the clothes I wore, knowing not what the future held in store, for now I had neither money, prospects, nor home.

For some time after my precipitous departure from the house of John Allan my mind was in a state of severe agitation and thus I wandered aimlessly, but at a brisk pace, through the streets of Richmond. By midday my excitation had turned to profound melancholy, for as I walked the desperation of my situation became all too apparent to me. Not only was I penniless and homeless, I was in danger of arrest at any moment, should bailiffs with warrants present themselves. And not to be ignored was the fact that the pangs of hunger were gnawing at my entrails—a sensation with which I was to grow intimately familiar, on frequent occasions, during the years which lay ahead.

As time passed, so increased my desperation. Then as the clock struck one, I resolved to call upon the one friend whose name came to mind in this hour of desperate need—Ebenezer Burling, for it was he who had often been companion to me during boyish escapades of happier years. I betook myself to his house on Bank Street, and fortunately found him at home. After I had recounted the unhappy events surrounding my breach with John Allan, he had his servant fetch me some food and volunteered to explore with me the full nature of my dilemma.

---

*You tasteless, ill-mannered deceiver.

During the course of my anguished peregrinations about the city after so hasty a departure from the Allan household, I had resolved to take passage to the city of my birth, Boston.[1] It was the literary capital of America, and surely, there, I would find a publisher for my poems and assume my rightful place in the world of letters. Ah, how simplistically runs the eager mind of inexperienced youth. But first, before I could embark on this voyage to a new life, it was necessary for me to take steps to ensure my survival from day to day, the acquisition of lodgings being uppermost on my list of priorities. I could not, however, merely present myself to some strange innkeeper or hosteler. There was the ominous matter of the warrants.

It was Ebenezer who provided a partial solution to my problems. Why not, he suggested, assume an alias, and make arrangements with some stranger to accept and hold correspondence for me? He recommended Court House Tavern, where he had a nodding acquaintance with the proprietor, but where I was unknown. I selected the European-sounding name of Henri Le Rennet. It was not my intention, however, to lodge at that establishment. I had no funds and therefore it would be impossible to establish the necessary credit, especially lacking a trunk or other travelling cases. It was distinctly possible, however, that I might take refuge at Mrs. Richardson's tavern, for she was kindly disposed toward me and looked upon Ebenezer and myself as favoured patrons. We were in perfect agreement that her discretion could be relied upon.

Having formulated our plans, we put them into execution forthwith, and by sundown I was comfortably ensconced in a small, but adequate garret chamber at Mrs. Richardson's. It was at this juncture that Ebenezer and I had our first disagreement. Exercising perfect logic, he pointed out to me that since I had neither money nor clothing, painful though it might be, I had no choice but to send a message to my guardian with a final request for assistance. At first I refused to hear of this, but at his insistence I reluctantly concluded that my friend was right. Not only was I without funds and clothing, but every one of my precious manuscripts was still in the room of the house at Fifth and Main. Thus, though it galled me to the very core of my soul, I took pen in hand, and wrote a dignified appeal, requesting that Allan send me my trunk and effects, with sufficient small funds to support myself until such time as I might obtain gainful employment in Boston. A softer heart, however desirous of ridding me from his life, would most certainly have replied to such a humble and desperate appeal. John Allan did not pen me so much as a single word.

I do not know precisely what events transpired in the Allan household during this unhappy period, but I can only presume to guess that a tearful episode came to pass between the wretch and the poor dear soul who had given so lavishly of her affection to an orphan scorned and loveless save for her own unselfish nobility. In any case I heard nothing, and was forced to endure the torture of waiting—yet hearing nothing. It was the first inkling I had of what prison must be like, thus strengthening my resolve never to allow myself to be so confined.

At the end of the day in my desperation I scribbled another letter to John Allan, hoping that he might undergo a change of heart, yet half-knowing, as I sat there in shadow and despair, that once again he would turn his back upon me. By midday of March twenty-first I could no longer endure another minute in the garret at Mrs. Richardson's for fear of going mad, so I repaired to the wharves to make enquiries of various ships' captains about the possiblity of my taking passage to Boston, even if it necessitated my working to pay for my passage.

In his reply to my second letter, John Allan refused me.[2] Although the twelve dollars I required would have been a paltry sum for him, it was the same as a fortune to me, for I had not even a penny. All that stood between myself and total destitution was the generosity of my friend Ebenezer. Though he did not belong to one of Virginia's first families, and was the son of a widow with a modest legacy, he was employed by a ship's chandler, and enjoyed a modicum of credit with Mrs. Richardson.

My excursion to the various ships in port proved fruitless. Even had I been in possession of the necessary funds for my passage, not a single captain bound for Boston would have me. Each vouchsafed that he had a full roster of passengers. It was as though there were a conspiracy against me, a supposition which proved to be true, although I did not learn of it until some years

later. As the story was related to me by a distant relation of the
Valentine family, with whom I became acquainted when I was
editor of *The Southern Literary Messenger*, my foster mother,
having learned of my intention to sail for Boston, pleaded tearfully with her husband, begging him to prevent me from leaving
Richmond. It was her fond but fruitless hope, that by ensuring
my continued presence, she could prevail upon him, then upon
me, and eventually effectuate a reconciliation between us.

Having failed so miserably in my efforts to arrange for a
passage to the North, I was in a greater state of melancholy than
ever upon my return to Mrs. Richardson's tavern. Imagine, then,
my surprise upon finding the familiar dark figure of Dabney
Danbridge awaiting me. As one of my favourite servants from the
Allan household, the sight of him had a cheering effect on me. He
greeted me cordially, in a manner reminding me of happier days,
and gave me an envelope containing a brief note from my dear
"Ma" pleading with me to come home and beg the forgiveness of
her husband by tendering my humblest apologies and promising
that I would acquiesce to his every wish. Enclosed was the sum of
seven dollars, enough to live on for a week perhaps, to be sure, but
not nearly enough to allow me to leave Richmond.

For a brief instant the temptation to return and throw myself
upon Allan's mercy was strong. But I could not bring myself to do
it. I was too proud, too determined. Instead I pressed two dollars
into Dabney's palm and asked him to bring me the trunk with my
precious manuscripts of verse, and whatever articles of clothing
he could pack, as well as some blank sheets of paper, pens, and
my inkstand and sandcaster. "Oh, Mars Eddy," exclaimed the
Negro, shaking his head from side to side, "yo mama she ebber so
hankerin for you to come home."

Although he would not confess to it, I suspected that she had
put him up to this attempt to bring me back. I finally convinced
him of my need to flee by appealing to the depths of his heart.
Said I, "Think of me, Dab, as you would a black man, striking off
his bonds of slavery and running away to freedom."

"But Mars Eddy," he protested, "you is a white man, you
neber been in chains like black folks has."

"Dab," I replied, "if I were to return to that house and bend to the will of its master, I would be bound by a form of bondage as wretched, as cruel, and as harsh as that which enslaves the lowliest field hand in all the South."

I do not think he thoroughly comprehended my words, but there was no question in my mind that I had touched his heart, and that he had grasped the emotions in them for, though he walked out muttering sadly to himself, he promised faithfully to perform later that night the task I requested of him. His intentions were obvious to me at once. He would enlist the aid of one or more other trusted servants; then under cover of darkness while the household slept, he would follow my instructions, stealthily remove my trunk, and deliver it to me in care of Mrs. Richardson.

There was something about the knowledge of having a small sum of money in my possession that helped to some degree in banishing my melancholy, and when Ebenezer came to join me— we had planned to sup together that evening—it was my intention to play the host. It was the least I could do in light of what he had done to give me succour in my time of need. And what a feast it proved to be: oyster soup with leeks, succulent fresh pork chops, roasted turnips, steaming baked apples with cinnamon, tender spring greens, and dessert of hot pecan pie, prepared by Mrs. Richardson's own hand, she having only recently received a barrel of fine pecans from her cousin in Georgia.

Having washed down our repast with hearty mugs of English ale, I must confess that the effect made me a trifle lightheaded. I will further confess here—for I have never made the admission to a living soul, and will not do so as long as I live—that strong drink was ever my nemesis. I did not like it. I seldom craved it, but once I partook I found it beyond my powers to stop, either until I was in a state of high nervous excitation or utter senselessness. As a rule, one drink alone was enough to undo me. I know that I have been called a drunkard by enemies and friends alike. That this is untrue can only be proven by history, and I leave the final judgement in the hands of those as yet unborn, who may regard me with more tolerant hearts.

But to return to that eventful evening. Perhaps because I had partaken of so hearty a meal, the ordinarily insalubrious effects

of the ale upon my constitution did not infuse me with the spark
which upon occasion ignited the troublesome side of my nature.
Temporarily gone were my emotions of melancholy. Vanished
were my fears, my apprehensions. My heart overflowed with love
for my fellow creatures. Like Tamburlaine the Great, if provided
with a sword and horse, I could have gone forth and conquered
the world.

Thus, when Ebenezer, somewhat more in his cups than I,
suggested that we adjourn to another place wherein we might
engage in greater revelry, I applauded his sagacity, and arm in
arm we sallied forth into the night. The tavern to which he had
alluded was one he attended infrequently, and which I had never
visited. Its name, as I recall, was *The Golden Bowsprit*. Located
on a well-traveled street near the riverfront, it was a haunt of
seafaring men and their women. Over the entrance swung its
sign, a large, weatherbeaten board bearing both lettering and a
large gilt picture of that for which it was named. Even before we
entered, the sounds of merriment within could be clearly heard,
and from the very moment we set foot inside, we found ourselves
in a world quite different from the one in which we dwelt.

Raucous laughter rang out over an incessant, lively babble of
hearty voices interspersed with clinking glasses, thumping on
tables, and occasional, high-pitched female shrieks, some in protest, most in glee. A thick haze of pungent smoke hung suspended
in the air like morning mists in the Ragged Mountains, and
though the dimness of the lamplight rendered the atmosphere
murky indeed, there was yet a decided ambience of cheer.

In this company of rough seamen and their fancy ladies, Ebenezer and I must have stood out in vivid contrast, but if such were
the case, no one took special note of us. All appeared too
concerned with the matter of their own merrymaking to pay us
any heed. Having found the ale I had partaken of with supper to
my liking, I ordered more here as did Ebenezer. Soon, between
the intoxicating effects of the ale and the infectiousness of the
revelry around us, we felt as though here, amidst the laughter,
song, and general good-natured tumult, was the real world,
whereas what we had left beyond the doors was but a fantasy
land of insubstantial unreality.

A rousing cheer arose in the far corner and we strained to see the cause of it. Two sailor-musicians, one with a guitar, the other with a recorder, struck up a chantey as a young woman leapt up and began to dance. What grace, what finely sculptured lineaments she possessed, and what excitement she inspired as she whirled and twirled and skipped and leapt in time with the music. Indeed, immodest though she might have been, in such a manner did she display herself, she brought every man to his feet. They jumped up on tables, they cheered and shouted their cries of approval. So tumultuous were the accolades, the woman was driven to even greater heights of frenzy, her eyes flashing, her pearly teeth bared in a half-savage smile. In the Dark Ages she would have been accused as a witch for she moved like one possessed by demons.

At length she finished her impromptu performance and all present—men and women alike—raised their voices in resounding cheers. Some threw coins; some thumped tabletops; others crowded to the far side of the room that they might obtain a closer glimpse of her. In the surge of humanity in that direction, the chair upon which I had been standing was jostled and I, being slightly unsteady on my feet in consequence of the ale I had consumed, fell over to one side, and by some strange act of Providence, instead of breaking some portion of my anatomy, found myself nearly horizontal on the floor, surrounded on all sides by an incessantly shifting forest of sturdy legs. It was only by exercising the greatest willpower and physical effort that I was able to crawl, let alone regain my upright footing.

It was while struggling to rise up from this ungainly and serpentine posture—with little success, I must add—that my eyes fell upon a soft, oval object, which at first I took to be a motionless rat. My initial impulse was to recoil from it, but upon closer examination I saw that far from being an animate creature, it was nothing more than a drab-coloured chamois pouch. Being momentarily unable to move either forward or backward, but moved in another direction by curiosity, I reached out and took the thing in hand. It was held shut by drawstrings of leather, and judging by the weight of it there was something of consequence inside. Then, while transferring it from one hand to the other, I recognised the unmistakable feel of coins within. My heart leapt with excitement! Although my first impulse was to open it and see what the goddess of fortune had cast before me, a *caveat* burst like an exploding rocket in my brain.

Were the rightful owner of this small treasure to discover me with it in my possession he would be justified in concluding that I had stolen it, and judging from the nature of the company here, it would not do for anyone, even over the most trivial matter, to arouse the ire of any from the youngest to the most grizzled of the lot. Thus exercising the discretion that would have inspired approval from François Villon himself, I thrust the pouch into one of my pockets and kept crawling until I found sufficient space to once again assume a proper relationship to sky and earth.

Looking about me, I tried to find Ebenezer, but his face was nowhere to be seen. It was as if he had been swallowed up in a sea of bobbing heads! For obvious reasons, I suddenly found myself anxious in the extreme to take my leave of this place. The chamois pouch was a heavy weight in my jacket. My heart now pounding wildly in my breast, I began moving against the flow of the crowd, which still pressed in the direction of the corner where the musicians and the dancing girl now struggled to collect the coins that had been offered to them in tribute.

Thank heaven! no one paid me the slightest heed, although I would have been willing to swear a solemn oath upon the Holy Bible that the beating of my heart was as loud as the sound of an African drum, and surely of sufficient volume to attract the attention of all who stood within hearing. But not a man of them even glanced in my direction as I moved steadily toward the exit. Not a thought did I give now to Ebenezer. The sole preoccupation of my mind was on the pouch and its owner. What if he suddenly discovered its loss, and looking about him, saw me attempting to make my escape? My life would not be worth a sou. If only I could slip away before I was noticed!

I had to make haste! The crowd was receding. As the spectators returned to their former places, the musicians made ready to strike up another tune. There was no time to lose. My brow felt fevered and damp with perspiration. My breath now came in short, hoarse gasps. The sole means of egress was now only a few feet from where I stood. I resolved to present the outward appearance of an innocent patron, who, having partaken his fill, was now prepared to take his leave, fade away, anonymous, into the night, and be seen no more. At last I reached the door, and with a deep sigh of relief, passed through it into the darkness of the night.

Now new fears overtook me. What if I were pursued by robbers, cutthroats who cloaked themselves in funereal black and lurked in dark places to pounce upon the unwary pedestrian and divest him of his worldly possessions? I broke into a run, but quickly resumed my accustomed pace. Running, I reasoned, would never do. Only those up to no good, attendants upon nefarious deeds, were to be found running in empty streets after dark. And indeed, in the eyes of the law, I was in truth a fugitive. Suppose I were recognised and arrested, then found to possess a bag of stolen coin? The penalty for such a crime was no doubt so severe that even its contemplation was too painful to dwell upon.

Were I to survive this ordeal it was of the utmost importance that I keep my wits about me, and so, by the exercise of only the greatest willpower, I finally found myself before the threshold of Mrs. Richardson's tavern. Breathing a sigh of relief, I entered, ascended to my chamber without delay, and removed the small pouch from my pocket with a trembling hand. For a moment I hesitated, contemplating it as Hamlet did the skull of Yorick. Then undoing the leathern thongs, I opened the chamois bag and emptied its contents onto my pallet.

I could hardly believe my eyes! The good fortune that had thus befallen me was my *deus ex machina*, my liberation from bondage. There, gleaming brightly in the dim glow of the flickering candlelight was a handful of English sovereigns with a value approximating sixty dollars.[3] It was enough to pay for my expenses at Mrs. Richardson's, for my passage to Boston, and, should I deport myself frugally, to support myself until I found gainful employment there. With this silver I was able to cast off the yoke of John Allan's subjugation. How brightly false hope gleams when all about lies the putrescent decay of despair festering in the gloom.

9

Now, when storms of Fate o'ercast
Darkly my Present and my Past,
Let my Future radiant shine . . .

M Y TIME during the next two days was spent attending to
the multifold details attendant upon my departure from
Richmond. As he had promised, good old Dabney had secured
the trunk containing my belongings and had carried it in secret
under cover of darkness to my temporary lodgings at Mrs. Richardson's. I bade him deliver some lines of verse to a certain Miss
Eulalie Elizabeth Simpson, with whom I enjoyed a passionless
friendship.[1] She aspired to become a poetess one day, and had
asked me for copies of some early poems I had composed that she
might study them. Although months before I had promised to
fulfill that request, I was delinquent in doing so, the turbulence of
my life during that period of time having prevented me. It was
one unpaid debt I was able to discharge before venturing forth
into the world.

There was another matter of honour I felt most obliged to
satisfy. My good friend Ebenezer Burling had given much of
himself during this time of need, and having in effect deserted
him on the evening I found the English sovereigns, I felt obliged
to stand for a final hearty meal before embarking on my journey.
Accordingly, on the night of March twenty-second, Ebenezer and
I adjourned to the Court House Tavern, and feasted on the best
the landlord had to offer.

During the course of the evening, due in part to our mutual
weakness for strong drink, we concocted a foolish and impetuous
scheme. Instead of my sailing alone to Boston, we would embark

together for foreign ports to seek our fortunes. We would climb to
the Pyramids and navigate the Nile. We would seek ivory and
gold in darkest Africa, traverse the hot sands of the deserts on
camelback, voyage to far China, India, and Araby. Then, after
having triumphed in manly conquest, we would return in a whirl-
wind of glory, laden with riches, and tales galore to keep generations of spellbound listeners enchanted.

Thus inflamed by our boyish fantasies, which in turn were
kindled by an overindulgence in the flowing cup, we rousted an
enterprising boatman of Ebenezer's acquaintance, who earned
his bread by navigating the waters of the James River in a
pinnace. He eagerly accepted the offer to transport us to Norfolk
for the sum of one sovereign, the only barrier to our immediate
departure being the necessity of having my trunk carried on
board his tiny vessel. While his servant attended to this urgent
matter, Ebenezer and I returned to Mrs. Richardson's, where I
settled my account, and let it be known that I was sailing for
Europe on the morning tide.[2]

Within the hour we were gliding over the calm waters of the
James, a fair breeze filling the sails of the pinnace. Soon all that
could be seen of Richmond was a small, dim cluster of twinkling
lights like fading fireflies suspended motionless in the air. The
starry sky shone down from above, reflecting a serene tranquillity
so rarely known in the lives of men, and ere long, soothed by the
gentle splashing of the water against the hull, comforted by the
soft roll and pitch of the stout little vessel, I drifted off into a
dreamless and peaceful sleep.

How different in aspect the world appeared to us when we
faced it alone, along the waterfront in the port of Norfolk. No
longer did we feel like bold adventurers about to embark on
voyages of exploration and conquest. Indeed, our earlier resolve,
now influenced by the harsh light of reality, dissipated like mists
in the breeze. Our thoughts, no longer distorted by the subtle
sorcery of spirituous liquors, were now directed toward the course
we were to pursue. Ebenezer, though as good a companion as ever
I had known, now wavered in his resolve. Emotions of guilt overcame him at the prospect of abandoning his poor widowed mother
in Richmond. Furthermore, though as a boy he had frolicked

joyously as captain of his own modest skiff when he and I pursued our youthful adventures on the river, he now had reservations. Would he suffer from *mal de mer* on the high seas? Would the cough that ofttimes troubled his sleep return to plague him?

Fond though I was of my dear friend, I knew at once that certain weaknesses in his nature, which I had perceived before, were now rising to the fore. He could not decide. Should he throw his lot in with me, or should he return to the hearth of the mother who loved him? I knew as he raised these and other questions, that our destinies lay along different paths. My resolve to burst into the world of letters like an ascending rocket was still un-dimmed. Therefore, in as kindly and understanding a manner as I could, I urged him to return to Richmond, whilst I pressed on to fulfill my destiny. I truly believe that his emotions were those of overwhelming relief to hear me address him thus.

He concurred with the wisdom of my recommendation and accepted my offer to pay for the cost of his transportation home, but he insisted upon remaining at my side until I had succeeded in arranging for my passage to Boston. This being accomplished, on Friday evening, March twenty-third, Ebenezer accompanied me aboard the packet *Providence* which was to sail the following morning, weather permitting. My stateroom was quite roomy, containing two narrow berths, one above the other, and I had the good fortune to be the sole occupant. There being a coastal collier bound for Richmond, which had put into Norfolk for mail, Ebenezer took his leave of me, and agreed that upon his return to Richmond he would promulgate on my behalf the fiction that I had sailed abroad to seek my fortune. I did not know that we were destined never to see one another again, for, though I did not learn of it until some time afterward, the poor fellow contracted the cholera, and died in the early part of 1830.

Good fortune smiled upon the *Providence*, and shortly after sunrise we unfurled our canvas and set sail on the high tide. We had fine weather, although the wind was dead ahead having dropped round to the northward immediately upon our losing sight of the coast. My fellow passengers were, consequently, in high spirits and disposed to be social. One gentleman, who unlike the others, displayed a rather solemn visage, suggested that after the evening meal of our first full day at sea, a game of cards be organised for the purpose of agreeably whiling away the tedium.

Falling prey to the false light of hope which illuminates the path of the gambler, I readily agreed. In view of my all too naïve willingness to accept the challenge, the stranger offered to engage me in a preliminary game of *écarte*,[3] to fill the time until it was possible for the others to join us. I might not have so readily agreed to this, for my skill was not exceptional, but I accepted his invitation out of pure, unmitigated avarice. I detected the unmistakable sweet aroma of spirits on his breath, and observed a slight unsteadiness to his gait. Were I to play without indulging in any intoxicating beverages, it was not inconceivable that I might increase my fortunes.

It was not my intention to cheat at cards, although I must confess to an awareness that the fine line between cheating and taking advantage of one less fortunate than one's self is difficult to discern. My process of ratiocination, however, was such that I absolved myself in advance of any conscious misdemeanor. I accepted a challenge, which, if having been refused by me would undoubtedly have been accepted by others.

We adjourned to his quarters, seated ourselves, and prepared to play. My opponent placed a bottle of port on the table, and produced two glasses. I declined for reasons of health, and noticed to my satisfaction that he emptied his glass before shuffling the cards. He then dealt and commenced playing with a wild nervousness of manner for which his intoxication, I thought, might partially, but not altogether, account. In a very short time he became my debtor by a large amount, and, having taken a long draught of port, he did precisely what I had been cooly anticipating: he proposed to double our stakes. With a well-feigned show of reluctance, and not before my repeated refusals had goaded him into some angry words which gave a colour of pique to my compliance, did I finally comply.

The result, of course, did but prove how entirely the prey was in my toils; in less than an hour he had quadrupled his debt. For some time his countenance had been losing the florid tinge lent it by the wine, but now, to my astonishment, I perceived that it had taken on a fearful pallor. That he was overcome by the wine he had been so steadily consuming was the idea which most readily presented itself, so that I was about to insist peremptorily upon a discontinuance of the play. But, alas! before I could speak a single word, the poor wretch clapped his hands to his head, uttered an ejaculation of deepest despair, and rising from his chair, fled from the cabin.

Alarmed by this unexpected behaviour, I hastened to pursue him onto the deck. A chill envelops me at the recollection, even to this very day. Reeling as he made his way to the starboard rail, he clambered unsteadily over before I could reach him and with a frenzied shriek, flung himself into the sea. Hardly able to believe my eyes I seized the rail and peered down into the darkness of the choppy waters. Before he vanished from sight forever, his gaze locked briefly on mine. Oh, what horror I perceived in those burning orbs, what anguish, what pain!

Having been seen by several others as he flung himself into the deep, the cry "Man overboard!" rang out. Those of us who had witnessed the melancholy event rushed to the rail and peered into the sable depths of the turbulent sea, but enveloped as we were by darkness, we could see nothing but the empty vastness of the ocean that surrounded us.

Although I had had only a casual acquaintance with the unfortunate deceased I was overcome with powerful emotions of grief and remorse. Would he have deemed it necessary to end his life had he not lost so heavily to me at cards? If not, then by reason of my having deliberately taken advantage of his insobriety, and being the instrument of his destruction, I was therefore, in the eyes of Almighty God, as much his murderer as if I had plunged a dagger into his heart. I was terrified lest I somehow betray my guilt, for it was announced, when word of the tragedy had spread throughout the ship, that in the morning the captain would conduct a formal inquiry into the matter in his quarters. In the meantime, to prevent the tampering with any evidence which might shed light upon the dead man's untimely end, a seaman was posted guard in his cabin.

My mind raced back to the game of cards. The two of us had been alone and his proposal to play had been made in the presence of others, whose intention it had been to join us later. I could not, therefore, deny that I was the last person to have been in the company of the unfortunate man before his precipitous and untimely departure from life. It was with understandable uneasiness, then, that I retired to the solitude of my cabin, for I had no desire to converse with any other of my fellow passengers at the moment. The state of nervous agitation in which I found myself made sleep impossible at first, but as I lay upon my berth listening to the incessant creaking of the ship and the splashing of the waves against her hull, I eventually drifted into an uneasy sleep, rendered painful by dreams in which the face of the deceased, dripping with brine, his corpse-eyes staring hideously, kept appearing before me as if in reproach for having driven him to his watery sepulchre.

When my summons to the captain's quarters came the following morning, my heart beat wildly and I fought mightily with myself to maintain an outward appearance of tranquillity. Were it necessary for me to defend myself in any manner, it occurred to me that the matter of the dead man's losses to me need never be known. He had not paid me in cash, but rather had given me a series of promissory notes, which, he assured me, would be honoured by his banker upon our arrival in Boston. Although it had been with a heavy heart, I tore them all to shreds, knowing full well the inculpating effect they might have had were their existence to become known.

The captain of the *Providence* was a stern man with a ruddy complexion and well-trimmed whiskers of iron-grey. To my relief he received me in private and brusquely proceeded to question me on a subject quite beyond my predetermined expectations. Had I observed anything strange about the manner of the deceased, he asked? I could think of nothing other than his predisposition to consume an inordinate quantity of wine. "Then he told you nothing about himself?" said the captain. "Nothing," said I. To which reply the captain shook his head sadly and emitted a deep sigh.

"For reasons that will be obvious to you," he then said, "you must swear not to reveal a word of what I am about to tell you." Puzzled by this turn of events, I gave him my word, at which juncture he went to his locker and fetched a hoary and weather-beaten Bible. Returning to me he held the holy book out and bade me place my hand upon it. "I must ask you to swear, sir!" he ordered. Sensing at once that I was in no way under any cloud of suspicion regarding the mysterious gentleman's death, I was overcome with relief, and readily obeyed the captain's command. This formality dispensed with, he returned the Bible to its place and invited me to be seated. Then he began to speak. His Yankee accent fell harshly on my ears, accustomed as I was to the softer quality of Southern speech, yet I hung attentively on his every word.

With solemn face and sombre voice he explained the tragic circumstances under which the ill-fated deceased embarked upon what proved to be the final portion of his earthly voyage. A week prior to sailing he had engaged passage for himself and his young wife. Shortly thereafter, however, she sickened and three days later she died. Disconsolate with grief, the husband resolved to take the remains of his adored bride back to his home in Boston for interment in the family plot. However, the universal prejudice which would prevent his doing so openly was well known. Nine-tenths of the passengers would have abandoned ship rather than take passage with a corpse.

Facing this dilemma the captain had arranged that the dead body, being first partially embalmed and packed with a large quantity of salt, in a box of suitable dimensions, should be conveyed on board as merchandise. Unluckily, upon being lowered onto the deck, the box was broken slightly, causing a substantial quantity of the salt to escape. Learning of this, the captain, fearing that decomposition of the corpse might betray its presence, ordered that late at night, under cover of darkness, it be buried at sea. Although it was with great reluctance that he was compelled to make this decision, it was, in his opinion as master of the vessel, imperative for the well-being of his passengers. Reluctantly, he announced his intention to the bereaved husband. Torn between his comprehension of the reasoning behind the captain's decision and a growing horror at having to surrender the mortal remains of his beloved to the deep, he began drinking heavily as darkness approached. Why he engaged me in a game of cards is a matter for conjecture. It was the theory of the captain that the gentleman had become deranged and believed that he had been irrevocably abandoned by the goddess of fortune upon learning that he must surrender the corpse of the wife he adored to the domain of the deep. It was my further conviction that upon gambling and losing, he confirmed this distressing opinion, and thus, further deprived of reason by the wine, plunged into the sea to await a final reunion with his beloved, when she, too, would be consigned to the dark waters.

Although the captain's melancholy narrative in part assuaged my feelings of remorse at having played a role, albeit minute, in the poor fellow's demise, I have never, even unto this very day, been able to forget the expression on his face ere he vanished forever beneath the waves. Often it has returned to haunt me in troubled dreams. It was in fact, this incident, having preyed upon my mind since its occurrence, that inspired me some years later to compose my tale "The Oblong Box."

10

So that the blade be keen—the blow be sure,
'Tis well, 'tis very well—alas! alas!

THROUGH THE GOOD offices of a fellow passenger on board the *Providence*, I was given the address of a modest rooming-house where I might obtain lodgings for a price well within my limited ability to pay. It was a large house in the North End, not far from the inner harbour where I had debarked. Old fashioned and rambling, the place had a gloomy air to it, with creaking staircases, long barren corridors, vestibules, windings, crannies, and seemingly interminable mysterious nooks. My room was a tiny chamber in a turret, from which I could see the top of the spire of the old North Church.

Once having settled in, I made up my mind to take a stroll about the city, it being a pleasant and balmy April afternoon. It was also my intention to seek, if possible, individuals who might have been acquainted with my late parents. After my uncommonly arduous sea voyage, the feel of *terra firma* beneath my feet was more than an inducement to brisk walking. As the hours passed I observed that there was much of the city that reminded me of London. Being older and far more populous than Richmond, it was invigorating, and the tumultuous sea of humanity excited me. Very soon, I became absorbed in contemplation of the busy scene around me.

With the gathering of dusk, pangs of hunger overtook me, influenced, no doubt, by the presence of street vendors purveying comestibles of many varieties: clams, oysters, fish fresh and smoked, sausages, cakes, loaves of bread, buns, yams, apples, condiments, and candies. To be surrounded thus by such an array of tempting edibles caused the mind to reel. As I strolled about sampling those things that appealed most to my palate, I learned that I was in the Haymarket. Lively though it was, I marvelled at the indifference to the street cries and din of vehicles from the natives going about their business. Immense charcoal waggons gave forth a clatter which I can liken to nothing earthly (unless, perhaps a gong), from some metallic, triangular contrivance within the bowels of the "infernal machine." To live in a district such as this would be disagreeable beyond measure.

It was quite dark by the time I had finished my modest repast and I was beginning to experience pangs of quite another hunger—those of loneliness—a need for the companionship of others. They were pangs I knew all too well, for one as young as I. Though my "Ma" had tenderly cared for me as a child, there was an underlying fear that every orphan knows—the vulnerability that springs from never knowing when one might be cast adrift. By never formally adopting me and bestowing his name upon me, my guardian had left me with no more true security than that of an empty bottle bobbing aimlessly on the waves.

Those sentiments of loneliness, which are always more strongly experienced when surrounded by strangers, had grown intense in me. As I wandered about the city, from time to time I had entered shops and accosted hackmen with enquiries concerning the possible whereabouts of friends who had known my father or mother. Having received not a single affirmative response, I knew that now I was more alone than ever I had been in my life.

Being still unfamiliar with the city of Boston, and observing that there were now fewer persons on the streets, I resolved to take my bearings and return to my lodgings. It was best that I retire early and in the morning commence a resolute quest for gainful employment. For a moment as I stood on the streetcorner, before venturing into what I believed to be the proper direction for me to follow, a gust of wind gave me a chill, and I gathered my cloak about me. At that moment I felt a hand touch my shoulder. Being somewhat apprehensive, having heard sombre accounts of cutpurses, gammons,* and other ruffians lurking in

---

*Pickpocket's accomplices

dark streets, I whirled around. To my astonishment and relief, I found myself facing a young woman. Although by now it was too dark for me to see her features clearly, they were visible enough. On the far corner was a flickering street-lamp, which bathed us both in the periphery of its soft glow.

That she was a fallen woman, a demimondaine, I was certain, for what respectable female would thus accost a stranger in the streets after nightfall. But there was an elusive quality about her which prevented me from dismissing her forthwith. As I gazed at her features I could detect early signs of dissolution. Yet, upon closer examination it became clear that she was unquestionably a woman who not long ago had been quite beautiful. Glossy, dark locks tumbled down about her shoulders and framed her face, which despite the faint blush of rouge upon her cheeks and lips, was smooth and translucent as the finest alabaster. Her distinctly aristocratic features were faintly reminiscent of my lost Helen.

Despite my innate revulsion at the knowledge of her profession, my heartbeat quickened, and disturbing, vaguely familiar longings stirred within me. Addressing me softly, she took my arm without invitation; and as though we were two old friends, we began walking. I believe that had I not been so starved for conversation I would never have permitted myself to succumb to her blandishments. I would most certainly spurn such improprieties today, being older and wiser in the ways of the world. But in the words of the Arabian poets, I was then but a "beardless youth," and blithely unaware of what was happening to me. Accepting at its face value the woman's amiability, and her outward appearance of interest in everything I had to say, I was mistakenly convinced that she was smitten by my youth, my good looks, and my erudition.

Having told her I was a poet, which was by no means a lie, she appeared excited at the prospect of hearing me recite, and proposed that I accompany her back to her apartment for tea. Eagerly accepting her invitation in my boyish naïveté, I was convinced that she saw in me the dream companion denied her by the vile profession she pursued. As we walked and gaily chatted, I saw myself becoming her true and loyal friend, providing her with respite from her onerous toils, and perhaps, in time, rescuing her from the dismal fate of the wretched Cyprian. Although I had not yet told her anything of myself, save that I was a poet, I instinctively knew that our souls were in harmony. We were of a similar stamp: she, a member of the oldest, most despised profession, an outcast from polite society; and I a friendless orphan, the offspring of poor players, a class held in equal contempt by the self-designated righteous of the world.

Suddenly, with an abruptness that nearly caused me to lose my balance, the young woman stopped and regarded me with what I could only construe as a deeply inquisitive expression. Then cocking her head to one side she said, "Are you truly a poet, or have you told me so merely to soften my heart, and pursue some other, darker purpose?" I was smitten by her words. "Dear lady," I said, "though I have yet to have the mantle of glory bestowed upon me, I am a gentleman, and upon my word as such, I assure you that I am indeed that which I represent myself as being." She contemplated my face momentarily; then, after pondering my words, she said, "Very well, sir, I accept your word, but in so doing, I throw myself on your mercy."

I was puzzled at first, but as we continued walking she bared her soul to me. I made no effort to embarrass her by confessing that I had deduced her calling in advance. Making no attempt to deny the low estate to which she had fallen, she related to me the story of her life. I will not presume to set down all the unhappy details. Her tale was a common one. Let it suffice to say that she was an orphan, like myself, and having been deprived of the tender love and guidance of a mother and father at an early age, she fell into the ways of impropriety from which there was no return for her.

A cousin, whose honeyed words and tender kisses blinded her to the vicious nature of his true character, left her with child and abandoned her. Homeless, in disgrace, and in abject poverty she lost the babe to disease on the eve of its third year.[1] Unable to resume a life of respectability she resolved to end her life by casting herself into the waters of the Charles River. But then she was stopped from this rash act by a "kindly" woman, who proved to be Mrs. Hester Markham, a notorious procuress. Choosing life over death, the young woman resigned herself to the fate of a woman of the streets.

How could my heart not go out to her, I, an orphan, whose own mother had died when I was so young? She confessed to me that she practiced her profession under the pseudonym of Nelly Flowers, but that her real name was Amelia Blackburn. She aspired to poetry writing herself, and on many a night (she said) she fell asleep with a slender volume of Byron on her lap. The reason for this unexpected outpouring, and the plea to throw herself on my mercy most certainly originated in her love of poetry. There was a small tavern, considerably distant from her bailiwick in the North End, located not far from the Common, called *The Philosopher's Stone*. It was Miss Blackburn's desire that I accompany her there, for it was, she told me, a gathering place for literati, who discoursed nightly upon the arts, and who frequently gave readings from their own works.

She further explained that occasionally she contrived to meet gentlemen who were unaware of her true calling. At those times she would suggest visiting the tavern for an evening of good conversation, poetry, and a respite from the demimonde to which she had to return, like Cinderella to the ashes. Upon those rare occasions when she visited *The Philosopher's Stone*, she employed still another pseudonym, a nom de plume, which she signed to the verses she composed, Ligeia Morelli.[2]

The tavern was a warm and friendly place with a large fireplace, fine paneled walls of dark rubbed wood, and lead glass windows which gave it a distinctive English flavour. The tables were oaken and round, so that patrons might sit in circular intimacy for the purpose of enhancing conversation. Hanging in simple but dignified frames were engravings of such literary greats as Shakespeare, Milton, Dante, and Petrarch. My heart leapt for joy as we entered, and the prospect that a new love, founded upon the pure principles of beauty and a mutual adoration of poetry, seemed closer than I dared to hope. Certainly the paradox of it made our prospects shine bright—the poet and the prostitute.[3] Indeed, why not? Without doubt she would welcome the tender moments of refuge that would free her from the base and sordid toils which provided her with daily bread.

We were greeted cordially by the proprietor, a rotund, balding man, with fine white hair and bright blue eyes, and a flowing moustache that fell below his chin. Barely had we seated ourselves than Miss Blackburn whispered something in the gentleman's ear, whereupon he contemplated me, his eyes twinkling, and announced that if I would consent to recite one of my poems for the assembled company, my companion and I would be his guests for dinner. It was customary thus to welcome new poets to the roster of regular patrons. I uttered a silent prayer of thanks, for I was hardly prepared to spend what little money I still had, and I readily consented, for I had a number of verses committed to memory. As we dined, I considered which poem I might select to serve as the proper vehicle for my debut in the realm of public recitation. I finally decided upon these lines, which I later deleted before the poem was published.

> *For being an idle boy lang syne,*
> *Who read Anacreon, and drank wine,*
> *I early found Anacreon rhymes*
> *Were always passionate sometimes—*
> *And by strange alchemy of brain*
> *His pleasures always turn'd to pain—*
> *His naïveté to wild desire—*
> *His wit to love—his wine to fire—*
> *And so being young and dipt in folly*
> *I fell in love with melancholy.*

Not only did my recitation bring on the applause of all those present but at its conclusion a young gentleman of approximately my own age presented himself and offered me his calling card. He was a printer named Calvin Thomas,[4] and he urged me to call upon him soon at his shop in Washington Street near State. The lovely Miss Blackburn was moved to tears, and when I had finished, she seized my hand and pressed it to her cheek.

The evening was filled with excitement and gratification. Though I had recited many times in the past for groups of friends, never had I done so before strangers, and the feeling of exultation was like none I had ever experienced. During those brief moments, as I stood there facing the friendly eyes of my listeners, I fancied that somewhere in the shadows stood the proud shade of my departed mother, nodding silent approval of her aspiring son.[5]

Before we took our leave, the proprietor enquired as to how soon we might return. I deferred to Miss Blackburn, for I did not know how often she might be able to devote an evening to her own private pleasure. She made no commitment, but assured the gentleman that it wold be soon. Afterwards, she explained, in her persona of Miss Morelli, she had let it be known that she did not reside in Boston, but in Worcester, some forty miles away.

Although it was nearly half-past eleven when we left *The Philosopher's Stone*, we were fortunate enough to secure a cab and in less than half an hour's time we arrived at Commercial Street some distance from the house of Mrs. Markham, where Miss Blackburn lodged. She wanted to dismiss the driver and walk the balance of the way, in order not to disturb anyone with the clatter of wheels and horses' hooves on the cobblestones. Not wishing to see her walk alone on the deserted streets at so late an hour, I insisted upon accompanying her, hoping that when I left I would not encounter too much difficulty in finding another public hackman. I was weary, and the prospect of walking from the house of Mrs. Markham to my own lodgings was not one I anticipated with relish.

I lingered at the doorway while she took the latchkey from a small purse, and when I enquired as to when we might meet again, she smiled sweetly, and suggested that I accompany her to her rooms that we might discuss the matter. Thinking nothing of the invitation, I agreed and followed her into the house. It was very dark and the vestibule was illuminated only by a single, dim, oil lamp above the balustrade of a steep, winding staircase. To prevent me from stumbling, she enfolded my hand in hers, led me up three flights of heavily carpeted stairs, and down a long, dark, passageway, until we came to a door which she informed me was the entrance to her private apartment. It was a suite consisting of a sitting room and a bedroom. The walls of the former, which was illuminated by a single lamp when we entered, were adorned with reproductions of romantic scenes depicting nymphs, satyrs, and fauns frolicking in bucolic settings. Heavy damask draperies hung over the windows, and on the floor were several thick Oriental rugs. The principal furniture in the room was a massive chaise of red velvet, upon which rested five or six pillows with ornate, embroidered patterns. Alongside was a morris chair with a purple cushion resting on the seat. Elsewhere in the room were several large ottomans, and on the other side of the chaise was a small table of adequate size to accompany a tray of refreshments.

After removing her coat and hanging it in an elegantly carved armoire on the far side of the room, Miss Blackburn bade me remove my cloak and be seated while she repaired momentarily into her boudoir. I observed a small bookcase against the wall behind the chaise, which had not caught my attention when I first entered, perhaps because of the dimness of the light. Unable to resist, I went over to examine its contents. There were *Sonnets* of Shakespeare, *Lalla Rookh*, *Gil Blas*, a volume of Byron, Disraeli's *Curiosities of Literature*, and a number of novels in cheap editions, by authors whose names were unfamiliar to me, including that of John Cleland, whose infamous *Memoirs of a Woman of Pleasure* was unknown to me at the time.[6] I had not quite finished perusing the bookcase when the lady returned from her boudoir in a white gown so immodest, so revealing of her feminine charms, that the sight of it must have brought a blush to my cheeks. She carried a tray with a cut-glass decanter and two long-stemmed glasses. "Before you take your leave," she said, "we must have some wine and toast our new-found friendship." Then, smiling as she placed the tray on the table beside the chaise, she said, "I could not possibly permit you to part company without reciting a few more of your beautiful verses."

I was flattered. What could I do? Although I experienced a slight feeling of apprehension, lest the wine have a deleterious effect upon me, I resolved to sip it slowly, instead of pouring it down as was my wont. She filled the goblets with the ruby liquid, insisting that I recline on the chaise like a Roman noble, whilst she placed herself at my feet like an adoring slave. Then bidding me make myself comfortable, she took her place on one of the ottomans and, smiling, gazed into my eyes. We raised our glasses and drank a toast to poetry. But I remained true to my resolve and took the merest sip, whilst she flung back her head and drained her glass.

Upon her ardent request that I commence reciting, I began by recalling the first lines that came into my mind.

> *In the spring of youth it was my lot*
> *To haunt of the wide world a spot*
> *The which I could not love the less—*
> *So lovely was its loneliness*
> *Of a wild lake, with black rock bound*
> *And the tall pines that towered around.*

She filled her glass and drained it twice as I recited the first stanza, yet hanging on my every word, her dark eyes burning with a fervid intensity. I continued.

> *But when the night had thrown her pall*
> *Upon that spot, as upon all,*
> *And the mystic wind went by*
> *Murmuring in melody—*
> *Then—ah then I would awake*
> *To the terror of the lone lake.*

Once more she poured and drank, this time filling my own glass to the brim, again not speaking a word, but fixing me with her now moistening, luminous eyes. Transported as I was by the music of the verse, I thoughtlessly drank my wine to the dregs as I continued to recite.

> *Yet the terror was not fright*
> *But a tremulous delight—*
> *A feeling not the jewelled mine*
> *Could teach or bribe me to define—*
> *Nor love—although the love were thine.*

Emitting a gentle sob, she gasped, "Oh, God!" her eyes now wild, her lips half parted and glistening. My heart began to pound. A nameless apprehension overcame me, I knew not why.

One half of my now reeling brain grew numb with terror, whilst the other seemed to explode with confused emotions of intermingling pleasure and pain. At that moment she leapt from the ottoman and flung herself upon me, enfolding me in a fierce embrace. Her mouth, half open in its passionate exhalation, revealed exquisite teeth, and I could feel her warm breath as her rosy lips descended to cover me with moist kisses.

The mounting terror that overcame me was akin to none I had ever known, save in my most dreadful nightmares. Though reason should have proclaimed that I had naught to fear, my reason had fled, and as I struggled, the icy hand of fear gripped my heart. Yet the fear I felt was not for myself, but for her! Surely to feel such an emotion was madness! I knew I was no threat to her. Indeed, I was prepared to love her deeply, but not with the burning fires of Eros, rather under the gentle guidance of Erato.[7] Surely, I thought, such love would be welcome respite from her joyless servitude at the shrines of Venus.

Would that I could have conveyed these sentiments to her! But alas, mistakenly taking my actions for signals of rebuff, of contemptuously spurning her favours, her visage was instantly transformed from one of beauty to an ugly mask of smouldering malignity. "Beast!" she cried. "I freely proffered you my love, my self! and you recoil from me as if I were some wretched vermin! Villain! Monster!"

Uttering a ululating scream of incoherent anguish, she seized the wine decanter and hurled it to the floor, smashing it into shiny splinters, at the same time shrieking a concatenation of vile epithets and obscenities, such as I had never heard from the lips of any other person. Then, a motion deceived me into thinking she was about to fling herself upon me again and I recoiled once more. But now I observed that she was apparently reaching beneath a certain pillow at the head of the chaise. I was about to leap aside when she loomed up above me, an ornate Florentine dagger clutched in her hand.

Her eyes, now blazing with hatred, a final curse upon her wine-stained lips, she lunged. Fearing for my very life, I twisted away, thus narrowly avoiding the point of her flashing dagger. "Die!" she shrieked in a voice that might have issued from a Fury incarnate. My previous fear became transformed into anger, not at this poor, insane strumpet, but at myself for having been foolish enough to fall prey to her seductive wiles. I parried her thrusts, employing techniques I had learned in the art of fencing.

But alas! her madness engendered a strength approaching the supernatural. We struggled amidst the crashing of objects, the smashing of glass, shrieks and cries, moans and curses, until, while defending myself, I involuntarily caused her to plunge the gleaming blade to the hilt into her milky breast. Then, Oh, God! with a fearful cry, half moan, half sob, she fell back upon the chaise, her dark eyes staring dimly upon the grim visage of Death himself, visible to me only in the reflection of her horrid expression.

As I stood there transfixed with horror, she clenched and unclenched her hands; then, convulsing in a single, terrible shudder, a cough escaped her lips, bringing with it a rivulet of ruby-red blood. At length the death rattle sounded in the depths of her throat, and as her spirit fled she moved no more. My heart now pounding wildly, my first impulse was to take flight, but reason prevailed. Such a rash move after such tumult would be madness. Certainly the impassioned exchange between us must have been heard. My only hope for salvation was to tarry a while and then, with the help of a sympathetic Providence, slip away from the house unseen.

Trembling with emotion, and moving as though in a trance, I lifted the morris chair to an upright position and slumped into it to contemplate the dead courtesan as she lay in repose on the chaise. The flickering lamplight cast an eerie glow across her pale features and I observed that they had returned to their former, gentle semblance. No longer were they contorted with hatred and pain. In death the fever'd madness of her brain had cooled once more to peaceful repose.

As I sat there gazing at her in the silence of the gloom, I felt as though some unseen force were mesmerising me. My emotions of horror ebbed and flowed like the tides, but in so doing commingled with sentiments of quite another sort. Smouldering sensations, not entirely unfamiliar, now kindled within me. The drumming of my heart, instead of subsiding to a more tranquil state, now thundered against my chest to the accompaniment of roaring and ringing in my ears. More than once I started, convinced that the pounding echoed from the walls around me.

My breath now came forth in tortuous gasps. Cold moisture formed on my throbbing brow. Remorse, oh fearful, anguished remorse and regret! Only moments before she had willingly offered her heart withour reserve. With searing passion unbounded she volunteered that prize held most dear by woman, driven by love alone. Yet I, though yearning for that love, but trembling in contemplation of its baser aspects, spurned her and destroyed her.

My eyes filled with tears. Plunging to the depths of despair I was enveloped by a melancholy unlike any I had known since the death of my beloved "Helen." As I trembled, thus enshrouded by my grief-stricken trance, there passed in mournful step before my eyes the images of both departed souls, torn from me by the cruel talons of Death's dark messenger. Then, as they faded from my mind's eye a sepulchral voice from afar, ringing with emotions of sadness, seemed to fill the room with its unearthly tones, "Her whom in life thou didst abhor, now, in death, thou shalt a-dore."

The words echoed through my fevered brain again and again, and as if guided by invisible hands I rose from the chair and knelt beside the lifeless Ligeia, the name she had given herself, and which now, in death, seemed somehow more fitting than any other. The dagger still protruded from her lifeless breast, a weltering stain of fresh blood surrounding it. Gently I withdrew the weapon of death and dropped it on the floor. Then contemplating her thus, in calm decease, my soul cried out in bitter anguish. Why? Why had I not enfolded her in my arms while she lived? I touched her smooth cheek, forever cooled by the exterminating angel, her soft swelling breast, never again to feel the caress of a lover.

Racked by sobs, I impulsively cradled her in my arms and pressed her cold lips to mine. In death she would receive from me what had been denied her in life. I was thus so overcome with emotions of such exquisite intensity that with a convulsive shudder I fell into a swoon.

When consciousness returned the lamp was flickering its last and I was swept back into the living nightmare from which I had been granted brief respite. A wave of horror overcame me, for the limbs of the poor dead creature beside whom I lay had become stiff with rigor mortis. Her lifeless eyes, still open and staring, were lustreless and seemingly pupilless, and the lips, now blood-less and shrunken, seemed parted in a smile of peculiar mean-ing.

Trembling as I withdrew from the couch, I touched the front of my shirtwaist, which was now stained with dry, stiff blood. I knew that if I did not quit this place forthwith, I should go insane with guilt and remorse. Having no idea of what the hour was I hurried to the window, pulled aside the heavy damask drape ever so slightly, that I might peer out unseen, and saw the new dawn reaching out from the eastern sky. I had to make haste so that I might leave unnoticed and make my escape under the blanket of what fleeting darkness remained.

I straightened out my garments, blew out the sputtering lamp, and wrapped my cloak tightly about me, making certain to reveal no outward signs of blood. Yet something held me back! Her eyes! I turned to take a final backward glance at the remains of my unfortunate victim, and knew at once I could not leave her thus. Retreating to the chaise upon which her cold form lay, I contemplated her once more. Then kneeling down, with trem-bling hand, my face averted, I closed her eyes. If I did not do so I knew that their hideous staring would haunt me till the end of my days. This accomplished, I rose, once again enfolded my cloak about me, and prepared to withdraw from the scene of my wretched crime.

Softly stealing from the room, I paused to listen for sounds, but there were none. Silently making my way through the dark corri-dor and down the steep staircase, giving unspoken thanks for its thick cover of carpet, I made my way to the front door. With studied caution I took the knob in my hand, turning and pulling with a single movement. But it would not open. The blood congealed in my veins. I was trapped as surely as tho' I had been buried alive in a sealed coffin. Had I come thus far only to be foiled in my quest for freedom? Was my escape to be effectively barred by the merest consequence of facing a locked door? My terror was incalculable. My wretchedness was beyond the wretchedness of mere humanity. Was I to be thus undone before I was given opportunity to flourish? But then my glance focused upon a small notice printed on a white card affixed to the moulding alongside the door. It read:

Gentlemen wishing to take their leave
before the household awakens may unlock
the door with the key in the tortoise-
shell box on the table alongside the
umbrella stand. Please be so kind as to
return the said key by placing it under
the door so that other gentlemen may
avail themselves of the convenience.

Breathing a sigh of relief, I reached into the box and found it empty. Assuming that another had indeed availed himself of the convenience before me, I reached under the door and there found the key. With trembling hand I inserted it in the lock, opened the door, stealthily removed myself, and hurried out into the darkness. Fortunately finding the street deserted, I struck up a brisk pace and returned to my lodgings ere day was breaking. Climbing wearily to my garret I undressed, crept into the welcome recess of my humble bed, and soon fell into a deep, exhausted sleep.[8]

11

That motley drama—oh, be sure
It shall not be forgot!
With its Phantom chased for evermore,
By a crowd that seize it not.

IT WAS NEARLY twilight when I awakened from my fitful sleep. It had been troubled by the old nightmares, those tormented visions, cast upon me by personal demons, chained to my soul by fetters stronger than iron. But with them, that terrible night, had come others, equally as dreadful, but perhaps for reason of their unfamiliarity, I could not recall them upon awakening. They eluded me like shadowy figures gliding through a thick, white mist.

My horrid recollections of the previous night's ghastly events filled me with suffocating emotions of remorse and self-reproach. I had shed the blood of another human being. Though I had slipped away from the scene of my crime unseen, and might well elude earthly punishment, I was irrevocably blackened by the baleful stain of guilt before the all-seeing eye of God. The shadow of that guilt would darken my path until the day I breathed my last.

I could not restore the dead to life, and the deed, having been done, there was naught for me to do but continue the tortuous pursuit of my hyperborean* goal. As I sat there, fearful and anxious, a peculiar sensation manifested itself to me, one of haunted dread, the sort that impels one to terror and flight. Yet it seemed to infuse me as well with a mysterious energy. As I pondered the nature of this extraordinary admixture of feelings, I observed the blood-stained shirtwaist I had worn the day before.

---

*A place beyond the cold north winds, a place of everlasting spring.

The sight of it gave me a sickening twinge of alarm. It had to be destroyed lest it become the instrument of my undoing, so without hesitation I tore it into shreds and consigned it to the dying embers of the fire.

Though my appetite had all but failed, the airless confines of my garret oppressed me. I felt the need to breathe some fresh air. After dressing I ambled to the Haymarket, where I broke my fast, then purchased a bottle of ink and returned to my lodgings. Darkness had fallen by the time I reentered my tiny chamber. I lit my lamp, opened my trunk, and took out pens, paper, inkstand and sandcaster. Then placing everything in a proper place on the small writing-desk, I seated myself and filled the inkwell.

At that moment it was as if Erato herself were poised at my shoulder. Like a man possessed I began writing verse as I never had before. A thrill of exhilaration swelled within my breast, and oblivious of time or place, I continued thus, fashioning, arranging, changing words until the grey light of daybreak began erasing darkness from the skies. As though emerging from a trance, I reread the stanzas I had written, softly to myself, in the solitude of the dawning day.

Take this kiss upon the brow!
And, in parting from you now,
This much let me avow—
You are not wrong, who deem
That my days have been a dream;
Yet if hope has flown away
In a night, or in a day,
In a vision, or in none,
Is it therefore the less gone?
All that we see or seem
Is but a dream within a dream.

I stand amid the road
Of a surf-tormented shore,
And I hold within my hand
Grains of the golden sand—
How few! yet how they creep

Through my fingers to the deep,
While I weep—while I weep!
O God! can I not grasp
Them with a tighter clasp?
O God! can I not save
One from the pitiless wave?
Is all that we see or seem
But a dream within a dream?

The fire had gone out and a damp chill permeated the room. My hand ached from the long hours of holding pen to paper, and the edges of my fingers were red and chafed from constant abrasion as I wrote. But a feeling of peace descended on me unlike any I had experienced. Yet a keen edge of uneasiness remained. Recollections evoked by the events which transpired on the night of my awful crime now pervaded my thoughts.

The first time that I had been in intimate contact with death and bereavement was on that night when I went to pay my last farewell to the beloved "Helen." For some days following that melancholy experience I had written feverishly and with little care for nourishment or sleep. Then there was the night when, inadvertently, I had come upon that poor, pathetic corpse of an unknown, lying in solitude in a rat-infested, tottering tenement. I knew her not, yet the very sight of her still, cold form had moved me deeply, and afterwards inspired the composition of verse. Why? How? Perhaps, having been born haunted by ghosts, I was, therefore, impelled by fate to search for beauty in darkness.

That I was a poet, and chosen by destiny to one day achieve greatness, was beyond question in my mind. There was a question of quite another sort that troubled me. I had shed the blood of a woman whom I might have loved purely and happily, her fallen estate notwithstanding. For the love I was prepared to offer transcended lust and carnal fire. Yet, howsoever unintentional the blow, it was by my hand that she was swept away by the dark, exterminating angel. Then, afterwards, what facile inspiration guided my hand as I wrote? Was I doomed by some dark and gloomy destiny to become an instrument of death as a condition of poetic creation? Was mine so savage a muse that she demanded I lay human sacrifices at her feet in order to satisfy *her* lust? I prayed that this was not so; yet I could not deny that in some strange way I was demon-ridden.

Why was I so drawn to beauty and love, with the passion of the mind; yet was without that passion of the flesh which most assuredly led the unfortunate Aspasian to her untimely death? It was a mystery to me then and it is one which binds me still. I shall no doubt carry it with me to the grave.[1]

I shall not dwell at length on any of the events of the weeks which followed, for most of my time was devoted to writing verse. I did, however, consider the possibility of seeking employment. I appproached the editors of all the Boston newspapers, but was universally rejected by virtue of my journalistic inexperience. When I asked these august gentlemen of the Fourth Estate where one might acquire such experience, I was given no answers, although one suggested that I retire to a garret with pen, ink, paper, a dictionary, and a copy of *The Times* of London. The latter, said he, represented the loftiest attainment in the journalistic profession. What would any of them have said had they known that he whom they so uncivily turned away from their doors was a principal in the "Most Atrocious Murder" about which they had raised such a hue and cry?

As the weeks passed, my meagre supply of cash dwindled to a pittance. Piece by piece I began selling my clothes. I took to eating but one meal a day in order to conserve what little I had. One evening, yearning for the warmth of human companionship, I resolved to pay a return visit to *The Philosopher's Stone*, where I was cordially greeted by the proprietor, who enquired as to the health of my friend, Miss Morelli. Exercising every caution to maintain a perfunctory manner, I told him that she had returned to her home in Worcester the day after he had seen her last, but that I had received correspondence from her wishing him and his patrons the best of health.

When he asked me if I had composed any additional verses since visiting last, I answered in the affirmative, whereupon he most kindly invited me to be his guest for dinner in return for the recitation of my latest poems. I consumed so much that I became quite ill upon returning to my lodgings later.

It was on the following morning that I took careful stock of my cash assets and remaining belongings, thereby arriving at the conclusion that my continued survival depended upon drastic measures. Upon perusing my possessions I came across the calling card of Calvin Thomas, the young printer whom I had met on my initial visit to *The Philosopher's Stone*. I recalled his appreciation of my poetry, and the thought occurred to me that he might be interested in publishing a collection of my works. I had completed "Tamerlane" and several others. Why not, I thought, pay him a visit at once?

His print shop on Washington Street was a considerable distance from my lodgings, but it was a pleasant day. The grass and trees on the Common were turning green. The signs of renewal and rebirth were everywhere, and I could not help but think of the Bohemian, Karel Hynek Macha,[2] poet of spring, May meadows, and blossoming trees. It was he who had written:

I love the flower for it withers and dies
The beast, for it will perish.
I love man because he ceases to live
To nevermore exist,
Because he is resigned to eternal extinction.
I live and prostrate myself before God
Because he, too, does not exist.

Mr. Thomas remembered me at once and received me most cordially in his shop. When I first suggested that he publish a volume of my poems he demurred on grounds that he was not a publisher, but only a printer. He had neither the means nor the experience. Barely a year older than I, he had only recently purchased his modest establishment and as yet had not succeeded in attaining a position of affluence in the community. Calling forth my most persuasive manner, I prevailed upon him, pointing out that were he to print a modest edition of my poems, I would exercise whatever efforts I could to assist him in producing it. Though I was a stranger to the mechanics of printing, I pointed out that by personally aiding him in the selection and setting of type, even operating the press, I might also simultaneously help him in other more immediately remunerative endeavours.

I next suggested that were the book to enjoy a rewarding sale, he would share in the profits, thereby earning substantially more than he might on the basis of printing alone. Were we to be successful in this venture, I declared, it was not at all inconceivable that we might, between us, establish some sort of literary journal.[3]

Fortunately he succumbed to my blandishments and soon publication of *Tamerlane and Other Poems* by "A Bostonian," my first book, was under way. Although I was far from anxious to conceal my literary light beneath a barrel, and had initially planned to sign my name to the title page, I reluctantly agreed to anonymity. Thomas pointed out, with undeniable justification, that there was no way in which we could sell the book beyond Boston and its environs. The name Edgar A. Poe, though simple enough, easy to pronounce and to remember, was completely unknown, and hardly an inducement to spend money. The cryptonym, "A Bostonian," however, might soften a heart or two and inspire a spark of sympathy for some unknown native poet, struggling for recognition. There was still another consideration—the outstanding warrants against me in Virginia. It would not have been expeditious for me at this time to render myself too visible.

Soon after we set to work I came to learn that poor Thomas was no less a novice than I, and it also became evident that my assistance was best left to the literary side of our venture. I laboured diligently preparing my manuscripts for the setting into type. Unfortunately, since Thomas, like all men, was faced with the necessity of earning his daily bread, he was not able to devote his full time and attention to *Tamerlane*. Thus, as time passed, my assets finally vanished, even my writing materials. All save for a single suit of clothing and a pair of shoes was gone, sold for a pittance.

Although my landlady was a woman of an amiable nature, I had observed that her hospitality was in direct proportion to the size of a boarder's purse. In my own case, I had exactly enough money to remain beneath her roof until the twenty-seventh day of May. I was, therefore, understandably disturbed as that day approached, for it was hardly my fondest hope to make a home beneath the stars. Indeed, the weather was now balmy and pleasant, but I knew all too well that Boston winters were of sufficient severity that each year a number of poor unfortunates froze to death.

On the night of May twenty-fifth I lay abed, unable to sleep, a pessimistic apprehension gnawing at my vitals. I was, for all practical purposes, friendless. Though I had a few acquaintances, there was no one to whom I could turn for the manner of assistance I now so desperately required. And I knew, just as surely as I knew that my name was Edgar Poe, that barring a miraculous occurrence, I would be homeless in the space of two days.

This melancholy prospect rendered sleep impossible for what I perceived at the time to be half of the night. At last, in desperation I arose from bed, dressed, and left the house. Perhaps, I thought, if I were to walk briskly for a while I might be overtaken by weariness, after which I could return and find sweet, brief solace in the temporary oblivion of slumber.

Boston's back streets and thoroughfares alike were deserted at that hour by all but denizens of shadow—scurrying rats, slinking cats, trotting dogs, and darting bats. Somehow I felt at one with these creatures of the night for, in sooth, was I not also a child of the darkness? As I walked, gazing at the dark and silent houses, my loneliness enshrouded me.

During the course of my musings I had paid little heed to where I was until I looked about me and found myself in the midst of the deserted Haymarket. How strange it looked at this hour, bathed as it was in the pale, lurid light of the moon. A faint breeze was blowing, creating tiny whirlwinds of dust that spun and danced about my ankles as I walked among them. Although the only sounds were the echoes of my footsteps and the occasional distant cries of night birds, I suddenly started at a faint rustling noise behind me. My heart leapt in alarm and I spun around only to observe the principal portion of a broadside, which had been torn or blown from a wall. It fluttered in the wind with a rising, falling, circular motion, and at first glance resembled a wraith dancing in the moonbeams. But upon recognising it for what it was, out of curiosity I picked it up and gave it a cursory examination. It was an advertisement giving notice that the First Artillery Regiment of the United States Army was seeking recruits.

In a brilliant flash of intuition I knew at once that my immediate salvation was at hand. It was as though the broadside had been delivered to me though the offices of some kindly guardian angel who had taken pity on me in this moment of direst need. Making a mental notation of the address at which to apply, a great feeling of relief overcame me, and along with it a powerful desire to rest. Ah, what salubrious affects have starry hopes on the human heart! I hastened back to my lodgings and ascended to my garret, where I tumbled into bed with the utmost alacrity. Sleep overtook me almost at once.

When I awoke it was mid-morning, and a glorious May day. Golden sunlight streaming through my tiny window accompanied by the cheerful warbling of the songbirds gave testimony to the glories of Nature. I had no real knowledge of what army life might be like. I had been following with interest news of the wars being fought in the distant corners of the earth—South America, Greece, Portugal. Perhaps it was this knowledge that prompted me at later dates to write several letters to my dear "Ma" in Richmond implying that I had become a soldier of fortune in Europe. Alas! I was in truth a soldier of ill-fortune, and had it not been for the execrable condition of my circumstances, I never would have enlisted.

The enlisted ranks of a peacetime army were hardly fitting for anyone of my heritage and upbringing. But immediate and decisive action was called for. As I made my way though the pleasantly greening streets that bright Saturday morning, the words of Titus Livius came to mind: *In rebus asperis et tenui spe fortissima quaeque consilia tutissima sunt.**

Thus, on the twenty-sixth day of May, in the year 1827, under the alias of Edgar A. Perry, I became a private soldier in the United States Army assigned to Battery H of the First Artillery, at Fort Independence, in Boston Harbour.

I shall pass lightly over the events which transpired during my

---

*In difficult and hopeless circumstances the boldest plans are safest.

career as a soldier, for, as I have stated, my principal intention in setting this narrative to paper is to confess certain misdemeanors which blacken my soul, and to leave behind a true account of those inner torments which drove me. Since, during that period in which I served flag and country, my behaviour was beyond reproach, there is little to say about it. However, for posterity's sake, I shall not abandon that portion of my life to unseemly speculation.

As a recruit, my life was harsh, and mostly devoted to training. The resounding boom of the sunrise gun aroused me daily from wearied slumber. Often cold and always in the company of my malodorous, groggy comrades-in-arms, I washed, shaved, and assembled for rollcall and breakfast. As an artilleryman I was required to familiarise myself with the mechanics and operation of the formidable cannon which constituted the principal defence of the harbour. I was also required to absorb the basic principles of infantry drill and musketry, the former essentially for cere-monial reasons, and the latter for the obvious. Though an atten-dant upon heavy and ponderous weapons, it would have been unthinkable for a soldier of any rank or station to be unfamiliar with small arms.

In the eyes of my superiors I was an exemplary soldier. By virtue of my having served in my youth as a lieutenant in the Junior Richmond Volunteers, the elements of drill were quickly remembered. But since I had imparted nothing of my true identity and past, my progress in their eyes appeared nothing short of miraculous. Furthermore, since I had given as my civil occupation the calling of clerk, and readily displayed an ability to read, write, and perform mathematical calculations, I stood out from my fellow soldiers. Indeed, although some enjoyed rudimentary literacy, many were barely capable of signing their own names.

The strenuous nature of my duties, though well within the limits of my endurance, were distasteful to me. I had not been brought up to engage in such manual labour, and it was impossi-ble for me not to associate the handling of cannon balls and powder-bags with the duties of slaves. I nonetheless refrained from making complaints, for they would have proved fruitless, and in time I was assigned to the commissary, and eventually designated as company clerk.

With a rigidity of purpose, I avoided all strong drink, and associated but minimally with my comrades, whose principal preoccupation during their leisure hours was drinking and wenching. Although I desperately longed for the gentle touch and soft voice of the fair sex, I was effectively barred from their agreeable company. To have associated with anyone on the level of society to which I was accustomed was unthinkable.[4] A private soldier, regardless of the quality beneath his incognito was socially unacceptable. As for the demimonde frequented by the lower ranks, I had neither the time nor the inclination. Yet I could not erect an impenetrable barrier between myself and those with whom I served.

Had I deported myself in such a manner as to convince them that I was a fop or a snob, they would have made my life unbearable. I therefore discovered a way in which I might ingratiate myself to them without compromising my own principles. Since it was de rigeur that each man maintain a healthy constitution, a certain amount of physical exertion was required of us. Being a better-than-average runner, jumper, and swimmer, I competed in these activities with my fellows on every possible occasion. For those whose education had precluded their having learned to read and write, I assumed the role of scribe, composing letters to parents, wives, sweethearts, brothers, and sisters.

Thus, though I was universally regarded as a fellow with queer tastes because of my preference for reading and writing over carousing in the fleshpots of Boston, I was accepted for myself, and permitted to go my solitary way. Of one circumstance I took advantage as often as I could. Due to my sober, obedient, and courteous disposition, in combination with my legible hand, I was accorded a great deal of personal liberty. I had, among other things, displayed a distinct ability to carry out all orders within a minimal span of time. These circumstances enabled me to have far more freedom than was ordinarily granted to a private soldier. Fortunately my fellow enlisted men knew nothing of this. They assumed my frequent excursions into the city to be on official business. Thus my comings and goings were never questioned by them. The greatest advantage accruing to me by this freedom was sufficient time to visit Calvin Thomas's print shop, and supervise the printing of my modest volume of poetry.

Tamerlane and Other Poems was published in mid-summer to a resounding silence by critics,[5] much to my deep disappointment. I was further chagrined that booksellers were, for the most part, loath to stock or sell the book, despite the fact that it was to be sold for the modest price of twelve and a half cents. I was handicapped by my position as a soldier, and was unable to go from shop to shop to distribute copies for sale, and my friend Thomas was too concerned with keeping his small shop in business to take the travails of a publisher upon himself. Though it caused me anguish, I sympathised with his plight. He had, at least, undertaken the task of publishing my book, which I appreciated deeply. I was hardly in a position to pay for paper, ink, binding, and his services.

I wrote very few lines of verse during those early months in the army, and those which I did compose, I destroyed, for I felt them to be inadequate. I also wrote from time to time to my dear "Ma," to let her know how much love for her was in my heart, and how often I thought of her. I confess that in these letters I permitted my imagination to run unfettered, dating them from Russia and other exotic places. In them I recounted my exciting "European adventures"—serving as a volunteer in the Polish army, fighting a duel in Vienna, paying homage in Paris to the heroes who fought for American independence, and having my portrait painted in London.

But alas! I was to know no such romantic climes or fabulous adventures. My restless spirit was burdened with the mundane encumbrances of the military existence. My dreams alternated between hideous nightmares and fanciful flights of boundless imagination.

Now and then, though I endeavoured to push them from my mind, waking fantasies occurred in which the unfortunate Cyprian, who had died by my hand, came back to haunt me. The vision was always the same. At first she came to me burning with reproach, but then her passions of anger changed to those of love. On those painful occasions it was all I could do to suppress the cry that seemed about to burst forth from my throat. Why? Why? Oh, why, had I repulsed her? Sometimes the answer appeared almost within my grasp, but then, evanescent as the foam on the breaking wave, it faded, dissipated, and vanished, ever to elude me.

Autumn approached, and with it the keen, cool northern air which slowly changed green leaves to brilliant oranges, reds, and gold. The long dark nights brought with them terrifying overwhelming sensations of despair that seemed to wrench my soul into a deafening purgatory peopled by raging spirits, howling ghosts, and restless shades of murderers, assassins, and victims.

Upon escaping from this place of horrors, I would imagine myself a murderous cutthroat, stalking darkened alleys, tangled woods, and murky tarns. Like a human ghoul I would seek virginal victims, to feed on their terror and devour their souls. With garrote and blade I would snuff out their lives; then, my terrible passions mollified, I would treat their cool, gentle forms with tenderness, before placing them in marble tombs to sleep the eternal dreamless slumber of oblivion.[6]

As the waters of the harbour grew chill and the skies above were blackened by flocks of migrating birds fleeing to warmer climes ere the frosts and snows came, I grew uneasy. The army had been good to me, but I did not relish the prospect of a New England winter. I had known cold in Richmond, to be sure, for though situated in sunny Virginia, it is not renowned for its tropical climate. Yet never did I experience a severe winter there. Having heard of Boston's howling gales and driving snowstorms, I was prepared for the worst. Imagine, then, the emotions of elation which overcame me when, on Halloween Day, my regiment received orders to relocate at Fort Moultrie, on Sullivan's Island, in Charleston Harbour, South Carolina.

12

For the heart whose woes are legion
'Tis a peaceful, soothing region—
For the spirit that walks in shadow
'Tis—Oh 'tis an Eldorado!

THE TREES WERE BARE and bent before the chill November winds, the skies and waters grey and angry, on that eighth day of the month. But as the bugler sounded reveille on the morning of our embarkation the raven wing of night still blanketed the city. Then after a hearty breakfast of plain but warming fare the men of Battery H gathered their belongings and boarded the brig *Waltham* for the journey southward.

Most of the enlisted men had never taken an ocean voyage before, and suffered greatly from *mal de mer* until we dropped anchor at our destination ten days later, on Sunday, November 18, 1827. Cheers rose from the throats of my comrades at the prospect of feeling solid ground beneath their feet once more.

The contrast between Boston and Charleston harbours was striking. As the late afternoon sun commenced its gentle downward arc to the west, the sky was splashed with brilliant-hued clouds of pink-tinged orange, red, and purple. Balmy breezes caressed the azure waters and, mingling with the fresh salt air, was the ineffably sweet scent of exotic blossoms. At the mouth of the harbour, facing our home to be, Fort Moultrie, was an island, upon which, rumour had it, was to be constructed still another fortress. There was apparently much contention over the matter in the Congress at Washington concerning funds and nomenclature.

As the officers and men of my regiment prepared to disembark, however, they were hardly concerned with the future of a

133

deserted island in Charleston Harbour, but rather with their new home. From our vantage point aboard ship the city of Charleston had an inviting look. Nestled along the shoreline were houses, steeples, and swaying palmettos. In the harbour and along the wharves were masts of ships from every continent.

Sullivan's Island consisted of little else than the sea sand and was about three miles long. Its breadth at one point exceeded a quarter of a mile, and it was separated from the mainland by a scarcely perceptible creek, oozing its way through a wilderness of reeds and slime, a favourite resort of the marsh hen. The vegetation, as might be supposed, was scant, or at least dwarfish. No trees of any magnitude were to be seen. Near the western extremity, where Fort Moultrie stood, were some miserable frame buildings, tenanted during summer by fugitives from Charleston dust and fever. The whole of the island, with the exception of this western point, and a line of hard, white beach on the seacoast, was covered with a dense undergrowth of the sweet myrtle, so much prized by the horticulturists of England.

To the east and north of our barracks stretched the empty, shell-strewn beaches, washed gently by the sea, and which during my term of service there I came to know intimately.

It was my good fortune to be garrisoned in such a languid spot, whose ambience contradicted the warlike aspect which our presence imparted. Fortunately, though war raged in such far-flung corners of the earth as Persia and Greece, peace reigned supreme in our sub-tropical outpost. Very quickly we settled into an easy routine. The bugle sounded at five-thirty every morning, after which we tidied our quarters, breakfasted, and performed an hour or more of infantry drill. Several times each week we engaged in exercises with the mighty cannon, although a certain amount of time was devoted daily to the cleaning and oiling of all weapons, a necessary procedure in consequence of the ever-present moisture of our environment.

As company clerk I continued to have more leisure time than my comrades-in-arms and I devoted much of it to solitary rambles about the island and its neighbor, Long Island.*

---

*Today known as the Isle of Palms.

I was most fortunate to make the acquaintance of Dr. Edmund Ravanel, a naturalist, who resided in a modest shack not far from the fort, and with whom I spent many long hours, during which he assumed the role of teacher and mentor in the science of natural history.[1]

Time passed slowly, and though periodic nightmares intruded upon my helpless soul to plague my sleep, I easily overcame their assault because of the opportunities afforded me to read and expand my knowledge of science and natural history. Thus on many a day I stalked the blue heron and the scurrying crab, the clicking beetle, and the fluttering moth. But I pursued them, not with the weapons of the human predator, rather with the thirsty eye of the scientist eager to drink in learning.

Not infrequently my nocturnal horrors led me to cool tombs and mossy graves where reposed the silent and eternally slumbering remains of those for whom my love would never fade. So real were these fantasies, it was as if my heartbroken spirit left my body and soared on astral wings to those ghoul-haunted regions where the living dare not venture. Sometimes on my solitary rambles the realities of the world affected me as visions, and as visions only, whereas the wild ideas of the land of dreams became, in turn, not merely the material of my everyday existence, but that existence itself. It was a happiness to wonder and a happiness to dream.

There was much in the real world around me, however, to inspire the composition of verse and tale, both during my sojourn there and elsewhere in years to come. A chance rereading of *Lalla Rookh* contributed in part to the exotic flavour of *Al Aaraaf*, which I began to compose at Fort Moultrie. And certainly, as any citizen of Charleston, familiar with *The Gold Bug*, knows, the tale surrounding that mythical insect was born en toto of my days there.

Charleston and the hinterlands surrounding it provided riches for me to put away in the personal vault within my mind wherein all images were stored. Gloomy woods and tangled swamps were never far. Snake-haunted fens and cypress-lined tarns bespoke of melancholy secrets known only to the dead.

Once whilst wandering alone in the wild and solitary Carolina woods, I came upon a mouldering mansion, tomblike, overgrown with vines, and festooned with Spanish moss. Its windows were black and empty rectangles, the peeling woodwork covered with lichens. The cracked and crumbling walls gave mute testimony to the impermanent nature of man and his works. Years later the memory of them inspired the lines.

> These crumbling walls, these tottering arcades,
> These mouldering plinths, these sad blackened shafts,
> These vague entablatures, this broken frieze,
> These shattered cornices, this wreck, this ruin,
> These stones, alas! these grey stones are they
> All of the great and the colossal left
> By the corrosive hours to fate and me?

Who had dwelt here, I wondered? What tragic ghosts trod nightly with silent step across its rotting boards? What secret might this scene of desolation and decay reveal were its mute components of wood and stone granted by divine decree the power of independent speech?

Mesmerized by the grim spectacle presented by this architectural corpse, I approached its once proud entrance, guarded on each side by worn griffins with broken wings. Hanging loosely on rusty hinges, a worm-eaten door was all that barred my way. Above the portal carved in weatherbeaten granite was an inscription, its letters barely legible, *Bibamus, moriendum est* ("Let us drink, Death is inevitable!"). Spurred on to further investigation by this sombre motto, I took the iron handle and pulled with all my strength. To the accompaniment of its own agonized groans the door swung open and I peered into the gloomy interior.

I fancied I saw a lizard or some other creature scurry into the shadows of a dark passageway. The room was enshrouded with cobwebs and in every way a scene of desolation and ruin. So forbidding and cheerless was the place that I could not bring myself to enter. Stepping back, I closed the door again and retreated, leaving the dusty salon to the more fitting company of its own familiar spirits. Still, I wished to explore further, restricting my investigation to the exterior grounds.

Accordingly I followed the path, now overgrown with weeds and overhung with dangling clumps of the ubiquitous Spanish moss. It led me around the mansion and beyond the ruins of several outbuildings until I came upon a small, stone chapel in a remarkable state of repair. Upon closer examination I perceived it to be not a chapel, but a sealed mausoleum, ornately carved, and surrounded by semi-feudal pomp, like so many of the great family tombs I had seen on the Carolina plantations.[2] Like them it harkened back to days of ancient glories, royal grants, and feudal fiefdoms of a grander era. I sensed an aura of mystery about the place at once; for above the entrance, where once had been a name, were jagged depressions, the result of some long-past deliberate defacement.

Although the sun was still close to its zenith, the tomb was overshadowed by a dense penumbra of gloom, surrounded as it was by a circle of tall, luxuriant trees whose foliage all but obscured the sky. Drawn as if by some unseen force beyond any mortal power to resist, trancelike, I approached the portal and grasped the brass handle, green with corrosion, and moulded in the shape of a Grecian column. My heart now beating wildly in my breast, I pulled with all my might, at first to no avail. Thus it was with the thrill of coming face to face with the unknown that I felt the heavy door swing slowly open sufficiently to permit my passage.

The only light beyond was that which was admitted through the opening of the doorway in which I stood. Several moments passed before my eyes became accustomed to the gloom, but then I saw clearly six coffins lying side by side in a row. Experiencing a sudden pang of guilt for having trespassed on the sanctity of the tomb, I prepared to withdraw when I observed something about the coffin nearest the entrance that made me start. The lid was noticeably askew at the upper portion, approximately above the occupant's head.

Unable to restrain my curiosity I knelt down alongside the coffin and examined the lid, which upon closer scrutiny looked as if someone had long ago tried to pry it loose. I glanced at the foot of the coffin. The lower extremity appeared to be perfectly secure. At the opposite end, however, the lid was raised a distance of approximately one and a half inches or more above the head. I reached out and grasped it on both sides with my hands to see if I could determine what might have caused this condition. It was my intention to work with the lid gently up and down, when suddenly, to my astonishment, due, no doubt to dry rot, at the first upward movement of the lid, it all but flew up in the air as if propelled by a spring mechanism.

As it clattered to the dusty floor of the sepulchre I looked down and beheld a sight so macabre, so awesomely horrifying, that it will haunt me until I breathe my last. Staring at me from the coffin was the withered, mummified corpse of what must have been in life a young woman.[3] Her tresses, even in death, were long, glossy, and of the deepest ebony hue, strewn about in wild *déshabille*. Nestling in the hollow eye-sockets were shriveled, dessicated orbs that once had gazed upon the beauties of nature. Drawn taut over the bony skull was parchment-smooth skin, surrounding brown, leathern lips gaping wide in a hideous grimace over the double row of perfect, pearly teeth. Ugly blotches of long-dried blood stained the shredded cerements, and the knees were drawn up as far as the coffin lid had permitted. The hands were clutched into tight fists.

I knew at once the tragic ending to the grim tale now communicated to me by the long-muted screams of this ghastly, pathetic corpse. Buried alive, she had revived in the smothering, sable blackness of her tomb. Her screams had gone unheard, her anguished cries for help, unanswered. Fruitlessly she struggled. Gradually as her waning strength faded, her sanity fled, to be replaced by fearful madness in the suffocating prison of her coffin. At last, her tearful face contorted in agony, her poor lungs burning in the final, horrid nightmare of dissolution, she rent her shroud and tore her flesh until the merciful palliative of death ultimately ended her sufferings.

Emotions of useless pity welled up within me, and on an impulse I reached down to smooth the tangled hair, to close the gaping mouth, restore a measure of quiesence to the mortal remains of this wretched, forgotten corpse. As I touched it, a soft, crackling, tearing sound fell upon my ears and what remained of the flesh disintegrated to dust before my very eyes. The jaws

snapped shut with an audible click. The knees fell back and the
fists unclenched. Lying there before me now was a shrouded skel-
eton in tranquil repose. Save for the disarranged hair and bloodstains on the lacerated cerements, she now appeared at peace.

Finishing what I had begun, I unraveled her hair. This task
completed, I replaced the coffin lid and returned to the moist and
fragrant outdoor air. By the time I made my way back to the
public road the shadows of dusk were lengthening and turning
purple. It was thus with sentiments of satisfaction that I returned
to Sullivan's Island. Long after nightfall, as I gazed up at the
star-strewn sky, I knew that in some distant corner of Paradise, a
beautiful dark-haired angel was smiling down on me, and would
cause the radiance of her countenance to shine upon me for all
the days of my life.

13

In visions of the dark night
I have dreamed of joy departed—
But a waking dream of life and light
Hath left me broken-hearted.

DOUBTLESS HAD I been garrisoned in cooler climes the rigours of military life would have imposed a heavier burden on my existence than that I bore in Charleston Harbour. The principal purpose of our presence there was to guard the coast, but in the absence of hostile sails our vigilance was never put to the test. As languid days gave way to warm and balmy nights the passage of time imposed an air of unreality upon my existence. I performed my duties, I read, I dreamed, I composed verses.

In the month of May of 1828 I was promoted to the rank of artificer and given additional duties, namely that of preparing shells and fuses in a small laboratory adjacent to the magazines. Since our warlike activities were confined to exercises, drills, and housekeeping, the labours attendant upon my elevated station hardly altered my way of life.

Passage by the Congress of the "Tariff of Abominations," the same month, brought about a reduction in the number of foreign vessels sailing into the port, and gave rise to an increase in the occupation of smuggling. Although decried in florid language by censorious gentlemen of the Fourth Estate,[1] even certain respectable citizens of Charleston engaged in this pursuit with enthusiasm. It was quite noteworthy to observe each evening at the approach of sunset a veritable fleet of boating enthusiasts, putting to sea in small craft, not to return until after the descent of darkest night.

With the passage of time and the tedium of life at this near-dormant military outpost, had it not been for the raging tempests in my heart and brain I might easily have fallen into the ways of idleness and vice which entrapped so many of my fellows. I enjoyed another distinct advantage: the circumstance of my somewhat bifurcated identity. My superior officers were unofficially aware of my true descent and, knowing me to have been ward of a rich and prominent Virginia citizen, treated me with a degree of civility ordinarily denied soldiers in the ranks.

In the course of my clerical duties I was privy to cryptograms and cyphers employed for the transmission of secret messages.[2] These afforded me many hours and days of absorbing activity, and though I often pondered on the innate foolishness of committing such trivial correspondence to secret writing in time of peace, I kept such thoughts to myself.[3] The great irony was that though I could demystify cyphers, I could not demystify my soul.

During the summer of 1828 my duties brought me into contact with a detachment of architects from the Corps of Engineers who were surveying the island site of the proposed new fort. It was my responsibility to keep a duplicate record of their measurements in a secure place among the papers of Fort Moultrie as a precaution, lest the original notations become lost or misplaced.

The island was a wild and rocky place, densely wooded from base to pinnacle and criss-crossed by ravines which spread out in all directions. The verdant foliage, like that on Sullivan's Island, attracted birds and insects of many species who found the place a peaceful refuge from the deadly presence of their common enemy, Man.

As I listened to these rigid military planners discussing their designs for the structures of stone and mortar to be erected on this site I was overcome with melancholy. What would become of the swooping petrel, the golden butterfly, the iridescent beetle? Where would the sea turtle lay her eggs? The evening song of the nocturnal creatures would be replaced by the harsh clatter of booted leather, the clang of iron, and the cannon's thunderous roar. Gone forever would be the gentle serenade of the cicada, the cricket, and the frog. The tulip tree would be felled to make way for bastions of rock. The relentless juggernaut of Science would drive the hapless tenants of the wood to seek new shelter in some more hospitable place.[4]

I believe that the highest point of the entire year for me was the happy day when my long-awaited copy of Dr. Webster's new dictionary arrived. For weeks afterwards I did little else but devour its pages, exploring the wondrous terrain of words. Every periodical that came into my hands I read and read again, endeavouring to absorb every iota of information available to me. For by devoting myself to the acquisition of knowledge I was able to suppress, to some extent, the pangs of guilt, the fears and the longings that burned within me.

At the Charleston Library Society, I came upon a body of material which had been published some twelve years before, following the death of still another European physician whose life and work had captured my fancy, Friedrich Anton Mesmer.

I had, of course, read previously about the subject of animal magnetism and the controversies attendant upon it. Never before, however, had I come upon such a rich body of writings on it. They excited my imagination for a number of reasons, not the least of which was a strange evocation, almost forgotten, of past experiences. From a passage describing minutely the trance state of certain individuals, I distinctly recalled having once witnessed a similar condition among the Negroes when I was a child.

My recollections were shadowy, but I vaguely remembered the sight of an aged black man, a gardener, reputed by his brethren to possess mysterious powers. While swaying to the rhythm of a small drum he made passes with his gnarled hands, and chanted sonorously in a strange tongue. Only brief images remained: flickering flames, clapping hands, swaying, swarthy bodies, and rolling eyes.

This ceremony was never spoken of beyond the slave quarters, and I never again witnessed another like it. My presence must have been tolerated at that time because I was very young, and in the care of my mammy, Judith. Now, in Charleston, while reading about the work of Mesmer and his disciples, I concluded that the arcane ritual I had witnessed among the Negroes was one of healing. As I read on, the clarity of my comprehension attending my flashes of recollection became greater. Several servants had participated in that ancient African rite, during which time each became entranced through the offices of the old man. And previous to this each had complained of some minor malaise. Was there not a relationship between the mesmeric phenomena induced by the Austrian physician and those by the ancient plantation healer?[5]

During the period of my most intense interest in this topic I read everything that I could find related to it. This necessitated considerable scurrying about the city, for no single library had all that was required by my insatiable appetite for the printed page. Thanks to the good offices of my friend Colonel Drayton, who was a trustee of Charleston College, I was granted access to that institutions's facilities. Otherwise, I spent most of my time in the Charleston Library Society, which, being the oldest repository of books in the city, now possessed close to fifteen thousand volumes. Nevertheless, the Franklin Library Society, on Chalmers Street, though newer, and in possession of fewer books, had a fine collection, especially in the fields of science and modern scholarship.

By the time I had completed reading everything I could find on the subject of mesmerism, there was no doubt in my mind that had I been able to find a willing subject, I, too, would have been quite capable of practicing the mesmerist's art. Though the opportunity never presented itself to me, I often wondered if a person approaching the final state of dissolution were to be placed in the mesmeric state, could it, perhaps, arrest death itself? Perhaps I was never able to obtain an answer to this question, but I was certainly able to speculate fictionally on the matter, to an extent beyond my original intentions.[6]

Some time afterwards another item of interest captured my attention as a result of a letter appearing in the *Southern Intelligencer*. The correspondent had visited the city of Leipzig, in Germany, many months before and while there had attended the performance of a new operatic work entitled *Der Vampyr*. Based upon a French melodrama, set in the Highlands of Scotland, the setting was changed by the librettist, Wilhelm August Wohlbruck, to Hungary. Although the writer of the letter said little about the performance itself, it was to his credit that he observed that the music of the eminent composer, Heinrich August Marschner, was most melodious.

He went on *ad nauseum* to express his disapproval of the subject matter on grounds of excess morbidity. He opined that the contemplation of vampires was more suited to the tastes of "mad-doctors,* papist theologians, and authors of grim German novels," rather than proper theatre lovers.

Once again my interest was aroused in an arcane and esoteric subject about which I had known nothing before, but which influenced me greatly when I began composing tales of my own. I therefore made enquiries at the libraries, and to my immense satisfaction, found a number of quaint and curious volumes on the subject, and for many weeks I applied myself to the study thereof. I marvelled at the antiquity and universality of it, for beliefs in this monster seemed old as mankind. I was astonished, not only at the great number of books devoted to vampires, but at their erudition.

I began by perusing the scholarly texts first, and was most fortunate in being accorded access to the personal library of a learned old priest, formerly of St. Finbar's Cathedral. Despite my professing to the Protestant faith he was most gracious to me. A man of great learning and wisdom, it gave him pleasure to see in a soldier, especially one as young as I, familiarity with Latin and a thirst for knowledge.

Certain superstitious shortcomings notwithstanding, I was transported by such works as Dom Augustin Calmet's *Traite sur les Apparitions des Espirits et sur les Vampires &c.* and *De Graecorum hodie quorundam opinationibus* by Leo Allatius. I read as well the infamous *Malleus Malificarum* by the deranged Dominicans, Sprenger and Kramer. Though concerned with the subject of witchcraft, it was nonetheless germane to my interests, and held me in fascination by its very loathsome precepts, as a serpent does its helpless prey.

I shuddered as I read accounts of reeking corpses, fetid with corruption, rising nightly from their graves to imbibe the crimson blood of their hapless victims. These unhappy sufferers, accord-

---

*An archaic term used to refer to doctors who treated the insane: psychiatrists.

144

ing to the learned authors, gradually wasted away, growing emaciated as they were nightly sapped of their strength, until they died of consumption. I read of horrifying Russian revenants, with eyes like burning coals, who lurked about graveyards to attack unwary passersby, then with hideous shrieks devoured their flesh and sucked their blood. Most chilling of all were accounts of historical personages who, inflamed by some fearful disquietude of the brain, loved nothing so much as to slake their detestable thirsts with the hot blood of human victims.

It was in the pages of poetry and fiction, however, that I lingered longest, for there I was not forced to endure the harsh imposition of facts or horrors purported to be true. The reporting of fact is the domain of the journalist, and though, out of necessity, for many years I followed this calling, the true inclination of my heart lay in pursuit of beauty and art. I was ever at odds with the definers of realism in art, who upheld this pitiable stuff on grounds of its truthfulness. In my view, this truthfulness is its one overwhelming defect. If an artist must paint decayed cheeses, his merit will lie in their looking as little like decayed cheeses as possible.[7]

The ballad _Lenore_[8] by Gottfried August Berger, inspired in me reveries and visions with its chilling, charnel horrors. With the clarity of crystal I saw enacted in my mind's eye the spectral Wilhelm sweeping the trembling Lenore onto his unearthly horse, and away to the graveyard to celebrate their weird, uncanny wedding feast attended by spirits of the dead. I shuddered over _The Vampyre_, the slim novel by Dr. [John William] Polidori, physician and companion to Lord Byron, and its melancholy plot about the depredations of the vampire nobleman, Lord Ruthven.

I studied [Robert] Southey's _Thalaba the Destroyer_, and vivid though its imagery was, I asked myself, is he who penned its lines truly worthy of the laureate's mantle? Was I guilty of excessive pride in knowing within my heart that my own _Tamerlane_ was far more worthy?

Many of the novels and tales that I read dealt with themes of mystery and supernatural dread. Some possessed such lurid nomenclature that, though their plots have deservedly faded into oblivion, the titles remain still in my mind: _The Demon of Venice,_

The Hag of the Mountains, The Abbot of Montserrat; or the Pool of Blood, The Midnight Groan, and *Tales of Terror,* or *More Ghosts.*

Of all the verse I so devoutly consumed those days, when time hung so heavy on my shoulders, none impressed itself upon me more than the terrible curse from Lord Byron's *Giaour.* In its grim words I thought I saw, in symbolic measure, a distorted image of myself as seen through some dark, imperfect looking-glass.

> *But first on earth, as Vampyre sent,*
> *Thy corse shall from its tomb be rent;*
> *Then ghastly haunt thy native place,*
> *And suck the blood of all thy race;*
> *There from thy daughter, sister, wife,*
> *At midnight drain the stream of life;*
> *Yet loathe the banquet, which perforce*
> *Must feed thy livid living corse,*
> *Thy victims, ere they yet expire,*
> *Shall know the demon for their sire;*
> *As cursing thee, thou cursing them,*
> *Thy flowers are withered on the stem.*

As the warm and fragrant autumn days wore on, memories of my transgressions against morality and law, though never to leave my thoughts, mercifully faded into the back recesses of my mind. When not attending to my military duties, or working on *Al Aaraaf,* I continued in my pursuit of knowledge by frequenting the libraries of Charleston. Tho' the dream of beauty never strayed far from my thoughts, I struggled to suppress those melancholy remembrances of lost love lest the talons of insanity seize and lacerate my mind.

Shortly after General Andrew Jackson's election, one evening, following a pleasant dinner at Colonel Drayton's house, my friend called me into the library and broached the subject of my future. Being aware of my true identity, though not personally acquainted with my former guardian, the gentleman declaimed at length upon the importance of proper alliances in high places.

He expressed the opinion that on account of my heritage and my upbringing it behooved me to pursue a career of public service. Poetry, he said, was, to be sure, a fitting avocation for a gentleman, but certainly not worthy of consideration as the sole occupation of a man's life. I despaired at hearing him speak thus, for though my affection for him was deep, and my respect without reserve, I knew that within his heart he could never understand the forces that drove me.

Regarding me as he did, however, much in the way he might a son of his own, I recognised his motives to be of the highest order. As our future cordial relations proved, his concern for my welfare was genuine and deep. It was his firm conviction that I must give serious consideration to a military career, but not, of course, in the enlisted ranks; rather as an officer and a gentleman. The only way to this "lofty" goal, said he, was for me to obtain an appointment to the United States Military Academy at West Point, New York.

I pondered Colonel Drayton's words for several days and nights. Though the prospect of obtaining a commission in the army held little appeal for me, the means of so doing was another matter. My present term of enlistment was five years. I had thus far served nearly two of them. If I could obtain my discharge and secure an appointment to the Academy, I might then put my time to much better use. My studies there would not be unlike those at the university, and in all probability, were I to become a cadet, it would hardly be necessary for me to attend for the full term.[9] My service as a professional soldier and my studies at the University of Virginia would undoubtedly stand me in good stead. After thinking the matter over carefully, I resolved to broach the subject to my commanding officer, Lieutenant Howard.

It was at this juncture, late in November, that fate intervened in a most extraordinary fashion. I was summoned to the lieutenant's office one afternoon, presumably to perform some minor clerical task. It pertained, I assumed, to the orders, recently received from Eastern Department Headquarters [in New York] for the relocation of the First Artillery to Fortress Monroe, Virginia. I was mildly surprised, therefore, to discover the lieutenant in conversation with an aristocratic-looking gentleman in civilian dress. I was even further astonished to hear the stranger say with a smile, "So this is the elusive Master Poe."

I could scarcely believe my ears. Never, from the day I had enlisted, had anyone at Fort Moultrie addressed me by any name other than my nom de guerre of Private Edgar Perry (though, as I mentioned, certain officers knew my true identity). The expression on my face betrayed my confusion, at which point the gentleman, a Mr. Lay, explained to Lieutenant Howard that he had come here with a message from "Master Poe's guardian, John Allan of Richmond." I was overwhelmed with emotions quite unbecoming a soldier. All the bitterness, anger, and hatred I had previously felt dissolved. In truth I had not wanted to break with my foster parents at the time I left Richmond. But boyish pride and the conviction that I was being sorely mistreated had prompted me to follow the course that I had chosen.

Imagine then, the emotions of elations that overcame me upon hearing Mr. Lay transmit a request to my superior for information as to my health and well-being. I did not question the means by which my guardian[10] had ascertained my whereabouts. I only felt again the heartwarming spark of hope that I would be restored to the bosom of the family which I regarded as my own. There was no longer any need for me to remain in the army. Oh, God! How often I was misled by the mendacious beacon-light of false hope.

In the clarity of sober retrospection, I know now that John Allan was moved by three powerful forces: the increasing awareness of his own mortality; the tearful melancholy of his poor, sick wife; and personal guilt for his infidelities. His letter made reference to an indisposition[11] and made a point of requesting that I be informed of circumstances in Richmond. Perhaps he did soften his heart towards me for a brief instant. In the guilelessness of my youth—I was still only twenty years of age—I believed that all dissension between us was over. Only one point in his letter brought a degree of discomfiture to me. I remember the words to this day. "Better," he wrote of me, "that he stay where he is until the end of his enlistment."

It was now that events began overtaking me more rapidly than ever I might have expected. On the following day, which was

Monday, the first of December, I was summoned to the presence
of Colonel James House, commander of the First Artillery. With
him was Lieutenant Howard. I was unprepared for the conversation which ensued. After being cordially invited to take a seat, I
was informed by the colonel that this interview was to be
regarded as beyond the boundaries ordinarily observed by soldiers in our relative positions.

Said he, "I was personally acquainted with your late grandfather, Quartermaster-General Poe. He was a gentleman and a
patriot, who sacrificed his fortune in the noble cause of our
nation's independence."

Though I dared not utter a word of disrespect, I wondered in
what circumstances had the colonel known my grandfather. The
year of our independence was 1776, fifty-three years past, and
dignified though he seemed, Colonel House was most certainly
not old enough to have served in the War of Independence.
Perhaps he met my grandfather under other auspices, at a later
date. His words concerning my immediate future were my principal concern.

Though he did not elaborate on the statement, he said, "I am
happy to say, young man, that several years ago I had the pleasure of meeting your guardian. I might add that your record of
service in Battery H indicates you have been a credit to him."

"Thank you, sir," I replied, I have always endeavoured to do
my duty."

"And so you have," he assured me. "But now, to the business at
hand. It has come to my attention that for certain personal reasons a
discharge from the army would be welcome to you now."

I began to explain that there had been a disagreement between
my guardian and myself before I left Richmond, but Colonel
House held up his hand and interrupted me. "It was not my
intention to intrude on your personal life, my lad. Rest assured
that the facts which I need to know are in my possession. I shall
speak frankly to you. A young man of your breeding has no business being a ranker. No good can come of it. But there is the
matter of regulations. You shall have your discharge on two
conditions."

I was overjoyed. "What are they, sir?" I asked.

Said he, "First you must obtain a letter from your guardian confirming the reconciliation between you. Secondly, you must obtain a substitute to serve out the remainder of your enlistment."

I promised to write the letter to my guardian that very day and asserted that upon its receipt I would go about seeking a substitute. Then, admittedly, employing a kind of guile, which I had never attempted before, I asked the colonel a seemingly innocent question. "In your opinion, sir, would the army be a suitable career for me, were I to secure an appointment to West Point following my discharge?"

I could see at once that nothing else I might have said would have pleased him more. "Spoken like a true soldier!" he ejaculated, his whiskers bristling, and his ruddy features now wreathed in smiles. "Be off with you now, lad! Write that letter to your guardian at once. Then, barring slave rebellion, invasion, or Indian uprising, we shall have you in the Corps of Cadets within the year!"

It was thus with mixed emotions that I returned to my quarters. I was elated at the prospect of being reunited with family and friends. I yearned to see my dearest [foster] mother again. I even entertained hopes of seeing the lost Elmira, if only from afar. Familial reconciliation banished the grim spectre of poverty, and my need to remain in the army was at an end.

Attending West Point in the cold north climes of New York State was not the most alluring of prospects. However, as I had reasoned before, my present station in the army would give my appointment as a cadet immense advantages. Having already passed thro [sic] the practical part of the artillery arm, my cadetship would, I was certain, be considered a necessary form which I could run through in six months at the most. After that I would be a gentleman by an act of the Congress, as well as by natural inclination.

Before sunset the letter to John Allan was written and posted. One week later, on Thursday, December 11, 1828, the First Artillery Regiment of the United States Army embarked on the ship *Harriet* for Fortress Monroe, Virginia. I was destined never to see sunny South Carolina again.

14

The happiest day—the happiest hour
My seared and blighted heart hath known,
The highest hope of pride and power,
I feel hath flown. . . .

PEERING ACROSS the gaping chasm of time separating the distant past from this place of wretched bitterness called "now," I ponder still the mysteries of life. By what strange alchemy of time does childhood's perception stretch a fleeting moment of joy to an hour of bliss, a fading summer of carefree pleasures to a whole eternity?

Why, I ask in deep reflection, do the first two decades of my life outweigh in substance the years that have intervened until this, my thirty-eighth? Why, in retrospection, do those earlier years seem resplendent with detail and of such greater duration than those which subsequently overtook me?[1] Though much transpired during the time between my arrival as a member of the First Artillery at Fortress Monroe, and my departure from West Point, only certain outstanding events are worthy of recording here. Should history choose to preserve my memory, it is to these events I must call attention, for they are the ones I deem worthy of preservation. If oblivion is to be my fate, what is written on these pages will never be seen by eyes other than my own.

In the months that have passed since I first resolved to place this record on paper I have given the matter much thought. My original intent was to unburden my soul rather than to reveal the story of my life, but some greater force has impelled me to do otherwise. In so doing I have violated one of my own cardinal rules of composition—never to sit down to write until I had made an end of thinking.[2] In writing for the vulgar public, with the need to earn one's daily bread uppermost in mind, such rules were and always will be a necessity for all scriveners of every time and of every place. What I have set on paper here has come from the depths of my soul. Every word flows according to the dictates of my fancy, unfettered by rules, and free as a bird finding freedom in the sky.

Of my sojourn at Fortress Monroe I need only say that it was during a time of cold winds and grey skies. Discipline was rigid, and lacking were the relative niceties of life which pervaded the atmosphere of Fort Moultrie. Furthermore, being less than a hundred miles from Richmond, my thoughts drifted more and more toward happier times there. But I grew restless, for I received no reply to the letters I had written to John Allan.[3] Why was he ignoring me, I wondered? Had I not proven to him—indeed to the whole world—that I was capable of facing adversity and defeating it with head high and banners flying? How much I still had to learn! I did not yet know the true meaning of adversity, though in my folly I often believed that I alone of all men had understood the meaning of suffering.

On New Year's Day of 1829 I had the honour of being appointed regimental sergeant major, thus by virtue of hard work and personal merit attaining the highest noncommissioned rank in the United States Army. But still no word from Richmond. I was especially concerned having had no letter from my dear "Ma," who must have had news of my whereabouts by this time. But I knew not that the gravity of her illness was such that she would never again rise from her bed of sickness. Meanwhile, on a wet and chilly Thursday, the fifteenth day of January, I was stricken with a fever and consigned to the hospital.

In a wild delirium I raved like a madman for several days, or so I was told, for I have no recollection of what transpired. However, when I regained my senses I knew at once that I had divulged a great many facts of a highly personal nature to the post surgeon, Dr. [Robert] Archer. At first I was in a terror for fear of having exposed myself to revulsion or worse, but until the day I was discharged from my sick bed the doctor was most cordial to me. He was acquainted with my guardian and promised to enlist his aid in procuring my release from the service.

Then on Saturday, February 28th, came the fateful summons from Richmond. It was dated one day earlier and consisted of the terse lines, *My wife is seriously ill and begs that you present yourself at her bedside with all due haste.*[4] Icy fear gripped my heart. Dire premonitions of tragedy engulfed me, and fighting to maintain an outward air of composure I hastily made arrangements for an emergency furlough.

Thus on the blustery late morning of March 1, I paced impatiently back and forth, waiting to board the afternoon stage from Norfolk to Richmond. Overwrought with anxiety, I cursed my impotency. Oh, had I only been capable of sprouting wings that I might soar like an eagle! Embittered and earthbound I had to bear the unbearable and wait helplessly in the midst of what I knew in my heart to be a race with death. Again and again during the sodden day and sleepless night of my arduous ride I prayed for her recovery to whatever gods might listen. Fierce gusts of wind rocked the stage like a small boat on a storm-tossed sea, and more than once the horses stumbled in the slippery mud of the rutted country roads. Each minute seemed to last for an hour; each hour, a day, a week. In the fantasies of my mind I leapt into the driver's seat, cast the teamsters aside, and whipping the horses to a frenzy of speed, drove them without respite to my final destination.

A gloomy, sunless dusk was falling when, at last, at eventide on March 2nd, I made my way through the gate and up the circular drive to the house on Fifth and Main streets. A rush of memories surrounded me as I broke into a run and dashed up the steps to the front door, hardly able to contain myself. The spark of hope still burned within my breast, and seizing the heavy brass knocker, I announced my arrival.

I had scarcely taken away my hand when the door was opened by a sombre-visaged Dabney Danbridge. "Mars Eddy!" he cried out, his eyes red and glistening with moisture. "You's too late. We done buried Miz Allan yesterday."

Had he plunged a red-hot dagger into my heart he could not have inflicted greater pain. The familiar sight of the rooms beyond reeled before my eyes. Words would not form. I burst into tears and uttered a single, anguished cry, which must have been heard from one end of the house to the other. Having not yet fully recovered my strength, having only so recently overcome the fever, I felt myself on the verge of falling into a swoon. But then I fancied I heard a familiar voice not far from where I stood, swaying to and fro. "Upon my soul, he's back! No, no. Stay where you are, I shall receive him."

An instant later I found myself enveloped in the ample embrace of Aunt Nancy, the old familiar scent of verbena that always accompanied her filling my nostrils. For a few moments our tearful emotions permitted neither of us to speak, and we stood there, clinging to one another like shipwrecked babes in a storm, racked with sobs and trembling. At length we both recovered our composure sufficiently to converse. "Please," I begged her, "tell me everything. Spare me not a single melancholy detail." My voice broke and I seized my head. "Oh, God!" I cried. "Why was I called so late?"

Instead of replying to my question, the good woman took my hand and contemplated me from head to toe. No doubt I presented a gaunt contrast to her own plump lineaments, made doubly imposing by the sable blackness of her mourning gown. "Dear Eddy," said she, "surely after so arduous a journey you must be hungry and fatigued. Pray, let me have one of the servants fetch you some supper."

Nothing could have been more remote from my desires than food. Shaking my head, I refused. "Please, Aunt Nancy, I will not rest until I know. Did she suffer, or was her passing peaceful?"

A sob escaped her lips as she raised a handkerchief to her eyes. "Let us go," she murmured softly. Then, turning to old Dabney, who had been standing there like an ebony statue, she said, "See to Master Eddy's things; then bring us some coffee and cakes. We will be in the drawing room."

Her voice trembled as she spoke and her eyes bore the scarlet stigmata of weeping. I followed her to the drawing room as tho' in a trance. Nothing in the house seemed changed; yet I could detect the grim presence of death in every nook and corner. Oh, how I fought the tears as I seated myself beside her, for no sooner did our eyes meet than she all but collapsed in a piteous fit of sobbing. It was only when Dabney entered, bearing a tray of light refreshments, that the unhappy woman succeeded in composing herself sufficiently to converse.

"Poor, gentle soul," sighed my "aunt," brushing away a tear. "How she pined for her 'dear Eddy.' How can you know of the days and nights she wept for you? Can you imagine the heartache she felt at the loss of you? Can you count the tears she shed over your likeness?" She hestitated and fixed me with an expression of disapproval, then continued: "What man can ever conceive of the suffering endured by the daughters of Eve on their behalf? Mark my words, young sir, the day you fled from this, your childhood home, was the day that she began to perish!"

"For the love of Heaven, madam!" I exclaimed. "Do not reproach me in this time of grief! I freely admit to many a youthful fall from the path of virtue, but never did my love for her falter."

"Indeed," retorted the bereaved woman. "And what token of that love did she ever see from you? For two long years she languished in misery, solicitous of your welfare, retiring nightly to a bed of anguish!"

"Please, forbear!" I cried, but she would not listen and continued with her fulminations against me.

"As the days passed she weakened. She faded like a spring flower in the summer's heat. How many sleepless nights she endured for the pains that gnawed her vitals! 'Twasn't a pretty picture, Eddy. And who do you think remained by her side till the end? Not you, nor that hypocritical Scotsman,[5] nor the doctors with their lancets and basins, and sanctimonious solicitude . . ." Here her voice broke and for a moment she sobbed as tho' her heart would break. But then, regaining something of her composure, she addressed me again. "No one. No one but her sister, Nancy Valentine, was there to offer solace and comfort. And then came December. May heaven shield me from ever being privy to such suffering again. The dark circles deepened beneath her eyes—more often filled with tears than not. Her poor cheeks grew wan and hollow. Do you remember how gay she once appeared?"

I could not suppress a sob. "For the love of God on high," I cried, "why do you torture me thus?"

"You asked to hear *everything!*" she retorted. "Did you expect some romantic tale of dissolution? No, my fine fellow, death is ugly. Death is pain. Death is tears. Never have I been so close to such lingering, melancholy death before. You accuse me of torture, dear Eddy. No, no. It was my poor beloved sister who knew the meaning of that accursed word. Had it not been for the opium I administered nightly, I tremble even now in contemplation of what she might have endured. You look pained, sir. And well you should."

"The opium eased her suffering, then?" I asked.

"It eased the sting of her pain and enabled her to bear it without screaming night and day. But it could not ease the anguish in her heart."

As she spoke, though I derived no comfort from the thought, I heard a voice, an echo from the dark side of my soul. *Why could it not have been him?* Tho' it had not been my intention, the words formed soundlessly on my lips. Aunt Nancy, perceiving them, fixed me with a sorrowful glance, shook her head, and sighed, "Oh, Eddy, had the bonds of love that once held you together not been rent asunder by pride and bitter words!" Once more tears flowed from her eyes, now crimson and puffed from copious weeping.

What painful emotions now intermingled in my heart. My grief was supreme; yet beneath the surface raging blasts of anger were tempered by recollections of happier, bygone times. Oh, if only by some miraculous means *she* could be restored to life and health.[6] If in some wondrous and mysterious way harmony and love might be given back to us. These and other futile sentiments passed fleetingly through the corridors of my brain, perhaps to the purpose of preserving my sanity. But again my wandering attention was summoned back by Nancy Valentine's words, tho' part of what she said was lost.

". . . I will avow in confidence, however, that I believe he should have summoned you at Christmastime."

"In heaven's name," said I, "please explain."

She paused long enough to dry her tears, then declared: "It was during the early days of the month that her suffering became so unbearable that her shrieks and cries could be heard throughout the house. I tremble still at the recollection. The lustre vanished from her eyes and her cheeks grew wan and pale."

I could not suppress a sob. "Oh God!" I gasped.

"Her once soft nature changed, and in place of the gentle dove-like creature she had been there emerged for a time a shrewish vixen who could not be pleased. She raged. She screamed. She heaped abuse on all who approached her bedside."

"I cannot believe this!" I exclaimed. "Surely, Aunt Nancy, you exaggerate."

She shook her head from side to side. "No, my dear," she said. "You must understand, it was not my beloved sister who abused us so harshly. It was the demon of agony that possessed her. Would you have wished to see her thus?"

I would have spoken, but she admonished me, saying, "I think not, nor would she have wished it either. Yet, because you were not here, it was your name she called out in her delirium. It was for her 'darling Eddy' she cried in her darkest hours of despair and greatest anguish."

"Why then? Why," I cried, "why did he not write me?"

"I cannot say," she said with a sigh, again shaking her head. "I do not know precisely for whom he feared the most. But this I can say with a certainty. There was terror in his heart, as there is deep remorse this night."

"As well there might be," said I.

"Yes, yes, I know whereof you speak, Eddy, but I do not refer to such delicate matters now. I speak of something else."

"What then?" I demanded, my curiosity now piqued beyond measure. She leaned close to me and lowered her voice. As she exhaled I recognised the unmistakable redolence of spirits on her breath. Though I had never seen her imbibe more than a genteel glass of wine with dinner, as I scrutinised her now I could detect at once that she had partaken of a goodly portion. I was struck that moment by remembrance of the ancient aphorism, *in vino veritas*.

She said, " 'Twas in December the doctors declared that she would not see another summer, and recommended extra doses of opium to ease her pain. With the diminution of her agonies the sweetness of her nature was to a great measure restored. I will allow that he was as generous as any man could be under such trying circumstances. He gave her whatever her poor heart desired. Everything but one thing. You know what that one thing was, Eddy, do you not? She wanted to see you, to hold your hand, to press it to her cheek, to press you to her poor, wasted bosom."

"Then in the name of heaven," I cried, "why did the wretch deny her this simple request? He knew I was at Fortress Monroe!"

"I will tell you what I think," said she. "He would not believe[7] that death was nigh. Before her fragile health abandoned her, tho' she spoke often of you to me, she eschewed all mention of your name in his presence for fear of arousing his displeasure. But then, on Friday morning [February 27, 1929], she began to sink. There was no longer any doubt that she would soon succumb. A calm descended on her, for she knew that her sufferings would soon end."

"Oh, that I could have been with her," I muttered.

" 'Twas her wish too. At high noon, before the doctor, her husband, and myself, she said, 'Oh that I might embrace my dear Eddy once more before I die.' It was then the note was dispatched to you."

At this mournful recitation the tears flowed freely down my cheeks. Tears of grief, tears of remorse I felt. Had it not been for my selfish and headstrong defiance of my guardian, she might have lived.[8] But I would never know for a certainty, and therefore, true or not, the shadow of doubt would hang darkly over me forever, increasing the burden of my guilt tenfold. Once more I focused my attention on the griefstricken woman in black beside me.

Said she, "Oh, how deep was her despair when you did not come, and in her final hour, as death's chill overcame her, she whispered to her husband, 'Promise me you will not forget my dear boy, Edgar.' "

"And what did he say?" I asked.

"He gave her his promise. But then she said, 'And should I die before he comes, I beg you, lay me not in my grave 'til he sees me one last time.' "

A chill as cold as arctic ice enveloped me before I spoke. Then, with all deliberation, fighting to maintain my composure, I asked, "And how did he respond to this plaintive plea? I pray tell me."

"He answered her not," Aunt Nancy said with downcast eyes, "for at that very moment she was stricken by the blast of death. She breathed her last. Her spirit fled."

Flushed with the heat of anger I leapt to my feet and trembled in my growing rage. "Why then, did he not obey her last wish?" I cried. "Why? Take me to him that I might hear the reason for this vile treachery from his own lips!"

To my astonishment she sprang to her feet with an agility I never would have suspected her to possess. Seizing my arms, her eyes blazing through the tears, she exclaimed, "Impetuous youth! Warlike words will not recall my poor sweet sister from her grave! Will further contention between you and John Allan accomplish any good? Hear me now! We are all prostrate with grief. He no less than you or I. Make your peace with him now, I say!⁹ I can think of no more fitting memorial to her, whom we all so adored."

Suddenly, overcome no doubt by emotion, her voice broke and she fell to sobbing piteously. Endeavouring to offer her what comfort I could, I gave her my arm for support, and at length escorted her from the room. I had not yet seen or spoken to John Allan, and I reflected on Aunt Nancy's words. There was wisdom in them. What purpose would I serve by pricking old wounds, by reawakening the ire of him to whom I was beholden. Yet, as if pursued by some nameless threat, I dreaded our first encounter after the passage of two years whilst at the same time wishing it to occur.

Being fully aware that he had not chosen to greet me when I arrived, I resolved to postpone our meeting until the morrow. It was my intention at [the] earliest opportunity to venture out to Shockoe Cemetery and place a wreath on the final resting place of my beloved "Ma."

As if I had never been gone I ascended the familiar staircase that I might retire to my chamber. I could not conceive of its not being exactly as I had left it. But something stopped me when I was in sight of another room, an empty room, one filled with memories of joy and gladness, laughter and tears. And as I stood bathing in the flood of my recollections, I found myself drawn to that once happy chamber as if under the influence of a powerful magnetic force.

As I drew near I became instantly aware of a dim, but perceptible beam of light issuing from the doorway. *Impossible*, I thought, but as I approached, its flickering presence became even more apparent to me. My heart commenced beating wildly. I could not hope. I was in no trance, no dream. The realities of what I knew to be true were all about me, yet for one fleeting precious instant I pretended that I might stand at the doorway and see her there. She would put down her needlework or her book, and her gentle pale features wreathed in smiles, she would welcome me with a tender embrace. Hovering about her would be the evanescent scent of lilacs or violets. Abruptly I closed my eyes and clapped my hands to my head.

Wretched fool! I told myself. Such fantasies are for children or madmen. She is gone. You will never see her again. But the light. From whence did it come? Approaching the door on tiptoe I observed that it was ajar, and gently pushed it open. Suppressing an outcry I stared in disbelief. Slumped in a chair alongside the empty, canopied bed was John Allan. His cane lay on the floor at his feet. His head, inclined sharply to one side, gave the illusion of a man recently hanged, and his jaw was slack, partially open. For an instant I envisioned him dead, but the rhythmic heaving of his chest and the wheezing rasp of his snores proved otherwise. But it was not his presence there that took me by surprise, rather his appearance. Indeed, though barely fifty[10] years of age, he appeared at the very least ten years older. The countenance I remembered as ruddy and full was now pale and emaciated.

How long I stood there gazing about at the familiar objects in that room which held such fond recollections I do not know. But it was the sight of her empty bed that brought fresh tears to my eyes. Never again would I behold her loving face, wreathed in smiles at my approach, as it rested in sweet repose upon that now cool, snowy pillow. As I stood, my eyes fixed on the bed, a stanza of verse took shape in my mind.

The lady sleeps! Oh, may her sleep,[11]
Which is enduring, so be deep!
Heaven keep her in its sacred keep!
This chamber changed for one more holy,
This bed for one more melancholy,
I pray to God that she may lie
Forever with unopened eye,
While the pale sheeted ghosts go by.

Unable to remain any longer, I hastened to my old room. The lamp had been lit, and the bed was turned down. What comfort I took in these familiar surroundings, that seemed to embrace me as I prepared to take refuge in slumber.

15

I stand amid the roar
Of a surf-tormented shore.

AFTER A NIGHTMARE-RIDDEN, restless night I approached my first meeting with John Allan with apprehension. Two years had exacted their toll upon him. His face was lined and his eyes were red, no doubt from secret effusions of grief in the privacy of his chamber. Beside him was the Malucca cane which he now required to ease the painful burden on his legs. As for myself, tho' no taller than when I had so hastily departed in the spring of 1827, I was lean and muscular. My complexion still bespoke a trace of the sunburn it had acquired in South Carolina, and I carried myself with an erect bearing commensurate with my military rank.

We met in the library after breakfast, he having arisen much earlier than I, and leaving word with Dab that I was to join him when I appeared. There was an awkwardness between us when first I entered his presence, for we both remembered all too clearly the acrimonious circumstances of our last conversation. Yet now, united by our common grief, there seemed a ray of hope that a true and lasting reconciliation between us might be effectuated. There was even a symbolic ray of sunlight that shone like a golden shaft through the window. Unlike the drear grey skies that had rendered the previous day so bleak, the morning brightness seemed to augur an early arrival of spring.

I greeted him formally, and as if it were the most natural thing to do, stood at attention before him. He contemplated me with what appeared to my perception as an air of mild approval, for after a moment of silence he said, "So the prodigal returns." Then nodding his head thoughtfully, without taking his eyes from me he added, "Sit down. Sit down. This is no army post."

"Of course," said I, hastening to take a chair and bring it into a position enabling me to face him. We both appeared to be at a loss for words at first, and if my instincts served me well, I believe that each of us was struggling to display a manly demeanour; to hide from one another the depths of our emotions. I took heart in the fact that my foster father addressed me not in the accents of his native Scotland, for whenever he did so it was certain that he was in a temper.

"The uniform becomes you," he said at length.

"Thank you, Pa," said I. "But I would gladly exchange it for civilian dress, and well I might if you were to but give me your word."

"We shall talk about that presently," he replied. "For the moment there is another matter I would discuss with you."

"Pray tell me what it is," I said.

Grimacing slightly as he shifted his position, he took a deep breath, then sighed deeply. "I want you to know, my boy, that I truly regret you were not here when . . ." He stopped speaking abruptly for he was unexpectedly overcome by a paroxysm of coughing, which necessitated his covering his face with a handkerchief. I leapt to my feet, but he waved me away with his free hand. As he replaced the handkerchief he finished the sentence: ". . . when the end came."

Not wishing to dwell on the subject of our grief, nor to impose upon either of us any undue discomfort, I assured him that I lay no blame upon him. My words seemed to offer him some small measure of consolation, for he nodded his head and said, "Now, on the matter of propriety, you must have mourning attire. The uniform will never do. I have sent a message to Mr. Ellis.[1] See him today so that the matter may be attended to." He fell to coughing again, but before I could answer he spoke again, his voice now hoarse and strained. "But I presume that you wish to visit — (here he hesitated) — your mother's grave first. Have old Dab see to it that a carriage is made ready."

"You are most thoughtful, Pa," said I, rising to my feet. "I shall go at once. But before I take my leave, if I may say so, please see to your health. It would appear that you have caught a chill. I know whereof I speak, for only recently I overcame an attack of the fever. I fully comprehend the perils and the consequences."

"Yes, yes," he muttered. "Now be off with you. I must attend to some matters that require my immediate attention."

"Of course, sir," said I, offering him my hand, "and God bless you."

We clasped hands and he replied softly, "May he extend his blessings to all of us, most especially the soul of that dear gentle lady who . . ." Once again he fell into a fit of coughing, and I knew it was best that I take my leave of him at once. I paused momentarily at the door to the library before making my exit, and though he was still racked by coughs, I thought that I could detect an affirmative nod of his head.

Though the songbirds warbled sweetly and the sun shone brightly on that unnaturally warm March day, I derived no comfort from them. What was there in this mortal existence that could offer me solace, especially as the carriage bore me through the portals of the graveyard? The silent shafts of marble and granite bore mute testimony to the fleeting nature of life. Unexpectedly, as we approached the final resting place of my poor dear foster mother, I caught sight of another tomb that nearly caused my heart to stop beating, the sacred spot where lay the mouldering remains of my beloved "Helen." But when we came to the fresh new grave, now blanketed with blossoms of every hue, unmarked as yet by any monument, my composure left me.

Dreadful awareness smote me like a thunderbolt from Jove's own mighty hand. The only mother I had ever known reclined, encoffin'd in suffocating blackness, a bare six feet beneath where I stood. Closer to me than the distance to my carriage, she was yet more remote than the most distant star in the firmament. I could bear the pain no longer. Caring not what any profane eyes might see, nor ears might hear, I flung myself to the ground above her and fell into a fit of convulsive weeping. Half maddened by my grief I truly believe that had two servants not been there to restrain me I would have torn at the earth with my two bare hands, in order to steal one final glimpse of her, whose shining love would remain imbedded in my soul forever.[2] My lamentations so sapped me of strength that when it came time to depart the necropolis, the servants had to assist me into the carriage.

The remainder of my ten days in Richmond was painful. The mourning clothes I wore, however, were the first civilian habiliments I had known in two years, and I confess that they offered a welcome relief from the confines of my uniform. John Allan was especially solicitous about my proper attire, tho' at the time, cloaked as I was in melancholy, I suspected nothing of his motives. I believe today that the true reason for his concern stemmed from quite another source. He was, after all, one of the most prominent men in the state of Virginia. It simply would not do for him to have a member of his family seen publickly [sic] in the army uniform displaying the insignia of a noncommissioned officer.

Tho' it consoled me not, I endured an endless procession of callers coming to the house that they might offer their condolences. I was subjected again and again to detailed interrogations about my "foreign travels," and my guardian never once said a word of contradiction about these mythical peregrinations. To have roved about Europe as a soldier of fortune was infinitely more socially acceptable in his circles than to have served as an enlisted man in the army of the United States. I was able to successfully answer every query most satisfactorily, either with a parry or a thrust. I could speak from first-hand recollections about England, and my reading about other places was so extensive that whatever I said was thoroughly convincing.

I spent most of my time in the bosom of the family, seeing my dear friends the Galts and the Mackenzies, who had adopted my sister, Rosalie. Though in blossoming health and in the ripe bloom of womanhood, she seemed to have no prospects of marriage, though her spinsterhood appeared not to have bothered her an iota. Upon several occasions I set out to pay a call on my old friend Ebenezer Burling, but my better judgement caused me to regretfully decide against it. Ebenezer was a great bon vivant, given to mighty consumptions of strong drink. I recognised my own weakness too well, and I knew that were I to see him I would be unable to restrain myself from joining him in a cup or two. I knew as well that if I wished to rely on my guardian's support in the matter of my discharge from the army, it behooved me to conduct myself in a manner that was beyond reproach.

One day I nearly abandoned my resolve, for I was returning to the house from a visit to an old university friend (to whom I was not indebted). As it happened, while strolling home I chanced to pass the house of Mr. and Mrs. Royster, the parents of my adored Myra. I hesitated before their gate and contemplated the house. For a moment I seriously considered paying them a visit and demanding to know the facts behind their having separated us. But then I reconsidered. Such an act would be too rash. Bitter tho' I felt at her loss, knowing as I did in my heart that she and I had been betrayed, I knew that were I to see her parents and raise my voice in anger, it would jeopardise the reconciliation with my foster father. And that I dared not do,[3] haunted tho' I was by dreams of her.

The most important accomplishment of my entire sojourn in Richmond was to receive assurance from John Allan that he would give his support to my endeavour to obtain an appointment to West Point. I will openly confess that had a completely free choice been mine, the last thing on earth I would have pursued was a military career. But, alas, the choice was *not* mine. Armed with the information I had received from Aunt Nancy, that my foster mother had wrested a promise from her husband to "remember" me, I proceeded with caution. I was older and wiser. What form that remembrance might take was for me to conjecture. If it consisted of being remembered in his will I would be saved. But I had no knowledge of what was in his will, or what changes he planned to make in it. That he would now do so was inevitable, his wife no longer being among the living.

I could hardly discuss the matter of his will with him, however, especially during this mournful period of our bereavement. The best that I could do was to remain in his good graces and make whatever compromises were necessary. To give the devil his portion, I truly believe that whatever his black machinations against me were before or afterwards, during this brief season of peace between us, his feelings for me were restored to their previous state of affection.

Two days before I was bound to leave and return to Fortress Monroe, we discussed the matter of West Point while riding home from a visit to the Galts. Although he was far from cheerful, his gloom appeared to be under control. For a time we rode in silence and I chose not to intrude on his reverie. Then he turned, contemplated me and said, "How long do you reckon it would take for you to secure an appointment to the military academy?"

"I should think not very long," I replied. "Once I have received my discharge from the ranks, and the necessary letters have been obtained, I daresay it should be no more than a matter of months."

Said he, "About your discharge, then. I believe you said something of a requirement that you must have a letter of approval from me."

"That is very true, sir," I answered, "but there is also the matter of a substitute. According to the military regulations, a substitute must be recruited to serve in my place. It is customary to pay all recruits a bounty of twelve dollars. When one of them is enlisted as a substitute, he who desires to be discharged must assume the financial obligation."

Nodding his head he said, "I see. But tell me, is there no way in which you might be appointed to West Point directly from the ranks, and thus avoid payment of this bounty?"

"Alas, no, Pa," I said. "Rankers are never granted appointments. To receive mine, I must first leave the service."

He thought the matter over for a moment, then declared with a sigh, "If those are the regulations, lad, then we must abide by them. You shall have your letter and a sum of money to purchase your substitute. You appear to have acquired sober habits, and a sense of responsibility in the army. We shall regard the expenditures as an investment in your future career."

Emotions of gratitude flooded my heart. Had it not been for the late tragedy which overshadowed us all, I should have felt happier than I had in a very long time. Consequently, when I took my leave on the morning of March 9, though still dispirited over the terrible loss I had sustained, I was at least confident of my future. The necessity of taking an early morning stage had

167

required my departing shortly before dawn, thus preventing me from wishing my guardian adieu. He was asleep at that hour and I had no wish to rouse him from the slumbers which gave him temporary respite from his grief.

Upon my return to Fortress Monroe on March 10, I informed Lieutenant Howard and Colonel House that a reconciliation had been effected between John Allan and myself, and that the required letter of confirmation would be forthcoming. Indeed, before another day dawned I, too, wrote a letter to my foster father, containing suggestions regarding certain influential individuals who might facilitate my appointment to West Point. By virtue of my position as regimental sergeant major, and the sympathy of my superiors to the cause of my discharge, a goodly portion of my time was spent attending to the numerous details pursuant to this end. Thus on April 8, 1829, Special Order No. 28 was received from the army's Eastern Department Headquarters in New York, authorising my discharge one week hence, Wednesday, April 15th.[4]

Although I cannot complain about the alacrity with which arrangements for my discharge were made, I can only ponder on the mysterious convolutions of fate which determine the course of our future. Under ordinary circumstances, on or about the day I was to be discharged, the first man to offer himself as a recruit would be named my substitute. I would pay him the twelve-dollar bounty, and I would be freed. But Providence decreed otherwise. Both Colonel House and Lieutenant Howard were away from Fortress Monroe and for several days no recruits had presented themselves to be mustered. I was disconsolate. Without a substitute the order for my discharge was a worthless piece of paper.

Racking my brain to find a solution, it suddenly occurred to me that a *new* recruit need not be found if I could secure the reenlistment of a man already in the army, who would agree to serve the extra three years of my time. The thought then presented itself to me that I knew of just such a man. He was a comrade, a sergeant named Samuel Graves. Known familiarly as "Bully" to his companions, he was a hearty bear of a man, several years my senior and one who had made no secret of his intention to make the army his career.

I rushed to regimental headquarters and searched for the papers relating to his term of service. Upon perusing them I learnt that he had two years yet to serve of his present enlistment, which in itself presented no problem. Since it was his intention to remain a regular, to serve the remainder of my three years would be of no concern to him. His becoming my substitute would be merely a formality, so I hastened to find him at once.

It was an unusually balmy day for April and I had difficulty locating the sergeant. He was the sort of soldier who possessed an uncanny talent which enabled him to appear industrious when, indeed, he was attending to matters closer to his own heart. Thus I found him playing cards with two corporals in one of the magazines whilst several sweaty privates busied themselves counting cannon balls and powder bags for the "inventory" desired by Sergeant Graves. Upon my arrival he looked up at me and said, "Ah, Perry,⁵ my hearty, you're just in time to join our game."

"Would that I could," said I, "but I have urgent business with you."

"Hellfire and damnation!" he exclaimed, his face clouding darkly. "Just when my luck was beginning to change."

Not wishing to antagonise him, for I desperately required his cooperation, I said, "Far be it from me to come between a man and his mistress, Dame Fortune. Our business is urgent, but an hour or more will not hinder its outcome. Meet me in my quarters after the midday meal."

"Bully fellow!" he ejaculated, employing the word that had come to be his familiar name. "I'll remember you in my will."

He returned to his game and I withdrew, confident that our arrangements could be settled before the end of the day. My assumption was correct. When we met at the agreed-upon time and place, Sergeant Graves said he was more than willing to become my substitute; however, he would not hear of the bounty of twelve dollars. "Damn it, Perry!" he exclaimed, thumping the table with his fist, "a sergeant of my standing is worth ten times that of a bloody recruit! But I'll strike a bargain with you. Make it seventy-five dollars. Shall we shake hands on it?"

"But, Bully, old man," I protested, "I do not have seventy-five dollars."

"Then here is what we shall do," said he. "Have you, shall we say, twenty-five?"

"Yes," I replied.

"Bully!" said he. "Give that to me and your note for the rest. You are an honourable fellow. You would not cheat an old comrade."

And with that exchange I agreed to his terms and he became my substitute. Had Lieutenant Howard or Colonel House been present, as officers customarily were during such transactions, I am certain I would not have paid so dearly. But business negotiations were never my forte. Little did I suspect, however, that this particular transaction, innocent tho' it was, would one day haunt me bitterly.

Had I foreseen the consequences, I would have awaited Lieutenant Howard's return from leave and enlisted his assistance. But I was eager to obtain my discharge, and upon that matter I was unwilling to gamble. As it was I remained at Fortress Monroe for an additional week following my formal release from the service, for I was eager to obtain letters of endorsement, which would, I hoped, assist me in securing my appointment to West Point.[6]

Not only were these letters given freely, but they attested quite frankly to the spotlessness of my conduct while serving in the army.[7] Having obtained them I gathered together my few belongings, which consisted of clothing, writing materials, and manuscripts. Then, after a few farewells, I departed from Fortress Monroe for the last time on Friday, April 24th and returned to Richmond. Although I was welcomed by my guardian with civility, I thought that I detected a certain element of aloofness in his manner. Nevertheless, he reiterated his promises to assist me in procuring the appointment to West Point and set about doing so.

16

Ah, by no wind these clouds are driven
That rustle through the unquiet Heaven
Uneasily, from morn to even.

VERY SHORTLY after my return to Richmond I received the distinct impression from my guardian that he was not eager to have me remain beneath his roof. I cannot say in truth that there was any rancour in his demeanour towards me at that time, but rather a certain nervousness of temperament, if you will, an air of discomfort in my presence. Neither he nor I knew the precise nature of the politics involving appointments to the academy; therefore, we determined to obtain a veritable bundle of endorsements from men of stature.[1]

Although I have no way of knowing this to be a certainty, I will nonetheless speculate that had my friend Colonel Drayton of Charleston been given the cabinet post to which he had aspired, my appointment would have materialised quite speedily. As it was, President Jackson awarded the position of secretary of war to an old crony, Major John Eaton,[2] of whom the less said the better, and it was to him the application had to be made.

The letters having been obtained, my foster father took pen in hand on May 6, and wrote an epistle of his own to the secretary of war.[3] He gave me his permission to read it along with the suggestion that before delivering it I take care to apply a seal. Although it did not deal with me in uncomplimentary terms, there was a chill quality in its words that were not lost on me. Referring to me, not as his ward, but as "this youth," he averred, "I declare that he is no relation to me whatsoever." Was this a subtle declaration to me that he intended to wash his hands of me?

Despite my apprehensions concerning the tone of this letter, I dared not criticise it, for in substance my guardian had kept his word. Though I had hoped to see in it some indication that some affection had been stirred, I was not unduly concerned. Had he not promised my beloved "Ma" on her deathbed to "remember" me? Surely, her meaning was an enjoinder to remember me in his will.[4] And why should he not have done so? Though he had sired one or more bastards, he had no legitimate offspring. Certainly, he would not deny me some small portion of his worldly wealth, after, as all men, he fell prey to the Conquering Worm.

Thus, girded with a measure of confidence and a single-mindedness of purpose, I departed Richmond and set forth to Washington. Having been provided with my letters and fifty dollars in cash, I prepared to have an audience with the secretary of war. I did not anticipate the bustling activity and the turmoil I encountered when I arrived in the capital. Much of this had been caused by the upheavals engendered by the President himself.

Not content to permit the government's functionaries to remain in place after his inauguration, he removed two thousand of them from office. In their places were appointed a coterie of cronies, sycophants, and others of such ilk from cabinet officers down to the humblest of clerks. A man of peculiar and inflexible character, President Jackson was said to have vetoed more bills sent to him from the Congress in one week than did all of his predecessors combined.

When I presented myself at the office of Major Eaton I was dismayed at the number of petitioners present. I had left Richmond fully confident of a personal interview with the gentleman. It would be granted eventually, I was told by one of his aides, but it would be necessary for me to endure a wait of no less than five, but possibly as many as thirty days.

"If you wish to commit the nature of your business to writing," said he, "I can assure you that it will receive the same consideration as that you would get from an interview with the secretary."

"Can I not see him briefly," I begged, "if only to present him my credentials by hand?"

"Impossible," replied the bureaucrat. "Why can you not see,

sir, how many have come before you? Indeed, were you to be given precedence I shudder to think of the consequences."

He lowered his voice and bade me glance with caution at the ranks of the other petitioners. I did so. "See," he whispered, "what a rough and uncouth lot most of them are? I reckon most of them are armed and ready to fight at the slightest provocation."

Whether or not he shared his observation for the purpose of discouraging me, I had to admit that a goodly number of them appeared to be mean- and scurvy-looking ruffians. Bearded, muddy-booted frontiersmen in stained buckskins predominated, but there were as well lean and scowling army officers, unkempt civilians, and a sprinkling of others whose habiliments gave rise to speculation that they may have been gentlemen. Perhaps had there not been such a malodorous stench of stale cigar smoke and unwashed bodies, not to mention the frequent streams of brown tobacco juice issuing from the mouths of the assembly, I might have chosen to await my turn. But instead I handed my petitions and testimonials over to the fellow, and upon being given a receipt, prepared to take my leave. He assured me that I would be notified "with all due dispatch." When I attempted to query him in an effort to obtain a more specific answer he volunteered nothing further. Recognising the futility of further conversation, and anxious to return once more to the fresh air outside, I left.

Having no further reason to remain in Washington, I resolved to visit Baltimore. I was anxious to make the acquaintance of a number of relatives there whom I had never seen. Furthermore, it was in Baltimore that my brother, Henry, resided. Though we carried on an irregular correspondence, it was many years since I had seen him and this was my opportunity to do so. The distance between the two cities being about forty miles, a journey from one to the other required a full day's travel. There were two morning stages daily, one at eight o'clock and another at ten. I lodged for one night at an inexpensive hotel, then arose at dawn and took the early stage to Baltimore, arriving there well before sundown.

My first necessity upon arriving was to secure cheap lodgings, for what little money I possessed had to be spent with extreme frugality. I harboured no illusions as to how or when I would receive additional funds from my foster father, and I was determined to do nothing that might arouse his displeasure. I must confess that I had a second motive for coming to Baltimore, of no less importance to me than the matter of making the acquaintance of relatives. As the third ranking city in America, it was a place of considerable industry and enterprise,[5] and occupied a respectable position in the world of American letters. Since I knew not how long I would be required to wait for my appointment to West Point, it seemed a most logical endeavour to devote what time I could to the pursuit of my literary career. As my all-consuming passion, I knew it was in this direction my true destiny lay, regardless of how tortuous the path.

As was my wont in an unfamiliar place, I spent the first day wandering about the city's broad streets, absorbing sight and sound, whilst acquainting myself with the environs. I found it to be a lively metropolis with pleasant thoroughfares and impressive public buildings. Above the rows of houses a number of lofty structures stood out in relief against the sky, the most impressive being the snowy marble shaft of the recently erected Washington Monument.[6] I made a particular point of visiting the fort which had so ably defended the city from the British in 1814. From its position of elevation I was afforded a sweeping view of the harbour, bordered on either side by a neat row of red brick warehouses and slips, giving it a look reminiscent of a piano keyboard. I must have lingered there for hours, gazing across the water, watching in rapt fascination the tall-masted clippers, the schooners, and the sloops. But it was the strange, naked-looking steamers that filled me with awe. How peculiar they appeared, devoid of sails, clouds of black smoke billowing forth from their stovepipe chimneys as they glided across the water. They were harbingers of the future, and I envisioned a day when they would dominate the seas.

One of the first persons upon whom I called after arriving in Baltimore was the Honorable William Wirt, formerly attorney general[7] of the United States, and author of *Letters of a British Spy*. It was my intention to show him the manuscript of *Al Aaraaf* in hopes that he might assist me, by virtue of his prominence, in getting the work published. Although he received me courteously, he declared himself unqualified to judge a work so modern in style, and recommended that I venture to Philadelphia and seek the assistance of some critic more versed than he in the matter of contemporary poetry.

Perhaps the proper thing for me to have done at that time would have been to first establish contact with my relations. Blinded, however, by the glittering beacon light of fame, which ever I pursued with a passion unmatched by any other, I postponed my familial obligations. Fame! How early in life I came to desire it, nay to require it for my very survival. I would drink to the very dregs the glorious intoxication it can offer. Fame! Glory! they are the life-giving breath and blood. I knew, even then—unknown, unwanted, unloved—that only fame and glory would justify my existence.

But alas! there were none, as yet, willing to recognise my gifts, save one, and he, tho' kindly disposed, could not assist me in the attainment of my dreams. Colonel [James P.] Preston of Richmond, father of a boyhood friend, wrote a letter to the secretary of war on my behalf, in which he went so far as to term me a "genius."[8] As for Mr. Wirt, I took his advice, ventured to Philadelphia, and sought the support of an editor, Mr. Walsh, of *The American Quarterly Review*. Next I called upon the publishers Carey, Lea & Carey, and tho' I was received courteously enough, that was all. *Veni, vidi, sed non vinci.*[9] These gentlemen offered to publish my poems if I would guarantee them against any loss. As the cost of publication was a mere one hundred dollars, the risk was virtually nil, and the likelihood of realising a profit was substantial.

Here I made a serious error in judgement. Knowing in my heart the superiority of my poetry, on my return to Baltimore I immediately wrote my foster father[10] asking him to offer this guarantee. In soliciting his support in this matter I assured him that I had abandoned Byron as a model, knowing him to hold the great romanticist in disfavour. All I received for my efforts was a strong censure prompting me to write back assuring him that I would publish nothing without his permission, hoping in the future to gain his approval of my work and some monetary aid.

175

Although John Allan continued to provide me with a meagre allowance, his letters were never without some form of reproach. On one occasion he suggested that "men of genius" such as myself ought not need to apply for assistance. This was a time of great trial for me, yet at the same time one of great revelation. I met my grandmother for the first time, the widow of "General" Poe. Aged and infirm, she was confined to her bed, and ofttimes not in full command of her faculties. I also met the dear aunt[11] and pretty little cousin, who (tho' I knew it not then) would come to occupy the principal chamber of my heart. I saw my brother, Henry, and was pained to observe the sorry state to which he had fallen. Displaying the ravages of consumption, he coughed piteously and often. Had he not so completely abandoned himself to the evil effects of excessive drinking, his life might have taken a different course.

Although none of my kin were blessed with riches, and indeed, some were wretchedly poor, they were nonetheless blood relations, and for the first time in my life I was not made to feel [like] an outsider. A second cousin, however, whose memory I will not perpetuate by mentioning his name[12] wronged me grievously and contributed to my impoverished state, by robbing me of forty-six dollars on a night when I had offered him the hospitality of my room. My meagre supply of cash was so badly depleted by his treachery, that when I was called upon at that time to satisfy the debt of fifty dollars to Sergeant Bully Graves, I could not do so.[13]

Late in July, having heard nothing from the War Department, and wishing to allay John Allan's fears that I was doing nothing to advance the cause of my appointment to West Point, I made up my mind to visit Washington once again. It was my intention on this occasion to see Major Eaton in person, with the hope of wresting an answer from him. The necessity of paying the greater part of my board bill depleted the principal portion of a small remittance which arrived from Richmond on July 22, so there was no recourse for me other than journeying to the Capital on foot.

The weather was hot and moist that time of the year, and as I trudged along the dusty roads, plagued often by swarms of mosquitos and flies, I cursed my lot. The only wardrobe I possessed consisted of my army uniform and the black mourning attire I had acquired after the death of my poor foster mother. My instincts told me that to appear before the secretary of war in the uniform of a noncommissioned officer would be detrimental to my cause; yet if I walked to Washington in my only respectable suit of clothes, I would resemble a vagabond on my arrival. Thus, my only recourse was to carefully wrap what decent attire I possessed into a bundle, and travel in the uniform. It was of heavy, coarse material so that every step I took was a sore trial. With the searing radiance of the sun blazing down on me from on high, I was soon convinced that I could understand the feelings of a soul burning in the infernal regions of hell.

Weary, hungry, and thirsty though I became as the hours passed slowly by, I did not abandon my resolve and pause by the wayside. At times, however, the temptation was strong, for it would have been easy to take refuge in temporary slumber beneath cool, shady trees along the road. To remain alert I recited poetry to myself and sang aloud as I walked. Only at high noon, or thereabout, did I seek temporary respite. Thanks to a kindly farmer I was able to slake my thirst with water from his well and assuage my hunger with apples from his tree. At sundown I found refuge in a haystack, because a warm-hearted tiller of the soil once again took pity on a poor footsore wayfarer.

I awoke early in the morning, for the tiny creatures with whom I had shared my nocturnal resting place, presuming me to have been provided by nature for their nourishment, allowed me little sleep. I arrived in Washington shortly before midday, at which time I sought a degree of rejuvenation at the facilities of the nearest public bath.

By the time I arrived at the War Department I was reasonably presentable. I was pleased to discover that there was less than a horde waiting to call on the secretary, and by late afternoon it was my good fortune to be ushered into his office. A florid-faced man of considerable girth, Major Eaton received me courteously and gave the impression of being personally acquainted with my case. He assured me that I would receive my appointment, but not as soon as I had hoped.

"You must understand," he declared, "that when your name was submitted, there was a surplus of candidates ahead of you."

"May I enquire as to how many?" I asked.

"Forty-seven," said he, shaking his head. But then he held up a finger, raised his ample eyebrows, and went on. "Your situation is not as bleak as it may seem. You see, sir, nineteen were rejected, nine dismissed, and eight have resigned. All that remain are yourself and the ten candidates before you."

My dejection must have been evident, for when I said, "Then I cannot be accepted until next year?" he shook his head and replied, "Not at all, Mr. Poe. You see, during the summer encampment there are always a number of resignations. It is quite possible that you might enter the Point before autumn. In any case, you are assured of enrollment by next year."

"But Major Eaton," said I, "will my age not bar me then? I shall be twenty-one in January."

At that he gave me a conspiratorial smile. "You forget," he said, "a man may consider himself twenty-one until the day of his twenty-second birthday. So you see, the very longest you must wait is until next September. On that, my lad, you may have my word as a gentleman."

His assurances did little to assuage my impatience and with the characteristic impetuosity of youth I asked him for the return of my epistolary testimonials, explaining, "Perhaps they might be of service to me elsewhere, until, of course, my appointment is confirmed."

I detected a fleeting expression of impatience on his countenance. "You may have them back at any time you wish," he told me. "However, if you take them, we must consider your application withdrawn. And frankly, sir, I would not recommend that. Be patient. You *have* been accepted, and you must bear in mind, as the President puts it, you cannot pour a quart of whisky into a pint bottle."

It was evident by his demeanour at this juncture that I was expected to smile. When I did so the secretary rose from his chair, extended his hand, and said, "I regret your having made a useless trip to Washington, but persevere and all will be well."

I shook his hand, thanked him, and masking my disappointment at the delays I envisioned ahead, bade him farewell, and tarried only long enough to endorse my papers with my address. I gave it as Richmond, for even tho' my guardian had written that he was "not particularly anxious" to see me, thereby wounding me deeply, his was the only home I had known. Furthermore, I had no definite residence in Baltimore. But there was additional method in my designating Richmond. I knew my guardian would look with favour upon the communication from Washington when it arrived, for it would be the confirmation of my appointment. Meanwhile, since he was determined to keep me away from Richmond, it would continue to be his responsibility to furnish me with financial support.

Although I could not bring myself to face the truth of it, I knew that John Allan bore me not a snippet of affection. I am certain that one reason he kept me at a distance from him at this time is that he knew I would resent his clandestine amours. With the wife who had devoted herself to him barely cold in her grave, he now carried on with greater frequency than ever.* I believe, too, he thought me half mad, and feared that were we to have even the slightest vociferous disagreement, I might do something scandalous.

These and other thoughts passed through my mind as I trudged wearily back to Baltimore. But it was not concern about my foster father, my relatives, or my appointment to West Point that preoccupied me. I was obsessed by a single, dominant theme: my determination to achieve immortality as a poet. Nothing would stand in my way. Nothing! No one!

Upon my return to Baltimore I was faced, therefore, with three pressing needs. First was the necessity of having my poems published; second, that of obtaining food and shelter; and third, the need to remain in my guardian's good graces. Each of these was painfully difficult. With the exception of my aunt Maria[14] [Clemm], who was poverty-stricken, none of my relations appeared exceptionally eager to offer the hospitality of their homes. I was thus forced to seek lodging in cheap quarters such as Beltzhoover's Hotel where my cousin had robbed me.

---

*And, as Poe was later to learn, was making active plans to remarry.

The summer was hot and oppressive. Forced to endure the agony of waiting for letters that rarely came, letters often filled with black reproaches, I fell into despair. There was no word from Washington. My meagre wardrobe fell into a state of shabby disrepair. I made no progress toward my immediate goal of publication. During the long, hot, stifling nights I lay abed pondering the state of my wretchedness, and upon occasion seriously considered ending my life.

All that ever came forth to alleviate my distress was an awareness that as long as I kept sleep at bay I was able to elude the nightmares which perpetually agitated my slumbers. Thus, due no doubt to my melancholy state of mind, I pondered nightly on the long and weird catalogue of human miseries. It was at that time I first came to the conclusion that the ghastly extremes of agony are endured by man, the unit, rather than by man, the mass.

So wretched was my poverty and in consequence my melancholy that perforce I accepted the kind invitation of my Aunt Maria to share her modest lodgings in Mechanics Row on Wilks Street. O God! When I think on it, even now, my heart bursts with gratitude. It was on a sodden August day of torrential rains and roaring thunder. I was no longer able to pay for another night's lodging, and with only the thought of seeking temporary asylum from the summer storms I had called upon Muddy[15] my aunt in late afternoon.

My clothes were so soggy that I presented a sorry spectacle. This I could see, having caught a glimpse of myself in a looking-glass. "Eddy, dear," said she, appraising my condition with concern, "you must get out of those wet things at once. Good heavens! Did you not know? This is the most perilous time of the year to take the chill—even worse than winter."

"But Auntie," I protested, "what shall I wear?"

"Hush," she said, "and go upstairs. I reckon you will find something there."

Then without affording me the opportunity to reply, she turned to my little cousin Virginia who had come skipping into the room, and said, "Now, Sissy, take cousin Eddy up to Henry's room and help him find something dry. But mind you, child, turn your back while he undresses. And bring me every stitch he takes off, you hear?"

"Oh yes, Muddy," answered the little cherub, then scarcely seven years of age. Rushing to me, her violet eyes sparkling, she seized my hand and tugged with all her might. "Come, Buddy!" she exclaimed, "come with me."

From whence she unearthed this sobriquet, I cannot say, but it offended me not. Her smiling face and dancing eyes, her dark rich curls and tinkling voice were a shining light in this otherwise dispirited household, of which I became a member that very day.

Were it not for the sunny disposition of my little cousin and the courageous fortitude of my aunt, we would have been a sorry lot indeed. In a dark, cramped, and rank-smelling room lay my paralytic grandmother, widow of "General" Poe. It was her annuity of $240—a scant twenty dollars a month—which helped to keep the family from utter starvation. A pittance was brought home by my nine-year-old cousin, also named Henry, a troublesome boy who was apprenticed to a stonecutter.

I shared a tiny, dark, back garret with my brother, Henry,[16] poor soul. Knowing full well that the consumption would soon deprive him of his life, he had abandoned himself to drink and shameful amours with women of low estate. It pained me to see his wasted body wracked with coughing each night as he lay fitfully yearning for the tranquillity of sleep. Upon occasion, when he came home sober, he would regale me with tales of his adventures as a sailor. A faraway look would creep into his eyes, and the waxen glow of his sunken cheeks falsely gave an appearance of heartiness. "Oh, Eddy," he would begin, "if only you could have been with me. What great adventures we might have had!"

And then would begin his spellbinding tales. He told of tropical isles, mountains of ice floating in the azure seas, of dusky savages with painted skins, of exotic birds with rainbow-hued plumage, and blossoms of such fragrance and beauty as to drive men mad. Of these and other wonders he would discourse until the candle sputtered and died, or until paroxysms of coughing rendered him too weak to utter another word.

On other nights, when poor Henry lay drunk, coughing blood, pleading with Death to stay his cold hand for another day, and groaning piteously, even after sinking into fitful sleep, I would write till I could work no more. Sometimes I helped little Virginia with her lessons. Ofttimes I brooded in silence, pondering my fate.

The month of September came and I did not receive my appointment to West Point. Deeply chagrined at this, my guardian hurled more bitter reproaches at me in his letters, but from time to time a small remittance was forthcoming. To obtain these, however, I was reduced to begging like a common mendicant. Then, with the suddenness of a thunderclap, the winds of fortune shifted in my favor. Thanks to the good offices of a cousin, George Poe, my poem *Al Aaraaff* was brought to the attention of the eminent editor John Neal, whose literary criticisms were received in the same light as holy writ. His response was favourable, the first encouragement I had ever been given by a man of letters.[17] As a consequence of this *imprimatur* by a man of such standing, the firm of Hatch & Dunning agreed to publish my collection, *Al Aaraaf, Tamerlane, and Minor[18] Poems*, at terms most advantageous to me.[19]

Mr. Neal then further advanced my cause by publishing in his prestigious *Yankee & Boston Literary Gazette* a letter carefully composed by me. It contained substantial excerpts from the forthcoming book, and to it was appended a preface[20] [by Neal] which established me without question as a poet with an ascendant star. Its propitious appearance had as well another unexpected and most salubrious effect. It was read in Richmond and brought to the attention of John Allan.[21] He responded by sending me a sum of money—eighty dollars, I believe—and an invitation to return for a visit at some time after the new year.

Oh, what a difference from the last was *this* homecoming. Indeed, I was welcomed with open arms, lionised by friends and family alike. I truly entertained the belief that now, at last, a final reconciliation with my guardian was at hand. I experienced an elevation of spirit unlike any I had ever known. My appointment to West Point was a *fait accompli*—only the date had yet to be announced. The recognition I so deeply craved was commencing to manifest itself. My horizons now appeared aglow with radiance. All that remained in some small measure to blight my new exultation was a lingering melancholy which had become a part of my soul.

It was a melancholy which had become a wellspring of inspiration, and tho' I knew it not, was destined to grow with the passage of time. Like a will-o'-the-wisp, its precise nature ever evaded me, but with the clarity of vision that comes only with retrospection, I can best describe it as an intangible sense of loss. Had not those whom I had loved most fervently been torn from me by circumstances beyond the sphere of my influence? I could not visit Shockoe Cemetery without experiencing renewed emotions of grief. Indeed, I could not even pass within sight of the Royster house, for the pain of loss of my adored Myra still lingered in my wounded heart.

Surrounded tho' I was by those whose effusions of warmth appeared outwardly to envelop me, I walked in shadow. I could not see the world as they saw it, could not feel their triumphs and joys. To the very depths of my soul I was alone. My vision of beauty was more intense than the brightest gold of autumn sunsets, more powerful than the thunder and lightning in the sky, but more intense than any words could then express was the loneliness which drew its strength from the raging elements of my stormy life. Tho' wild were my passions and deep my desires, an unquiet demon, lurking in the shadows of my soul, rendered me restless and uneasy.

17

I wrapp'd myself in grandeur then
And donn'd a visionary crown—
Yet it was not that Fantasy
Had thrown her mantle over me.

BOREDOM OVERTOOK ME during those early months of 1830. I wearied of hearing the same drear questions: "From whence came my inspiration?" "How many lines do you compose in a single day?" Most writers, I explained—poets in especial—prefer having it understood that they compose by a species of fine frenzy, an ecstatic intuition. They would positively shudder at permitting the public a glimpse behind the scenes at the elaborate and vacillating cruelties of thought, at the true purposes seized only at the last moment. It would never do, I invariably said, to reveal the fully matured fancies discarded in despair as unmanageable. Certainly no reader would care to fritter away time examining cautious selections and rejections, or the painful erasures and interpolations—in a word, the wheels and pinions, the tackle and scene-shifting, the stepladders and demon traps, the cock's feathers, the red paint and the black patches, which in ninety-nine cases out of a hundred constitute the properties of the literary *histrio*.*

In order to conceal the disgrace which would have accompanied any revelation of my service in the army, I revived the wild tales of my "foreign adventures."[1] I was able to embellish them admirably by including fanciful stories told me by my brother when he recounted his own exploits as a sailor. Indeed, even if I had been caught in a bold-faced lie, by someone who knew that

---

*An arcane word used to denote the writer who dramatizes his material.

these narratives were all humbug, I would have been held in higher repute than if I had openly admitted having been a common soldier. On a level with imprisonment, the very contemplation of enlistment was regarded at best as a cowardly alternative to suicide.

In spinning these fables I was not above perpetrating an occasional harmless jest, which I suspect must have caused a great deal of whispering. I refer to a rumour I spread on more than one occasion, namely that I was a descendant of the traitor Benedict Arnold. In that the fallen general shared a surname with my mother, it was an easy "revelation" to make. Invariably I did so with lowered voice, solemn countenance, and after extracting a sacred oath that this awful secret, this blot on my family escutcheon, never be revealed. Human nature being what it always has been, I soon bathed in the dubious splendour of infamy twice removed.

Although relations between my guardian and myself remained to all outward appearances cordial, I began observing what struck me as an alarming eagerness on his part to see me absent from the house. It began with such casual suggestions as "Have you thought of going down to the Byrd for a spell?" or "The Mackenzies[2] have been asking for you. Perhaps you ought to spend a few days with them."

These suggestions were so offhandedly made and, as a rule, at times when I had planned either to write or read, that it never occurred to me there might have been some devious, underlying reason for them. One day early in the month of March, he had another suggestion. "Edgar, my boy," said he, "the Galts are going down to the Springs for a fortnight. I think they might enjoy your company and you theirs."

"I appreciate their kind thoughts, Pa," I replied, "but in truth I prefer it here, near books and my manuscripts. Besides, should I receive favourable word from the secretary of war . . ."

To my astonishment he interrupted me abruptly, something he rarely did when in a good temper. His voice was coloured with sarcasm, and his words tinged with a bit of a burr. It was an ominous sign to me. "Weel," quoth he, "I'd been thinking that you had all but forgotten about West Point."

"Not at all, sir," I hastened to assure him, selecting my words with caution. "I have been awaiting my appointment with utmost eagerness. But truly, Pa, do you not agree that I have been putting my time to good use?" I hesitated for emphasis, waiting for a certain quizzical expression to appear on his countenance. Then I continued. "You have seen with your own eyes favourable critical comments on my work, have you not?"

Grudgingly he nodded his affirmation. "Aye, that I have," he said.

Then, pressing my case, I said, "And have I not arisen early each morning, and put my time to good use? Have I not avoided the temptation of carousing and drinking in favour of perfecting my art? I do avow, were I to go with our cousins to the Springs, the temptation to fall into mischief might be too great for me."

My words had been intended to be lighthearted, but evidently they struck a painful chord in his breast. A black scowl appeared on his face, his eyes narrowing, and the lines deepening on his furrowed brow.

"I shall give your regrets to *my* cousins," quoth he. "Now, if you'll excuse me I have some business to attend." I would have sworn a solemn oath that I detected the sweet aroma of spirits on his breath.

I soon learnt what sort of "business" was making such demands on him. His comings and goings at hours ordinarily reserved for more homely activities had aroused considerable whisperings among the servants. By employing a bit of the subterfuge I had learnt as a soldier, I succeeded in discovering that John Allan was engaged in a romantic intrigue with a certain Mrs. Elizabeth Wills, who, being rather inconveniently with child, had laid the responsibility of paternity at his feet.

I further discovered, to my chagrin, that he had been slyly paying certain improper attentions to Aunt Nancy.[3] As his maiden sister-in-law, she was the legitimate mistress *pro tem* of his household. Under the circumstances, her residence beneath his roof was beyond reproach. On several occasions I saw them together whispering and laughing in the drawing room. On others, though I witnessed nothing with my own eyes, I learned beyond question that they had gone off for afternoon *tête à têtes* in the carriage.

How could he behave thus? His wife, my sorely missed foster mother, was in her grave barely a year, and now he was conducting himself like a schoolboy with her own sister. Even more reprehensible were his frequent nocturnal peregrinations to the abode of his mistress. I could contain myself no longer. Out of respect for the memory of that gentle soul who had showered me with love from the moment I was orphaned, I determined to act.

Admittedly I employed a cunning ruse, calculated with Machiavellian guile to accomplish my ends. One rather chill and gloomy morning, shortly after my guardian had taken his leave, I suggested to Aunt Nancy that we ride out to Shockoe Cemetery, to place flowers on the grave of our departed loved one. She appeared reluctant at first. "But Eddy," she protested, "it is still cold and blustery. I am certain it will rain."

"I must go," said I. "I may be summoned to West Point at any moment. I cannot take the chance of permitting another day to pass. If . . ." Here I deliberately permitted my voice to break and I feigned the actions of one about to be overcome with emotions of grief before continuing. ". . . If such a melancholy journey appears more than your constitution can bear, I understand. I shall go alone."

"I am perfectly fit," she insisted. "No, you are right. I have not visited my poor sister's grave since autumn. I welcome the opportunity to do so now in the company of one I know loved her as dearly as I."

By agreeing to accompany me, Aunt Nancy fell into my snare as surely as if I had been a fisherman and she a finny denizen of the briny deep. Influenced by the chill of the weather, the grey of the sky and the all-pervasive gloom of the graveyard, she soon succumbed to tears. I sought to comfort her by recalling happier times in bygone days, although in so doing, I fell victim to my own wiles. I will freely admit that I had undertaken to deliberately prey upon the lady's emotions, that I might gain a certain influence over her. But as is so often the case in life, my plans were overtaken by events. It had been my orginal intention to bring up—with utmost discretion—the matter of my guardian's amours. I truly believed that, under the circumstances, it would have been most inappropriate for him to form a matrimonial liai-

son with his sister-in-law. The need to do so, however, never
arose.

As we stood by the mossy grave, tenanted scarcely one year,
Aunt Nancy burst into tears. "Oh, Eddy," she cried, "how
wicked I have been! I must pray that God will forgive me for the
dreadful thoughts I have entertained of late. Alas! What a stain
besmirches my poor soul!"

Proffering my handkerchief, I said, "Dear lady, pray what
brings about this lachrymose outcry, this effusion of dismay?
You, of all women, have led a spotless life."

"That may have been so until now," said she. "But of late I
have fallen from grace. For some days past I have been giving
grave consideration to the possibility of marrying my brother-in-
law. Please, please, do not judge me too harshly. I am a poor,
weak woman, who has never known the gentle touch of a husband, or the tender joys of motherhood. I confess his blandishments had all but overcome my resolve to remain steadfast."

"Villain!" I muttered. "How could he bring himself to behave
thus, and compromise your virtue? Has he no shame, no self-
respect, no regard for that poor clay which lies mouldering in her
grave—she, whom we all so dearly loved!"

The good woman sighed and placed a gentle hand on my arm.
As tears welled up in her eyes, she shook her head and offered me
a wan smile of conciliation. "Judge him not too harshly, Eddy,
dear, nor me either. His heart has been troubled sorely, too, of
late. Illness has weakened his constitution. He is filled with
remorse over certain affairs which have been troubling his conscience." A blush spread over her countenance and she softly
added, "Affairs of far too indelicate a nature to be openly
discussed."

An involuntary expression of astonishment gave away my
emotions. She smiled once more, and again placed her hand on
my arm, a note of *weltschmerz* clearly detectable in her voice.
"You are still young, Eddy, and you have much yet to learn about
the foibles of your sex—and of mine. Though we grow old, a
certain spark of youth burns eternally within us. And fruitless
tho' the attempt may be, upon occasion we try to retrieve it."

I attempted to speak, for my heart was overflowing with a

flood of sentiments I wished to express. But Aunt Nancy put a finger to her lips, and said, "Now hush up, boy," How often she had used those very words when I was a child, and as if the clock had been mysteriously and abruptly reversed, I stood there mute, awaiting her words.

"I have not made up my mind," said she, pensively, and with quiet deliberation. "I shall examine my conscience, and consider the rules of propriety. I give you my word on it."

"Aunt Nancy," I said, with all the composure at my command, "can you not see the error in such a rash act? Can you not visualise the dangers—forgive me if I speak frankly—of suffering grievously for the sins of others?"

Gasping at my words, she averted her eyes. I pressed my advantage, making certain to address her only in tones of utmost compassion. "And can you be assured in advance that the purity of your own motives will be fully understood? I implore you, absolve yourself of remorse! As the great bard said, 'To thine own self be true,' and to thy sister's memory as well."

A sob escaped her lips and I took her by the arm. "Come," I said, "the winds are rising. Let us return to the house before we take the chill."

"I shall pray for divine guidance," she murmured as we hastened back to the waiting carriage. There was a quality in her manner which led me to believe that she would ultimately make the choice I deemed favourable. My intuition proved to be correct, but my reasoning, having come from the heart, contributed enormously to my eventual undoing.

My guardian, whose infirmity caused him increasing discomfort as it worsened, took greater solace in the Highland whisky he imported by the barrel. To give the devil his due, he never, to my knowledge, drank himself senseless; yet he was, in these days, often less than sober. His demeanour toward me grew increasingly more distant, and I cannot say what might have transpired had not my appointment to West Point been confirmed by letter in March.[4] I was to report for the entrance examinations in June, and it was unquestionably this knowledge of my eventual departure that made my presence more tolerable to him.

Upon receipt of the confirmation I embarked on a period of

intensive reading and composition. Insofar as it was possible, I withdrew from the company of others, especially that of my foster parent. His increased drinking inspired him to unprovoked bouts of bad temper, and it was my fervent wish to avoid any unnecessary confrontations with him. I had been cursed with a bad temper of my own. It was hardly my intention to provoke him then, for I could foresee that the time when his infirmity might carry him off was in sight. If only I were to maintain sufficiently cordial relations with him until his inevitable rendezvous with the dark angel, my future would be assured. Oh, God! how desperately we mortals cling to futile hopes.

On the third day of May, the confrontation I had so dreaded came to pass. It was a Monday and my guardian returned home from his place of business shortly after midday. There was a slight stagger to his gait, a ruddiness to his complexion, and a pained expression in his eyes. I was in the library, reading a notice of Stendahl's new novel, *Rouge et Noir*, in *The Times* of London.

Understandably startled at his unheralded appearance, with all due solicitude I said, "Pa, you are home early. Are you feeling a trifle fragile today?"

"How dare you make such insinuations?" he exploded.

"I assure you, sir," I replied, "I insinuate nothing, I merely wished . . ."

"Ye merely wish'd tae let me know ye tho't I was drunk! Confess it now!"

The unfortunate fact might not have been so apparent to me before he spoke, but now there could be no doubt as to the state of his sobriety—or the lack of it. Knowing something of the terrible changes that can be wrought in a man by the influence of spirits, I determined not to arouse his ire further.

"Please, Pa," I said, "I know that you have been in poor health of late and . . ."

Once again he interrupted me. "I dinna want tae hear yer bloody false solicitations. Now, get out o' tha chair, it's my favourite!"

With those words he lunged forward and would have lost his balance had I not leapt to my feet and seized him, turning him

around, so that when he fell backwards, it was into the chair.
Then retrieving his cane, which had fallen from his hand, I held it
forth and said, "Are you all right, Pa? Perhaps I should have one
of the servants fetch the doctor."

"The doctor be damned!" he exclaimed, his voice heavy with
bitterness. "What ails me now no doctor can cure, and
you . . . you bloody meddler . . . I'll say no more!"

I knew not precisely to what he alluded, but I felt a chill in my
heart, for I could see at once that he was regaining control of his
faculties. "You mystify me," I said.

A mirthless ejaculation escaped his lips. "Mystify indeed!
Since I would not condemn even the lowliest nigger without
evidence, I'll not accuse you directly. But I would wager a goodly
sum, my fine poetical lad, that you had a hand in a recent disappointment of mine."

"Sir," I protested, "I do not . . ."

"Sir me no sirs!" he replied sharply. "I'll have none of your
sanctimonious blathering." Then pointing a long bony finger at
me and narrowing his eyes, he said, "But if I ever learn that there
be a grain of truth to my suspicions, I'll make ye regret it till your
dying day. Now leave me be. I have no more wish to converse."

Having no desire to continue this painful exchange[5] I hastily
took my leave of him and repaired to my chamber. I knew the
nature of the matter to which he had alluded. Aunt Nancy's
refusal of his hand in marriage had gnawed at his entrails until he
could no longer contain his growing suspicions of my part in it. A
man of overpowering self-esteem, John Allan could never have
accepted the possibility of being refused on his own account. In
order to preserve that self-esteem, he had to find an external
cause. I thanked Providence that his evidence was nonexistent,
for his reasoning, his powers of deduction, had been without flaw.
The most monstrous flaw of all was my own imperfect judgement.

It is well and good to cast backward glances at one's errors if
one intends not to make them again. But it is fruitless to brood on
them. Had I voiced no objections to this marriage, and had it
come to fruition, I know that Aunt Nancy would have been a

moderating influence on John Allan. But such speculations do not change the past; all they may do is alter the future of the wise. And wisdom, at that juncture of my life, was not an attribute with which I was excessively endowed.

Impetuosity being the trait with which I was most generously laden, I committed a grave indiscretion. On the previous day I had received a letter from my old army comrade, Bully Graves. He expressed concern about the fifty dollars of which I was still in his debt. His concern was heightened since he had learned that another creditor, who had presented his claim to John Allan, had been turned away. To allay his fears I exhorted him to be patient a while longer, and explained that my guardian was not always sober these days. I assured him, however, that soon all would be right with our respective worlds. I also informed him that I had been accepted as a cadet at West Point. What a poor judge I was of human nature then. This letter was destined to haunt me like Banquo's ghost, and doom me as surely as that spectre did Macbeth.

18

John Locke was a notable name;
   Joe Locke is greater; in short,
The former was well known to fame,
   But the latter's well known "to report."*

IT WAS ON Friday, the 21st day of May, that I departed the house of John Allan, as a member of the family, for the last time in my life. Perhaps it was for that reason I felt a pervasive sense of melancholy, for tho' no words attesting to the matter had been spoken, I had a premonition that it was the case. My guardian accompanied me to the steamboat landing, and appeared to be in reasonably good spirits, for his manner was cordial. During the carriage ride to our destination we chatted amiably about inconsequential matters, and when I was ensconced on board, he shook my hand warmly and said, "Deport yourself well, my boy. Work hard, avoid temptation, and never forget the honour that has been bestowed upon you."

"I shall make you proud of me, Pa," said I.

A curious expression appeared briefly on his countenance, but quickly vanished; then, with a nod of his head he turned and descended the gangway. I watched him as he climbed into his carriage and drove off without so much as a single backward glance. I remained at the railing of the steamboat, gazing at the bustling activity along the wharf, but seeing nothing, for my mind was in the stars. Tho' I was embarking on a new adventure that other men might regard as a stepping-stone to glory, I did so without illusions.

---

*An allusion to Locke's tendency to spy on cadets for the purpose of catching them in violation of the rules.

The military life was no mystery to me. I knew it in the starkness of its naked, raw crudity. The fife, the drum, and the fluttering banners held no charms for me. I had seen with mine own eyes what lay beneath the facade of boots and braid and shining brass buttons. Yet what other choice was open to me? All that enabled me to retain my sanity, in contemplation of the ordeal before me, was the misapprehension that my superior education and previous military experience would enable me to complete my term as a cadet in six months at most. Once commissioned as an officer, I assumed, I could serve my additional four and a half years, devoting my free time to the perfection of my art. There had been soldier-poets before. It was a compromise I was willing to accept.

I was not required to report for entrance examinations until Thursday, June 24, for they were to take place on the 25th and the 26th of the month.[1] I therefore stopped briefly in Baltimore to visit members of my family, after which I journeyed to Philadelphia that I might pay respects to several acquaintances there. From Philadelphia I went directly to New York City to board the Hudson River steamer, which would take me to West Point. Unfortunately I missed it and had to wait until the following day for the next one. I was thankful to have given myself enough time to allow for such a contingency. Had I been tardy for the first day of the examinations I know not what might have been my fate.

My initial impression of New York was that it was a metropolis in dire need of cleaning and repairs. A local gentleman, with whom I became engaged in conversation, confided that the community had fallen prey to "political philistines" determined to destroy all traces of the past. "I do declare," said he with indignation, "at the rate these scoundrels tear down the fine old houses, there will soon be nothing left but modern ugliness. Why, even Trinity Church is no longer safe. Mark my words, sir, any city with functionaries named Coffin, Graves, and Bloodgood is destined for evil times. And now I bid you good-day." At first I believed the fellow to be a trifle mad, but driven by curiosity, I learned that much of what he said was true. Indeed, I even discovered that Messrs. Coffin, Graves, and Bloodgood were respectively assistant city inspector, street commissioner, and superintendent of streets.

Having a certain amount of time on my hands and nothing of particular urgency to do, I went to the City Hall and enquired of the clerk if I might have permission to peruse a city directory. I was curious to see how many publishers did business in New York. Observing that one, who was situated near the front of the alphabet, Elam Bliss, was within walking distance, I resolved to pay him a visit. His office at Number 111 Broadway was in one of the modern buildings I had heard so soundly deprecated, and though it was hardly the epitome of aesthetic architecture, neither was it the nadir of ugliness. Unfortunately, Mr. Bliss was not present, so I penned him a brief note, expressing the hope that we might meet at a later date, and took my leave.

It was such a glorious spring day that my original determination to call upon publishers dissolved. Instead I walked to the Battery, which afforded the pedestrian a superb, panoramic view of the harbour, especially on such a glorious day as this. Knowing all too well what sort of restrictions would be imposed upon me once I had taken the oath, I abandoned myself to the enjoyment of what tiny parcel of liberty was left to me. As I stood there at the tip of Manhattan Island, watching the gulls wheel and swoop and dip, I was momentarily overcome by envy of them. It was the envy known to all men since man first trod the earth. I dreamed the dream of Icarus, then transferred my attention to the billowing sails of the tall-masted ships in the harbour. How graceful they appeared as they slid gracefully thro' the waters; how they contrasted with the squat, ugly steamboats, belching black smoke into the clean, unsullied air. The sight of those fire-breathing monsters disquieted me. They marred the symmetry of Nature's beauty. Tho' they bespoke of mankind's relentless conquest over the beasts of the field, the fishes of the sea, and his own savage brethren, they nonetheless gave me a vague feeling of apprehension for the future.

I arrived at West Point on the appointed day and was greeted by Captain Ethan Allen Hitchcock, the commandant of cadets. He took me quite by surprise, for unlike most men of the military calling, he was both sensitive and well read. "Mr. Poe," he said, when we were alone, "I trust you understand that once you have taken the oath, your lot will be a hard one."

"I fully understand, sir," said I. "But do you not agree that my service in the ranks will stand me in good stead?"

"I fear not," replied the good captain, a wistful smile playing over his countenance. I could hardly believe his words. He continued, saying, "Let me clarify my words. I do not mean to imply that your knowledge of the military life is of no intrinsic value. It is that here at the academy, rankers are looked upon as the meanest, most contemptible species of humanity."

"But why, pray?" I asked, dumbfounded.

Said he, "West Point turns out officers. Professional officers. For the most part—and I am sure you know this—enlisted men are rabble. Not a few of them have been recruited from the dregs of the barrel—thieves, pickpockets, cutthroats, and worse. To command men such as these, officers must inspire respect, and if not respect, fear. We are often hated, but so it must be." He paused and put his hand to his head, then continued: "I cannot recall which of the ancient Romans said it—*Oderint dum metuant*—but it is a motto every officer must carry with him in peace and war. You do know Latin, do you not, Mr. Poe?"

"Yes, sir," I replied. "I believe the quotation is from the pen of Lucius Accius, the tragedian and critic. The sentiment is apt indeed for an officer: 'Let them hate me, as long as they fear me . . .' I shall remember it."

Captain Hitchcock smiled. "Capital, capital!" quoth he. "I am certain you will do splendidly on the examinations. Now, a word of caution. Once you have become a cadet, never reveal to your fellows the truth concerning your previous service—unless, of course, you trust them implicitly. You are older than the others. Profit by your experience, by your knowledge. Create the illusion that your capacity to learn the military sciences is prodigious. But take care to conceal your secret at all costs."

"If that is your advice, Captain, I shall most certainly follow it."

"Good," he replied. "A final word now. We shall be hard on you here. Very hard. We shall be rigid and unbending. But we shall be impartial as well. For those who do not fail or falter, the rewards are enormous." With those words he clasped my hand, lowered his voice, and said, "By the by, sir. One day, after you have joined the brotherhood of officers, you must explain the significance of *'Al Aaraaf'* to me."

Pleased at learning that he had knowledge of my work, I said, "Permit me to do so now."

"No," said he. "In view of what our relations must be over the course of the next four years that would not do. I fear that we have been overly familiar as matters stand now. But I address a former soldier and I know I may be straightforward."

His words sliced into my heart like blades of steel. Struggling to maintain an outward air of composure I said, "But Captain Hitchcock, in view of my university attendance, not to mention my military service, is it not possible that I might complete my cadetship in a shorter span of time?"

"Good heavens, no!" he exclaimed. "The regulations are quite specific on that point."

'Twas as tho' he had sentenced me to a term at the oars in a Roman galley, but I betrayed no emotion. I understood precisely what he meant. Bearing my pain with all the stoicism at my command, after the exchange of the necessary courtesies I took my leave of him. My mood following this conversation would have been of the utmost blackness had I not received a letter from my guardian immediately on my arrival. It contained a twenty-dollar-bill and a formal expression of his good will. Nonetheless, I was deeply concerned over Captain Hitchcock's revelations. My dream of completing the prescribed course of studies in six months, or even a year, was now shattered. The prospect of spending four full years as a cadet filled my heart with dismay. Yet, what choice did I have? I had no income, no means of support, only the anticipation of an inheritance when my foster father went to meet his Maker. Since my sole hope of remaining in his good graces rested on my becoming a cadet, there was nothing else for me to do.

The entrance examinations were, in my opinion, simple beyond belief. Certainly, anyone incapable of passing them was barely more than an illiterate,[2] yet a number of candidates from illustrious families were disqualified. With a heavy heart I took the oath on Thursday, July 1, 1830, and girded my loins for the coming ordeal of the annual summer encampment.

It was in many ways reminiscent of the days I had spent as a recruit in the First Artillery. There was one noticeable exception. As "Plebes"—the word applied to the new underclassmen (derived from the Latin *Plebs*, or common people)—we were subject to a variety of vicious persecutions known collectively as "hazing." These were unlike any mistreatment I had ever experienced in my life. Indeed, the lowliest black servant in Richmond was never, to my recollection, the victim of such continuous, malicious mistreatment. We were told it was for the purpose of moulding character, of instilling discipline, of making men. To me it was humbug. What enabled me to endure it was my experience in the ways of the enlisted men.

The matter of drill and parade was child's play to me. My fellow cadets were awestruck at my apparent ability to learn so rapidly. Even the upperclassmen were astonished at my skill in performing the manual of arms and all the other idiotic trappings of military show and display. There was another cunning I possessed of which my comrades were thoroughly ignorant. I was skilled at avoiding onerous tasks and creating the impression of diligence where none existed.

It was not until the commencement of the academic year at summer's end that I began to fear for my sanity. To my dismay I encountered a faculty member, a lieutenant, with whom I was, alas, all too well acquainted. His name (which will remain engraved forever in my personal book of infamy) was Joseph Locke. He had known me as an enlisted man at Fortress Monroe, where he was thoroughly hated by one and all in the ranks. A Cassius[3] of a man by the look of him, he possessed deceptively pleasant features, which did not reflect the overpowering cruelty of his nature. An unbending martinet and merciless disciplinarian, Locke struck terror into the hearts of cadets, for he had the nature of a ferret and the disposition of a serpent.

When first he noticed me at parade, an expression of astonishment crossed his countenance, for he had never known me by any other name than Edgar Perry. At first he was not certain, but after fixing me with his cold, uncompromising stare, recognition came. A triumphant sneer spread over his lips and with a snarl he said, "Fall out and follow me." My comrades trembled for me (I was told later) for they were certain that I had committed some unpardonable breach of conduct. Locke marched me to a lonely spot overlooking the river and burst into laughter.

"Well, well, well," said he, "as I live and breathe! How did a bloody, stinking ranker the likes of you crawl up from the slime into the corps of cadets? Speak up!"

I was mortified, but at the same time enraged at the scoundrel's insinuations. Yet, my personal feelings notwithstanding, I dared not reply with insolence. "I was appointed by the secretary of war, sir," I answered, fighting desperately to disguise my true emotions.

"And what filthy lies did you tell him to obtain his appointment?" he said, sneering.

"None, sir," I muttered.

"Speak up!" he barked.

"None, sir!" I repeated loudly.

Instead of replying, he narrowed his eyes and placed his face so close to mine I could smell the foul essence of his breath. For moments he contemplated me thus, then withdrawing to a more natural distance, and shaking his finger in my face, he said, "Now hear me carefully, Sergeant—I beg your pardon—Cadet Edgar Poe. Commit a single breach of the rules, make one misstep, try any of your ranker's tricks, and I shall broadcast to the length and breadth of the academy the truth about your lowly background. Do I make myself understood?"

"Yes, sir," I replied, my heart now pounding with hatred as I struggled to control my temper. How easy it would have been to seize him and throw him into the river. But I remained at attention, my face impassive and expressionless, seething tho' I was inside.

"We shall see," said Locke. "And mark me well, scum. I make no idle threat. Now, get out of my sight. Dismissed!"

Executing a smart "about face," I ran to the barracks as fast as my poor feet could carry me. And that night, unable to contain my rage, I took a step which was to me like that of a condemned man ascending the gallows. After "lights out," accompanied by my two barracks mates, I ventured off limits to Benny Haven's[4] tavern and drank myself into a stupor. I have no recollection of what transpired that evening after I downed my first brandy, but I knew, when I awoke in the semi-darkness of morning, that only a miracle—indeed, a series of them—would enable me to finish my term.

Tho' there was naught I could openly do to vent my true feelings against this scurvy wretch, I did compose anonymous satires against him to the delight of my fellow cadets. However, in time to come, I wreaked my vengeance on Joe Locke[5] in quite another way. Whenever I composed a tale involving dark and bloody deeds, his was the countenance upon which my destruction rained. His was the face of Fortunato in "The Cask of Amontillado." His was the visage of the old man in "The Tell-Tale Heart." He was even in part inspiration for the despicable king in "Hop Frog."

It is strange. I, who from earliest days of youth, found greatest freedom in the use of words, joy supreme in the expression of ideas, now stumble as tho' tongue and pen were mired in some frightful bitumen, rendering me mute. The mere recollection of those baneful days induces my hand to tremble, even after passage of so many years. The quarters were barren and cold, inferior to those occupied by the lowliest slave in Richmond. Water had to be drawn in buckets and conveyed by hand from a distant well. The food was swill, and were it not for stolen chickens and other clandestine fare roasted illicitly over an open fire, I shudder for what might have been.

Weariness was my constant companion, and again, shades of my days at Charlottesville, the spectre of poverty dogged the dust of my every footstep. Novels, poems, and games were forbidden in cadet quarters. Drinking, smoking, and card playing were similarly proscribed. Perhaps beyond the prison-like precincts of this dreary place men were free to pursue the happiness supposedly guaranteed them by the Constitution. Here, however, we were in bondage as oppressive as that endured by the Israelites in Egypt.

By some caprice of human nature, when former companions gather in convivial reunion, their recollections are inclined toward happy memories. Why, then, is the opposite my inclination? Indeed, my memory fails me not. I recall a boisterous prank

or two,[6] but for the most part my reminiscences consist of bitterness and gall. Save for the Virginians, with whom I enjoyed a
certain degree of intimacy, I remained aloof from my fellow
cadets. Being the oldest member of my class—indeed, one of the
eldest cadets at the entire "Point"—afforded me a certain slim
advantage. I deliberately encouraged the rumours[7] which ran
rampant about my past, and whenever possible created new ones of
a more imaginative stripe. Unfortunately, I was forced to endure a
certain amount of abuse, as well, even from my fellow sufferers. An
idiotic jest was circulated, which stated that my son was the one who
had received the appointment as cadet, but upon his death, I took his
place. I was often addressed as "Old Poe," and behind my back
referred to as "Father Time," and "Old Pa."

I was unable to conceal my unhappiness. I was concerned only
with my studies and my true work, which of necessity had to be
attended to after hours. At times I drank heavily to ease the pain
and disquietude. But for this brief respite I paid dearly by suffering consequences of a more tangible nature afterwards. Although
I was once visited by General Scott, and treated with great
cordiality, I felt as tho' I had been forgotten by all who knew me,
most especially by my guardian. The single incident that saved
me from falling into total madness was a visit from the New York
publisher, Elam Bliss. He had been an admirer of *Al Aaraaf* and
he agreed to publish my next collection of poems.

Despite the hope for future blessings that this prospective
publication offered, my immediate burdens were not lessened.
My salary, which consisted of barely ninety cents a day, was
hardly enough to provide me with funds for such necessities as
books, blankets, soap, and candles. I fell into debt again, and had
I not received permission from Colonel Thayer, superintendent of
the Academy, to take up a subscription from the cadets toward
the purchase of my forthcoming book, I would have been lost.

It was in the month of October when I received the news that
signalled the end of my term as a cadet. It was a season of great
beauty alternating with sombre gloom. Upon occasion the brilliant oranges, yellows, and encrimsoned golds of the autumn
foliage transformed the Hudson valley into a multicolored won-
derland of breathtaking beauty. Other times, all-engulfing fogs

enshrouded the countryside, leaving a damp chill and miasmic sombreness on everything it touched. It was the latter which most reflected my sentiments when I learned what had occurred on Tuesday, the fifth day of the month. My foster father journeyed to New York, where he married Miss Louisa Patterson, a spinster relation of his friends the Mayos, of Virginia. Later I learned that the wedding was a gala affair, attended by friends, relatives, and even strangers, but I was not even accorded the courtesy of a post-matrimonial announcement. If ever I had felt alone and cast aside, it was the day on which I learned of this alliance.

As the chill winds of November gave way to the bitter storms and snows of December, my lot at West Point became more melancholy. When my fellow cadets were granted Christmas leaves to visit their families, I took none. For where was I to go? Indeed, tho' I knew that I would have been more than welcome in the bosom of my family in Baltimore, I had not the means to journey there and back.

I did receive a solitary gift, but hardly one of beneficence. It was a letter of vile invective and outraged recriminations from John Allan. He heaped curse upon curse, and declared that I was disowned, and henceforth a pariah, forbidden to enter his presence again. The spark which kindled the flames of his savage abuse was a single statement made by me, and one I could not deny. It was part of a multifold indiscretion, which I freely admit, and which, had I not made it, might have altered the entire fabric of my existence. The wretch, Bully Graves, impatient to recoup the fifty dollars I owed him, sent my foster father the letter I had written with the revelation of his excessive drinking.

Indeed, he had cause to be angry, as any natural father might, upon learning of his son's indiscretion. But was he fair in casting me adrift without a penny? Even were I to complete my course at West Point and earn my commission in the United States Army, I could not survive without independent means. The officer corps was never intended as a place for poor men. I resolved to resign from the Corps of Cadets. However, in order to be honourably released, I had to obtain the permission of my guardian. Without it I would not receive the pittance due me for the journey that would enable me to return whence I came.

Accordingly, on January 3, 1831, I wrote him a letter[8] defending my position and requesting, as a final gesture of our severed relations, that he grant me that permission. Though a cold, impersonal note from him would have enabled me to depart from the academy with dignity, he answered me not. My only recourse was to absent myself from lectures, to neglect my duties, and subject myself to court martial and dismissal. My melancholy was overpowering. A growing weakness of constitution had caused my strength to ebb. Indeed, had I not been certain that my life would soon be over on account of declining health, I would have plunged into the icy waters of the Hudson River.

Thus, my life a shambles, my health failing, alone and friendless, I stood court martial, knowing full well what the outcome was to be. Upon my conviction, I was formally dismissed from the Corps of Cadets. On a bitter cold Sunday, February 20, 1831, I bade my comrades a final farewell, and with what few belongings I still possessed (having sold what I could to obtain a small quantity of cash), I boarded the steamboat *Henry Eckford* bound for New York City.

19

M ERE WORDS are not adequate to describe the horrible suffering I endured immediately following my departure from West Point. I had caught the most violent cold. My lungs were congested, my ear discharged blood and matter continuously, and my head ached so dreadfully I was barely able to lift my feet from the ground. Blustery winds whipped through my clothes, chilling me to the marrow. It was only by the exertion of near superhuman effort that after I debarked I found temporary lodgings in a shabby seafarers' boarding house in the vicinity of the wharves, where I took to my bed for several days, uncertain as to whether I would ever rise from it again.

Burning with fever, yet trembling in the chill of my dank and cheerless room, demon-haunted dreams tormented my nights, delirium and nameless fears my days. All the wretchedness I had ever known seemed now to envelop me, to suffocate me, to crush and to destroy me. Death would have been preferable to the tortures I endured.

On the third day,[1] overcome by desperation, I took pen in hand, abandoned my pride, and wrote a letter to John Allan, appealing for temporary succor. I would as well have applied to a marble statue for assistance. I wrote to my brother, Henry, but he, too, was unwell and unable to help.

Thanks to a merciful God, my strength returned to me after a week of suffering. Thanks to Mr. Bliss, my publisher, I was able to survive in New York for a full month, until my book [of]

Poems saw the first light of day. The night before we were to receive the first bound copies of the volume, Mr. Bliss very kindly invited me to his house on Dey Street for dinner. During the course of the evening I had broached the subject of employment in New York. "Certainly," I declared, "somewhere in this city there must be a salaried position I might occupy. I have no wish to be idle."

"In all truth, my friend," said he, "you would be ill-advised to remain here. There are more journalists than there are journals. The publishers of periodicals are loath to pay for contributions when there are so many amateurs in the country willing, nay, anxious to see their names in print. In my opinion you would do best to return to Baltimore. There at least you may find refuge in the bosom of your kith and kin. You will not be alone and prey to temptation or melancholy."

Tho' I wished not to agree with him, I own I had to respect the verity of his words. I returned to Baltimore with a few dollars advanced to me by Mr. Bliss, and a determination to seek employment. Thank God for the bountiful heart of my dear aunt [Maria]. Poor tho' she was, I was welcome in her humble abode on Wilk Street. Once again I found myself sharing the familiar garret with my brother, whose health had severely declined since last we saw one another. The fatal flush was on his cheek, the pallor on his brow. Barely twenty-four years of age, he was resigned to his approaching appointment with the Dark Angel, and he abandoned his nights to wild bouts of drinking and futile amours.

The only ray of light in this melancholy household was my little cousin Virginia. Languishing in her rank and airless room was my grandmother, often babbling incoherently about days long past or holding conversations with ghosts waiting for her to join their company. The mortar that bound us together, the foundation which afforded us support, was my aunt. Occasionally then, and ofttimes in years to come, I would watch her sitting in her chair reading, mending, or busying herself with any one of a thousand womanly tasks. How I wondered what thoughts were locked within her gentle heart. Those enigmatic eyes, ringed with cares and sadness—did they shed silent lonely tears in the solitude of her chamber?

Had it not been for my grandmother's pension, and the charity of a few friends and relations, I know not how we could have survived. Our meals were meagre, our habiliments threadbare. Henry was too ill to work, and there was nowhere I could find employment. Thus, rather than fall prey to the sin of sloth, I busied myself at writing. Often when my hand was cramped to the point of immobility, during the dead hours of the night I gazed into the flickering candle and was transported on wings of fancy back to happier times. What contrast was this life of poverty to the affluent and carefree days of Richmond! How I pondered on the cruel alchemy of fate that had thrust me into this barbarous modern age. Oh, that I could have been born in a gentler age, when poets and painters had wealthy patrons, when romance flourished, and beauty was valued for the joy it brought to mankind. Had it only been my fate to live the *Bios Theoreticus.*[2]

My melancholy increased with the passage of time. I truly believed I would not live to see the new year. Perhaps this morbid obsession was due to the influence of two dying relations beneath a single roof. I dreaded the night, the coming of sleep with its ghastly nightmares, and so I wrote furiously and demoniacally— like one possessed. I paused only occasionally to help little Virginia, or Sissy, as we called her, with her lessons, or to converse with Henry on those rare nights when he came home sober.

At the beginning of the month of July a change came over Henry. He became weaker and took more frequently to his bed. His attacks of coughing became more protracted and more terrible. Some days one would begin ever so slightly, but then it would erupt into a continuous spasm of choking and rasping and expectoration of blood. His breathing became laboured. At every intake of air he would be seized by a deep and hacking cough that appeared to issue from the depths of his diaphragm. With each dreadful spasm his legs would kick convulsively as he clutched his throat with his hands.

After the first of these terrifying and protracted attacks, such as I had never seen before, I learned that the only way in which I could afford him any relief was to administer wine of opium (laudanum). This eased his pain, lessened the spasms, and after inducing a vacant glaze in his eyes, carried him mercifully off to sleep.

The last week in June, poor Henry grew gaunt and cadaverous. Dark rings encircled his eyes and the flush on his cheeks gave him a preternatural look of fevered vitality. His appetite decreased, perhaps because of the opium, but thanks to the soporific qualities of the drug his attacks were less frequent. I accomplished very little that week, for I spent most of my waking hours in conversation with Henry. Only when he slept did I write, and even then very little, for exhaustion and nervous excitation had taken their toll of my energies.

On Sunday, the 31st of July,[3] Henry seemed to rally, and tho' somewhat unsteady on his feet, he insisted upon taking his evening meal with Sissy, our aunt, and myself. Our repast was sparse, as usual, consisting of a tasty but watery fish soup, boiled potatoes, mustard greens, and cornbread. It had been a hot day, but a gentle breeze had blown in from the bay, and we looked forward with hopeful anticipation to respite after nightfall.

With her usual cheeriness, Virginia contemplated my brother and said, "Oh Henry, do tell us a sea story tonight. Please."

"I'll make a bargain with you, Sissy," said he. "There are some matters I must discuss with Eddy tonight. But tomorrow I shall oblige you." With that he was overcome by a brief but violent fit of coughing.

"Do you promise?" she asked, making no effort to conceal her disappointment.

"Indeed I do," he gasped.

"Cross your heart and hope to die?"

An expression of momentary anguish crossed Henry's countenance, but before he could speak, Aunt Maria declared reprovingly, "For shame, Sissy. For shame! Why, 'tisn't proper to ask your cousin to swear at the supper table, 'specially when he feels so poorly."

The sweet child lowered her eyes. "I'm truly sorry," said she softly. Then casting her eyes pleadingly upon Henry, she added, "But you will tell me a sea story tomorrow, won't you?"

Opening his mouth to speak, poor Henry was seized once more by a fit of coughing so violent that it behooved me to rush to his side. Clutching his aching chest with one hand, while clapping the other over his mouth, he staggered from the table.

As he gasped and hacked I helped him up the stairs to our room and to my horror I could see the effusion of blood through the fingers of the hand he held over his mouth. Once in the room he flung himself upon the bed and I turned to fetch the opium bottle, but Henry seized my sleeve and restrained me. Struggling for breath, he shook his head and waved his bloody free hand at me in a frenzied fashion.

"No opium," he croaked. "Come Hell or high water I shall have a drink this night!"

In alarm I tried to protest, but he would not let me continue.

"Please, Eddy, hear me. . . . In my sea chest, there is a bottle of fine old Spanish brandy. . . ." Again his body was wracked by violent coughing. "Please!" he cried weakly. "The brandy . . . I am dying, Eddy, but by God! I'll toast the Devil and Death together before I go. . . . Quickly now!"

"You are *not* dying!" I insisted, suppressing a sob as I flung open the lid of his sea chest to find the brandy. I knew he was speaking the truth, but I could not bear it. At first I feared I would not find the bottle, but then I came upon it and I rushed back to my brother's bedside. His coughing had stopped but he was wheezing horribly. His face was flushed. His forehead gleamed with sweat, and his lips and teeth were stained with fresh ruby blood. Wiping his mouth with the back of his sleeve, he exercised what must have been a supreme effort and raised himself to a sitting position as I uncorked the bottle and poured two glasses, thinking nothing of the consequences.

Raising his glass with a trembling hand, Henry contemplated me with wildly gleaming eyes and gasped, "To Death and the Devil, and all the imps in hell!"

I repeated his ghastly toast and we drained our glasses.

"Another!" he demanded, holding forth his empty goblet.

Again I poured and again we drank to the dregs. Now I could feel the fiery liquid infusing every part of my body, and I did not wait for him to call for another.

I do not recall what happened after I downed my third drink. I only know that when I awoke, as the first feeble light of dawn was creeping in through the garret window, my brother was no more.

"O God!" I cried. "What have I done?" In the confusion that now distracted my brain, my head throbbed as from the impact of a thousand beating hammers. My mouth was dry and I burned with thirst. The room spun and whirled as tho' rocked by a turbulent sea. Fighting to overcome the nausea which threatened me, I contemplated the cold, motionless form of my brother, still clasping the empty brandy glass in his pale, dead hand. His jaw hung slack and open, gone was the flush from his cheeks, the expression of pain from his countenance. His eyes were closed and I knew his poor soul was at rest. All ambition for him was o'er. Like the thunder-blasted tree, he would bloom no more.

So distraught was I upon the awareness of this melancholy encounter with the Angel of Death, a particle of the madness that has always lurked in the dark corner of my soul escaped. Tho' I was an adult, and she a child, my little cousin and I wept inconsolably in each other's arms, while Aunt Maria, that tower of strength, attended to all the painful necessities pertaining to the funeral. The mournful obsequies took place on the 2nd day of August, and after Henry's burial in the graveyard of the First Presbyterian Church, our little family gathered for a sad funeral dinner at the Herrings.[4]

Between exhaustion and depression of the spirit I resolved to retire the moment we returned to our humble little house on Wilk Street. I could not endure the spectacle of Sissy's weeping or the intermittent cackles, curses, and cries of Grandmother Poe, so I repaired at once to the garret I had so recently shared with my departed brother. But I was overcome with a terrible fit of trembling at the prospect of sleeping on the bed in which he had died. It was not fear, but rather an overpowering sensation of grief intermingled, perhaps, with a particle of guilt.

Indeed, in retrospect I know that Henry could not have lived another day, but at the time there was the lingering doubt that perhaps, had I not shared that bottle with him, he might have survived. Certainly, knowing now the truth of what terrible suffering must be endured by those cursed with the affliction of consumption, I know, too, that death is the greatest blessing God can bestow.

On that melancholy evening, however, I could not face the prospect of sleep. I longed to take a drink, yet I dared not. Tho' I knew it might provide me with temporary relief, I could not face the prospect of the sickness which invariably followed an excess of drinking. Yet, if I did not do something to soothe my nerves, I feared for my sanity. I suddenly remembered the wine of opium. Perhaps if I were to take a small draught of it I might find some measure of forgetfulness and rest.

Taking the bottle from its customary place, I was about to pour a small quantity into a glass when a large bee flew in through the window, startling me, and causing me to drop the bottle, whereupon it shattered into a thousand pieces. I cursed my ill fortune. Had I been singled out by fate to don the mantle of Job? I then remembered something that Henry had told me once. During his days at sea he had acquired the habit of smoking opium upon occasion. Indeed, he had even shown me the hookah he used to smoke the narcotic. Perhaps a quantity of it still remained in his sea chest.

The hookah I found with little difficulty. The packet of opium took longer, as I found it necessary to rummage about the disarrayed contents of the chest. But at length I discovered the drug as well, carefully wrapped in a piece of silk in a leather pouch, which also contained a quantity of uncut leaf tobacco. Henry had mentioned that when he smoked the opium he preferred to mix it with the leaf. Accordingly I filled the water bowl of the hookah, then its smoking bowl, with opium and tobacco cut and mingled half and half.

At first inhalation, after I had ignited the mixture, I experienced nothing. But soon a sensation of well-being enveloped me, a euphoric warmth. Tho' I knew at all times where I was and what I was doing, I imagined myself embraced by a gentle, white mist which protected me from all the misfortunes which clambered at my heels like a pack of gaunt and hungry wolves. My cares appeared to dissolve like the friendly vapours in which I fancied myself to be surrounded. Then, as I sat there, Henry's ghost materialised on the very bed where he had breathed his last.

"Henry!" I cried, calling out to him in disbelief. But he answered me not, instead beckoning as he rose from the bed and glided toward the window, smiling and beckoning, beckoning and smiling. I was too startled to follow him at first, but just as I resolved to do so he was obscured by the swirling mists and vanished. A deep drowsiness came over me now, and the words formed in my mind, "What a heroic drug,[5] which can bring its user such peace," and reclining on the bed I drifted into a deep sleep, but one filled with dreams such as I had never experienced before.[6] They were dreams of opulence and grandeur, and of such vivid character I am certain that they exerted a certain influence on my future literary works.

20

They speak ill of him
As One who entered madly into life,
Drinking the cup of pleasure to the dregs,
Ridiculous! . . .
He is a dreamer, and a man shut out
From Common passions.

AFTER THE DEATH of my brother I embarked on an impassioned devotion to my writing. What assurance did I have that I, too, would not soon meet with an untimely end? A new phase of my life began. I took to composing tales of the grotesque and of satire in addition to poetic verse.

But I must avow again, it is not my intention to present a detailed literary history of myself. Having attained notoriety and, indeed, the fame to which I so ardently aspired, long before I began this unburdening of my soul, I know that the events germane to my achievements will survive long after I have gone my way into the region of shadows to my sad and solemn slumbers with the worm. There will, no doubt, be distortions and lies, for I have made legions of enemies.[1] Yet I have been assured by those few whose opinions I respect that the ape, the bug, and the bird[2] alone are sufficient to earn me immortality (if not, alas, to escape from poverty). Tho' I covet the end, let the means be judged by loftier accomplishments.

On the matter of those who winced beneath the barbed sting of my critical judgements, let me say that had the Fates seen fit to provide me with independent means, I would never have stooped to toil in the vineyards of common journalism merely to survive. As the mantle of the critic was thrust upon me I had no choice. I could not help but expose the faults of those whose pens produced inferior works. It was my obligation to literature and to the future.

I would have been far happier had I been able to court my muse and nothing more and adhere to the philosophy of [Robert] Herrick, when he wrote:

Ile write because Ile give
You criticks means to live
For sho'd I not supply
The Cause, th'effect wo'd die.

And indeed, tho' many in the ranks of those who gave me the means to life inspired me with admiration, too many, alas, incurred my scorn. I never clung to the erroneous belief that two standards of excellence for literature in the English language existed. Too many of my predecessors and contemporaries, amateur literateurs at best, judged works on the basis of Christian morality rather than the quality of content. American works of a high moral tone were given praise merely because they were moral and American. Thus *e.g.*, the injustice done in America to the magnificent genius of Tennyson is one of the worst sins for which the country has to answer.

In my mind there was, and is, only a *single* world of letters, and a single standard on which to judge. The good, the great, and the beautiful must be praised. The inadequate, the superficial, and the ugly must be condemned. It must be the business of the critic to soar that he shall see the sun, even tho' its orb be far below the horizon.

As the year 1831 wore on I withdrew more and more from the society of others, to devote virtually every waking moment to my work. But our poverty was so severe that I was unable to keep myself from falling into desperate fits of melancholy on occasion. Had it not been for the unswerving devotion and loyalty of my aunt and little cousin, I know that I would have perished.

I sank to such depths that I swallowed my pride and wrote several letters to John Allan, groveling—yes, groveling like a common mendicant—before him. And as he would with any beggar in need, he tossed me a few scraps. The affection and recognition I craved from him were never forthcoming. I could not bear to be unloved, unwanted, yet I could not love as others loved. I did not crave the love they craved, for mine was ever a loftier star, my dreams of another world. I shared not a shred of commonality with the man of the crowd.

The meagre rewards for my labours were painfully slow in coming to me. When I was not writing in my garret I frequented the library and Coale's bookstore on Calvert Street, where, because of my standing as a poet, the proprietor was generous enough to lend me books and provide me with outdated periodicals. It was when I visited Widow Meagle's oyster parlor on Pratt Street I succumbed (infrequently, however) to the conviviality of my companions and drank to excess. It was easy for me to fall thus, for I was often called upon to recite poetry there. Upon the occasions I did so I was, as a rule, offered the hospitality of the house which sometimes led me to indulge.

But it was only upon *rare* occasions that I drank intoxicants. I was far too concerned with crafting my tales to abandon myself to drink, which made it all but impossible for me to write. I did, however, resort to the occasional use of opium so that I might calm my troubled nerves and attain the tranquillity which hastened sleep. My poverty was the cause of near perpetual distress exacerbated by frequent hunger and the extremes of heat and cold. I learned quickly, tho', that too frequent use of the drug was inadvisable, for it produced an utter depression of the soul, an afterdream, a bitter lapse into everyday life, a dropping off of the veils. Tho' the visions it produced were often opulent and luxurious, transforming my bare garret into a palatial setting of multicolored wonders, it produced as well unspeakable horrors.

I knew always that one day I would conquer alcohol, though despite its distressing after-effects, the temporary balm it provides my spirit has saved me from insanity.[3] Indeed, it was during this period I came firmly to believe that were I to pour my own glass I would never suffer from the ills of intoxication. Unfortunately, it was ever my misfortune to drink in the presence of at least one unknown enemy, who purposely increased the strength of my libations so that I might innocently overindulge and thus become the subject of ridicule.

Many were the occasions when I knew I should have resisted

the temptation. But always I fell, ever falling victim to the misguided belief that this *once* I would not be overcome by drink. I was like the young St. Augustine (was it he who said it?): "Please save me from temptation, God—but not yet!"

Very often even now in the twilight of my life, I tremble violently when I reflect on that painful, dismal time. Now and then I fell into fits of melancholy so deep I feared that death would *not* overtake me. Tho' I would gladly have been consumed by the fever of this life, I had not the courage to take steps to end it. When the dread cholera reached the shores of America, why it did not smite me I do not know, but to die thus was not my destiny. Trapped as I was in the strangling grip of adversity, it was no wonder that my awareness of death was so acute. Thus, when I read that the philosopher Hegel was no more [1831], I felt an emotion of personal loss. The death of Sir Walter Scott in 1832 was especially painful to me, for I remembered with great affection the wild and beautiful Scotland of which he wrote so eloquently.

I grew more dependent upon my aunt and my pretty violet-eyed cousin, each for quite different reasons. Both of these noble females adored me and nurtured me as tho' I were some rare and exotic creature of value, the only survivor of its species. They nursed and consoled me when I was sick. They fed me when I was hungry, and they kept my threadbare garments clean and in good repair. Their love was to me what sunshine and rain are to wild-flowers. They were the nutrients of my soul, fuel to the flames of my life.

Were I ever to utter a word, or commit an act which might destroy their devotion to me, I would have perished. Yet I could not kindle in my heart a fire to match the blazes burning in theirs. Tho' the capacity to love had once existed in every chamber of my wounded heart, adversity had made that organ a passionless lump of ash and ice. But I was not totally lacking in warmth for them; I was as fond of them as I could have been of any human beings. Thus, that I might not lose them, I employed my genius with words, and cultivated the players' blood that flowed through my veins to convince them, as well as the outside world, of my undying love. And what harm was there in this deception? It brought them happiness. It provided them with the assurances that their sacrifices, their deep affections, were not in vain.

Not infrequently, tho', it pained me to be so smothered with love that it was beyond my capacity to reciprocate. At such times it was easy to succumb to the gift of Bacchus, for then the consequences of my words and deeds were no longer mine, but the fault of the alcohol.

My twenty-fourth birthday [January 1833] came and went; yet wretchedness was still my lot. I had attained the age at which my only brother had perished of the consumption, and I had wondered whether the Dark Angel would claim me ere the dawning of another year. The prospect of such a melancholy possibility brought indescribable agonies, for I had not yet achieved a fraction of that which I still hoped to accomplish.

In the month of April my aunt suggested that I try once more to prevail upon John Allan for some assistance. I did not wish to do so at first. "But Eddy dear," said she, smoothing her widow's cap, and addressing me in that familiar supplicative[4] tone for which she was so well known, "our needs are not great. If you appeal to Mr. Allan respectfully, perhaps he will take pity on us."

The words of this letter[5] did not come easily to me, for my heart was not in its composition. Yet I wrote it, and as I had anticipated, it was never answered. In fact, it ended forever the correspondence between myself and the villain who could have saved me from a life of misery.

I remained diligent during most of this year, and abstained from drink entirely. The inclination (which I resisted) nearly overtook me when I learned that an autobiography, supposedly written by the nearly illiterate bear hunter, Davy Crockett, had been published with great financial success. How galling it was to learn that Yahoos were in the majority of Americans who called themselves readers. I took heart at another piece of news, however. An announcement was made that a new daily newspaper, called the *New York Sun*, was born. It was to sell for a penny, a reasonable price, and I hoped for its success, for to me it meant the prospect of a new outlet for my writings.

The highest point of my life that year came in the month of October when the Baltimore *Saturday Visiter* [sic] awarded me first prize of $50 in its literary contest, for my tale, "A MS. Found in a Bottle." Of equal importance to the prize was the opportunity it afforded me to form a friendship with the novelist John Kennedy,[6] whose future encouragement did much to advance my career.

In January of the next year I received a letter from Richmond. It was written by my boyhood friend John Mackenzie. There was little of consequence, merely an avowal of friendship and an assortment of news and gossip about old friends. It contained one sentence, however, that arrested my attention. "I fear that John Allan is not long for this world." I could not help but wonder what manner of legacy he might have left me had we not quarrelled so.

I made mention to this to my aunt over supper that night and she folded her hands piously and said, "Did he not relent toward you when his poor wife died?"

"Briefly," said I. "But alas! it took precious little time for his true feelings to manifest themselves."

"Ah, but Eddy dear, now it is he who must prepare to meet his Maker. Perhaps if he were to see you now, there might be a final reconciliation."

Her words were earnest and her expression wistful as she spoke. I suppressed a sardonic laugh. My aunt had never met John Allan, but I doubted not that had such a meeting ever taken place, her decorous wheedling might well have extracted a few coins from his tightly clenched fists. But it was too late for such idle speculation. Nevertheless, I was unable to convince her of the futility of my venturing back to Richmond at this time. With that exasperating, yet gentle, manner of hers, she kept pressing me until she unveiled her *pièce de résistance*. Taking me by the hand like a wayward child, she led me into the kitchen and pointed to a cupboard. "Open it up, Eddy," she said gently, yet with a certain firmness.

Curious as to what her intention was, I did as she told me. A green enameled spice box was the most prominent object in sight, and when I spied it she repeated her injunction. Once again I followed her instructions, and this time I was astonished. For there inside the box was the sum of ten dollars in gold coins. "Muddy!" I cried, "I can hardly believe my eyes!"

Smiling benignly she said, "I have been saving three years for just such an occasion. A penny here, a half-dime there. Now, my dear, you must take it all and go to Richmond. Call on Mr. and Mrs. Allan. Make your peace, and perhaps, God willing, Mr. Allan will include you among his heirs."

"A likely possibility," I scoffed. But it was impossible to dissuade her, and early in February I found myself embarking for Richmond.

The journey itself was unremarkable. When I arrived it was with distinct emotions of trepidation that I approached the mansion at Main and Fifth. How would I be received, I wondered? There was naught for me to do but attack the situation with boldness and hope for a favourable outcome. A thousand thoughts raced through my mind as I walked up the familiar curved driveway to the front door. How many happy days I had spent in that house. What love, what comfort, and what joy I had known there! And yet, what dark reproaches, what bitter quarrels had I endured beneath that roof.

For a February day the weather was surprisingly mild and the sky was nearly devoid of clouds. Somehow the brightness gave me courage and I strode confidently up the steps to the portico and rang the bell. I wondered if old Dab was still there. He was a good-hearted soul, my favourite of all the servants. What would he say when he saw me, I wondered? And Aunt Nancy? I had not had one word from her since my days at West Point and I hold to the opinion even now that she deliberately severed relations with me for fear of offending her benefactor. I could hardly blame her. She was, after all, a helpless female of genteel upbringing, who would have foundered and sunk had she been cast adrift like a rudderless vessel.

I rang the bell a second time and speculated on how I would be received. To my surprise the door was opened by a woman whose face I had never seen, but whose identity I surmised to be the present Mrs. Allan. A plain matron whom I judged to be in her late thirties, she contemplated me with a quizzical expression.

"May I ask what your business is here, sir?" she asked in the unmistakable accents of the North.

"I am Edgar Poe and I must see my foster father at once," I replied. Out of habit rather than arrogance, I waited not to be invited in, but swept past her and made for the staircase.

"God in Heaven!" she ejaculated, rushing after me and seizing the sleeve of my coat. "You must not go up there! My husband is too ill. The doctors have forbidden him to have visitors save for the immediate family!"

Her manner irritated me. I turned and fixed her with a baleful stare. "Madam," said I, "for better or for worse, I have been part of this immediate family since the third year of my life."

"You are no longer, sir!" she exclaimed, "and I order you to leave this house at once!"

I was infuriated at her insolent, Yankee arrogance. The man I had called "Pa" for more than twenty years of my life was dying in his room upstairs, and this shrilling harpy would not keep me from him. I deigned not to address her further, save to announce my intentions. "If you will excuse me," I said, "I have business with my foster father." And without awaiting her next shrill outcry, I brushed past her and ran up the stairs as quickly as I could.

Immediatley she commenced shrieking and screaming as tho' the house were on fire, or she had been assaulted by a gang of ruffians. Above the clamour of her strident cries I could hear the slamming of doors, the clatter of feet, and the agitated voices of alarmed servants coming to see the cause of their mistress's distress.

Meanwhile I betook myself directly to John Allan's room, where I found the door slightly ajar. I could not help myself, but my heart began to beat wildly in anticipation of our meeting. Rarely, since I attained manhood, had we ever confronted each other without one of us becoming greatly agitated. I gave the door a premonitory knock and boldly threw it open. The sight that befell my eyes was shocking. Seated in a chair, propped up by pillows, was a gaunt and wasted-looking John Allan, a veritable spectre of his former self. His hair was grey, his cheeks sunken, and his once flashing eyes, bloodshot, watery, and ringed by circles of sooty shadows. His appearance was thus the caricature of some strange bird, for his hawk-like nose seemed, in proportion to the rest of his face, immense. His badly swollen legs rested on cushions atop an ottoman, and he was engaged in reading a newspaper.

At my intrusion he looked up and his jaw fell like a shot. At the same moment the blood drained from his face and for an instant he stared at me in disbelief. The newspaper fell from his trembling hands and he seized his cane.

"Pa . . ." I began, but I was not permitted to utter another word.

Livid with rage, he raised his cane and as if propelled by some supernatural agency, struggled to his feet. "Ye blasted, no-account scoundrel!" he roared. "Get out o' my sight or I'll beat ye bloody! Get out o' my sight, I say! Get out!"

Before I could utter a word I was seized from behind by sturdy black hands and bodily pulled from the doorway. "Throw him out!" I heard John Allan cry. "I'll thrash the nigger tha' ever lets tha' blackguard in here again! Out wi' him! Hear? Out! Out!"

Mrs. Allan was nowhere in sight now, and if Aunt Nancy was present she did not reveal herself. "Unhand me!" I demanded. "How dare you use a white man like this!" But the servants heeded me not and dragged me roughly to the front door whereupon I was ignominiously ejected. So deep was my humiliation I left Richmond forthwith, without so much as calling upon a single friend.

I never saw John Allan again. I received word less than a month later that he was blasted by the hand of Death on Thursday, the 27th of March, 1834. And need I say that the name of Edgar A. Poe was not mentioned in the will?

21

Would God I could awaken!
For I dream I know not how,
And my soul is sorely shaken
Lest an evil step be taken,—
Lest the dead who is forsaken
May not be happy now.

WHILE JOHN ALLAN lived, there had always burned within my bosom a spark of hope that when he fell prey to the Conquering Worm I would receive a legacy. This hope now extinguished, I knew that I had no choice. Either I must succeed or perish. The only avenue open to me was that which led me to the world of letters, a precarious path at best. Now more than ever before I had to rely on the strength and patience of my aunt for survival while I perfected my craft and struggled for recognition. Strange as it may seem, and thank God for it, she regarded me as the future provider for her old age. By nurturing me now, she hoped to guarantee the warmth and comfort of her declining years. But I did not know this yet.

I feared that she might one day resolve to abandon me abruptly to ensure the comfort of her declining years. Virginia was on the verge of blossoming into mature womanhood. Her amiable disposition and her delicate beauty would soon attract suitors. Could I in all honesty find fault with my aunt if she chose to arrange a marriage for her only daughter—a marriage with someone who would cherish, protect, and keep them? Yet it was a prospect I did not relish, and which inspired me with disquietude.

Rather than fall prey to melancholy I cloistered myself in my chamber and devoted my waning energies to the composition of fanciful tales. All the while, living within my own heart, I was addicted, body and soul, to the most intense and painful meditation.

The realities of the world affected me as visions, while the wild ideas of the land of dreams became the material with which I wove fantastical tapestries of words. From time to time my health failed me so miserably that I was confined to my bed and unable to work. What malady affected me[1] I knew not, but the fever, the nausea, and the pitiless pain were torments that would have been unbearable had it not been for the ministrations of my darling little cousin. It was during this time that my cool affection for her underwent a metamorphosis into love. But it was a pure, ethereal love, untainted by the smoking embers of Eros. And she, a pretty child, artless and innocent, loved me with no guile disguising the fervor of the devotion which animated her heart.

Thanks to my heaven-sent talent and the unselfish efforts of the generous John Kennedy, by the spring of 1835 I found myself a regular contributor to the *Southern Literary Messenger* of Richmond. Tho' Mr. [Thomas W.] White, the publisher, could pay me only eighty cents per column I was grateful for the opportunity he afforded me to be read. I was thrilled beyond all measure, however, when he wrote, asking me if I would be interested in coming to Richmond to avail him more extensively of my contributions.

On Tuesday, July 7, 1835, calamity struck. Grandmother Poe died, thereby depriving us of the pension[2] which had been the principal means of our support. Although there was one less mouth to feed and much less drudgery for my aunt, she was disconsolate. It was the first time I had ever seen her so distraught. "What will become of us?" she wept. "Without Aunt Elizabeth's pension we are lost."

"Don't cry, Muddy," said Virginia, her violet eyes glistening. "Eddy will take care of us now, I know he will."

Assuming all the bravado I could muster, I stood between them and clasped them to me. "Unless I am sorely mistaken," said I, "our privations are all but over. I shall soon be working for Mr. White in Richmond and he has promised to pay me regular wages."

"But Richmond is ever so far away!" exclaimed Virginia, an expression of alarm appearing on her countenance.

"Fear not, Sissy dearest," I assured her. "I shall send for

you soon and you will become the fairest flower of Richmond society."

I kissed her hand and executed a courtly bow in the most polished European manner, whereupon she flung herself into my arms and cried, "Oh Eddy, I love you ever so much! Really and truly I do. I shall miss you so when you have gone."

Hearing these words, my aunt contemplated me and asked, "When do you plan to take your leave of us, Eddy?"

"In a few weeks," I replied. "I wish to settle this matter with Mr. White as quickly as possible."

"Could you not contribute to his magazine from here, as you have been doing?" she asked.

"Perhaps," said I. "It is only a matter of details. Mr. Kennedy feels that it would be to our best advantage for me to meet with Mr. White first. I promise you, Aunty dear, I shall act only in our own best interests."

I did not leave Baltimore for Richmond until Sunday the 9th of August. The night before my departure, after Virginia had gone to bed, my aunt came to me, and the following conversation (as approximately as I can recall it) took place between us.

"I am worried, Eddy. I have a premonition of evil."

"Nonsense, Aunty dear. I am embarking on a great adventure, and one on which you and our beloved Sissy will soon be joining me."

"It is about Sissy that I am especially concerned. Do you know that she wept all afternoon when you were out?"

"But Aunty, surely she knows that I love her passionately, devotedly."[3]

"Does she, Eddy?"

"Most certainly. May heaven be my witness! I have told her so many times. She is more than cousin, more than sister . . . why, no man could love a *wife* more deeply than I love that darling child. The very thought of being separated fills my heart with grief. But it must be so. Mr. White will be paying me ten whole dollars a week. Do you realise what that means? Soon we shall be together again, but in Richmond."

"I pray to God that what you say will come to pass, Eddy!"

"Your prayers will be answered, I promise you."

I slept badly that night. The conversation with my aunt troubled me. Why was she worried? Did she fear I might not keep my promise to send for them ere long? Certainly she knew I could not live without them now. Sissy and she were part of me and I part of them. Our three hearts beat as one.[4] I pondered over my emotions concerning them. Did I love them, or did I not? Was I confusing that tenderest of all passions with the element of need? When Virginia flung herself into my arms, was I not infused with sentiments of warmth and affection for her? Did I not often hold her like a babe in my arms and recite poetry to her? O God! What was this phantom nightmare beyond the reach of consciousness that plagued my soul? Why did I feel terror while in contemplation of matters which involved it not?[5]

Although I did not return to Richmond as might a conquering hero astride a white charger, I was not only well received, but regarded with new respect, for most of my friends and acquaintances had read my contributions to the *Southern Literary Messenger*. My poems and criticisms were praised, universally, but my tales, understandably, met with an admixture of reactions that did not surprise me. "Berenice" and "Morella" were considered so shocking, indeed, bordering on bad taste, that the few ladies who read them complained of experiencing terrible nightmares afterwards. A certain dental surgeon, having read "Berenice," declared me insane, and vowed he would never enter into my presence unless fully armed.

Mr. White was a most amiable man, and he had a pretty, charming daughter, with admirable literary inclinations. I was to assume the duties of editor on a one-month trial basis, after which we would make mutual decisions as regarded the future. Officially, however, I was engaged as his assistant. I have no doubt that all might have gone well, for I produced more work than two lesser men. But several incidents occurred which unleashed the frenzied demon that raged in the darker recesses of my soul.

I was invited to be present at a fashionable party one evening. It was a glittering and gala soirée attended by the very cream of Richmond society. Several of the guests looked askance at me, for they were friends of the second Mrs. Allan, who had discreetly sent her regrets, knowing that I was to be present. There were, however, many old friends eager to see me. I had arrived early, and while standing in the drawing room at a vantage point which enabled me to see who came and went, I beheld a vision that arrested my heart.

Ascending the graceful, curved staircase, alone and clad in an elegant gown of creamy satin, a ruby necklace encircling her snowy throat, was Elmira Royster, now Mrs. Shelton. She was as lovely as she had been nine years ago when last we saw one another. At the sight of me the colour drained from her face! Her crimson lips parted, as if in contemplation of a sheeted ghost. For an instant we stood there, our eyes locked in silent embrace. The years melted away and the dormant love that once had bloomed between us erupted resurgent like the flames of Vesuvius. At that moment everything about me, except my lost Myra, faded into nothingness. It was as if the two of us had been plucked out of Time and Space by some preternatural agency. There was no world except that in which the two of us existed, each for the other, burning with love, serenaded by choruses of winged seraphim. Neither of us spoke. There was no need to do so. Our eyes exchanged caresses more passionate, more tender than ever mere words could convey.

What might have transpired had we spoken I will never know. Barely had our eyes met when her husband, Mr. Shelton, arrived at her side. Though he and I had never met, an electric spark of recognition passed between us. An expression akin to panic intermingled with indignation crossed his countenance; then, without a word, he flung his wife's cloak about her shoulders, seized her by the arm and made a hasty departure.

With the scent of her perfume still lingering in my nostrils and the imago[6] of her lovely features imprinted on my brain, I was seized by an uncontrollable fit of trembling. Exercising a super-human effort to maintain an outward appearance of tranquillity, I descended the staircase and sought out the host. Upon offering my apologies on grounds of pressing duties the following morning I took my leave. Tho' I had resolved not to approach the bottle while in Richmond, I knew at the moment that if I did not have a drink at once I would succumb to a fit of nervous prostration.

I found no pleasure in it, but I drank, and it took hold of me and abused me even as a terrier does a rat. Yet I could not stop myself. There ensued a period of abysmal melancholy. For me, life in a common boarding house was hell 'twixt papered walls. The imbecilic questions and fatuous platitudes to which I was subjected were more than I could bear. To preserve my sanity I avoided meals and devoted myself to work. This unquestionably did damage to my nerves, and weakened my already sensitive constitution. Only alcohol enabled me to survive. It was not in gaiety of spirit that I partook of these stimulants, but as crutches for my survival. Knowing how ill I appeared to others I thus exposed my life, my reputation, and my very reason to jeopardy.

I soon fell into such a wretched state I knew not who I was. There were two Edgar Poes residing in a single corporeal form. One was the editor,[7] author, and poet. The other was a tormented soul wallowing in misery, sick in body and mind. Late in August I came to understand in part the true cause of my anguish. I am convinced that, unknowingly, I had developed a supernatural clairvoyance. On the surface of matters I had every reason to be of good cheer. My writings were being regularly published. I was slowly but certainly attaining reputation, achieving respect. Why then, should I be so miserable?

The answer came in a letter from my aunt declaring that my cousin Neilson Poe had offered to take Virginia into his home and provide for her education. I was stricken as if by a thunderbolt. I was blinded with tears. I had no wish to live another hour. I was incapable of thinking. The mere thought of my little family being torn asunder was more than I could bear. I became insane with grief and I wrote an impassioned letter,[8] baring my soul to my aunt. It was embellished a trifle, perhaps, by the fact that I wrote it while drinking brandy. But there is no doubt in my mind that it expressed to both of them my need for their love and companionship.

At first I heard nothing. In the weeks that followed, I felt a growing terror that I had lost them forever, and was again to be cast adrift like a bottle on a stormtoss'd sea. I drank more heavily. What transpired next was inevitable. Mr. White called me to him and said, "Edgar, my boy, I must speak to you plainly."

"Please do, sir," said I, struggling to keep my hands from

trembling, and fighting the nausea and headache that troubled me.

"I believe that you are sincere in all the promises you have made me," he began. "But I fear that once you leave this office, you will sip the juice that will steal away your senses."

"But Mr. White," I said plaintively, "I assure you . . ."

He did not permit me to finish. Closing his eyes and shaking his head sadly, he said, "I cannot believe that you are able to rely on your own strength. You must look to your Maker for help. Believe me, my boy, I regret having to sever our relationship. I was deeply attached to you . . . I am still. Willingly would I say that we must not part, if I did not dread the hour of separation again."

Tears welled up in my eyes. I knew that he spoke the truth. If only I could convince him that if given another chance I would reform. "Is there no way, sir," I pleaded, "that you might change your mind?"

"Only if you would take up quarters in my family, or in some other, where liquor is not used, might there be some hope. But if you go to a tavern, or any other place where it is used at the table you are lost. I speak from experience."

I tried to speak, but words would not come to me. I opened my mouth but no sound issued forth. Mr. White continued: "You have fine talents, Edgar—and you ought to have them respected as well as yourself. Learn to respect yourself and soon you will find that you are respected by others. Separate yourself from the bottle and drinking companions forever. Tell me that you can, and will do so. Let me hear that it is your fixed purpose, that you will never again yield to temptation, and your position will be restored to you."

He paused, placed a hand on my shoulder, and fixed me with a penetrating look into my eyes. "Promise me that you will heed my counsel and all will be as before. But remember, it must be expressly understood that all engagements between us would be dissolved the moment you succumb to drunkenness."

"I have never meant to get drunk, sir!" I exclaimed. "I have never derived pleasure from drinking. I speak the truth."

"I do not disbelieve you, Edgar," said he. "But remember, no man is safe who drinks before breakfast. No man can do so and attend to business properly. Yet I have seen you do this. Now go, meditate on what we have discussed. Take what time you require, then advise me of your decision."

He clasped me by the hand and we bade each other a melancholy *au revoir*. That no one in the office might see the tears in my eyes, I hastened out into the street and back to my lodgings. There, knowing not what to do, I packed my few belongings and resolved forthwith that I must return to Baltimore.

Tho' I felt a desperate need to take just one drink to bolster my nerves before embarking on my journey I refrained from doing so. I feared the consequences, and concern lest I cause discomfort to my aunt and cousin gave me the strength to abstain.

My return to Baltimore on Sunday, September 20, proved to be a curious admixture of joy and sadness. Virginia flung herself into my arms, weeping copious tears and smothered me with tender kisses. "Oh, Eddy!" she exclaimed. "Eddy! I feared you would never come back to us. I cried myself to sleep every night you were away . . . and I prayed to God that he would send you home again."

The soft lisping tones of her sweet gentle voice were like music to me, and I knew then I could never bear to be parted from her. Tho' she chattered gaily, and asked me a thousand questions about Richmond, I observed my aunt, on the contrary, to be sombre-visaged and silent. "There is not enough food to put on the table, tonight, Eddy," she said at length, upon which she fell to sobbing piteously.

My heart went out to her. "Fear not, Aunty dear," I assured her. "I have almost eight dollars. That will feed us for a while, and surely good fortune will overtake us before it is exhausted."

The sorely needed money induced her to stop weeping, and it enabled us to feast lavishly that evening. It was after we had dined that, being infused with the emotions of well-being which accompany a full stomach, we solemnly resolved never to part. I said in a light-hearted fashion, "You shall be the fairy godmother, Sissy, the princess, and I the prince charming. How could we not then live happily ever after?" To which the darling child exclaimed, clapping her hands with glee, "And you will bundle me up in your soldier coat and carry me off on a noble white steed!"

It was the hand of fate that led us to such playful discourse, for from it emerged the resolution that Sissy and I should marry. Tho' she was just thirteen, and I exactly twice her age, it was a marriage truly made in heaven. Our love was pure and chaste, free of the baser passions that have ever throughout the ages caused beauty to fade and love to change into bitter hate.

"You know, Eddy," said my aunt, smiling benignly, after my child bride-to-be had retired to her bed, "I knew in my heart that you wanted to marry our dear Sissy, even before you went down to Richmond."

"Then for the love of God," said I, "why did you nearly cause my heart to break when you sent me that letter? Why, by heaven! the thought of my own beloved little cousin going to live in the household of that pompous ass, Neilson Poe, nearly drove me insane!"

She nodded sagely, a mildly conspiratorial gleam in her eyes. "I know, Eddy," quoth she. "I know. It pained me to cause you even those few weeks of unhappiness, but I felt in my heart that if your desire was strong enough to be with your little family, my words would help you to make up your mind. Oh, I prayed you would do as you did, for you need us as much as we need you. Now you may rest easy, and devote your God-given talents to the matters closest to your heart."

Had it not been for the devotion I had for my sweet little cousin, I might have taken some measure of offence at having been subjected to such anguish. But I knew that my aunt had only our best mutual interests at heart. She was and is still, a simple woman, not customarily given to guile [?], but having been fated to live forever on the brink of poverty, she was all too frequently forced to employ her wits. I believe with all my heart that had it not been for her singlemindedness and gentility, we all might have perished long ago.

Two days later, on the 22nd of September, I obtained a marriage license, and that evening Sissy and I were quietly married by the pastor of St. Paul's Episcopal Church in the parlour of his house. We agreed among us to keep the marriage secret for a while. Sissy wept, having read in one of the ladies' magazines about the grand and lavish weddings of the rich, and I promised her that before another year went by I would see to it that she celebrated another, more public, and more cheerful nuptial ceremony. We also resolved to live as we had always lived together, excepting that the bonds of matrimony would now bind us more closely than ever we had been bound before.[9]

On the following day I wrote a letter to Mr. White, promising faithfully that I would forswear the bottle were he to reinstate me at the *Southern Literary Messenger*, explaining that my aunt and cousin were soon to join me. I was now prepared (I wrote) to embark on a new life of serious endeavour, hard work, and renewed responsibility. So confident was I of his response that three days later I returned to Richmond without awaiting word from Mr. White. My aunt promised that she and Sissy would follow me to Richmond as soon as I sent them the necessary money. Thus I put Baltimore behind me with a sense of exhilaration and brave hope for the future.

22

I will not madly dream that power
Of earth may shrive me of the sin
Unearthly pride hath revell'd in
I have no time to dote and dream:
You call it hope—that fire of fire!
It is but the agony of desire.

UPON MY RETURN to Richmond I was restored to grace. Not only did the good Mr. White receive me cordially, he elevated me officially to the position of editor, and tho' my salary of ten dollars a week was not a princely sum, with extras it came to nearly eight hundred per annum. It was adequate for my needs, and sufficient to bring my aunt and wife from Baltimore. But since our marriage had been performed in secret, the true nature of our relationship perforce had to remain hidden.

We boarded at Mrs. Yarrington's house, a pleasant brick structure with green shutters on the southeast corner of Twelfth and Bank Streets, overlooking the Capitol Square. From our quarters above the parlour we enjoyed a charming view of the Capitol grounds as well as an ample amount of sunshine from early morning till dusk. Our sojourn soon became a happy one. My employer was pleased with my industry and sobriety. My aunt and bride were content with their lot of comparative ease, and I set about to make a name for myself, and in consequence, for the *S.L. Messenger*.[1]

I need not go into detail about the sum of my accomplishments, for they were of sufficient magnitude to have become part of American literary history in my own lifetime. For me to discuss them here, therefore, would be pointless. Suffice it to say that before my tenure as editor, the magazine was a pleasant, Southern journal, a platform for genteel amateurs whose literary effusions were at best insipid twaddle, destined for oblivion. In my hands it grew into a periodical that transcended parochialism and inspired the pursuit of excellence.

Oh, I made enemies. I engendered outrage, and possibly placed my life in jeopardy.[2] But I cared not if I was accused of critical savagery. I was rapidly becoming a personage to be reckoned with, and I found it a heady experience. In December of 1836 I made plans to visit New York for the purpose of becoming personally acquainted with some of the better known literati there. But on the 16th of the month that tragic fire broke out which destroyed all of the city's east side from Wall Street to the river. As a result of this dreadful catastrophe I cancelled my journey.

Because of her immaturity, Sissy did not participate in the increasingly active social life into which I was drawn. But it disturbed her not. She contented herself with childish pleasures and appropriate female pursuits, at the same time developing a most pleasing singing voice. She was admired by all who came to know her, for her manners were the ideal of gentility, her graceful form and pretty features presaged the blossoming of a woman who would, ere long, be the object of universal admiration.

She received many a flowery compliment for the pure, Parian marble-like quality of her complexion, and the limpid sparkle of her eyes. But I grew inwardly alarmed upon those occasions when I saw the unnatural blush on her cheek and heard the cough which bode the ominous warning of weakening lungs. They were symptoms I knew and dreaded all too well, but I refrained from saying anything to alarm the dear child, hoping that with the departure of winter's icy blasts they too would vanish.

With the coming of the new year I had reason to rejoice. My friends in Richmond received me with open arms. I was soon to receive an increase in salary that would bring me to $1,000 per annum, and my reputation was soaring, especially in the South. Contrasted with those circumstances in which I found myself a scant year before, I had reason to be grateful.

During the cold winter months Sissy's health declined somewhat. She succumbed to fits of fainting. Her manner became more languid than ever before, and she found it necessary to take more often to her bed. But with the warming spring breezes and the appearance of new flowers, she, like the fresh blossoms, appeared to bloom and to regain her strength. Often, however (so I was told), when I was away from home she grew morose and melancholy, behaviour most uncharacteristic of her.

One evening as I was about to leave for a dinner party she burst into tears and wept as if her heart were about to break. "Oh, Eddy!" she cried, throwing her arms about me, "if only I could come with you. How proud I would be if only all of Richmond knew I was in truth your wife."

"You have not betrayed our secret, have you my dearest?" I asked.

"Oh no!" she exclaimed, bringing one hand to her mouth. "I would never do anything to make you angry with me."

"The world will know soon, my dearest," I promised.

"Indeed?" she pressed me. "Oh please, Eddy, tell me! How soon?"

"We will discuss it tomorrow after dinner. I promise you," I said. Thus I committed myself. I was not averse to making the revelation, but I was at somewhat of a loss as to how it might be accomplished without stirring up a scandal. There was nothing that so delighted the gossips of Richmond than to turn the ears of their listeners into the graves of others' good names.

My little Sissy's expressed desire to be recognised as my wife prompted me to give the matter serious thought. Although my love for her knew no bounds, and I had no desire to cause her any unhappiness, she was, after all, a female and a child, incapable of making decisions for herself. Just as I might were I her older brother, or father, it was my responsibility to think for her and guide her along the path that was most beneficial for her.[3] I asked myself, would she be happy in the company of her intellectual superiors? Would she enjoy discourse which consisted of subjects far beyond her interests or, indeed, her capacity to comprehend? I discussed the matter with my aunt the next morning and asked for her opinion on the matter.

She smiled benignly, put down her sewing, and said, "Oh, Eddy, Eddy, how little you understand the female heart. Tender creatures such as our dear Sissy live only to love and be loved. She cares not a fig for what *Blackwood's*[4] might say on any subject. She may have sighed over *Tamerlane*, but only because you wrote it. I am certain she could not understand a word of it. I declare, I scarce can say I do myself. No, my dear, you are the idol at whose shrine she worships night and day."

"If that be so, Aunty," said I, "then why is she not content to let matters remain as they are?"

She shook her head, still smiling, and sighed. "How blind you men can be, even men of genius, to what is plain to the simplest of our sex. Can you not understand? There is no subterfuge, no jealousy in her fair heart. There is not even a desire to mingle with fashionable society."

"Then, by Heaven, what does she want?" I asked, somewhat annoyed at the enigma of it.

"She merely wishes to spend more time at the side of the man she adores. She wishes to bask with pride in the reflected radiance of your presence."

So eloquent was her simple explanation that it melted my heart. Still, I was concerned about what manner of malicious gossip might ensue were we to suddenly reveal our true relationship. We finally hit upon the scheme of announcing an "engagement," and then having a second marriage performed. Sissy was beside herself with joy, for she had been more than disappointed the first time.

Accordingly on May 16, 1836 we were married once more in the parlour of Mrs. Yarrington's boarding house in the company of several guests, including Mr. White and his daughter, Eliza. Garbed as she was in a traveling dress, wearing white hat and veil, Sissy looked far older than her fourteen years. A note of merriment was struck soon after the ceremony by the chance remark of a young lady, Miss Jane Foster, who was one year the bride's junior. During the nuptial ceremony itself she had fixed her eyes on Sissy with a penetrating stare that seemed to increase with intensity after the marital knot was tied. Approaching us after all of her elders had offered their good wishes, she tugged at Sissy's sleeve and said, her eyes wide with astonishment, "Why Mrs. Poe, you look no older now than you did before the wedding began!" Her remark was greeted by gales of laughter. It appeared that the child was of the opinion that the ceremony of marriage somehow mystically thrust brides from youth to maturity.

Our honeymoon consisted of a brief sojourn at Petersburg [Virginia], where we called upon a number of literary acquaintances. Sissy deported herself admirably and thoroughly enjoyed the parties and entertainments given in our honour. Tho' she frequently sat demurely in a corner smiling, without uttering a word, she was often called upon to sing for the company, which she did most sweetly, thereby earning the admiration and affection of all.

It was the first time we had been alone together for any length of time and, many times afterwards, she insisted that this had been the happiest journey of her life. Only once was there even the suggestion of a discordant note, and that passed quickly. It was on the first night in Petersburg. We were ushered into our suite, which was surprisingly elegant for such a provincial hotel. The moment that we were alone the dear child came to me, took my hands in hers, and looked up into my eyes. Tho' her complexion was waxen and pale, a slight flush came over her features and she said, "Sweet Eddy, there is something I must ask you."

"Pray, do so, my darling," I replied.

She lowered her eyes and struggled to find words. "I have heard," she said softly, "that there is some terrible secret, some painful knowledge which all brides must discover on the night of their wedding day. I am ready to learn of this if you wish to teach me."

I knew, of course, to what knowledge she alluded and I was indignant to hear that anyone might have been so base, so indelicate and thoughtless as to mention such matters to one so young, so virginal and innocent. Then with the unexpected swiftness of a flash of summer lightning, I was smitten by an inspiration. Clasping her to my bosom I stroked her head gently, and said, "But Sissy, my love, this is not the first day of our wedded life. Have you forgotten, we have been married for months? There is no terrible knowledge to be acquired, no mysterious or painful duties to be performed. All is as it has ever been between us. No matter where we are, no matter where we journey, when we are together we shall always dwell in the valley of the many-colored grass."

"Oh, Eddy," she murmured, "you say such beautiful things. I do love you so! Tell me that you love me, too!"

I kissed her hair and said, "I love you as I never loved before, and never will love again."

"Oh, my heart!" she exclaimed, "if a crown of jewels were offered [to] me now, I could not be happier."

How much happier would have been her lot had she never set eyes on such a wretched soul as her cousin Edgar! Irony of ironies! Were it within the realm of possibility to weigh happiness, what pitiful quantity I provided during her sweet, short life would be likened to a feather measured against a bag of gold. Certainly the love, the sweet, unselfish love she gave me was more precious than any object gold could buy—or any amount of gold itself.

Our brief sojourn in Petersburg had a profound effect on me. The provincial tastes, the narrow horizons, the distant unworldliness infused me with discontent. It was a discontent that had long lain dormant in my breast. As it grew I came to know as surely as the sun rose and set each day, that the South no longer afforded me that wider stage toward which my muse propelled me. The maggots of disquiet commenced gnawing at my soul, and the old, familiar demons once again began to haunt me.

Oddly enough, one small incident which befell me during the year 1836 remains vividly etched in my mind. I exchanged a brief correspondence with one Jeremiah N. Reynolds, a visionary man of action, whose words and deeds inspired me to no small degree. Having participated in several voyages of discovery in the South Seas, he now desired to explore the frozen expanses of the Antarctic regions.[5] I was thrilled beyond measure when he suggested that were I able to spare the time, I consider accompanying him on such a voyage were it to become a *fait accompli*. He wrote, "I can think of no other journalist whom I would rather have at my side to chronicle such an endeavour." This adventure never came to pass for me, but the flights of fancy mere thought of it inspired contributed in great measure to [*The Narrative of Arthur Gordon*]*Pym*.

Unhappily for me, and for those around me, I began to give way, at long intervals, to the temptation held out on all sides by the spirit of Southern conviviality. My sensitive temperament could not stand an excitement which was an everyday matter to my companions. In short, it sometimes happened that I was completely intoxicated. For some days after each excess I was invariably confined to bed.

I truly believe that had I remained editor of the *S.L. Messenger*, some disaster would have followed. Tho' certainly an amiable and well-meaning man, Mr. White had not the intellect to be proprietor of a serious literary magazine. It mattered not to him that I had single-handedly turned the *Messenger* from an unknown Southern journal into a prestigious periodical, with seven times the circulation it had when I undertook its guidance. Thus, at the beginning of the year [1837] that Queen Victoria ascended the throne of England, I resolved to storm the literary bastions of New York.

How I thanked God for Virginia and our dear "Muddy," once we arrived in the city of Gotham. We were utterly alone. There were no friends, no relations, only hundreds of thousands of strangers who cared not a fig whether poets lived or died. We first took lodgings in a shabby rooming house located in a bucolic section of the city at Waverly Place and Sixth Avenue. There we made the acquaintance of a bookseller named William Gowans, a most warm-hearted Scotsman, who came to board with us when we moved to better quarters at [113½] Carmine Street.

Although Mr. Gowans was well acquainted with most of the city's editors, he was unable to assist me in the procurement of gainful employment. Those of them upon whom I called greeted me cordially, but offered me no hope. The winter was cold. The nation was in the grip of a terrible financial panic. By spring thousands were ruined.

So that we would not starve, my aunt took in sewing and Virginia assisted her. But alas! my poor, dear little wife's health faltered. Tho' she never once voiced a murmur of complaint, the hacking cough that sapped her strength brought pain and sleeplessness. Our constant companions were cold and hunger and disappointment. That the entire city was in a state of gloom and despair did nothing to alleviate our private distress.

Having not the wherewithal to afford public entertainments such as theatrical performances and concerts, work occupied the principal portion of my time. Occasionally, when the weather was more pleasant, and my Sissy appeared to be on the mend, we would take long walks, sometimes along the banks of the Hudson, occasionally at the Battery and around the Bowling Green. I finished writing *Pym* and continued casting about for employment, but to no avail. I was intrigued beyond all measure when I went to see Mr. [Samuel F.B.] Morse exhibit his new invention, the electric telegraph, which when put into universal use would revolutionise communication between cities.

Finding it no longer possible to survive in New York, we finally packed our meagre belongings and removed to Philadelphia in the late summer of 1838. Deeply in debt and with no immediate prospects, we were given shelter by the sisters of Mr. James Pedder, a fellow author and editor. We had been introduced by Mr. Gowans, and it was at Mr. Pedder's suggestion that we changed our residence to the Quaker City. I was hopeful, for it was an important center of American publishing, and with my now established reputation, I was confident of finding work.

When we arrived, there flourished in the city such periodicals as *Godey's Lady's Book*, *Atkinson's Casket*, *Burton's Gentleman's Magazine*, *Alexander's Weekly Magazine*, and many others, not to mention a host of annuals and newspapers. I soon learned that my reputation was not quite what I had assumed it to be. In certain quarters I was regarded with apprehension because of the severity of my literary criticisms. I pondered the irony of my dedication to literature. I endeavoured to impart professionalism to it as well as art. I did not dilute my talents by teaching as did Professor Longfellow. I was not distracted from my creativity by ministering to the spiritual needs of others as did the Reverend Dr. [Ralph Waldo] Emerson, nor was my time divided between my life's chosen work and the demands of a government sinecure, as was that of Mr. Hawthorne. Perhaps, had I been a physician as was Dr. [Oliver Wendell] Holmes, I might have been able to prolong the life of my darling Sissy. But speculation upon what might have been was always a fruitless endeavour. In any event, I was skilled in no other profession and I cared for no other.

I was happy to see the work of a fellow American succeed, as in the case of Mr. Hawthorne's *Twice-Told Tales*. Similarly, I felt no envy at the immense popularity of Mr. Dickens' latest works, *Oliver Twist* and *Nicholas Nickleby*. But I felt a sharp pain in my heart at the lack of an existing copyright law in America. The firms that published Mr. Dickens, and indeed all the distinguished English authors, profited immensely therefrom. Yet these selfsame publishers were no better than pirates, for not a penny of the proceeds was ever paid to the originators of any works from abroad. For this reason, Americans were discouraged from entering the literary profession. Why, reasoned the publishers, pay good money to unknown fellow countrymen when we can print and sell the finest literature England has to offer for nothing? Thus, only untalented dilettantes and madmen such as I persisted in the pursuit of our goals.

It was for the above stated reason, among many others, that I desired nothing more fervently than to be the proprietor of my own magazine. But the bitter pain of my failure in that endeavour to date prompts me not to speak of it at all. Tho' my efforts toward that end occupied a considerable portion of my time, I continued to work on my own productions. At times the noise which assaulted my senses was enough to drive me into a state of distraction. Not a day went by when there was not a conflagration in some part of the city. The ears were nightly assailed by a cacophony of clanging bells, the resounding baritone din of gongs, and nerve-shattering, ear-splitting bugle calls. These, of course, were all unleashed upon Philadelphians' sensibilities to the accompaniment of waggon wheels rattling over cobblestones and the sharply echoing clatter of horses' hooves. But I persevered. I endured sleepless nights and hungry days. I watched with grim and helpless despair as my poor Sissy's health declined, but I would not stop writing. The fruits of my labours, however, provided less than a bare subsistence.

It was in the spring of 1839 that my fortunes began to improve and I became a regular contributor to *Burton's Gentleman's Magazine*. I did so with reservations, however, for it was a periodical of doubtful literary quality. The proprietor, Billy Burton, was an Englishman who had made a sizable reputation for himself on the stage as a comedian, before emigrating to the New

World. He had consequently met with considerable financial success. A large buffoon of a man with heavy jowls that shook when he spoke, he had founded his magazine two years before. I had applied to him for employment with some misgivings, when he invited me "to cut mutton" with him early in the month of May. With mixed emotions I accepted.

He was direct in his manner and addressed me thus: "Knowing you by reputation, sir, I can think of no one more qualified to assist me than yourself."

"I am happy to hear that," said I. "And what terms do you propose to offer?"

"Very good ones, my dear Poe. I shall pay you the sum of ten dollars per week, and I daresay that two hours a day will be more than sufficient to discharge your duties on my behalf."

"And those duties will consist purely of writing for your magazine," I declared. "Is that correct?"

"Quite correct," he replied, adding, "of course it is to be understood that you will not exercise your talents on behalf of any publications which compete with mine."

In view of my generally low opinion of the *Gent's Magazine* I was not aware that it had any serious competitors, but because of my dire state of want I kept such opinions to myself and agreed to his terms. The rationale behind my accepting this employment, aside from financial necessity, was that I could lend its pages a quality they had not attained before.

To my astonishment, on the July number Mr. Burton had placed my name on the title page as co-editor, undoubtedly to attract a better class of readers. I was not entirely pleased with this, for the plans I had been formulating to establish my own magazine, *The Penn*, were uppermost in my mind. I did not wish, therefore, to become too closely identified with *Gents*. Nonetheless, I gave Burton his money's worth,[6] and diligently refrained from touching stimulants of any kind. I produced critical reviews, poems, and tales of the grotesque, which were very much in the public favour then. In so doing I infused the pages of the magazine with a degree of quality it might never have achieved otherwise.

In *The Fall of the House of Usher*, which appeared in the September number, I attempted something that painters had often done with their canvases. I deliberately created, in the character of Roderick Usher, a verbal self-portrait, but a portrait only in the physical sense.[7] I was curious to see if anyone of my acquaintance would observe this and comment on it. None, however, did so. I now embarked upon a period of intense productivity.

Tho' I was relieved somewhat from my previous financial burdens by virtue of my association with Burton, I was far from content. I felt an ominous stirring from deep within, as my personal demons again grew restless.

My own health was far from perfect, and the sensitivity of my nerves was an ever-growing source of distress. Increasing bouts with illness confined me to bed for weeks on end. I could not bear the slightest criticism of my work, especially at the hands of my intellectual inferiors, who understood me not. I was falsely accused of producing a species of tale whose nature was borrowed from the so-called Germanic brand of terror. The fools! How could they have known that the terror was not of Germany, but from the very depths of my own tormented soul?

Thus, even tho' the end of 1839 saw publication of my book[8] *Tales of the Grotesque and Arabesque*, I was frequently beset by moods of deepest depression. My relations with Burton deteriorated severely. Where before there had been an abundance of warmth, there now existed between us the narrowest strands of cool civility. A strain of considerable weight was now more frequently pressing upon my nerves. I spent a good deal of time in the company of two friends,[9] Henry Hirst and John Sartain, both of whom were imbibers of no mean might. Consequently my resolve to abstain was often sorely tried.

As the year drew to a close I reflected on the past seven months during which I had been associated with Billy Burton. Tho' my efforts had been prodigious, and I had published a substantial amount of my own work, I was deeply dissatisfied. What I still yearned for most was my own magazine, *The Penn*. Oh, that I had a dollar for every letter I wrote to prospective backers of this project so dear to my heart. But alas! even as the curtain descended on 1839 my dream was no closer to fulfillment than when I first envisioned it.

I truly believe that in view of my growing disillusionment with Burton, my lack of success with *The Penn*, and increasing anxiety over Sissy's failing health, I might have plunged over the brink into madness, had it not been for certain external events. In contemplation of science's awesome accomplishments alone, I could not help but lose sight of my own vicissitudes, if only for brief periods of time. Mr. Goodyear's new chemical progress was bound to have a profound effect on the increased application of India rubber to a multitude of new uses. And how exciting was the photographic process perfected by the Frenchman Louis Daguerre. Now, *actual likenesses* of illustrious individuals could be made and preserved for the edification of future generations. What treasures we would possess today had such a science been known to the ancients!

The Opium Wars in China augured ill! Already the price of laudanum and morphine had risen by five and seven cents an ounce respectively. What would the poor do if the cost of these necessary and soothing drugs soared beyond their means? I was disappointed to see that on account of shortsighted bickering by ignorant provincials in the Congress, Americans would not be the first to explore the Antarctic. Two English vessels, the *Erebus* and the *Terror*, set out on the first voyage to that mysterious, frozen region. No doubt poor Reynolds was even more disappointed than I. Announcement of that event prompted me to investigate the possibilities of republishing *Pym*.

My gloom increased as my health declined. My work suffered, and to stave off a total collapse into insanity I began drinking cider. As winter gave way to spring, Burton appeared to renew his old interest in the theatre and spent a good deal of time away from the office. This, contrary to our original understanding, forced more work upon me than I deemed fair. I therefore devoted more of my own time to the preparation of a prospectus for the *Penn*. Then an altercation erupted between Burton and myself in April, and by June I had severed all connections with him. I promptly suffered a complete nervous collapse, and only because of my devoted aunt's exertions and ministrations did I survive. Indeed, tho' I gave no hint of it to a living soul, I seriously contemplated suicide at this time.[10]

242

23

If late, eternal Condor years
So shake the very Heaven on high
With tumult as they thunder by,
I have no time for idle cares
Through gazing on the unquiet sky.

THE MONTHS following my disassociation from *Gent's Mag* were hellish. I could hardly write. I could hardly speak or think. My hands trembled. I was subject to fits of such unspeakable melancholy that my reason all but fled. I experienced long periods of oblivion which exist even to this day as gaping black holes in my past.

I feared that my end had come, and that of my poor Sissy, too. The doomish flush of dread consumption spread over her cheek. The unnatural luminosity of her eyes and the terrible cough gave all too visible evidence of the disease about which all were cognizant, but which none dared call by name.

As the golden days of autumn gave way to winter's cold and sombre grey, only a single thread of hope that *The Penn* might come into being kept me from sinking into irreversible despair. Then, in November, an event occurred which was to have great bearing on a new direction for the winds of my fortune. George Rex Graham, publisher of a magazine called *Atkinson's Casket*, purchased the *Gent's Mag* from Billy Burton and sent me a note, requesting an interview. I was suffering from a terrible cold at the time and my body was wracked by fever and chills. Nevertheless, I went to see him.

An amiable man several years my junior,* whose appearance and demeanour indicated a predilection for *le bon vie*, he received me most courteously.

---

*Graham was twenty-seven at the time.

243

"Tell me, my dear Poe," said he, after the usual preliminary amenities had been attended to, "what are your feelings about becoming editor of my newly organized magazine?"*

"Very honestly," I replied, "my chief interest at this time is to start my own magazine."

"Yes, yes," he answered, nodding his head, "I have read your prospectus and I find it most interesting. But tell me, have you any financial backing as yet?"

Had our communication been via written correspondence I might easily have convinced him that I was on the verge of success. As matters stood, however, my threadbare attire gave sorry testimony to the true state of my finances. "No," I told him, "I fear that my health has not permitted me to pursue my prospects as actively as I might have desired."

"Then by all means give serious consideration to joining me," said he. "I have a grand scheme in mind, which I daresay will meet with your approval. I shall speak frankly, Poe. Not another editor in the country possesses talents such as yours. How many of them are authors in their own right, as you are?"

I would have replied, but he interrupted me gently, saying, "No, no, my friend, the question was purely rhetorical. Now, here is my proposition. Assume the editorship of the new magazine. Supply stories, poems, criticism, whatever you wish. Guide the magazine into the hands of every literate person it can reach. Seek out the most gifted and celebrated literary figures. Dazzle the readers with your own most glittering works, as well as the finest writings of your peers. What say you?"

Tho' flattered by his words, they did not bring joy to my heart. The "grand scheme" of which he spoke differed little from what I envisioned for my *Penn*. Yet what was I to do? I was poor. I had no prospects, and I faced the grim reality of another bleak winter. I was feeling so sick on that particular day, however, that I seriously doubted my capacity to survive until spring. I reflected. Since, to my way of thinking, to coin one's brain into silver at the nod of a master was the hardest task in the world, why end my

---

*Graham combined *Burton's Magazine* with *Atkinson's Casket* and called it *Graham's Lady's and Gentlemen's Magazine.*

days in such misery? I therefore said, "I must think on it, sir. I shall consider the matter for a while and give you my decision presently."

Graham sighed, then nodded his head, and declared, "Very well, I do not wish to impose undue pressure on you. But I urge you, pray give my offer serious consideration. And bear in mind *this* thought. If you will abandon your own scheme for six months—a year at the most—and become salaried editor of my new *Lady's and Gentlemen's Magazine*, I will unite with you as a partner in the *Penn*. Think on *that*, sir."

Had I not been so sick I would have accepted his offer at once. But I could not think. Only one thought preoccupied my mind: to get home and into bed lest I collapse in the street. Graham and I parted on most cordial terms, and I hastened home. I would make up my mind when my strength returned. Unfortunately I experienced a severe episode of nervous and physical prostration, and was thus confined to my bed until the beginning of January [1841].

By then, even tho' I had regained a substantial portion of my strength, I was once again a victim of the caprices of fate. Perhaps my reputation in the world of letters was not insubstantial. Yet that alone would not put food on our pitifully bare table. It would not provide us with coal or wood to keep the cruel winter's cold from our bones. Had I only myself to provide for I might have chosen another path, but such was not the case. I sought out Graham and upon learning that his offer was still open to me, accepted his terms. I was to be paid a salary of approximately $800 per annum with extra payments for contributions above and beyond my regular duties.

Soon after public announcement had been made concerning my new position, I began receiving letters from friends expressing disappointment at my abandonment of *The Penn*. I hastened to write them all with assurances that the project was far from abandoned, merely in temporary abeyance for one year at the most.

Wretched tho' I was at the beginning of that year, it proved to be one of the most comfortable of my older years.[1] Our house on Coates Street was a pleasant one, but it was not until now that we were able to furnish it adequately. Soon, as my fortunes improved sufficiently, I was able to buy my darling wife a harp and a pianoforte. But alas! despite her cheerful disposition and enthusiasm for life, the ravages of disease were slowly consuming her. The dark shadow of the Worm was ever behind her. Each time she suffered a painful paroxysm of coughing, I was seized by dread apprehension. Often on these occasions my aunt's eyes would meet mine and I could detect beyond her usual expression of tranquillity one of fleeting anguish. Indeed, the only member of our little household completely free of care was Cattarina, the cat. Yet not a word was ever exchanged among us concerning our gnawing fears. We dared not breathe them aloud.[2]

My tenure with *Graham's* had its share of rewards. Graham and his wife were both *bon vivants* who entertained lavishly as they prospered. Being a businessman, rather than an artist, Graham was concerned primarily with money. I truly believe that had he discovered that he could become richer by selling pictures without words, or blank pages of paper, he would have done so without hesitation. I do not fault him for this. It was his nature.

Under my guidance the magazine prospered beyond my employer's wildest aspirations. Every morning, he and his wife would come to the office and eagerly open the bundles of mail that had accumulated. As my assistants and I attended to matters of an editorial nature, the two of them would extract the banknotes with mutual ejaculations of glee. The volume and intensity of their vocal effusions were in direct proportion to the quantity and face value of the currency thus harvested.

Mrs. Graham would stack the bills into neat little piles when she was not chortling and clapping her hands like a child contemplating a platter of sweets. Her husband would then inspect them and sort them according to denomination, after which he would tie them into bundles with a piece of string, place them carefully into a large carpetbag, and bid us all adieu for the day.

I was a fool. So engrossed was I in the pursuit of my aesthetic ideals I failed to think enough of my own material needs. There was a roof over my head, my wife and aunt were reasonably well clothed and fed, and I was a force to be reckoned with in the world of letters. It concerned me not that Graham spent as much as $200 for a *single* engraving, that he paid Longfellow $50 and more for a poem, while I was never paid more than $25 for any contribution outside of my salaried duties. How can I look back without tasting bitterness? Were it not for my efforts, Graham would never have acquired a penny of his wealth.

By the beginning of 1842 the circulation, which had begun at 3,500, was a full 40,000. If, instead of a paltry salary, Graham had paid me a tenth of his magazine, I should have become a rich man. But I permitted myself to be seduced by the false glow of my own celebrity. I similarly deceived myself into believing that *The Penn* would soon become a reality with George Graham's help.

It was on Thursday, the 20th of January [1842] that my final descent into darkness began in earnest. Tho' the frosty blasts of winter wind howled about the eaves and rattled the shutters, a cheery blaze crackled on the hearth. Cattarina lay curled up dozing in its warmth, dreaming no doubt of some happy place inhabited by sugar-covered mice and shortsighted dogs. Several guests were present, including my recently widowed cousin Elizabeth and her father. My aunt, dear Muddy, hummed to herself as she bustled about pouring coffee and dispensing freshly baked muffins.

"I hear that our lovely Sissy has a new song for us," declared Uncle Henry [Herring], in a stentorian whisper calculated to be heard by all.

"Eddy taught me the words," responded the dear creature modestly. "They are French, you know."

"I trust they include no hidden indelicacies!" declared Uncle, his eyes twinkling mischievously.

"Father!" exclaimed Elizabeth. "You are making poor Sissy blush."

But it was not a blush that coloured the cheek of my beloved wife; rather a precursor of the horror that was about to befall us. Upon finishing our coffee and muffins we gathered about in a circle as Virginia seated herself behind her harp. As she plucked the strings she filled our ears with sweet music, which was heightened by the melodious tones of her voice. How lovely she appeared.

Indeed, I reflected on the beauty of her face. It was akin to the richness of an opium dream—an airy and spirit-lifting vision more wildly divine than any fantasies which hovered about the slumbering soul. I listened as she sang and examined the contour of her lofty, pale forehead—it was faultless. How cold indeed was that word when applied to a majesty so divine! The skin rivaling the purest ivory, its commanding sweep, the gentle prominence of the regions above the temples; and the raven-black, glossy, luxuriant and naturally curling tresses.

I looked at the delicate outlines of the nose, and nowhere but in the graceful medallions of the Hebrews had I beheld a similar perfection. There were the same luxurious smoothness of surface, the same scarcely perceptible tendency to the aquiline, the same harmoniously curved nostrils speaking the free spirit. I regarded the sweet mouth from which now issued melodious sounds. Here indeed was the triumph of all things heavenly: the magnificent turn of the short upper lip, the soft, voluptuous slumber of the underlip, the dimples which charmed, and the colour which blossomed. Her teeth reflected, with a brilliancy almost startling, every ray of light, and her serene, yet most exultingly radiant smile, enchanted everyone who glanced at her.

But it was in her eyes[3] that her ultimate spirituality resided. They were larger than the ordinary eyes of our race. They were even fuller than the eyes of a gazelle. As she sang, her beauty, in my heated fancy, appeared to be that of beings above or apart from the earth. The hue of the orbs was the most brilliant violet, and far over them hung jet lashes of great length. The brows, slightly irregular in outline, had the same tint. Ah, but those eyes! those large, those shining, those divine orbs! They became to me twin stars of Leda, and I to them the devoutest of astrologers.

Suddenly her eyes widened. An expression of indescribable horror distorted her features. Her hands flew to her throat. Then to the accompaniment of a frightful gurgling, she leapt to her feet. Blood and gore began welling profusely from her parted lips, trickling through her fingers, and spreading its crimson stain

across the bosom of her snowy gown. My cousin Elizabeth emitted a single shriek and fell senseless to the floor as I rushed to my
darling's side. She gasped so horribly I feared she might drown in
her own blood. O God! Only a miracle kept me from going insane.
Lifting her into my arms I *flew* up the stairs to her bedchamber,
Muddy following hard on my heels.

I laid her gently upon the bed on her side, so that she might not
choke on the flowing blood. Her eyes were open and her poor face
contorted with terror as she coughed and gasped and tried to
speak. Muddy took a wetted towel in hand and did her best to
wipe away the bloody effusion. Then, turning to me, her features
fixed with sober determination, she exclaimed, "Fetch the doctor!
Hurry, Eddy! For the love of God, hurry!"

Seizing my greatcoat I ran down the stairs, not even stopping
to speak to the others, who were gathered in solemn silence in the
parlour. The physician, Dr. Mitchell, lived on the far side of
town, and how I succeeded in reaching his house, or how long it
took me I cannot recall. What an apparition I must have seemed,
spattered with clotting blood, wide-eyed, almost incoherent as I
stood there in a frenzy, pulling on his doorbell, pounding at his
door. When I was finally admitted and cried out the nature of my
errand, I was in such a state of nervous excitation that the doctor
administered a powerful draught of laudanum to me. I very
quickly fell into a state of unconsciousness, for I recall nothing
until I awoke in my own room the following morning.

How thankful I was when I learned that my beloved still lived!
But the crisis had not passed, and we knew not whether she would
survive to see the flowers bloom in spring. I was so disconsolate I
could not work. I wanted only to remain by her side, to hold her in
my arms, to give her comfort and solace in this, her darkest hour.

Despairing of her life as I did, it was now my deepest wish to
fulfill her most ardent desires, no matter what they might be. It
was my duty now to be in her eyes what I had not been. Locked in
each other's embrace, we spoke few words that day, and by
sundown we felt that we had enkindled within us the fiery
passions of our forefathers. Together we breathed a delicious
bliss, and her simple chamber became magically transformed
into the Valley of the Many-Coloured Grass.[4]

At the approach of darkness Muddy came with steaming broth, freshly baked biscuits, roasted chicken, and buttered greens. The three of us supped together so that my darling need not arise from her bed and further strain her fragile constitution.

I slept badly that night. My slumbers were tormented by phantasms of the past. It was as tho' I had been shackled in some dank and pestilential dungeon as a mournful procession of wailing ghosts and mouldering corpses came one by one to reproach me.

My face was damp with sweat when I awoke; my breath came in short, hoarse gasps, and I thanked the living God that my ordeal was over.

But was it over, I asked myself as I sat up, trembling in the chill of the morn's early light. The fever that maddened my brain, the fever, called living, that burned in my brain, still tormented me. I could not get up. Yet I could not remain in bed for fear I might fall back into sleep and tumble once more into that dread nightmare world of madness and despair from which I had barely escaped with some vestige of sanity. Wine! That was it! I would drink a little wine. But no! If I drank a single drop of spirits I might be seized by a fit of nervous excitation. My heart would pound as it had before, and its mesmeric rhythm would entrance me and dispatch me back to that chamber of horrors. No! No! I wanted peace. I desperately required tranquillity to preserve my sanity, and to maintain what measure of strength I possessed for Sissy's sake. Only the juice of the crimson poppy would alleviate my distress. A spoonful. A few paltry drops of laudanum and I found temporary respite.

In the weeks and months that followed, tho' Virginia appeared to regain a portion of her health, I sank into a decline. I experienced periods of absolute unconsciousness. I drank. How often, how much, I cannot say. I had fits of melancholy. How I survived I do not know. How I managed to continue functioning as editor of *Graham's* Magazine, I cannot say. Between my despairing of Virginia's life during those horrible intervals when she sank— and they were frequent—I became obsessed with the persecution of authors.

With no copyright law in America, we could be trampled,

pirated, despised, and defied by all those who profited by our labours. For a brief period I devoted a portion of my time reading the law in the office of my friend Hirst.

Back in the year 1831 I had experienced a horrible nightmare in which a spectral black bird came to me and spoke in frightful, sepulchral tones. The ghastly creature spoke of the cholera—the details elude me. Now I was reminded of the incident upon reading Mr. Dickens' *Barnaby Rudge.* Something there was about the feeble-minded Barnaby, with his tame, talking raven, Grip, that captured my imagination. I began formulating in my mind a plan to compose a poem incorporating such a bird. Yet how could I devote my energies to the fulfillment of my artistic destiny when I was driven by poverty to perform the most menial of literary chores?

I was forced by circumstances to live among the masses, but no power on heaven or earth could ever make me one of them. O God! Why had I not been born in happier days when nobility of [illegible] was recognised for its superior qualities, and in consequence accorded its just privilege. But such was not my destiny, alas! It was rather to languish upon Despair's unhallowed bed.

Much of the trouble which beset me at this time was due directly to the presence of enemies on all sides. I could hardly let the world know that I was aware of this, however. Thus, by feigning ignorance of their foul machinations, I could guard against any moves they might make against me. I was not always successful.

Early in May [1842] I arrived in the office one morning feeling especially fragile. Virginia had experienced a very bad night and had it not been for a strong cup of coffee laced with brandy, I might never have succeeded in making my departure from the house. Imagine my chagrin, no, my outrage, upon entering [the office] and seeing the Reverend Dr. Rufus Griswold ensconced behind *my* desk. Exercising superhuman effort to conceal the fury I felt at his effrontery, I greeted him in my most civil manner, adding, "Now, tell me, to what circumstances do I owe the honour of your visit?"

"Why, my dear Poe," said he, "surely you jest. I am not here as a visitor, but as your assistant. Did Mr. Graham not inform you that he had engaged me?"

"My dear Griswold," I replied, mocking his manner somewhat, "I was *only* the editor here, My sole responsibilities were for the literary content of the magazine. Such dreary matters as the engagement and dismissal of employees never concerned me."

"But Poe!" he exclaimed, rising to his feet, an expression of astonishment spreading over his countenance. "Surely you do not propose to leave? Why, together we can . . . ."

"Do nothing," I interposed, taking care still to conceal my blistering rage. Such a fury now blazed within my breast, I own, I could easily have dismembered him and fed the pieces to rats in the streets. "My tenure here has expired. Yours has begun. Be assured that I made my decision long ago. And now, sir, if you will excuse me, I have business elsewhere."

Without uttering another word I turned on my heels and left the office of *Graham's,*[5] never to return again in any other capacity than that of a free-lance. Once again I was at liberty to pursue my own interests. I was both elated and smitten with a depression of the spirits at the same time. In order to bolster them I hastened forthwith to the office of my friend Hirst. Upon hearing the news he thumped the desk with his fist and exclaimed, "To hell with the Grahams and the Griswolds of the world with their shopkeepers' souls and petty, narrow minds." With that he produced a fresh bottle of brandy and two glasses, and declared, "Let us drink to the noble brotherhood of poets and the Devil take the others."

How could I refuse? I remember nothing after swallowing my second drink.

24

The sickness—the nausea—
The pitiless pain—
Have ceased with the fever
That maddened my brain—
With the fever called "Living"
That burned in my brain.

I T IS PAINFUL to confess, even to the silent foolscap that points no finger of disapprobation, but the time of fictions has long since passed. The madness to which I gave way was a dreadful affliction, for I knew not where I went nor what I did. I rambled and dreamed away several weeks. Then, during the brief periods between, I fell into a mania of composition. During these attacks, I would scribble all day and read all night as long as the disease endured. I knew not what was real and what was unreal.

Often I would awaken as if from some terrible dream and I would find myself abroad on the streets, knowing not how I had come to be there. For a moment—and upon each occasion I experienced the same emotions of panic—I would be overcome by terror. Then I would feel an arm about my shoulders. It was always my dear aunt, her careworn face a mirror of concern for my well-being. "Come, Eddy," she would say softly, "it is time to come home now."

Upon one such occasion—I believe it was midsummer of '42—instead of taking me home, as was her wont, she brought me to the house of Dr. Mitchell, and left me there with him. While his servant was preparing tea (the good doctor made it clear he would permit me to touch nothing stronger) we seated ourselves in his library.

"Edgar," said he, "I speak both as your physician and your friend. What demon drives you to the very edge of suicide?"

"Do I appear *that* mad?" said I, suppressing a shudder.

"If I thought you to be entirely bereft of reason," he replied, "I would have committed you to the lunatic asylum. No, my friend, *I* do not think you mad, tho' others indeed may. But this I know as a certainty. If you continue on the path you now pursue with such a frenzy, you will destroy yourself."

"I cannot help myself," I muttered with downcast eyes. "I am sick at heart. Daily I see my beloved Sissy grow weaker. I see her fade before my eyes, yet I can do nothing to save her! I have failed to establish my magazine. Poverty dogs my every step. So I drink to numb the pain. I admit it."

At that the doctor leapt to his feet and contemplated me, his eyes flashing with anger. "Humbug!" he ejaculated. "You are wallowing in the most contemptible species of self-pity I have ever seen. And you do so because alcohol is destroying your brain. A man of your talent, nay, genius, should be in far better straits than you are now . . . "

"The fault is not mine!" I interrupted. "Why, do you know, while Graham paid me a paltry eight hundred a year, he hired that ass, Griswold, at one thousand? To my twenty-five he paid that plagiarist, Longfellow, double and sometimes more! And Fenimore Cooper he paid a thousand—a thousand!"

"More self-pity," declared the doctor, his tone cold and un-sympathetic. "Your worth will never exceed the value you your-self place on it. You flaunt your poverty like a badge of honour! You declaim with eloquence on the subjects of beauty and art, but you do not demand your pound of flesh!"

"You dare to compare *me* with a Shylock?" I cried, hurt and confused. I had never observed a physician behave thus before. But then he placed a hand on my shoulder and said gently, "It was my express intention to anger you, Edgar. Can you not see? You are ill-paid *because* you are poor, because they know you will accept whatever paltry bones are thrown at you. You must change your ways. You have a mother-in-law and a dying wife to support. You must come to your senses. Abandon the bottle! And above all, insist upon fair compensation for the fruits of your genius. If you do not follow my advice—and I speak now as a physician only—you may not outlive your wife."

Had he plunged a red-hot dagger into my vitals he could not

have wounded me more severely. I cared not for myself, but the
words, "dying," and "may not outlive your wife," stung me to the
quick. I had often despaired of her, given her up as lost to me
forever, but never had I heard the finality of her doom so directly
expressed. "How much more time can I hope to have her with
me?" I asked.

"The consumption is a treacherous disease," said he. "She
could be carried away in a month; she might survive for years."
He stopped speaking and fixed me with a penetrating stare.
"Much of the matter depends upon you. When you drink yourself
into a delirium and wander the streets, raving like a madman, she
worries. She frets. She weeps for you. And I can tell you that
each tear, each sob, each gasp of apprehension for you brings her
one step closer to the grave. Her anxiety for you is as harmful to
her health as liquor is to yours; ergo, every drink you take hastens
her end."

"Oh God!" I exclaimed. "You must help me. You must advise
me."

"Only you can help yourself, my friend," quoth he. "That is
the best advice I can give you. Now heed it! Go to her. Cherish
her, and protect her from the anguish that has brought so many
bitter tears to her fair face. But above all, abstain! Abstain! Or
you both may be tenants of early graves."

His admonition both strengthened my resolve to mend my
ways and heightened my fears concerning the insalubrious effects
of the dissipated ways into which I had so ignobly fallen. After
tea I returned to my house determined to observe Dr. Mitchell's
advice to the letter. But alas! That night my darling little wife
suffered another hemorrhage. Driven nearly wild with terror that
I was losing her, I sought refuge in drink, and know not where I
went or what I did during the next eight days.

Praise be to a merciful God, Virginia recovered from the
attack, but Dr. Mitchell, fearful for both of us, insisted that I
leave Philadelphia for a while.

One especially bleak day when there was nothing to eat in the
house save bread and molasses, I resolved to sell *The Raven* to
Graham's Magazine. Although it was far from perfect in its still
unpolished state, my own state of desolation led me to abandon

caution. Griswold had been dismissed, and I had resumed my contributions to the magazine. I truly believe that Graham wished to have me back in the editor's chair. He greeted me with warmth when I arrived at the office and said, "My dear Edgar, how good to see you. I trust that Mrs. Poe and Mrs. Clemm are in good health."

"Alas!" said I, "would that I could answer 'yes.' But Virginia had a very bad night and languished in her bed. As for my mother,[1] she too, is a trifle under the weather. We have not had the money to buy extra wood and the house is woefully cold. The poor soul has a sore throat, and I pray that she will not become worse."

"Heaven forbid!" he exclaimed, adding hastily, "but tell me my friend, what brings you here? Is it possible that you have brought a new tale for us to publish?"

I reached into my pocket and took out the manuscript of *The Raven.* I had copied it out in the most ornamental hand at my disposal. Handing it over to him with a flourish, I said, "I offer you something far more lofty than a mere tale. Here is a poem I daresay will enjoy as long a run as any I have ever composed."

"The Raven?" quoth he, taking the manuscript from my hands. "Am I to suppose that you have recently become a disciple of Mr. Audubon?"

Tho' it was a weak jest I replied with as light-hearted an answer as possible in light of how wretched I felt that day. Our funds had run so low that we had been unable to afford any tea or coffee. With her usual resourcefulness, my aunt had been brewing a beverage made of toasted, dried chicory leaves mixed with ground, baked acorns. It was hearty enough, but it did not compare to the rich flavour of real coffee. There as I sat with George Graham, I began to inhale the aroma of coffee that was being brewed on a stove elsewhere in the office. Oh, how desperately I yearned for a cup of it, but I was too proud to ask, and as no offer was made I perforce held my peace.

We fell silent as my former employer read the poem. I had no preconception as to what his reaction might be. Therefore, I was shocked when, upon finishing it, he looked at me with an expression of bewilderment and said, "An interesting piece of work to be sure, but quite frankly, Edgar, it does not measure up to your usual standards of excellence."

"You do not like it?" I returned, crestfallen.

He appeared genuinely uncomfortable, for as he struggled to find words, shifting his posture as he spoke, he finally said, "It isn't that I do not like it . . . I . . . I feel that it has too many—how shall I put it—yes, arcane references. Our readers, I fear, could not possibly understand it."

"But surely," said I, "there is nothing obscure about the poem's meaning. It is quite clear. It concerns the unutterable melancholy of a lover, yearning fruitlessly for his departed beloved. Surely, my dear Graham, you can conceive of nothing more poetic in tone than that of romantic melancholy?"

"Perhaps," he conceded, "but somehow, the idea of a talking raven seems hard to imagine. What is it doing there, where has it come from?"

"Why, it has flown in from a tempestuous night to seek refuge in the serenity of the unhappy lover's chamber. Oh, I own I might have chosen a parrot. The parrot can be an admirable conversationalist. But the raven is a symbol of death, and is certainly capable of speech. Now, when this ill-omened bird utters the word 'Nevermore' again and again by rote, knowing not the meaning of the word, this merely reminds the unhappy lover that he will never see his lost sweetheart again. His melancholy increases. And without doubt the most poetical topic in the world is the melancholy arising from the death of a beautiful woman. Can you not see?"

I could tell from his expression that my words were as far above his head as the full moon at its zenith. But I was desperate. In dire need of funds I *had* to convince him that *The Raven* must be published. "Suppose," I suggested, "that I read it aloud to you. Perhaps then, when you hear the music and the metre, its meaning will become clear."

He thought for a moment, then said, "You may be right. But I think I shall call the entire staff together. Let them hear it, too. Their tastes are not unlike those of our subscribers. If it meets with their approval, and they comprehend it, then we shall publish it forthwith."

What could I do but agree? Yet in my heart I protested. What did this gaggle of tradesmen know of art and beauty? How could Graham be so deficient in imagination, so indecisive. Was it not the place of a publisher to *lead* the public in the matter of taste? Was it not his place to guide his readers toward that which was meritorious, and away from the banal and trivial? But no, apparently he did not think so. Instead he and all too many of his colleagues were of a single mind, to pander to the lowest tastes. Thus is the state of art in modern America. I pray that at some future time such will no longer be the case, and that the shade of Sydney Smith[2] will be made to recant.

Humiliating tho' it was for me to assume the role of a performing bear, to strut and fret upon a stage before my intellectual inferiors, I had no alternative. The indignity I was forced to endure was heightened by the arrival at that moment of Mr. [Louis A.] Godey,[3] who had come to pay a social call on George Graham.

At length the groundlings[4] were assembled and Graham offered a few gratuitous remarks about Virginia's infirmity, and the deplorable state of my finances. On my oath I would rather have faced a firing squad at that moment, but the die was cast. Tho' I burned with humiliation, I took my place before them and began to recite. How ironic! It was a bright and cheery morning, with sunshine streaming through the windows. Could this be a fit setting to induce in the hearts of common folk a proper picture in the mind's eye? Did the words, "Once upon a midnight dreary," convey their true image to them? Were they capable of visualising "each separate dying ember" that "wrought its ghost upon the floor"? Could they be swept away by the gloom "And the silken, sad, uncertain rustling of each purple curtain"?

They stood before me, listening politely, but upon most of their faces I perceived vacant expressions of blankness. The office boy thrust his little finger into one nostril and probed vigorously as if he were searching for gold. The printer's devil, his cheeks smudged with ink, rubbed his chin several times, thereby besmirching it and rendering it a shade darker than it was before he touched it. Peterson, the editor, scowled throughout my recitation as he chewed on an unlit cigar which he kept shifting from one side of his mouth to the other. The two lady editors, with whom I was not acquainted, appeared somewhat more receptive tho' slightly baffled. But the clerks were thoroughly mystified. One of them rudely punctuated at least four "nevermores" by loudly blowing his nose into a filthy handkerchief. Godey fiddled with his gold watch-chain, and George Graham merely looked uncomfortable.

Immediately after I had uttered the final "nevermore," there was a strained silence, followed by a shuffling of feet interspersed with considerable coughing and "aheming." Sensing an embarrassment on the part of my erstwhile audience virtually as strong as my own, I broke the impasse by suggesting that I withdraw for a moment in order to save them the further discomfort of discussing the merits of my poem in their presence. With that I hastily removed myself to another room with a copy of the magazine's latest number, that I might pass the time.

As was my wont, I became so engrossed in my reading I cannot say with any certainty how long I was out of the office. I was in the midst of a perfectly wretched story by an anonymous female authoress of the "Laura Matilda"[5] school of writing, when I heard my name called out. It was Peterson informing me that Graham would see me in his private office. I hastened to that *sanctum sanctorum* and found the publisher seated behind his desk, a distressful expression betraying his feelings. My heart sank, for I knew precisely what he was going to tell me, or, at least, so I thought when I entered.

"Sit down, old man," said he. I knew at once that something was amiss, for he never addressed me as "old man" unless that were the case. "I fear," said he, "that no one understood your *Raven*. Oh, they all praised its sonorous rhythms, and the ladies in particular admired the timbre of your voice."

"Then you are not going to publish it," I said. There was no need for me to question him on the subject.

"I cannot," he replied, shaking his head and looking genuinely sorrowful. "It is too mysterious, too obscure. Why, even Godey agreed that the most starry-eyed of his subscribers would never fathom it. Have you thought of revising it, clarifying it?"

"I have been revising it constantly for nearly a year," I told him, rising to my feet. "But I can see that I have clearly failed to produce a work of sufficient quality to find favour in the eyes of the *mob*." I must confess I could not prevent a touch of the bitterness I felt from making itself known. Graham flushed and reached for a small oilskin pouch on his desk. "This is for you, Edgar," said he softly. "Here, take it." He held the pouch out to me.

"What is it?" I asked. "I do not understand."

"Everyone here knows of the unhappy state of your present circumstances, the deplorable condition of your poor Virginia's health. A small collection was taken. Let us call it a small token of our esteem and affection for you. I know you will see better days ere long."

O God! how I hated to accept this. What a crushing blow it was to my pride! But what could I do? Unable to hold back the tears that were welling up in my eyes, I muttered a hasty expression of thanks, accepted the charity in the sense that it was offered, and hurriedly took my leave.

I did not open the pouch until I was home. It had been my original intention to stop by the office of Henry Hirst, but I knew that were I to have done so I might fall prey to the clutches of the bottle, and I dared not face the temptation. My aunt was worried to see me home so early. "Eddy!" she exclaimed, "you aren't feeling sick now, are you dear?"

"No, Muddy," I assured her. "Perhaps a little sick at heart, but nothing more."

She searched my face with those soft, sad eyes of hers, and guessed at once what was wrong. Her face went pale. "Don't tell me," she said, "*The Raven* . . ."

"It will not be published, " I said, adding, "yet. . . . But look what I have for you." With those words I handed her the unopened pouch and told her what had transpired at Graham's office. With trembling hands she opened the pouch and emptied its contents onto the kitchen table. Being all in coins of assorted denominations with the exception of two dollar bills, it appeared to be a fortune. Eagerly we counted it together and found it to be a total of fifteen dollars. Then something happened that was an uncommon occurrence. The good woman began to weep. Tears streamed in profusion down her care-lined cheeks, and her eyes became as red as spring cherries.

"Praise be to God!" she cried, enfolding me in a tender embrace. "I declare, we were down to our last thirty cents! Why, heaven help us, had it not been for this we would have had no fire tonight!"

"Not only will we have a fire on the hearth tonight," I declared, "we shall have a feast."

"Oh, and our Sissy will not have to shiver through the night. Praise be to God!"

Indeed, I was more than willing to offer up praises, too, tho' silently I hoped that the good Lord would be more lavish in His munificence next time. In truth, *Graham's Magazine* turning down *The Raven* proved, in the long run, to be a blessing after all. I did extensive revisions, and when the poem was eventually published in 1845, it was infinitely superior to the version I read that day.

25

I have reached these lands but newly
From an ultimate dim Thule—
From a wild weird clime that lieth, sublime,
Out of SPACE—out of TIME.

A FULL YEAR has passed since first I resolved to record on paper the story of my life and, indeed, began to do so. I remember well the night on which I first took pen in trembling hand and then commenced to write. It was in the bleak month of February [1847]. My beloved Virginia had been gone barely one month. Having just recovered from an assault of brain fever I was now wretched as never before in my entire life. I felt that I had been driven to the very gates of death myself. I had fallen into an abyss of despair *more* dreadful than death. Thus, to preserve what gossamer strand of sanity remained I occupied my mind by reconstructing the principal events of my past. But in my despondency and feeble health, I held forth little prospect of living even until this very day.

It was, therefore, my intention to present little more than a sketch. Yet how vast a dissimilarity exists always between the germ and the fruit—between the work and its original conception. In this instance I sat down to write with no fixed design, trusting to the inspiration of the moment. In so doing I violated my own principle that pen should never touch paper until, at least, a well-digested general purpose be established. However, since my overall purpose was to keep from succumbing to total insanity, I grant myself forgiveness.

Perhaps I err in breaking the continuity of my narrative, but as its author I claim the privilege of so doing. There is an unbridgeable chasm of difference between a passionate effusion from the depths of one's heart and a deliberately constructed fiction. I say this because, upon examining certain passages, written when I was in a frenzy, like a man in a trance, I remembered not having written them. Indeed, tho' I recognised the events, the *style!* that was the thing. Often it appeared to be the style of a fiction, not a memoir. But where does fiction begin? Is it not born out of reality?

Fighting as I was to hold at bay the relentless assaults of madness, I plunged into my work as never before. How I laboured—how I toiled—how I wrote! Ye Gods, did I not write? I knew not the word ease. By day I adhered to my desk and at night I consumed the midnight oil. You should have seen me—you *should*. I leaned to the left. I sat forward. I sat backward. I sat upon end. I sat *tête baisée*,* bowing my head close to the alabaster page. And, through storm and heat—I wrote. Through sunshine and through moonshine, I *wrote*. What I wrote you have read so far. How I wrote it is unnecessary to say. Like one possessed I fell into the ways of the tale-spinner rather than those of a disciplined reporter of facts.

Now, thank heaven! the crisis is past and the lingering illness is over at last. I know I am short of strength, but no matter, I feel I will be better soon. I shall resume my story, and throw myself on the mercy of future generations to determine the extent of my failings and my pain.

The poverty which had stripped us of nearly all our worldly possessions convinced me that I could no longer remain in Philadelphia. What meagre dollars I earned were supplemented by the efforts of my beloved aunt,[1] now mother, without whose loving care I would have died. As the winter of 1844 drew to a close my Sissy seemed to rally again, and in March we decided among the three of us that the time had come to leave the Quaker City for good. I was well enough known among the literati of Gotham to assume that if I were in their midst my fortunes would improve.

"Take Sissy with you, Eddy," said my aunt. "The change may do her good. Why, who knows, perhaps the climate there will improve her health."

---

*Literally headlong, precipitously.

My darling's eyes glistened in anticipation at her mother's words. She clapped her hands and said, "Oh Muddy, I should so love to go! You will take me with you, Eddy, won't you?"

"Well," said I, feigning a frown and stroking my jaw gravely, "perhaps, if you promise to regain your strength, to laugh and sing and dance again. . . ." Oh, God! how I loathed myself for uttering such futile words, for I knew that my beloved wife walked ever in the shadow of death. Was it not kinder to offer her even the illusion of hope, rather than the grim prospect of an early grave?

It was decided that she and I would leave as soon as the weather improved. Muddy would stay behind and sell what she could, then join us the moment we found suitable lodgings. "Don't forget, Eddy," she reminded me, "as soon as it's time for me to come, you must find a nice little house so that we may take in boarders." Even as that saintly woman was preparing to endure a period of solitude, away from the children she loved, she was yet capable of making plans for our future happiness together.

Thus after a fair share of tearful embraces and farewells, which did not exclude Cattarina, and with a princely eleven dollars, we embarked for New York [on Saturday, April 6, 1844].

It was raining hard when we arrived the next morning, so I left Sissy aboard the boat with the trunks in the ladies' cabin and went ashore to buy an umbrella and look for a boarding house. I met a man selling umbrellas and bought one for twenty-five cents. Then I went up Greenwich Street and soon found a place to lodge. It was on the west side going up, just before Cedar Street.* I made a bargain with the landlady, Mrs. Morrison, and hurried back to the wharves to fetch Sissy. She was astonished to see me back so soon.

Altho' the house was old and buggy-looking, the board was the cheapest I ever knew. For supper the first night we had the nicest tea ever, strong and hot—wheat bread and rye bread, cheese, tea cakes, a great dish (two dishes) of elegant ham, and two of cold veal, piled up like a mountain and large slices—three dishes of

---

*Today that would be about one block below the World Trade Center.

the cake and everything in the greatest profusion. There was no fear of starving in this place. The landlady seemed as if she couldn't press enough food on us, and we felt ourselves to be at home.

That night Virginia had a hearty cry because she missed Muddy and Cattarina. Then, in leaning over to comfort her I tore my pants against a nail and had to go out and buy a skein of thread, and while about it I also bought a skein of silk, two buttons, a pair of slippers, and a pan for the stove. That night my darling hardly coughed any and had no night sweat.[2] The fire kept in all night and our room was warm and cosy. Exhausted by our journey, we slept well and awoke in the morning with voracious appetites. They were soon assuaged at breakfast which consisted of excellent-flavoured coffee, hot and strong—veal cutlets, elegant ham and eggs, and nice bread and butter. I never sat down to a more plentiful or better breakfast. What eggs, and great dishes of meat!

Tho' our stomachs were full, and there was a roof over our heads, still a cloud loomed heavy on the horizon. We had exactly four and a half dollars left, and in order to survive and send for our mother I had to take drastic action at once. Now, I had in my possession a manuscript, which I had written some time earlier, but which had never been published, or indeed, shown to a single soul other than Virginia and my mother.[3] It was a caricature of the lurid journalism so popular in the press, a flight of fancy concerning the alleged crossing of the Atlantic Ocean in a balloon.

Daring not to consider what the consequences might be if I were not able to have it published, I approached the editor of the *New York Sun*, Gotham's first penny newspaper, and suggested to him that he publish it as a hoax without my name affixed as its author. He knew me by reputation, and was flattered that an editor and author as formidable as I should offer one of his works, and he accepted my proposal at once. "By God, Poe!" he exclaimed, thumping his desk with an ink-stained fist for emphasis, "if this doesn't flummox them out of a fair bit of coin, I will eat the entire first edition for dinner. I shall pay you ten dollars now, and if we succeed, a handsome bonus afterwards. Agreed?"

I was perfectly satisfied with his terms, and we sealed the agreement with a hearty handshake. The article was not published until the morning of April 13th [1844]. It carried the following headings:

ASTOUNDING
NEWS!
BY EXPRESS VIA NORFOLK!
THE
ATLANTIC CROSSED
in
THREE DAYS

———

Signal Triumph
of
Mr. Monck Mason's
FLYING
MACHINE!!!!

The "Balloon Hoax" made a more intense sensation than anything of that character since the "Moon Story" of Locke.[4] On the morning of its announcement, the whole square surrounding the *Sun* building was literally besieged, blocked up—ingress and egress being alike impossible—from the period soon after sunrise until about two P.M. In Saturday's regular issue, it was stated that an "Extra" was then in preparation, which would be ready at ten A.M. It was not delivered, however, until nearly noon. In the meantime, I never witnessed more intense excitement to get possession of a newspaper. As soon as the first copies made their way into the streets, they were bought up, at almost any price, from the newsboys, who made a profitable speculation beyond doubt. I saw half-dollars given, in one instance, for a single paper,

and a shilling⁵ was a frequent price. I tried in vain, during
the whole day, to get possession of a copy. It was excessively
amusing, however, to hear the comments of those who read the
"Extra."

The *Sun's* editor, an honourable man, was true to his word,
and gave me a bonus of twenty-three dollars in addition to the ten
I had initially received. Sissy was overjoyed, for it gave us the
means to send for our mother. After the passage of a few weeks'
time, the truth about the authorship of the "Balloon Hoax"
became known, and thus I erupted, as it were, on the literary
scene of New York. Nevertheless, the wolf continued to bay at
our door.

Our poverty notwithstanding, the presence of her mother and
Cattarina made Virginia happy and for a while her health even
appeared to improve. The small sums I earned were once again
supplemented by Muddy's nimble fingers, and tho' we enjoyed no
luxuries, and could not avoid presenting a certain air of shabbi-
ness, never did we lose the gentility which was a part of our very
nature.

During the spring of 1844, I devoted myself assiduously to
family and work. Tho' I occasionally met a colleague or two at
Sandy Welsh's wine cellar, *not a drop* [?] of anything stronger
than tea touched my lips—malicious falsehoods to the contrary
notwithstanding. I was eager to complete my revision of *The
Raven* and, as the warm weather approached, I became a veritable recluse, leaving the house only occasionally for solitary rambles about Manhattan. When I embarked on one of these, invariably my poor little wife would look at me plaintively and sigh,
"Oh, Eddy, how I wish I could come with you. I so miss the sight
of trees and the singing of birds."

I would gladly have taken her with me, but her weakened lungs
would not permit the strain. She was too much of an invalid now
to venture far from home. Before leaving I would embrace her,
stroke her ebony tresses, and vow in my heart to bring her some
"surprise" when I returned. Alas! I was too poor to buy her any of
the objects I yearned to bring her, but never did I return without
a spray of fresh wildflowers to brighten her lonely hours.

One day while working on *The Raven* in my head, I traversed the entire length of Fifth Avenue, beyond the Croton Reservoir at Forty-Second Street, and out into the country beyond. So absorbed was I in my reveries, I did not realise how far I had come. Indeed, I was a good three miles north of the reservoir and five miles, at very least, from our lodgings[6] on Greenwich Street. What a beautiful, bucolic setting it was! All about me were gentle slopes covered with a profusion of grass and blossoms, trees and shrubs. It was impossible to take a step without inhaling their delicious fragrance. From where I stood on Bloomingdale Road[7] I could see the blue waters of the Hudson River to the west, and the green New Jersey shore beyond.

It was late in June, I do not recall the exact day, but it was one of exceptionally hot weather. I suddenly became aware of a terrible thirst, and observing a plain, tree-shaded, but sturdy looking farmhouse atop a rocky promontory not far from the road, I resolved to knock on the door and ask if I might have a drink of water from the nearby spring. To reach the front entrance it was necessary to climb a long, wooden, exterior staircase, as the high location of the house made any access path impossible. The shade offered by surrounding trees, especially by an immense weeping willow,[8] was oh, so welcome.

My knock was greeted by a tumultuous barking of dogs and clatter of feet within. Moments later the door was thrown open and a pleasant matron with classical features of Ireland on her face appeared. In her arms was an infant, and around her was an exuberant entourage of assorted children, dogs, cats, a raccoon and, if I am not mistaken, one small, wriggling green snake tightly clutched in the hands of a golden-haired boy of about six summers. Mrs. Brennan (for that was the lady's name) greeted me most graciously, invited me in, and insisted that I partake of some freshly made fruit punch.

I will not endeavour to set down all the details of what transpired next. Let it suffice to say that early in July, Virginia, our mother, and I took up lodgings with the Brennans as their boarders. They were a good-natured and hospitable family, and their table was lavish. We hoped and prayed that the rural setting would have a salubrious effect on Virginia's health. It was an enchanting spot, a perfect haven. Not only was this lovely and peaceful environment a blessing for my Sissy, but it offered me an ideal refuge and quiet, away from the clatter and tumult of Manhattan. And indeed it was there that I eventually completed my final revision of *The Raven*.

Although it is hardly of any importance, I recall that I received a modicum of my inspiration at the Brennan's. Above a door which opened into an inner hallway was a small shelf, nailed to the casing of the door. Resting upon this shelf was a small plaster bust of the goddess Pallas-Athene. Seeing it as I did, day in and day out, I was struck with the idea of contrast between the "pallid bust" and the ominous black bird perched upon its head. Not only was there alliteration, there was visual imagery.

Once we had settled in at the Brennan's farmhouse, our life was tranquil as never it had been before. I had not known such a peaceful existence since my boyhood days. I welcomed the seclusion and only once ventured into Manhattan. The five-mile walk in either direction was tiring, and I hardly relished the prospect of such a trudge after the cold of winter descended.

Because of my inability to call upon editors, and being forced to rely on the mails, scarcely enough money remained to pay for our board and lodgings. Consequently, one Sunday morning early in September, my mother, who had been concealing her growing apprehension, could contain herself no longer. It was after breakfast when all the Brennans had departed for church, leaving us alone. Muddy was sitting in the parlour, rocking back and forth. Her black dress, tho' old, worn, and oft mended, appeared as elegant as if it were new, and the spotless, neat widow's cap blended harmoniously with her soft, snowy hair. But there was a grave expression on her gentle, careworn features.

"Something is troubling you, Muddy," I said. "I see it reflected in your eyes."

Heaving a great sigh, she nodded her head. "I do declare, Eddy dear, I tremble to think of the months ahead."

I endeavoured to reassure her. "Certainly our lot will soon improve," I said.

But she would not hear me, and insisted upon unburdening herself. "Eddy, Eddy," she said again, sighing, and shaking her head sadly, "will you never be of this world? Can you not see? If we do not lay hands on some money soon, we are lost! How shall we exist? There is nothing left for October. And I *must* have some wool, so I can knit Sissy a shawl. The almanac predicts a *dreadful* hard winter this year."

"You must not worry, Muddy," I insisted. "I shall publish *The Raven* soon, and I have other things in mind. You will see. I promise!"

Perhaps because it was she who attended the "wheels and pinions" of our daily finances the dire state of our situation was more apparent to her. My heart went out to the poor, loving soul. Had it been within the realm of possibility I would have helped her to bear the burden. But how could I concern myself with figures and accounts, when I was fighting to maintain my sanity, and devoting the full capacity of my mind to writing?

Her concern proved to be even greater than I had expected, for two days later, unbeknownst to me, she journeyed to Manhattan and paid a call on Mr. [Nathanial Parker] Willis, editor of The *New York Mirror.* It proved to be a most fortuitous call, for he was at that time planning to expand his readership by bringing out both daily and weekly numbers.

Shortly afterwards I was engaged as a mechanical para-graphist.[9] Tho' the position entailed a miscellany of writing duties of no appreciable literary significance, it served admirably to keep the pot boiling. I was, however, able to reappear before the public as a critic again, and most important of all, I knew there would be funds to purchase the necessities to care for my family. Virginia's health had begun to decline again, and she experienced a series of frightful coughing fits which, upon each occasion, made me despair for her very life.

Between the cost of lodgings, board, medicines, and other necessities, I did not always have the omnibus or boat fare and I had to walk the five miles to and from the *Mirror*'s office. My constitution was not up to such strenuous activity on a regular basis, and therefore, tho' it pained us to do so, we removed from the Brennan's farmhouse and took rooms back in the city at 15 Amity Street.* At first the cramped quarters were a source of

---

*Now West Third Street, Greenwich Village.

deep concern to me. On our first night there, poor Sissy was so
melancholy that she cried nearly till dawn. She tried to convince
me that her tears were due to some irritation of her eyes, but alas!
I knew the true source of her weeping to be an aching heart.

Our deplorable poverty notwithstanding, I was not given to
great spells of melancholy as long as I was able to work. But
whenever my darling succumbed to those terrible attacks of
choking and coughing and effusions of blood, part of her seemed
to wither and die, and so thus did a portion of myself perish.
Early in January [1845] I resigned from the *Mirror* with the best
wishes of Mr. Willis for I was engaged in discussions with the
proprietors of a new publication, *The Broadway Journal*, concerning an editorship. The position did not materialise, however,
until February [22].

Later that month a momentous event occurred which was to
change my life. If heaven sees fit to so favour me, it may even one
day earn me immortality. I refer to the publication of *The
Raven.*

The sale of *The Raven* came about by means of such an
extraordinarily peculiar set of circumstances I feel that I should
relate them here. It is incumbent upon me to explain, however,
that I must, perforce, reconstruct a certain portion of the story,
since I was not privy to the entire affair. It all began in early
autumn when my faithful friend [James Russell] Lowell wrote a
letter to Henry G. Colton, editor of *The American Review*,
suggesting that he offer me a position. I am told by someone[10]
who had been present when he read the letter that he frowned,
and uttered a coarse epithet, then exclaimed, "I would sooner go
to bed with a scorpion under my pillow than to have any dealings
with that venomous vituperator, Poe!" Thereupon he sat down
and wrote Lowell a peremptory refusal. I fault him not, for in the
course of excoriating me he had the good taste to be alliterative.
Furthermore, we eventually became good friends.

Because of Colton's initial dislike of me, however, *The Raven*
was offered to him as the work of an anonymous "amateur."
Willis, who by now had become a good friend, sent a note to
Colton, declaring that he had heard of "an extraordinary new
poem," soon to be published in the pages of *The American*

Review. "If you would do me the honour, sir," wrote Willis, "it would give me great pleasure to give my readers an advance glimpse of this opus." Colton, flattered at being thus addressed by so eminent a man of letters as Willis, immediately assented.

When *The Raven* first appeared in *The Evening Mirror,* on January 29, 1845, it was, indeed, published under the *nom de plume* of "Quarles." It was such an overwhelming sensation that Willis published it again on Saturday, February 8th. This time, he preceded it with a glowing notice[11] identifying me as the poem's author.

Thus, by the time that I had reached the thirty-sixth anniversary of my birth, the fame that I had so desperately craved was at last mine. It was then that I knew beyond a doubt how dubious a prize it was. To be sure I was pleased at the adulation, the deference, and the lionising. I was even pleased with the ten dollars I received in payment. But did this achievement, for which I now heard myself so lavishly praised, bring me happiness? It did not alleviate my impecuniousness. It did naught to improve the health of my dying wife. Indeed, it propelled me into a rush of activities—lectures, literary teas, and a thousand other things of questionable value. But in the end I had to conclude that man is now only more active, not more happy nor more wise than he was many thousands of years ago.

26

I dwelt alone
In a world of moan,
And my soul was a stagnant tide.

REPUTATIONS, like empty bottles tossed on the ocean, move with the tides. Some soar to the zenith of the firmament and blaze gloriously forever. Others, like dying autumn leaves wither and fall, only to be blown from obscurity to anonymity, and thence to oblivion. To recall the remark of a former colleague,[1] the entire country went "Raven-mad," and ere long even Europe fell under the shadow of the dark bird's wing.

Finding myself thrust precipitously into the glow of celebrity, like any ordinary mortal finding himself in similar circumstances, I basked in its dubious glitter. At first I was flattered by the breathless praises and fluttering eyelids of the adoring females who flocked about me. I was guilty of an excess pride[2] as I strode about amongst my admirers, dispensing *ex cathedra* bits of wisdom, bestowing *bon mots* on the favoured. What a wretch I was! Instead of treasuring the precious dwindling months left me of my fading wife's time, I squandered them in the company of fawning sycophants and well-wishers alike.

Knowing in my heart that poor Sissy's days were numbered, I failed to give enough of the one commodity it was within my power to bestow upon her—my own poor company. For literary lion tho' I had become, I was at best a sickly one, whose ribs stood out beneath his coat. I could not bring her precious jewels or other costly gifts, and yet she did not complain. When the time had passed beyond which I could remedy the fault I learned that rather than hurl reproaches in my absence, she merely wept and prayed for my safety. O God! Can I ever be forgiven for the grievous manner in which I so neglected her? Must I forever be tormented by the omnipresent sting of remorse?

But I cannot alter the past. Now I live in continuous hope for the future, and carry on. Only by setting words to paper as I do here, am I able in some small measure to ease the melancholy which envelops me. Why I was chosen to endure such earthly suffering is certainly the greatest mystery of my life, and one I fear I shall never fathom. Would that by some strange and miraculous means I could materialise a living Dupin[3] from the recesses of my brain to emerge and illuminate the dark corners of my soul.

Why, as I sit here alone in my study, listening to the wind howling about the rooftop, do I feel as tho' my reason is about to desert me again? My hand trembles. My heart thuds dully in my breast, and only the steady bright beams of lamplight convince me that some terrible doom is not descending from without—like the comet of death in *Eiros and Charmion.*[4] Does this mean that the ultimate dissolution is upon me, that even at this moment I am on the verge of tumbling into the region of shadows?

But I must retrieve the riband of my narrative, which appears to have slipped from my grasp, for in so doing I will prevent the thread of my sanity from unraveling, and abandoning me in the tangled skein of madness. In contemplating my very recent past, I can truthfully state that during the wild incandescence of exhilaration that swept over me following the flight of *The Raven*, I became two men. Perhaps I was always thus. In the bosom of my family I was the same "Eddy" I had always been. As the public man, I sat in the exalted eyrie of my editor's chair, hurling down verbal thunderbolts in Jovian fashion at all who aroused my displeasure. Tho' I said it not aloud—and know there were many who would dispute me—I regarded myself in secret as the uncrowned poet laureate of America.

One evening—I believe it was in June—immediately following a tea in the home of a well-to-do matron who aspired to the starry sisterhood of female poets, I returned home[5] to find Virginia pale and breathless, languishing in a chair, clutching Cattarina to her breast for warmth. She was alone, and having sustained a painful fit of coughing, was too weak to traverse the distance from where she sat to her bed. Thanking God that I had not touched a drink that day, I lifted her into my arms and carried her there.

Her face was flushed and her eyes glistened with the ghastly luminosity characteristic of her disease. Fresh bloodstains on the bodice of her dress gave mute testimony to the severity of the attack she had just sustained. "Oh, Eddy, my dearest," she murmured weakly, "what a joy it is to have you by my side. Will you stay home this evening?"

Tho' she expressed her wish in the simplest of phrases, there was such an expression of longing in her eyes, indeed upon the whole of her countenance, that teams of horses would not have torn me from her side that night. I assured her that I would remain with her, leaving only long enough to brew her a cup of tea. When she had finished it she took my hands in hers—how cold they were—and said in so plaintive a tone it brought tears to my eyes, "May I ask you something, Eddy, my dear love?"

There was a melancholy music in her voice, an angelic expression upon her features, so beauteously affecting that had she asked for a star I would have gone at once to climb the highest peak in hopes of fetching it for her. Embracing her before I answered, I wiped away my tears, then whispered, "My very soul is yours if you wish it, my darling."

"Will you promise me not to be sad?"

"How can I be sad when I am with you?"

She smiled a wan smile and said, "Oh what joy it is to hear you say that is so. Then I know I can ask you the question that has been troubling me. You are so wise, Eddy. Surely you will know the answer."

"Ask me then, dearest heart."

"If I should die before summer comes, please make my grave among the trees and flowers, so the songbirds can serenade my lonely slumber."

My heart could have burst asunder but I chided her gently, "Hush, my darling! Speak not of death and graves! Love will heal your lungs. We will find a little cottage away from the world with all its care."

"Oh, if only that could be, I should be the happiest girl in all

275

the world. But I am so afraid. I feel so weak. Tell me, Eddy, truly now, does it hurt to die? I have known so much pain, I pray that when the hand of Death touches me it will be gentle."

Tho' I knew not what to tell her, I could not bear to hear another word on so melancholy a subject, and I said, "You will know no pain, my darling. The greatest pain we ever know is the pain of life itself."

Then I tenderly kissed her and caressed her until she fell gently to sleep. Once I was certain that she slumbered peacefully I slipped from her chamber and burst into tears. Our mother had not returned yet from whatever errand had taken her away from our lodgings. No longer able to contain myself, I rushed headlong out into the gathering darkness. I had to have a drink or I would go insane! Would that Death had reached out his gaunt claws to me that night.

Heaven help me! Merely contemplating in retrospect the events which transpired from that day on make me ill again. While the *Broadway Journal* flourished I wielded my pen with alternative strokes of ferocity and loving tenderness. In either instance I was excoriated by enemies, and they were legion.[6] When I was not prostrated by sickness[7] I worked with a demoniacal intensity for fifteen, sixteeen hours a day. I was torn between emotions of professional triumph and personal agony. I was famous. My words, my company, were constantly sought, yet my poverty remained an inescapable burden. For me to watch helpless as the wife I loved more than my own life itself moved daily closer to the yawning pit of Death, was more than my nerves could withstand.

My soul will burn for all eternity in the fiery depths of hell for what I did that year. Instead of remaining resolute by the side of my beloved, unable to bear the spectacle of her ever-present suffering, I took refuge in the company of the literati. Often, when held captive by the vicious toils of drink, I behaved abominably to my unhappy Virginia. Nothing that I can ever say or do will expiate my sin or shrive me of my guilt.

From time to time when her failing health permitted, she accompanied me to the salon of a Gotham bluestocking. There she would remain adoringly by my side, saying but little, but smiling sweetly at all who greeted her. Upon one such occasion, fool that I was, I accepted a glass of port. Then, my passions excited, my sentiments of loyalty confused and misdirected, I resolved to escort a certain poetess to her home. I will not mention her identity, for her mediocrity was so monumental that to name her might preserve her memory for posterity. I announced my intention to Virginia, who voiced not a whisper of complaint. I declared that I was certain she would not object to taking herself home as Mrs. —— was too important to be left unattended.

Did my darling reproach me? No, she fixed me with a wan smile, nodded her head, and assured me that I had made a proper decision. Yet I learned afterwards that the moment she took her leave, unescorted and afraid, she was seen making her way down the street coughing, her eyes glistening, and the tears streaming down her poor, flushed cheeks.

Had this been my only transgression against her I might look forward to a day when my guilt might be washed away, my remorse softened. But no! I did what no man may do and remain in a state of grace in the eyes of God. I lost my heart to another woman—*but I could not help myself*. I was smitten by her charms as surely as if ensnared by the spells of Circe. Oh! had I only lived at a time or in a place wherein it was not regarded by Society as a sin of enormous magnitude to love two women at once. I did not love my Sissy the less, nor F[rances] O[sgood] the more, for my love for F.O. was chaste as it was intense. She was a married woman, a poetess of divine talent, a great beauty that evoked my own dear mother's grace,[8] and a disposition of such sweetness that she might have tempted the heavenly angels to fall. All men who entered her presence fell under her mesmeric spell, and even most members of her own sex worshipped her.

I had previously known her only by means of her poetry. But one evening we met at a brilliant gathering of literary lights. Longfellow was there, as were others such as [William Cullen] Bryant, [Fitz-Greene] Halleck, Griswold, [Horace] Greeley, Mrs. [Elizabeth] Ellet,* and Margaret Fuller. When F.O. first

---

*A minor poet of the time.

entered the room I was in conversation with the laconic Bryant on the subject of *The Raven*'s meter. Suddenly I saw her. Our eyes met, and as our gazes thus locked together my heart began to pound and a roseate blush spread over her features. At that moment there were no others in the room save the two of us. All other conversation ceased for us and we were drawn together as tho' by a powerful magnet of immutable force.

A gentle smile akin to that of the immortal Gioconda played over her mouth as I took her hand and brushed it with my lips after the European fashion. "So we meet at last," she said in tones as sweet, nay sweeter, than those that must have come from the Aeolian harp. "I have met you in my dreams," I said softly, so that none but she might hear. "Since first I ever read your poetry. Permit me to tell you, my dear Mrs. Osgood, you have turned this night into a waking dream."

Her blush deepened. "You are too kind, Mr. Poe," said she. And tho' I longed to pour out my soul and tell her what powerful emotions now stirred my passions and overflowed my heart, the only reply I could make was, "You are everything I had hoped you would be." I felt awkward, tongue-tied, like a beardless schoolboy at his first dress ball. I cannot say precisely what might have happened next, but at that moment we were joined by Griswold, whose face betrayed beyond the slightest doubt that he was hopelessly smitten.

Her grace transcended her beauty, and tho' we dared not give voice to the emotions we both felt in our hearts,[9] we published verses expressing our mutual love, which perforce had to remain pure. Thus its very essence rendered it honest and above reproach. But alas! viperish tongues and pens dipped in vitriol later created a scandal[10] which injured poor Mrs. O. and at one point even prompted her to flee the city.

The fearful heat of summer that year was one step removed from the blasts of hell's furnace. However, our having relocated to more spacious quarters at 85 Amity Street, near Washington Square, made it more bearable. At this time I had published my poem "Eulalie," which was in truth a paean of love to my darling Sissy, and which provided a small measure of balm to my stricken conscience. I was now called upon to give lectures and readings, many of which I had to cancel due to increasing episodes of illness.

In autumn my poor wife's health worsened again, and I became frantic with worry. My despair reached such depths that I was driven to more furious drinking. Thus, in the month of October I suffered a total collapse and was forced to spend the better part of the month confined to my bed. I was obliged to cancel a speaking engagement at the Boston Lyceum, where I had planned to read a new poem, but having been temporarily deserted by my muse I remained in New York.

My body wracked with pain, my brain assaulted by the ravages of alcohol, and my nerves strained to the breaking point, I resorted from time to time to the use of laudanum to alleviate my distress. Tho' my friend Chivers[11] cautioned me against the use of stimulants, I could not do without them during this dreadful, trying time. My responsibilities were immense. Having acquired sole proprietorship of *The Broadway Journal*, I fought to keep it alive. Perhaps it was not *The Stylus*, but it was my own magazine. Unfortunately, by the end of December it foundered for lack of financial support. In the final number, which appeared on January 3, 1846, I bade a regretful farewell to friends and foes alike. Only one pale gleam of hope remained to illuminate an otherwise bleak and melancholy year. A little volume, *The Raven and Other Poems*, was published by Wiley & Putnam on December 31.

For the rest of that dismal winter I sought respite from the vicissitudes of life where and when I could find it. Inspiration often eluded me, giving rise on such occasions to a terror more horrible than any I had ever confected in my fictions. Indeed, what could be more frightful to a poet than the prospect of being unable to write? I paced the floors, shivering with cold as the icy blasts of winter winds rattled the windowpanes and doors—as my adored wife lay sweating and trembling, gasping and bleeding.

"Eddy," she murmured through chattering teeth one frosty March morning, "if I live till the May flowers bloom, will you take Cattarina and me to call on the Brennans? It was so lovely there."

"How you do talk!" I exclaimed in tones of mock light-heartedness. "You will live to see your locks turn grey. Remember the sweet words of the valentine[12] you gave me? "Perfect ease we'll enjoy . . . Ever peaceful and blissful we'll be."

I knew not whether she would live to see another sunrise, but I resolved that were she granted the gift of continued life till spring, I would do as she had asked. I was acquainted with several medical men with literary aspirations. Two of them, Doctors Valentine Mott and John W. Francis, had met Virginia, and recognised the gravity of her condition. On separate occasions each of these gentlemen had confirmed my worst fears: that my beloved was not long for the world.

Accordingly, with the first arrival of springtime's green buds, our little family returned to the farm on Bloomingdale Road, but only for a brief sojourn of three weeks. Mrs. Brennan, warm and tender-hearted soul that she was, could not bear the spectacle of poor Sissy's coughing spells without bursting into tears or falling to her knees in fervent prayer. The effect of this good woman's emotions and supplications had an unsettling effect on the unhappy invalid, and we moved to another farm cottage in Turtle Bay.*

Despite the pleasant surroundings, Sissy was now so weak she rarely left the house. Pale as death, she coughed and lost blood daily. I so despaired of her life I marvel that I was able to accomplish anything of consequence at all, but with the spectre of poverty continually lashing at me with its icy scourge, I was driven. Is it any wonder, then, that on occasion I partook of stimulants? It is here that I must make a confession concerning the ill effect of drink upon my nature.

Lurking deep within the inner recesses of my soul there is a perversity of spirit which, in benighted days of yore, might well have been termed a demon. When sober I am able to keep it imprisoned where it belongs. But once the glass has touched my lips I am powerless to contain this beast, which takes command of my senses and transforms me into a raging replica of itself. It blusters and roars. It is ever prepared to do battle, even over the

---

*Now approximately 47th Street and Second Avenue in Manhattan, a short walking distance from the United Nations.

most trivial affronts. In its zeal to defend me from all enemies, imagined and real, it is in truth the most terrible enemy I have ever known. And it is bound to me as irrevocably as the bonds of Prometheus.

One hot May day, in what I must in all honesty describe as a flight of drunken madness, I borrowed my landlord's skiff, rowed out into the river, and tied up at the southern tip of Blackwell's Island.* I removed my clothes and dived into the crystal waters of the East River for a swim. My inebriated condition notwithstanding, I was still more than capable of breasting the current. While frolicking about thus, I failed to observe two fishermen in a small scow. Upon inadvertently becoming entangled in their lines I was seized by panic. In my frantic efforts to free myself I began flailing about fearfully and for a moment I thought I should drown.

By some miraculous twist of fate I succeeded in freeing myself and rising to the surface, but in so doing I grazed my shoulder against the fishermen's boat. "Hoo-hah!" exclaimed one of them. "What sort of creature is this we've caught?"

His infantile attempt at a jest, when I had nearly lost my life, infuriated me. "Imbeciles!" I cried, sputtering and treading water as I shouted. "Had I a screw-auger I would drill a hole in your hull and sink you to the bottom!"

"A talking fish!" retorted one.

"And a blusterer, too!" declared the other.

They both burst out laughing, and had it not been for the fact that the cold water had begun to bring me back to sobriety, I do believe I might have attacked them with my bare hands, and attempted to swamp their craft. Fortunately reason prevailed and, after flinging a final curse their way, I dove beneath the surface and returned to my skiff.

I must have caught a cold that day, for I was terribly ill through most of the spring and well into summer. Poor Muddy, what a burden we must have been! Her beloved little Sissy was slowly dying of the consumption. Each gasp, each cough, each effusion of blood was like a dagger plunged into her loving moth-

---

*Now Roosevelt Island.

er's heart, yet she persevered. And I, confined to my bed ofttimes for days on end, cried and raged in my deliriums, begging for a drink, begging for laudanum or morphine, and, yes, even begging for a dagger that I might plunge it into my own heart and bring my misery to an end. This last request she tearfully revealed to me many months later.

On those occasions when I was lucid and felt capable of working, I often toiled furiously through the night. Always, my dear mother remained by my side, leaving it only from time to time to look in on Sissy, or to fetch me a steaming cup of hot black coffee.

By midsummer I began to recover and from John Valentine, whom I had met during a brief excursion to Baltimore early in spring, I rented a snug little cottage at a village called Fordham* about thirteen miles out of town. The rent was a reasonable eight dollars a month and our surroundings offered the rural charm and isolation we had yearned for so long. The pillars of the small porch were wreathed in jasmine and sweet honeysuckle. Pots of gorgeous flowers abounded on all sides and the vivid green of an old tulip tree overshadowed the cottage. Around us were orchards and woods, and from the rise upon which we were situated we could see the Hudson River to the west and Long Island to the east. Spread before us to the south was the distant aspect of New York, bounded on the north by the flatlands of Harlem.

Weak tho' she was, dear Sissy loved our little cottage and took great delight in the cherry tree, the lilac bushes, and the other verdant shrubs that made it an oasis of tranquillity and beauty. As for me, it was akin to an earthly paradise. No longer were we strangers in the homes of others. No more were we forced to endure the ear-splitting, window-shaking, mind-shattering rumbles of the city. Instead of being blasted from the gentle embrace of Morpheus by the clatter of wheels and horses' hooves on paving stones, we were gently awakened each morn by rosy fingers of dawn and the sweet music of songbirds.

Barely had we settled into our sweet new home when visitors and well-wishers began descending upon us like locusts. Al-

*Now 192nd Street and Kingsbridge Road, Bronx, N.Y.

though she was the very picture of propriety and hospitality when they were present, Muddy was in the habit of reading aloud some of the female poets' more passionate epistolary effusions. In hopes of obtaining my approbation, many of them wrote fervid letters to me which might readily have been misinterpreted as declarations of undying love. Sissy would listen to her mother attempting to impose a jocular note, and burst into gales of merriment at the gestures, the inflections, and the grimaces, all punctuated by sighs and groans and gasps and moans. My darling knew she occupied the throne of my heart, and regarded these impassioned outpourings with deep amusement.

One day in June a visitor, Mrs. Elizabeth Ellet, a chattery, gossipy, magpie in the guise of a human female chanced to overhear one of her missives being read in the next room. Leaping from her chair in most unladylike fashion, nearly toppling the teapot in her haste, she dashed from my presence. Livid with rage, she snatched the letter from Muddy, who was startled nearly out of her wits.

"How dare you intrude on the privacy of my correspondence?" exclaimed Mrs. Ellet. "Wicked, wicked woman!"

Before Muddy could utter a word, the enraged poetess charged back into the kitchen, where I stood transfixed with astonishment, not knowing whether to laugh or frown. Fixing me with a baleful glare, she drew in her breath and shrilly declared, "You, Mr. Poe, are a wretch and a scoundrel! Not only do I never wish to see you again, I demand that you return every letter I have ever sent you!" Whereupon she stamped her foot, uttered a choked little cry, and ran from the house, never to return again. Muddy and Virginia laughed till the tears rolled down their cheeks.

Having always regarded myself as a gentleman, I hastened to comply with Mrs. Ellet's request. I tied her letters into a bundle, made a special trip to New York, and left them on the doorstep of her house. But there were repercussions. In a fit of hysteria, she complained of the matter to her brother, a pompous ass named Colonel Lummis. Not knowing that the letters had been returned, he came to me and demanded them.

"I fear you have traveled here in vain," I told him coolly. "The letters you seek are not in my possession."

As tho' I had not said a word, he repeated his demand. "I am not accustomed to being defied, Mr. Poe. I *will* have my sister's letters at once!"

"Are you deaf, sir," I retorted, "or are you calling me a liar?"

He roared, "You are a liar, a drunkard, and a spoiler of ladies' good names, and if you do not return the letters immediately I shall . . ."

"Bay at the moon? Froth at the mouth? Perhaps you might prefer to stamp your feet and bite your cheeks for all the good it will do you. I no longer have the damned letters! If you want them so badly, I suggest you ask that semi-literate fishwife who sprang from the same womb that spawned you! And as for you, sir, you have the manners of an orangutan, the smell of a billygoat, and the intellect of a mouse! Now, if you will excuse me."

His face turned crimson. Clenching his fists and baring his tobacco-stained teeth, he sucked in his breath with an audible hiss and roared, "You swine! You villain! . . . I . . ." Then composing himself with some effort, he lowered his voice, narrowed his eyes, and said, "You had better obtain a pistol, Edgar Poe, for my seconds will be calling on you presently!" With that he turned on his heels and stalked off in high dudgeon.

Such an imperfect challenge I had never heard of in my life! Why, even the tenderest schoolboy in the South knows that the gentleman who is challenged has the choice of weapons. Did he intend to stalk me like an animal in the streets? For my personal safety I resolved at once to obtain a pistol at the earliest opportunity.

The duel, however, never came to pass. But while contemplating it I became excited and overindulged in drink. The fool did not know what an excellent marksman I was; I had not spent all that time as a soldier for naught. But I made an error in judgement in the matter of procuring a weapon. While in my cups I paid a call on a literary acquaintance, Thomas Dunn English,[13] to ask for the loan of a pistol. He refused me and there ensued harsh words, which led to blows. The villain had the temerity to spread the false rumour that he had thrashed me within an inch of my life, when the truth is that *I* beat *him* quite badly.[14] Nevertheless the encounter proved to be of sufficient severity that afterwards I was obliged to take to my bed for several days.

The summer of '46 was one of the hottest, most oppressive in all my recollection. I was thankful for our Fordham residence. Tho' we were given a measure of relief with the coming of faint evening breezes, it was a time of trial. Virginia weakened steadily. My health was further debilitated by the nervous excitation arising over the libel suit I had instituted against the *Mirror*,[15] no longer owned by my friend Willis.

Other than a visit from my sister, Rosalie, at a time when I was confined to my bed with another episode of delirium, little transpired during those months. It was a time of decline and despair. One day in August when Virginia and I both felt strong enough we ventured forth for a stroll. My head throbbed with pain, but I said nothing of it to her. The suffering she had endured was far too great for me to impose my own on her. Yet she knew; perhaps it was betrayed by a grimace, an inadvertent touch of the head. I cannot say. Nevertheless, she knew that my insignificant pain was the result of an enduring soul sickness and she endeavoured to comfort me. But she was seized by a paroxysm of coughing which, thank God, ceased after a short passage of time. It so exhausted her, however, that we seated ourselves beneath a shade tree in a leafy glen along one of the wooded pathways that led from our cottage. We sat there, my arms around her as she rested, saying nothing, when unexpectedly she looked into my eyes and murmured softly, "Eddy, we know the truth, don't we?"

Somewhat mystified by her words, I was about to speak when she held a dainty finger to my lips. "Hush, my darling," she said. "I know in my heart that you are truly brave. Why, I am certain, if I were a man and I were beset with such misfortunes as you have known, I could never have faced them with such fortitude. But now I must die soon . . . no, no, my dearest. Say nothing. I am resigned to my fate. It is God's will, and it must be done. And I want you always to remember, when I am gone I will be your guardian angel. And if at any time you feel tempted to do wrong, just put your hands above your head, so . . ." She lifted her hands and smiled, oh, so sweetly, then said, "and I will be there to shield you."

I could not hold back the tears and pressed her to my bosom and wept. Had I not been so overcome with emotion at that moment I might have risen to my feet and shaken my clenched fists at heaven. "Why, God?" my heart cried. "Why hast Thou chosen to ravage me so? Why was I chosen to live out my life in the grim shadow of so dark and baneful a star?"

What more is there for me to say? As autumn came, the skies darkened and the cold winds blew. Tho' the spark of life remained, the icy fingers of Death now tightened their grip on my beloved wife. Not once did she complain, tho' she trembled from morn till night, and her poor teeth chattered as if the chill of the tomb had already stolen into her frail bones. As she lay on her straw pallet shivering, uncomplaining, she would hold Cattarina tightly to her breast for warmth. Her wasted limbs appeared almost lifeless. Having naught but a thin, patched coverlet that could not keep her warm, I spread my worn and mended greatcoat over her as Muddy and I sat by holding her hands and feet to warm them.

The days were not so bad. From time to time a visitor came. I was barely able to work, however, and for days on end we were reduced to eating but one meal a day. Were our situation not deplorable enough as it was, Virginia began receiving scabrous, anonymous letters, which inspired the deepest distress, tho' we were certain of the source. Each of them was without doubt penned by the venomous hand of the vicious Mrs. Ellet, and once read they were consigned to the flames.

Had it not been for the tender concern and efforts of two saintly women, Mrs. Mary Gove and Mrs. Mary Louise Shew,[16] I shudder to think what my beloved's last days might have been. Until my own dying day I will regard that winter as the most melancholy season of my life. It was bitter cold. As the snows piled high into high, white drifts, and the skies grew ashen and grey, fewer visitors crossed our poor threshold. None of the literary ladies dared brave the wintry blasts to warm us with the radiance of their presence. Occasionally a kindly neighbor came bearing some small necessity to help us ward off utter starvation. But mostly we were alone. How humiliating it was to be thus!

Christmas Eve saw me drinking weak coffee from thrice-used grounds, and working feverishly through the night like a man possessed. The only gifts to grace our hearth on Christmas day were a small bag of coal, a sack of potatoes, and a dressed wild duck which was ambrosia to us.

In mid-January Dr. Mott came to call. Virginia was now failing rapidly and suffering great pain. He gave her morphine to ease her distress, then drawing me aside the moment she became drowsy, he said gravely. "My friend, I can offer you no more hope. Virginia cannot last another month, if indeed she survives that long. She is in the hands of the Almighty."

A sob escaped from Muddy's lips and her eyes shone with tears. She said, "May the good Lord grant her a gentle death."

On the 28th day of January, after supper and after we had given Virginia her medicine so that she might have a peaceful night of sleep, Muddy came to me, fresh tears in her eyes, and declared mournfully, "Oh the cruelty of fate, that such a saintly child should be snatched from us by death."

My heart sank. "Do not tell me that she has gone!"

"No, no. She still lives, but she knows that her time is running out. Do you know, even as the hour of her final agony approaches, her only thoughts are of you. When you had left her side, she said to me, 'Darling, darling Muddy, you will console and take care of my poor Eddy—you will *never, never* leave him? Promise me, my dear Muddy, and I can die in peace!' "

Unable to answer her lest I burst into tears I turned and ran to the chamber of my beloved Sissy. So peacefully was she slumbering now in her poor little bed, that any beholder might fancy her dead. Fresh ruby bloodstains darkened her nightdress. I knelt by her side and prayed to heaven that her sleep would be peaceful, her dreams filled with sweetness and tranquillity. How deathly was her pallor! How troubled her breathing! Fearful lest I inadvertently arouse her, I backed from the tiny chamber on tiptoes and ascended the stairs to my study. Oh, God! how desperately I was in need of a drink, yet how thankful I was that there were no spirits in the house.

Only one relative came to console us in our hour of dreadful trial, my cousin Elizabeth. She sat all day with Sissy, talking of Baltimore, holding her hands for warmth. Mrs. Shew came also. Her cheeks and nose were cherry-red from the cold outside. She carried a bundle which she gave to Muddy, saying, "I have a white linen dress for Virginia . . ."

When I heard her finish the sentence, ". . . it will be her burial gown," my heart seemed to stop beating. I could contain myself no longer. Not wanting a stranger to behold me in such a state of distraction—even so beloved a one as Mrs. Shew—I flew up the stairs and flung myself upon my bed. I was seized with an uncontrollable fit of trembling and weeping. Unable to stop, a terror seized me and, to calm my nerves, I took a small draught of laudanum. Very quickly I fell into a deep slumber inhabited by strange beings in even stranger places.

I was awakened in the morning by a piteous cry which chilled my blood, for tho' I knew not from whose lips it came, I knew what it heralded. Virginia was no more! Stricken with remorse for having been absent during her final moments, I hastened down the stairs. Standing about her bed, weeping softly, were Muddy, Elizabeth, and Mrs. Shew. "God forgive me!" I gasped. "In my own wretched weakness I abandoned her in her final moments. I am accursed . . ."

"No, you are not, Edgar," said Mrs. Shew, fixing me with a stern glance. "No one was with her in her final moments . . ."

"But how can that be?" I interrupted her.

"She smothered in her sleep. It was a painless and fortunate way to die. Don't you see? You have no reason to feel remorse."

"How can you speak thus?" I demanded. "She lived all through yesterday, and I saw her only in the morning. I should have been by her side! I should have been with her till the end but I was not. Oh, God! What have I done?"

In my grief I tried to fling myself on the bed and clasp my lost beloved in a final embrace, but they seized me with cries of horrified protest. For one brief instant I experienced a black rage unlike any anger I had ever known. It was so terrible, so all-consuming, I know that had it continued to hold me in its grip I would have become a wild beast. It was enough, however, to make me struggle against their efforts to restrain me. "For the love of heaven, no!" cried Muddy.

I threw back my head and uttered a ululating wail of anguish and plunged forward. I lost my balance and fell against the wall, striking my head a powerful blow. Mercifully I lost consciousness.

Of the days that followed I will, indeed I can, say nothing. I was obliged to take laudanum before and after my darling was laid to rest in the vaults of the Valentine family, the owners of our cottage. My recollections of her solemn obsequies remain dim and shadowy as tho' enshrouded in mist. Huge moons wax and wane. The sounds of weeping mingle with sobbing winds. Sorrowful figures drift silently through mounds of snow.

For days, for weeks, I hovered over the edge of madness. I wept, I wailed, I babbled, I wandered about like a lost soul. Gradually I recovered my senses, but they were burdened by a leaden melancholy. I was full of dark forebodings. Nothing could cheer or comfort me. Then I was stricken with the brain fever. I was totally deranged and during the interval I imagined the most horrible calamities.

I have recovered my sanity now. I have begun to write again, and God willing, before the Dark Angel comes to convey me to the region of shadows I shall triumph over my many enemies once and for all time. If good fortune chooses at last to favour me with a smile, I may yet establish *The Stylus*, and enjoy one final blaze of glory before I die. To begin with, I must write a new prospectus. I say this because my destiny has always been to strive thus, tho' I care not whether I live or perish the moment I put down my pen. I am tired of the world. Indeed, I have often thought that hell itself would be a better place for me than the society of heartless men and women.

Indeed, I even care not whether this narrative is ever seen by other eyes than mine. For it to perish with me would be a fitting punishment for one who has transgressed in life as grievously as I. But should fate decree that it be seen by future generations, so be it. And if that day should come to pass, let these words be my valediction:

I ever spoke the word, "farewell"
With heavy heart and sombre brow.
And now as I await my knell,
I fold my cloak, take one last bow.

EPILOGUE

THANKS to the compassion and medical skills of Mary Louise Shew, Poe soon recovered from his serious bout with "brain fever" following Virginia's death. Mrs. Shew recalled some time afterwards that he had raved wildly during his periods of delirium, claiming to have had all sorts of adventures that were, in truth, figments of his vivid imagination. She made another comment about Poe that has been given credence by some medical authorities and discounted by others. Nevertheless, it is worth mentioning. Based upon certain irregularities she detected in his pulse, it was her opinion that he was suffering from a brain lesion that caused his erratic behavior.

While nursing him back to health Mrs. Shew gave Poe what we would call "occupational therapy" today. Recognizing his gifts for visual imagery, she suggested that he come to her home in Manhattan (in what is now Greenwich Village) and help her decorate her apartment. He did so and was constantly annoyed by the tolling of the bells from nearby Grace Church. As a result of this experience he wrote his poem, "The Bells."

Whatever the state of his mind, he continued to write brilliantly despite his physical and emotional deterioration. In June 1848 George P. Putnam published Poe's prose poem, *Eureka*, in which he expressed his theories about the universe. He received an advance of $14 for the volume and continued to live an impoverished life with his aunt in the cottage at Fordham. He left briefly

291

in July on a trip to Richmond, where he hoped to raise money and get subscribers for *The Stylus.*

It was about this time that Poe began a series of fugues which eventually ended with his death. Through a series of romantic poetical exchanges of verse he became involved with a mystically inclined widow, Sarah Helen Whitman, whom he visited, and proposed to in September 1848. She was a fairly well-known poet of the time. She lived in Providence, Rhode Island, was financially well off, and had a tendency to get herself tipsy on ether, with which she continually soaked her handkerchiefs. Contemporary accounts describe how her presence was invariably heralded by the distinctive scent of the anesthetic that she exuded the way other women did perfume.

Mrs. Whitman almost married Poe, but her family thwarted the affair by insisting that Poe sign a waiver forfeiting any rights to her estate. He was highly indignant at this. Besides, he was also in love with another woman, Annie Richmond, who was married and therefore tantalizingly unavailable. Despite impassioned love letters to both women, no marriages, no clandestine affairs developed. Whether consciously or unconsciously, Poe remained faithful to his dead mother and dead wife.

More attempts were made to finance and establish the *Stylus*, all unsuccessful. There were brilliant and triumphant lectures, drinking sprees, and a brush with death in Providence from an overdose of laudanum. It may have been a suicide attempt that failed. He wrote of it to Annie Richmond on November 16, 1848 saying in part: "... how shall I explain to you the *bitter, bitter,* anguish which has tortured me since I left you? You saw, you *felt* the agony of grief with which I bade you farewell. You remember my expressions of gloom—of a dreadful, horrible foreboding of ill. ... As I clasped you to my heart, I said to myself: 'It is for the last time, until we meet in heaven.' I remember nothing distinctly, from that moment, until I found myself in Providence. I went to bed & wept through a long, long, hideous night of despair ... the demon tormented me still. Finally I procured two ounces of laudanum & without returning to my hotel, took the cars back to Boston. When I arrived, I wrote you a letter. ... Having written this letter, I swallowed about half of the laudanum . . . but I had not calculated on its strength for, before I reached the Post Office my reason was entirely gone & the letter was never put in. . . . A friend was at hand, who aided & (if it can be called saving) saved me. . . ." Whether or not he was trying to commit suicide here, his obvious lack of knowledge about the effects of the laudanum in the strength he took it proves that, though he was a "user," he was never an "addict."

Despite his suffering from severe headaches and general depression, Poe continued to work when he returned to Fordham. Among the works he produced was his science-fiction tale, inspired by the California gold rush, *Von Kempelen and His Discovery*. Then, after publication of his sonnet in tribute to Maria Clemm, "To My Mother," he suffered one of his worst nervous breakdowns. Alarmed as she had never been before, Mrs. Clemm wrote to Annie Richmond, "God knows I wish we were both in our graves—it would, I am sure, be far better." Poe himself was now totally unable to explain his depressions; he specifically denied that recent failures and rejections had anything to do with them. He wrote: "No doubt, Annie you attribute my 'gloom' to these events*—but you are wrong. It is not in the power of any mere *worldly* considerations such as these to depress me. . . . No, my sadness is *unaccountable,* and this makes me more sad. I am full of dark forebodings . . ."

In the spring of 1849 a total stranger, Edward H. N. Patterson, of Oquawka, Illinois, offered to finance a magazine for Poe and promised him total editorial control. Poe was overjoyed. He saw at last, looming on the horizon, the fulfillment of his fondest dream. But Patterson recommended that first Poe go on a three-month lecture tour in order to drum up interest in the new publication.

Poe agreed to this and embarked, in high spirits, but a series of drinking sprees wrecked the tour and he suffered another complete breakdown. His self-destruct mechanism was working now as it never had before. After a partial recovery he went to Richmond in July 1849, and delivered a brilliant lecture on his essay, "The Poetic Principle." While in Richmond he attempted to

---

*Most of his income had stopped. All the magazines to which he had recently contributed failed to pay him, offering a variety of excuses.

revive the romance with his now widowed childhood sweetheart, Elmira Royster Shelton. Although she still loved him, she had become somewhat of a religious zealot, and had doubts about his affection. She voiced her suspicions that perhaps he was proposing marriage only for her money. After all, she was no longer the vivacious teenager with whom he had originally fallen in love. He promptly had another breakdown and she relented and agreed to marry him in October 1849.

Late in September he developed a fever, got drunk, and wound up in Baltimore looking for a friend, Dr. Nathan C. Brooks, who was not at home. At that point Poe wandered away and vanished for five days.

On October 3, 1849 he was found unconscious, lying outside a polling place on East Lombard Street. There was an election on at the time and it has been conjectured that he fell into the hands of some crooked political connivers who got him drunk and used him for the purpose of illegally stuffing ballot boxes. A friend, Dr. J. E. Snodgrass, was summoned by Joseph Walker, the man who found Poe. Apparently Walker brought Poe to consciousness, offered his help, and Poe asked for Snodgrass.

Snodgrass described Poe's condition thus: ". . . his face . . . haggard, not to say bloated, and unwashed, his hair unkempt, and his whole physique repulsive. His expansive forehead and now lusterless eyes were shaded from view by a rusty, almost brimless, tattered, and ribbonless palm-leaf hat. His clothing consisted of a sackcoat of thin and sleazy black alpaca, ripped, faded, and soiled, and pants of a steel-mixed pattern of cassi-nett,* half worn and badly fitting, if they could be said to fit at all. He wore neither vest nor neckcloth, while the bosom of his shirt was both crumpled and badly soiled . . . "

Poe was always scrupulously careful about personal cleanliness. At his poorest he always had an elegant bearing. Obviously, someone had robbed him of his clothes.

Snodgrass, or someone else, sent for Poe's uncle by marriage, Henry Herring, and they decided to take him to Washington College Hospital, where he was admitted at once.

---

*A material made with a cotton warp and a woof of fine wool or silk.

Dr. J. J. Moran, the resident physician on duty wrote the following report to Maria Clemm concerning his patient's final days:

"When brought to the hospital, he was unconscious of his condition, who brought him, or with whom he had been associating. He remained in this conditon from five o'clock in the afternoon—the hour of his admission— until three the next morning. This was on the 3rd October.

"To this state succeeded tremor of the limbs, and at first a busy but not active delirium, constant talking, and vacant converse with spectral and imaginary objects on the walls. His face was pale and his whole person drenched in perspiration. We were unable to induce tranquility before the second day after his admission.

"Having left orders with his nurses to that effect, I was summoned to his bedside so soon as consciousness supervened, and questioned him in reference to his family, place of residence, relatives, etc. But his answers were incoherent and unsatisfactory. He told me, however, he had a wife in Richmond (which I have since learned was not the fact), that he did not know when he left that city, or what had become of his trunk of clothing. Wishing to rally and sustain his now fast-sinking hopes, I told him I hoped that in a few days he would be able to enjoy the society of his friends here, and I would be most happy to contribute in every possible way to his ease and comfort. At this he broke out with much energy, and said the best thing his best friend could do would be to blow out his brains with a pistol, that when he beheld his degradation, he was ready to sink into the earth, etc. Shortly after giving expression to these words, Mr. Poe seemed to doze, and I left him for a short time. When I returned I found him in a violent delirium, resisting the efforts of two nurses to keep him in bed. This state continued until Saturday evening (he was admitted on Wednesday), when he commenced calling for one 'Reynolds,' which he did throughout the night until *three* on Sunday morning. At this time a very decided change began to affect him. Having become enfeebled from exertion, he became quiet, and seemed to rest for a short time; then, gently moving his head, he said, *'Lord help my poor soul,'* and expired."

The next day, Monday, October 8, 1849, after a simple burial service conducted by a distant relation, the Reverend W.T.D. Clemm, Edgar Allan Poe was buried in the cemetery of the Presbyterian Church at Fayette and Green Streets in Baltimore. Only four men were present as mourners, to see him consigned to his grave: his cousin Neilson Poe; Henry Herring; his friend Dr. J.E. Snodgrass; and an old schoolmate, Z. Collins Lee.

The poet was finally reunited with the spectral lovers who had haunted and inspired him throughout his life. And they, the raven-haired, dark-eyed phantoms, by whatever names they were known—Helen, Lenore, Ligeia—were now one with him for all eternity. He had finally found his Eldorado "over the mountains of the Moon, down the Valley of the Shadow."

—B.J.H.

CHRONOLOGY

BIBLIOGRAPHY

NOTES

CHRONOLOGY

Jan. 19, 1809	Edgar Allan Poe born in Boston, Mass.
Dec. 8, 1811	Poe's mother, actress Elizabeth Arnold Poe, died in Richmond, Va. Young Edgar becomes foster child of John Allan and Frances Keeling Allan.
June 1815–July 1820	In England and Scotland with the Allans. Poe received important early education here.
July 1820–Feb. 14, 1826	Adolescent years in Richmond, Va.
Feb. 14–Dec. 1826	At Charlottesville as student at the University of Virginia.
Dec. 1826–Mar. 1827	Returned to Richmond from university; went to Boston.
May 26, 1827	Enlisted in the army under name of Edgar A. Perry. As member of First Artillery, stationed in Boston Harbor at Fort Independence.
Summer, 1827	*Tamerlane and Other Poems,* Poe's first book published in Boston by Calvin F.S. Thomas.
Nov. 8, 1827	Poe embarked with his battery to Fort Moultrie, South Carolina, located in Charleston harbor.
Dec. 11, 1828	Poe transferred with his battery to Fortress Monroe, Virginia.
Feb. 28, 1829	The death of Poe's foster mother, Frances Keeling Allan.

April 15, 1829	Poe discharged from the army and returned to the home of John Allan in Richmond.
May 1829	Went to Washington and Baltimore. In Baltimore met his aunt Maria Clemm, and other blood relatives.
Dec. 1829	*Al Aaraaf, Tamerlane, and Minor Poems* published in Baltimore by the firm of Hatch & Dunning.
ca. Feb. 1830	Returned to the house of John Allan in Richmond.
May 21, 1830	Having received confirmation (in March) of his appointment as a cadet at the U.S. Military Academy, Poe left Richmond for West Point via Baltimore and Philadelphia.
June 2?, 1830	Arrived at West Point, sworn in as cadet on July 1st.
Feb. 20, 1831	Left West Point for New York after deliberately forcing his own court martial and dismissal.
Spring, 1831	*Poems* (which had been partially subsidized by the cadets at West Point) published by Elam Bliss of New York.
May 1831	Went to Baltimore and remained; began living with his aunt Maria Clemm
July 31, 1831	The death of Poe's brother, Henry.
Oct. 1833	Won first prize in the Baltimore *Saturday Visiter* contest with "A MS. Found in a Bottle."
Mar. 27, 1834	The death of Poe's foster father, John Allan.
July 7, 1835	The death of Poe's grandmother, Mrs. David Poe, Sr., thereby ending her government pension of $240 per annum.
August 1835	Joined the *Southern Literary Messenger* as editor, remained until early September, when he was discharged for drinking.
Sept. 22, 1835	Poe secretly married to his first cousin Virginia Clemm. He was 27, she was 13.

298

Sept. 26, 1835	Returned to Richmond, reinstated as editor of the *Southern Literary Messenger,* which position he retained until January 1837.
May 16, 1836	Poe officially married to Virginia, in Richmond.
Feb. 1837	Poe tried unsuccessfully to survive in New York until the following fall.
Sept. 1838	Went to Philadelphia, then an important publishing center. He remained there until 1844.
Winter 1839	*The Conchologist's First Book* published under Poe's byline, the subject of great controversy as the work was not 100 percent his. It is significant that he does not refer to it.
July 1839	Poe became co-editor of *Burton's Gentleman's Magazine.* During this period Poe concentrated less on poetry and developed his skill as a short story writer.
Dec. 1839	Poe's first collection of short stories under one cover, *Tales of the Grotesque and Arabesque,* published by Lea and Carey.
June 1840	Resigned from *Burton's* to concentrate on starting his own magazine.
Feb. 1841	His reputation now expanding significantly, he became editor of *Graham's Lady's and Gentleman's Magazine.* Under his editorship it became the first mass-market, general-interest magazine in the world. Its circulation was the highest of any magazine, and its publisher became a wealthy man.
Jan. 20, 1842	Poe's wife, Virginia, suffered a severe hemorrhage, the first of many that eventually marked her steady decline and early death at age 24, in 1847.
1843 (?)	*The Prose Romances of Edgar Allan Poe* published.
June 1843	Won literary prize offered by the *Dollar Newspaper* for *The Gold Bug.*

299

Spring 1842	Relinquished editor's chair of *Graham's*, but continued to contribute on a freelance basis.
April 6, 1844	Left Philadelphia with Virginia and went to New York.
Dec. 1844	Became columnist and general editorial writer for N.P. Willis's *New York Mirror*.
Jan. 29, 1845	*The Raven* first published in the *New York Evening Mirror*.
Feb. 22, 1845	Joined Bisco & Briggs as an editor of the *Broadway Journal*.
June 1845	*Tales* published by Wiley & Putnam.
July 12, 1845	Briggs departure left Poe as sole editor of the *Broadway Journal*.
Oct. 24, 1845	John Bisco relinquished all rights, and Poe became publisher and editor of the *Broadway Journal*.
Dec. 31, 1845	*The Raven and Other Poems* published by Wiley & Putnam.
Jan. 3, 1846	The last issue of the *Broadway Journal* published, it having failed for financial reasons.
Feb. 1846	*The Raven & Other Poems — Poe's Tales* a double volume published by Wiley & Putnam.
Jan. 30, 1847	Virginia Poe died of tuberculosis at their home in Fordham, N.Y.
Feb. 17, 1847	Poe won his libel suit against the *New York Mirror* and was awarded $492 in damages and costs.
Jan. 1848	Still pursuing the dream of his own magazine, which he now called *The Stylus*, he printed a new prospectus.
June 1848	The prose poem, *Eureka*, published by George P. Putnam.
July 1848	Journeyed to Richmond to promote financing and subscribers for *The Stylus*.
Sept. 1848	Returned to New York.

Sept. 1848	Went to Providence, R.I., to propose marriage to Sarah Helen Whitman.
Oct.–Dec. 1848	During this period, Poe shuttled back and forth between New York, Providence, R.I., and Lowell, Mass.
May 1–June 1, 1849	Went to Lowell, Mass. to see Mrs. Annie L. Richmond. Then returned to New York.
June 29, 1849	Went to Richmond, Va. from New York.
June 30, 1849	Went from Richmond to Philadelphia and remained there until July 13.
July 14, 1849	Returned to Richmond with a side trip to Norfolk, Va. to deliver a lecture. He renewed the acquaintance with his childhood sweetheart, Elmira Royster Shelton, and discussed marriage.
Circa Sept. 26, 1849	Took steamboat from Richmond to Baltimore.
Oct. 3, 1849	Poe found unconscious outside Ryan's Fourth Ward polls at 44 East Lombard Street, Baltimore. He was taken to Washington College Hospital.
Oct. 7, 1849	Edgar Allan Poe died, aged forty.

BIBLIOGRAPHY

THERE HAVE PROBABLY BEEN more scholarly and critical books written about Edgar Allan Poe than about any other American writer. If we were to count personal reminiscences and novels, the list would very likely fill an entire volume. Included here are only those works actually consulted for the purpose of researching *My Savage Muse*.

Allen, Hervey. *Israfel, The Life and Times of Edgar Allan Poe.* 2 Vols. (George H. Doran Co., N.Y., 1926).

Benet, William Rose. *The Reader's Encyclopedia,* 2nd Edition (Thomas Y. Crowell Co., N.Y., 1965).

Bittner, William. *Poe, a Biography* (Little, Brown and Co., Boston, 1962).

Bonaparte, Marie. *The Life and Works of Edgar Allan Poe,* translated from the French by John Rodker (Imago Publishing Co., Ltd., London, 1949).

Campbell, Killis. *The Mind of Poe and Other Studies* (Harvard University Press, Cambridge, Mass., 1932).

*Chivers, Thomas Holley. *Chivers' Life of Poe* (E. P. Dutton & Co., Inc., N.Y., 1952).

Didier, Eugene. *The Poe Cult and Other Poe Papers* (Broadway Publishing Co., N.Y., 1909).

Fagin, N. Bryllion. *The Histrionic Mr. Poe* (Johns Hopkins Press, Baltimore, 1949).

---

*Chivers, the eccentric physician-poet, and friend of Poe, wrote this memoir shortly after Poe's death, but the manuscript was never published. It was unearthed in the Huntington Museum at San Marino, California, and published for the first time in 1952.

Grun, Bernard. *The Timetables of History* (Simon and Schuster, Inc., N.Y., 1975).

Lauvrière, Emile. *The Strange Life and Loves of Edgar Allan Poe,* translated from the French by Edwin Gile Rich (J. B. Lippincott Co., Philadelphia, 1935).

Lindsay, Philip. *The Haunted Man* (Philosophical Library, N.Y., 1954).

Mabbott, Thomas Ollive. *Poe, E.A. 1809–1849 Collected Works, edited by T.O. Mabbott* (Harvard University Press, Cambridge, Mass., 1969).

Ostrom, John Ward, ed. *The Letters of Edgar Allan Poe.* 2 Vols. (Harvard University Press, Cambridge, Mass., 1948).

Poe, Edgar Allan. *Complete Poems and Tales of Edgar Allan Poe* with an introduction by Hervey Allen (Modern Library, N.Y., 1938).

Quinn, Arthur Hobson, *Edgar Allan Poe, A Critical Biography* (Appleton-Century Co., N.Y., 1941).

Spannuth, Jacob E., ed.; with preface, introduction, and comments by Thomas O. Mabbott. *Doings of Gotham in a series of Letters by Edgar Allan Poe as described to the Editors of the Columbia Spy: Together with Various Editorial Comments and Criticisms by Poe* (J. E. Spannuth, Pottsville, Pa., 1929).

Stedman, Edmund Clarence & Woodberry, George Edward, eds. *The Works of Edgar Allan Poe,* Vols. 6 & 8 (Stone & Kimball, Chicago, 1894–1895).

Symons, Julian. *The Tell-Tale Heart* (Harper & Row, N.Y., 1978).

Weiss, Susan Archer. *The Home Life of Poe* (Broadway Publishing Co., N.Y., 1907).

Williams, Neville. *Chronology of the Modern World 1763 to the Present Time* (1965) (David McKay Co., Inc., N.Y., 1967).

Winwar, Frances. *The Haunted Palace, A Life of Edgar Allan Poe* (Harper & Row, N.Y., 1959).

OTHER SOURCES

Directory and Strangers Guide for the City of Charleston, S.C. 1826

Directory of the City of New York, 1830

Southern Literary Messenger, Richmond, Va. September through February, 1836.

The Broadway Journal, N.Y. January through December, 1845.

NOTES

CHAPTER 1

1. Although there is little doubt as to the essential truth of what Poe wrote here, there is another essential to consider. On one level he was writing to achieve the catharsis he so desperately required. He was always trying to unravel that "fearful mystery" which darkened his soul. Yet he was not fool enough to devote so much time to a manuscript for his eyes only. He simply didn't have the time. That he didn't want it to be read by anyone who lived during his own lifetime was his chief concern, and he probably didn't trust anyone, even those closest to him. There had to be another consideration. Much of what he was saying was far too shocking to be published in his day, and he certainly had no intention of hurting anyone he loved, especially Maria Clemm, the aunt who, in his final days, was more mother to him than any he had ever known. His opening comments on approaching death probably combine a deliberate attempt to achieve a dramatic effect, and the genuine depression he still felt over the death of his wife, Virginia, in January 1847.

2. This should clear up any speculation—or at least some speculation—on the paternity of Poe's sister, Rosalie. Although he does not name the actual father, the implication is clear that he was someone other than David Poe. But what does he mean by the words concerning wine? Perhaps a "close friend" came to the young actress and in the guise of offering sympathy during one of her husband's drunken flights, plied her with wine and seduced her. This is certainly the implication.

3. This may well be a perfect example of Poe's exaggerations. There can be no doubt that he read Hakluyt at some time during his life. He was too voracious a reader to have missed that important work on the subject of exploration. It is doubtful, however, that he read it when he was this young.

4. Again the question arises: did Poe actually read the works he describes here and understand them as thoroughly as he claims? He may be telling the truth. After all, he was a genius. His education was far superior to that which

passes for it nowadays. That he was a precocious scholar has been more than verified. (See *Edgar Allan Poe, A Critical Biography* by Arthur H. Quinn. D. Appleton Century Co., New York, 1941. Chap. 3, p. 65.)

CHAPTER 2

1. The intensity with which Poe excoriates John Allan here and elsewhere is not entirely justified. As Poe himself acknowledges, Allan was beset with financial problems. His wife was in delicate health and in all probability incapable of indulging in a normal sex life. This can be one explanation for her childlessness and Allan's extramarital affairs. The love that Frances Keeling Allan lavished on young Edgar was needed and reciprocated, for John Allan was a reserved and undemonstrative Scot, a product of his time and culture. He regarded young Edgar's leanings toward poetry and romanticism as frivolous, even dangerous. Their constant bickering, Allan's constant reminders that his ward was fully dependent, was the early stage of a prolonged clash between two strong wills and opposing personalities. Had Poe given in to his guardian's wishes and behaved as an obedient son was expected to in those days, there is strong reason to believe that he might have been eventually named as John Allan's heir. That Allan was not hatching "insidious schemes and plots" against Poe at this time is supported by many biographers. Emile Lauvriere in *The Strange-Life and Loves of Edgar Allan Poe* [(English version trans. by Edwin Gile Rich), J. B Lippincott, Philadelphia, 1935] wrote, "With regard to these relations between Edgar Poe and Mr. Allan, which altogether were rather tense, most biographers make it their duty to exalt the great man at the expense of whoever finds himself in conflict with him. They prefer blind partiality of apology and even the delirious enthusiasm of dithyrambics to the simple or rather complex inquiry into real facts. So they blame heavily the cruel conduct of Mr. Allan in respect to his delicate ward of genius . . . If Mr. Allan took advantage in fixing Poe a career of his own choice, in seizing a favorable occasion to get rid of an ingrate, who had himself left him, after he had singularly deceived, cheated, and insulted him, was he more blameworthy than so many fathers of families in other respects rigorous to their own sons? We do not think so; we believe this the less that despite all these annoyances and a more or less justifiable antipathy, Mr. Allan never completely abandoned the being who had, in spite of everything, acquired indefeasible rights to his protection."

A clue to Allan's feelings for his rebellious charge can be found in a note written by him just six months after the death of Mrs. Stanard on the occasion of Lafayette's visit to Richmond. ". . . never was I prouder of him than when dressed in the uniform of the Junior Morgan Riflemen, he walked up and down in front of the marquee erected on the Capitol Square, under which the old general held a grand reception in October, 1824."

2. Although great strides had been made in the medical specialty one day to be called psychiatry, the term "insanity" was still an all-encompassing blanket obscuring too many corners. Thus, then, even more than today, "insanity" was a disgraceful condition. Even though it was recognized as a medical problem, there still lingered the pre-eighteenth-century concept that "insanity" was divine punishment for sin. It was regarded in much the same light as venereal disease. Although we don't know today precisely what caused Mrs. Stanard's death, judging by what little we can ascertain it is possible that she died of a brain tumor which caused outward manifestations of erratic behavior along with physical debilitation before death.

3. This orgasmic experience was clearly, by Poe's own description, non-genital. But it established in his mind a psycho-sexual precedent determining his entire future sexuality. Although some authorities have asserted that he was a sado-necrophile (see Marie Bonaparte, *The Life and Works of Edgar Allan Poe: A Psycho-Analytic Interpretation.* Imago, London, 1949), this is really an oversimplification. As Prof. Vladimir R. Piskacek, a psychiatrist on the staff of Cornell University Medical College has theorized, Poe was not sexually attracted to corpses *per se.* He was attracted to beautiful women. But he also knew, as did virtually everyone at that time, that sexual intercourse was potentially lethal to women. There was no antisepsis. Fifty percent of all pregnancies terminated in the death of the mother in childbirth. There was also the danger of venereal disease. Thus the prevalent taboos against sexual promiscuity of the day were founded on valid medical theory. Consequently, Poe, after having had this intense sexual experience at an early age, without being fully cognizant of what was happening to him, was never able to contemplate or enjoy a "normal" sexual encounter with a living woman. He loved them too much, he idealized them too much, he worshipped them as creatures who transcended ordinary mortality. Yet, knowing that they were mortal, knowing that by means of sexual intercourse with them he might be responsible for their premature deaths, he strenuously avoided it. However, when a woman was dying, his sexual desires were unconsciously aroused. When a woman he adored was dead, she was safe. He was safe from guilt were he to make love to her, for he had not been responsible for her death.

CHAPTER 3

1. On the surface this might appear to be a confession of drug use. It also appears to be one of those instances of Poe's romanticizing and exaggerating. When he refers to the "cup that brought dreamless oblivion," he is romanticizing the favorite drug of all Americans since earliest times—alcohol. His drinking problems are extensively documented in all the major biographies and reminiscences. The "ethereal trances" of opium to which he refers are partially wishful thinking and partially the result of extensive reading. Although tincture of opium

was easily obtainable, and quite legal in Poe's day, he was not addicted to it. He used it from time to time, in much the same way that some twentieth-century Americans occasionally take tranquilizers or sleeping pills. By his own admission Poe once swallowed two ounces of laudanum and became so ill that he threw it all up. More than one doctor who knew him—even one who had no great affection for him—testified that Poe was definitely never an opium addict.

2. This graphic description of his visit to Mrs. Stanard's grave clears up a point that has been troubling scholars for many years. Some believed that he did indeed go forth alone to "haunt" her grave; others considered the story apocryphal. He was known, however, to have visited the site with her son, Rob. That he also went there alone, we know now to be a fact.

3. This mention of passion and apprehension is a clear example of Poe's unconscious fear of a sexual relationship.

4. This is one of those vague statements that is difficult to verify. Poe makes no specific reference to what these slanderous statements were. He had a fairly good idea that Allan was partially responsible for alienating Elmira's parents. However it came about, the fact is known that Elmira's parents arranged a marriage for her with A. Barrett Shelton. It is also known that this marriage did not substantially diminish the affection Poe and Elmira felt for one another.

CHAPTER 4

1. Since there is no tangible evidence of any validity to this claim that Allan was scheming against his fifteen-year-old ward at this time, we must either assume that by the time he began writing this autobiography, Poe had convinced himself that this was true, or he was deliberately attempting to blacken the memory of his former guardian. Poe was impulsive, mercurial, passionate, and given to exaggeration. He also had no qualms about stretching the truth when he felt it would suit his purposes. But he was a decent person, and though quick to anger, was equally quick to forgive and make peace. He was not vicious. Therefore, he probably had a paranoid fixation which convinced him that everything he said about John Allan was true.

2. There is more truth in this statement about the relationship between Poe and Allan than in most of the others. It is almost as if Poe took time between the earlier parts of this section and this paragraph, mellowing somewhat in the process. Whatever the case, Poe craved love and affection, but he was driven by forces more powerful than his immediate needs. Allan was neither better nor worse than any foster parent of a brilliant, defiant, and exasperating teenager.

3. This apprehension is further indication of the terrible conflict Poe experienced when his normal sexual desires clashed with his unconscious fear of becoming the destroyer of his loved one should their love be consummated sexually.

307

CHAPTER 5

1. Placed in its proper perspective, this comment about a daily "exchange of acrimonious words" is probably quite valid, but overemphasized. Allan was still experiencing financial difficulties. He knew he would inherit a fortune when his uncle died, but there was no guarantee that the old man would not live to be a hundred. Allan was also probably concerned about the maintenance of his mistress and illegitimate son. Then there was the omnipresent specter of his wife's ill health. Though he was still fond of Edgar he was growing impatient with his adolescent ward's incessant defiance and elitist airs. Allan's continual reminders to young Poe of his humble origins were most likely meant to instill a proper respect, which he lacked. It probably galled Allan to recognize that in this brooding young genius was an aristocratic air that was not supposed to exist in the offspring of mere actors.

2. This work is regarded by medical scholars as the first serious treatise on psychosomatic medicine. It is very interesting to see that Poe recognized the possibility that Frances Keeling Allan's condition might have been psychosomatic in nature.

3. The Creon to whom Poe refers here is the mythical King of Thebes, brother of Jocasta, who condemned Antigone, daughter of Oedipus, to death.

4. These paranoid accusations that he was treacherously entrapped also point to the inventiveness of the creative genius's mind. He is correct in asserting that he did nothing more than behave in the manner to which he had been brought up. What he fails to state and/or realize is that he miscalculated the extent of his guardian's rigidity.

5. It is clear from this statement and corroboration by scholars that Allan did not regard Poe's attendance at the university as a matter to be taken lightly. Although there is ample evidence to indicate that he was more penurious than he should have been when it came to his ward, it is also possible that he honestly believed that austerity would be healthy for young Edgar. Unfortunately he was incapable of recognizing literary genius, and Poe was incapable of understanding how anyone could be so dense. Theirs was a perfect example of "the immovable object meeting the irresistible force."

6. Poe's propensity for enigmas is probably what kept him from being specific about the particular nature of these "more dangerous seductions." But it is safe to guess that they included English and French pornography, opium, and cannabis. The smoking of hemp was well known to affluent young Southerners of the day, for they learned about it from the slaves who were forbidden to drink alcohol.

7. Poggius, or Giovanni Francesco Poggio Bracciolini was the renaissance humanist and apostolic secretary responsible for the preservation of the lost plays of Plautus, the lost orations of Cicero, and many other works of scholarship. He was best known, however, for his *Facetiae*, the first collection of bawdy

stories in Western literature to become a best seller by virtue of its coinciding with the invention of movable type. He was also a master of the invective with such measured verbal acid as the following, written during a feud with his fellow humanist, Francesco Filelfo:

> *You stinking billy-goat, you horned monster, you*
> *malevolent vituperator, father of lies and author*
> *of chaos. . . . May Divine vengeance destroy you as*
> *an enemy of virtue, a parricide who tries to ruin*
> *wives and decency by mendacity, slanders, and most*
> *foul, false imputations. If you must be so scorn-*
> *fully arrogant, write your satires against those*
> *who debauch your wife. Vomit the putrescence of*
> *your stomach upon those who put horns on your*
> *forehead.*

This reference is typical of so many bits of arcana Poe loved to quote to demonstrate his immense erudition.

CHAPTER 6

1. Poe states that he "did not deduce the facts" until years later. Although he was a master of puzzle-solving as is evidenced by the fact that he is universally acknowledged as the father of the modern puzzle mystery story, the "facts" referred to here are purely supposition. He may be absolutely correct in his assumption. He was, however, a master at the choice of words, and had he had specific proof there is no doubt that he would have so stated.

2. "John Allan did not hate me": this is an interesting statement. After all the emphasis that has been placed on their animosity, this seems contradictory; yet it is probably closer to the truth. We must bear in mind that this manuscript was written in the period covering 1847 and 1848. All of Poe's *sturm und drang* vis-à-vis his relations with Allan is very likely retrospective amplification. It may also be a projection of Poe's own feelings after years of reliving painful experiences.

3. This is probably the most accurate appraisal of what Allan had in mind for his ward at that time. If Poe could be made to see the errors of his ways, abandon his foolish preoccupation with romantic nonsense, and assume the role of a productive Southern gentleman, he might yet become heir to the Allan estate.

4. This is extremely significant, although it is doubtful if he had any but the vaguest recollections of his mother, if any. But with the miniature he carried as a constant reminder, he created an idealized image of her in his mind. Bonaparte (see Bibliography) is certainly on the right track when she points out that all the women to whom Poe was attracted had dark hair, eyes, and pale

complexions. All of their photographs and paintings verify this, and certainly all Poe heroines fit that description. The miniature of his mother, Elizabeth Arnold, however, must have had an enormous effect on him, especially because of its unearthly quality.

5. This reference gives us a fascinating insight into some of Poe's early influences. His mind was like a sponge. Imagine, then, the lasting impression made upon him when as a child he was privy to the after-hours recreation of the blacks, to whose quarters he was taken by his "mammy," Judith. Few biographers give any significant attention to this phase of his development, which is a serious oversight, as his own words offer as proof. One writer, Frances Winwar (*The Haunted Palace*, Harper & Brothers, N.Y., 1959) had sufficient insight, when she wrote, "She [Judith] would carry him off to the servants' quarters and, of a winter's evening, as he grew older, he would sit spellbound at her knee among the Negroes and listen, half in wonder, half in terror, to the rich lore which the transplanted race had accumulated from native memories and the New World. Suffering, hardships, and death played their part in the tales and chants, as the narrators took turns telling what they had heard from the mouth of truth itself. The inborn genius of the Negro to dramatize lent reality to the most incredible tales and filled with 'haunts' and ghouls the receptive young mind, already predisposed to belief by the evidence of his own experience. Had he not perhaps witnessed, in an age when childhood was not spared the grim realities, the lowering of the coffin into that gaping hole in St. John's burial ground? Certainly, as a small boy, he had a horror of everything connected with death; but the horror also held its own kind of fascination, renewed each time his mammy took him walking under the old trees of St. John's."

Although Poe's use of the name Guede was slightly incorrect, it indicates a first-hand knowledge of ancient West African ritual that he probably witnessed as a child.

6. Historical records indicate that during the flogging of slaves, the victims frequently cried out, "More, master!" They dared not curse their oppressors, and rather than merely screaming in pain, they applied a kind of reverse psychology. By begging for more pain there was a good chance they might in reality receive less.

7. Sawney Beane was a Scottish highwayman and cannibal who was burned at the stake with his family in the fifteenth century. Jonathan Wild was an eighteenth-century London master criminal, one of the most successful fences in history, who frequently arranged the robberies. He hobnobbed with the rich and the powerful as well as the underworld until he slipped up and was hanged in 1725.

8. In voodoo, a *loa* is a spirit, who, when possessing a person behaves in a recognizable fashion enabling observers to call it by name. A *loa bossal* is a wild, or untamed spirit that has not been baptized.

CHAPTER 7

1. There is considerable consensus among biographers that at this stage Allan might well have been waging a war of attrition against his ward. He could not easily eject Poe from the house without making his wife more unhappy than she already was, but he could make life so miserable for the young man that he might leave of his own accord.

2. Legba and Agwé are gods from the Yoruba and Fon pantheon, having their origin in West Africa, principally from Togo, Benin, and Nigeria. Baka comes from the same culture. He is an evil spirit who manifests himself in the form of a black dog.

3. The mention of feeling mesmerized is very significant here. In all probability, some of the rituals he observed in the slave quarters as a child involved ceremonies where certain participants entered trance states, possibly as part of a healing ritual. It is possible that because of his highly impressionable state, he may have gone into the trance state himself on occasion. Certainly the imagery here, the evocation of Africa and its culture points to that.

4. The phrase "when I regained my senses" further strengthens the theory that he actually entered a trance state when recalling his experiences in the slave quarters. His earlier statement in which he recalls mesmeric chants that so entranced him may very well be taken at face value.

5. Although no correspondence between the two brothers during this period exists, Poe's statement here corroborates the theory that they were in contact.

6. Henry had visited the Allan household in Richmond, and was overwhelmed by its affluence.

7. Henry's concern for Edgar may very likely have stemmed from fears arising out of a letter he received from John Allan dated November 1, 1824, in which Allan says in part that Edgar "has had little else to do for me he does nothing & seems quite miserable, sulky & ill-tempered to all the family . . . The boy possesses not a Spark of affection for us not a particle of gratitude for all my care and kindness towards him. I have given [him] a much superior Education than ever I received myself . . ." Henry knew poverty all too well, and he did not want to see his brother throw away what he had. (Ellis-Allan Papers, Library of Congress, Poe Volume)

CHAPTER 8

1. One of the few tangible items Poe inherited from his real mother was an amateur painting of Boston harbor that she had once executed, and on the back of which was inscribed in her own hand an injunction to her son to "love Boston, the place of his birth, and where his mother found her best and

most sympathetic friends." (See Hervey Allen, *Israfel*, N.Y., 1926. Vol. 1, pg. 24.)

2. Allan's letter to Poe, dated March 20, 1827, was obviously in reply to Poe's first letter. Poe was incorrect in assuming it was a response to his second letter. Its tone was cool and devoid of emotion. It said in part: "I am not surprised at any step you may take, at anything you can say, or anything you may do, you are a much better judge of the propriety of your own conduct. . . . It is true and you will not deny it, that the charge of eating the Bread of Idleness, was to urge you to perseverance & industry in receiving the classics, in perfecting yourself in the mathematics, mastering the French, &c &c how far I succeeded in this you can best tell, but for one who had conceived so good an opinion of himself & his future intentions I hesitate not to say, that you have not evinced the smallest disposition to comply with my wishes, it is only on this subject I wish to be understood. . . . Your list of grievances require no answer the world will reply to them—& now that you have shaken off your dependance & declared for your own Independance—& after such a list of Black charges— you Tremble for the consequences unless I send you a supply of money." (Ellis-Allan Papers, Library of Congress, Poe Volume)

3. Poe's account of finding the bag of sovereigns in the tavern clears up a mystery that has puzzled scholars until now. There was never a clue as to how or where he obtained an amount of money sufficient to sustain him until he enlisted in the army in Boston. Poe's statement that the coins he found were worth approximately sixty dollars would indicate that the pouch contained exactly fifty-four sovereigns, for at the exchange rate of the day, the British sovereign was worth $1.11 U.S., and fifty-four would add up to exactly $59.94.

CHAPTER 9

1. More than one biographer asserts that the servant, Dabney Danbridge, carried "love notes" for Poe to a young lady somewhere nearby. Poe's statement that he was sending "some lines of verse" to a young woman who aspired to become a poet would refute this supposition. We can only speculate on how they knew each other. The fact that her name was Eulalie Elizabeth is interesting. In the early 1830s he wrote a sonnet, "Elizabeth," to his cousin Elizabeth Rebecca Herring, and for all we know, some lingering memory of this other Elizabeth might have remained in his mind. Regarding "Eulalie—A Song," there is no way of knowing if any connection existed at all. We must always remember that Poe never wrote a word of poetry without taking into consideration the way it sounded, and the euphony of Eulalie is obvious.

2. This verifies the supposition that Poe planted the seeds of rumors concerning his "exploits" in Europe before he even left Richmond. His manner of reaching Norfolk also explains why there has always been a question as to how he actually journeyed from Richmond to Norfolk.

3. *Ecarte* was a popular two-handed card game that Poe probably learned while at the University of Virginia.

CHAPTER 10

1. Whether or not she was telling him the truth, her statement that she had been orphaned "on the eve of her third year" clearly struck a responsive chord in Poe. That was the exact age at which he was orphaned.

2. The significance of this young woman's nom de plume is beyond question, for it explains where Poe derived the names of the title characters for two of his horror tales, *Ligeia* and *Morella*, the former, by his own admission, being one of his favorites.

3. This statement is another solid clue providing a key to the romantic, asexual quality of Poe's attachments to women.

4. Here is the first tangible explanation of how Poe first met Calvin F. S. Thomas, the young printer who published *Tamerlane and Other Poems*. This slim volume, which as Poe states, sold for twelve-and-a-half cents, is today one of the rarest and most sought-after nineteenth-century American books. In 1979, were a copy to be found, it would easily command a price in the neighborhood of $50,000.

5. Throughout his literary career Poe was an enthusiastic lecturer and "elocutionist." (See *The Histrionic Mr. Poe* by N. Bryllion Fagin, Johns Hopkins Press, Baltimore, 1949.)

6. This seems hard to believe. One would think he had seen or heard of *Fanny Hill* at the university. Being the consummate storyteller, he could conceivably have made this point here in order to emphasize the extremity of his unworldliness at this time of his life.

7. This is the most recurring theme in Poe's literary depiction of love, and of course, it reflects his own nature. Unfortunately, the muse Erato, patroness of love poetry, exacted a harsh tribute from him instead of exerting the "gentle influence" he so desired.

8. No doubt when he recovered from the initial shock of what had taken place that terrible night, Poe began scanning the local newspapers to see what would be written about the young woman's tragic death. The journals of the day were given to even more purple prose than our most outrageous contemporary scandal sheets. Evidence of this fact may be found in the following, a newspaper clipping found in the box containing the original manuscript pages of *My Savage Muse*. It was extremely difficult to read in spots because of partial decay and moisture damage. The date was illegible, but judging by the spacing, it was a single digit, indicating that the date was probably April 9, placing the date of the slaying itself on April 6. The newspaper story says "on Friday"

which is our clue. In 1827, April 6 fell on a Friday, a date which would certainly fit in with Poe's arrival in Boston from Norfolk.

From *The Boston Post*, April [?], 1827:

Most Atrocious Murder

The good name of our fair city was besmirched on Friday by a foul murder more properly belonging to the licentious environs of Paris than of these hallowed regions where once the noble blood of American Patriots flowed in defence of freedom. The following are the circumstances as best we can ascertain them.

The deceased, Miss Amelia Blackburn, better known to denizens of the demimonde as Nelly Flowers, was a notorious courtezan [sic] who dispensed her favours in the taverns and grog shops frequented by seafaring men in the vicinity of the Haymarket. On the night of her demise, Miss Blackburn returned to her lodgings on Commercial Street, in a house kept by Mrs. Hester Markham, formerly a common demirep in the notorious establishment of Mrs. Susan "Little Belt" Bryant, of whom the less said the better. It is definitely known that Miss Blackburn entered her rooms in the company of a "gentleman" considerably after the hour of midnight, having been observed by another occupant of the house who assigned that particular social status to the alleged assassin on the basis of his fashionable attire.

What matters transpired between Miss Blackburn and her "gentleman" can only be surmised, and we hesitate to proffer any theories thereof. Let it suffice to say that after a brief period of tranquillity the clamour of strident voices was overheard issuing from the chambers of the unfortunate young woman, a clamour that was dismissed by those who heard it as nothing more than a drunken exchange of base passions quite commonplace within the walls of Mrs. Hester Markham's house.

Once again, our informants tell us, a period of calm descended upon the premises and no further thought was given to the intimate transactions taking place behind the closed doors of Miss Blackburn's quarters. We must now concentrate our attentions on the events of the following day. As you may surmise, the nature of the nocturnal activities in the house of Mrs. Markham preclude any possibility of early retiring and rising of its inhabitants. Indeed, according to those familiar with the customs of the demimonde, it is a rare occasion when its denizens relinquish the tender embrace of Morpheus before the sun has reached its zenith.

So matters stood in Mrs. Markham's venereal fiefdom on the fateful day after the crime. By early afternoon the house was abustle with activity, preparations being in progress for the weekly Saturnalia which is said to have no rivals in this city insofar as the extent of the debaucheries are concerned. Approximately an hour before dusk, it being observed that Miss Blackburn had not yet descended from her chambers, Mrs. Markham dispatched Miss Augusta Powell, one of her younger boarders, to summon the sleeping Cyprian and bid her make ready for the anticipated revels of the evening.

One can imagine the emotion of icy terror that gripped the heart of this young woman, scarcely more than a child, when she crossed the threshold of that heavily curtained room and beheld in its gloomy recesses the awful spectacle of her unfortunate sister in degradation lying lifeless upon the chaise, her mouth agape, and an ornate, blood-stained Florentine dagger lying on the floor below. Her once warm and palpitating breast was still, and marked by an ugly wound.

Uttering a single piercing scream, Miss Powell fled from the apartment of the deceased and stumbled down the staircase whereupon she flung herself into the arms of the startled Mrs. Markham, to whom she related the nature of her dreadful discovery, sobbing piteously all the while.

It was our solemn duty to attend the scene of the crime and glean the pertinent facts in order that the public be properly informed of all the sordid details. Nothing is known of the identity of the assassin himself save that the wretch was garbed as a gentleman and that in his haste to flee from the chamber of his unfortunate victim he left behind a single black kid glove.

Miss Blackburn was laid to rest in Potter's Field on Sunday following a simple service at the North Church attended by a number of Boston's most prominent Aspasians,* gentlemen of the press, and representatives of the police.

[Susan "Little Belt" Bryant, mentioned in the newspaper article, was one of those notorious characters of nineteenth-century America whose activities were considered so scandalous that they were excluded even from the folklore. Mrs. Bryant acquired her nickname, it is said, during the days when she was a popular Boston prostitute. According to the legend, the entire crew of a British warship, *The Little Belt*, visited her and personally enjoyed her favors in a single night.]

CHAPTER 11

1. The mystery to which he alludes was inextricably tied to the conflicts, the desires, the insecurities, and the frustrations that plagued Poe's personal life. The Freudians make a strong case of the unconscious wish fantasies concerning his dead mother. The theory that he unconsciously wished to be reunited with her and was therefore attracted to women who resembled her is not implausible. The theory that he refrained from sexual activity unconsciously fearing to violate an incest taboo, seems a bit too much to accept. The matter of this mystery, however, is discussed by Bonaparte (Book II, pg. 209) when she writes: "Baudelaire has observed that love, as such, plays no part in Poe's tales. 'Mrs. Frances Osgood's idea of Poe's chivalrous respect for women,' he writes, 'is

---

*Archaic euphemism for prostitute

corroborated by the fact that, in spite of his phenomenal skill in portraying the grotesque and horrible, there is never in his work one passage that might be called licentious, nor one that deals with sensuous pleasures. All his women, as it were, are drawn wearing haloes; they shine through a supernatural aura, and are strikingly delineated as though by an adorer.' An adorer, we might add, who dare not approach the object of his adoration, since he feels it surrounded by some *fearful, dangerous mystery."* [Italics mine]

2. For Poe to quote Macha [1810-1836] is quite remarkable, for it is doubtful that the Bohemian poet was translated into English during Poe's lifetime since they were roughly contemporaries. In all likelihood, Poe read Macha in German some years later, but in writing his memoir placed these lines at a point in time he felt appropriate. It is also interesting that he would be drawn to the writings of someone who expressed a sentiment akin to existentialism a century early.

3. Although little is known of Calvin F.S. Thomas, it is worth noting that he did enjoy a long and productive career as a printer and publisher. (See *Edgar Allan Poe* by Arthur Hobson Quinn, Appleton-Century, New York, 1941. Chap. VI, pg. 122, f.n. 7.)

4. This is one of the many offhand references pointing to the fact that in truth Poe was a staunch elitist. It is to his credit that though he was very much a snob, he took pains to cover up the tendency.

5. The publication was mentioned by two magazines: *The United States Review and Literary Gazette*, August 1827; and *The North American Review*, XXV, 47. October 1827. Neither, however, made critical comments. (See Quinn, Chap. VI, pg. 128.)

6. This revealing necrophilic-sadistic fantasy may well suggest that had Poe not been able to sublimate his darker impulses in literature he might have channelled them into frightful, anti-social acts.

CHAPTER 12

1. It was during this period that Poe underwent considerable ferment. Under the tutelage of Ravanel he obviously learned a great deal about natural history. With all the free time he had, his voracious reading was extensive. His romantic imagination was certainly sparked by legends of buried pirates' treasure. With his photographic memory and sponge-like mind he absorbed impressions that fueled his genius in years to come. He also, very obviously, became more interested than ever in the other sciences, but he had mixed feelings. His sonnet, "To Science," which was written during this period, definitely illustrates that he possessed a streak of prophetic vision. The sentiments he expresses presage the very omnipresent ills of the late twentieth century being attacked by contemporary environmentalists.

2. It has been suggested that one of these old Carolina mansions might have provided inspiration for the physical description of the "melancholy House of Usher."

3. This traumatic experience could certainly explain, in part, Poe's fears concerning premature burial. It could also offer a clue to the thought process leading to some of the plot elements of *The Fall of the House of Usher*, specifically the premature burial of Lady Madeline.

CHAPTER 13

1. The Charleston newspapers at the time were *The City Gazette, The Charleston Courier, The Charleston Mercury, the Southern Patriot*, and *The Southern Intelligencer*. There can be no question that Poe was familiar with all of them.

2. This casual recollection would clearly indicate that point in time when Poe first developed his deep interest in cryptography, which manifested itself so prominently in *The Gold Bug*.

3. Keeping such thoughts to himself must have been especially difficult for, as we know today, Poe was in many ways a thoroughgoing rebel at heart.

4. Here again Poe displays his prophetic vision. From his vantage point he could foresee the devastating effects of progress on nature. This is especially evident in the last six lines of his "Sonnet—To Science."

> *Hast thou not dragged Diana from her car?*
> *And driven the Hamadryad from the wood*
> *To seek a shelter in some happier star?*
> *Hast thou not torn the Naiad from her flood,*
> *The elfin from the green grass, and from me*
> *The summer dream beneath the tamarind tree?*

5. Anthropological and psychiatric studies have explored this subject extensively. The use of the trance in healing is extensive, and Poe's speculation on the subject is correct. (See *The Artful Healing of the African Witch Doctor* by B. J. Hurwood, *Washington Post*, August 13, 1978.)

6. Poe refers here to his horrific tale, *Facts in the Case of M. Valdemar*. In the story, the subject, M. Valdemar, is hypnotized while terminally ill. He dies, but remains in the trance state, answering, when asked, in an unearthly voice, "I am dead." When finally brought out of the trance, months after his death, the narrator says, "As I rapidly made the mesmeric passes, amid ejaculations of 'dead! dead!' absolutely *bursting* from the tongue and not from the lips of the sufferer, his whole frame at once—within the space of a single minute, or even less,—shrunk—crumbled—absolutely *rotted* away beneath my hands. Upon

317

the bed, before that whole company, there lay a nearly liquid mass of loathsome, of detestable putrescence."

So realistic was this story that it was taken seriously and accepted as fact in England, where it was reprinted as a pamphlet entitled, *Mesmerism, "In Articulo Mortis," An Astounding and Horrifying Narrative. Shewing the Extraordinary Power of Mesmerism in Arresting the Progress of Death.* By Edgar A. Poe, Esq. of New York [London, 1846, Price threepence].

In a letter dated Dec. 30, 1846, to a correspondent named Arch Ramsay, Poe wrote.

Dr Sir,

"Hoax" is precisely the word suited to M. Valdemar's case. The story appeared originally in "The American Review," a Monthly Magazine, published in this city [New York]. The London papers, commencing with the "Morning Post" and the "Popular Record of Science," took up the theme. The article was generally copied in England and is now circulating in France. Some few persons believe it but I do not, and don't you.

Very Resp[y]
Yr Ob. S[t]

Edgar A. Póe

7. Certainly the impressionists of the nineteenth and twentieth centuries, and especially the abstract expressionists would applaud Poe for this sentiment. One wonders, is it possible that Picasso may have read this statement of Poe's before he said, "The art is a lie which tells the truth."

8. It has been generally agreed upon by the Poe experts that the poet's "lost Lenore" was Elmira Royster Shelton. However, he always idealized the objects of his romantic adoration by assigning them alliterative or euphonious names. It is quite possible, then, even though he doesn't say so here, that Berger's *Lenore* inspired him at least to use the name.

9. This error in judgment, that he could breeze through the U.S. Military Academy in less than the prescribed period of time was a major one. It is very likely that had he known the facts he would never have sought the appointment.

10. It is interesting to note that earlier, when Poe was convinced the break with Allan was permanent, he refers to him as his "former guardian," but the moment he felt a reconciliation was possible he reverted to "guardian."

11. Allan was suffering from dropsy [edema] as the condition was called in those days. In his case it manifested itself as a painful swelling of the legs due to the accumulation of excessive water. Not recognized as a symptom of something more serious, the "dropsy" was regarded as a disease in itself. Although we cannot be certain precisely what killed Allan, judging by the symptoms, he was

suffering from a liver malfunction, heart disease, or both. Often, when edema manifests itself as it did in Allan's case, it may be related to congestive heart failure.

CHAPTER 14

1. Psychologists have often pointed out that the earlier years in our lives, the formative years, are invariably more memorable. Whether happy and secure or unhappy and insecure, children are less aware of their own mortality and the passage of time appears to be of much greater duration. The older we grow, the faster we seem to be rushing through our temporal journey.

2. In one of his critical essays, Poe wrote, "I believe it is Montaigne who says 'People talk about thinking, but, for my part, I never begin to think until I sit down to write.' A better plan for him would have been never to sit down to write until he had made an end of thinking."

3. One letter was written on December 22, 1828 and the other on February 4, 1829. (See John Ostrom, *The Letters of Edgar Allan Poe*, Harvard University Press, Cambridge, Mass., 1948, Vol. I, pp. 11-14.)

4. Until now there was nothing on record to indicate the content of Allan's letter summoning Poe to his dying foster mother's bedside. Its combination of cool formality of style with urgency of content is typical of Allan's correspondence.

5. Miss Valentine had to express her feelings to someone, and obviously she could not do so to John Allan. Her position in his household was a fragile one, for she was totally dependent upon his charity.

6. This sentiment is one of the most important underlying themes in Poe's psychodynamics, one of the great sources of his *angst*, a desire to be reunited with the departed loved one.

7. Unconsciously Allan probably felt that Poe's presence at this time symbolized defeat in their personal, ongoing rivalry and battle of wills. More important, however, by keeping Poe away, Allan was able to cling to the futile conviction that his wife would recover. Also, the closer she came to death, the more guilt he most likely felt about his own infidelities, and of them, because he was aware of them, Poe was a constant reminder.

8. This represents another of the *leitmotifs* running through Poe's writing, an unconscious fear that he was in some mysterious way responsible for the death of his real mother. His unfortunate accident involving the death of the prostitute in Boston reinforced this feeling, and now, with the death of Frances Allan, the fear surfaced.

9. Nancy Valentine's personal grief notwithstanding, she knew where her security lay, and knowing Poe's mercurial nature all too well, her own

practical nature prompted her to give what she regarded as extremely sound advice.

10. Actually John Allan was forty-seven when his wife died, but Poe had a tendency to add or subtract years when it suited him.

11. The stanza from *The Sleeper*, Poe claimed to have written when he was a boy. (See Ostrom, Vol. II, pg. 232, letter dated Dec. 15, 1846 to George W. Eveleth.)

CHAPTER 15

1. The message read: "Mr. Ellis—Please furnish Edgar A. Poe with a suit of clothes, 3 pairs of socks or thread hose. McCrery will make them. Also a pair of suspenders, and hat and knife, pair of gloves." (See *Israfel*, Vol. I, Chap. 12, f.n. 318, pg. 232.)

2. Psychiatric studies have indicated that death does not necessarily terminate a deep and strong relationship. Consciously or unconsciously, the survivor often keeps it very much alive. Poe was a prime example of such an individual.

3. Some biographers, notably Hervey Allen (*Israfel*, Vol. 1, Chap. 12, pg. 234) assert that Poe did indeed pay a visit to the Roysters, during which time a bitter scene ensued. This, of course, is all based on unconfirmed reports, and Poe's own account would indicate that such an encounter never took place.

4. The order was actually dated April 4, 1829, but we must remember that Eastern Department Headquarters was in New York. It must have taken at least three or four days for the order to travel by sea from there to Fortress Monroe. Poe's discharge date was set on the fifteenth of the month to give him the advantage of an additional week's pay.

5. The regimental NCOs knew him only as Edgar A. Perry.

6. Letters were written by Lt. J. Howard, Poe's company commander, Capt. H.W. Griswold, Regimental Adjutant, and Lt. Col. W.J. Worth, Commandant of Fortress Monroe.

7. In his letter, Lt. Col. Worth, not only attested to Poe's good conduct and superior qualities as an enlisted man, but he wrote, "Understanding he is thro' friends, an applicant for cadet's warrant, I unhesitatingly recommend him as promising to aquit [sic] himself of the obligations of that station studiously and faithfully." (See Quinn, Chap. VI, pg. 136.) It is also worth noting that all three officers providing Poe with letters of endorsement used his real name, Edgar A. Poe, rather than the alias of Perry, under which he had enlisted and subsequently served.

NOTES

CHAPTER 16

1. In addition to the letters written by Poe's officers he collected an impressive array of references. They included Judge John T. Barber of Richmond; Major John Campbell, a friend of his foster father; Andrew Stevenson, Speaker of the House of Representatives; and James P. Preston, the congressman from Richmond.

2. Eaton, a former senator from Tennessee, an extremely powerful man in the Jackson administration, was connected with many of the scandals that rocked it, not the least of which was one allegedly involving his wife.

3. Allan's letter said in part: "The youth who presents this . . . left me in consequence of some gambling debts at the University at Charlottesville, because (I presume) I refused to sanction a rule that the shopkeepers and others had adopted there, making debts of honour of all indiscretions . . . Frankly, sir, do I declare that he is no relation to me whatsoever; that I have many whom I have taken an active interest to promote theirs, with no other feeling than that, every man is my care, if he be in distress. For myself I ask nothing, but I do request your kindness to aid this youth in the promotion of his interests." One can imagine Poe's sentiments upon reading this letter, which was hardly a document overflowing with warmth and generosity.

4. This expression was an unfortunate miscalculation based purely on wishful thinking.

5. "Owing to the development of ship canals between it [Baltimore] and Philadelphia, and the building of the Baltimore and Ohio Railroad, it was like many other American towns of the time, just entering upon a period of surprising enterprise. Along with this there was a considerable publishing business of newspapers and more or less intermittent periodicals sponsored by various literary groups." (*Israfel*, Vol. 1, pg. 317.)

6. The Washington Monument in Baltimore as described by Poe was either just finished or close to completion. Construction began in 1815 and was completed in 1829.

7. Wirt had known Poe's grandfather and probably young Poe himself while the poet was a student at the university. It was at that time Wirt was offered the institution's presidency. (Quinn, Chap. 7, pg. 138.)

8. Preston was the father of one of Poe's boyhood schoolmates, and he had read a good deal of the youthful poet's early works. The letter, dated May 13, 1829, said:

Sir: Some of the friends of young Mr. Edgar Poe have solicited me to address a letter to you in his favour, believing that it may be useful to him in his application to the government for military service. I know Mr. Poe and am acquainted with the fact of his having been born under circumstances of great adversity. I also know from his own productions and other undoubted proofs that he is a young gentleman of genius and taleants [sic]. I believe he is destined to be distinguished, since he has already gained reputation for taleants [sic] and attainements [sic] at the university of Virginia. I think him possessed of feeling and character peculiarly intitling [sic] him to public patronage.

Very respectfully your obt., serv't,
JAMES P. PRESTON

9. This is obviously a Latin paraphrase of Ceasar's immortal *"Veni, vedi, vinci"* ("I came, I saw, I conquered"). By adding two words, Poe tells us, "I came, I saw, but I did not conquer."

10. The letter said in part: "I am aware of the difficulty of getting a poem published in this country.... The cost of publishing the work, in a style equal to any of our American publications, will at the extant be $100—this then, of course, must be the limit of any loss supposing not a single copy of the work be sold. It is more than probable that the work will be profitable & that I may gain instead of lose, even in a pecuniary way." (Ostrom, Vol. 1, pg. 19, letter #13.)

11. He is obviously referring here to his aunt Maria Clemm, who, though she eventually proved to be one of the most important women in his life, had not yet stepped into the spotlight.

12. There is some disagreement among biographers as to the cousin's name. Some call him James Mosher Poe and others Edward Mosher Poe. His act of thievery seems to be his only claim to fame.

13. It is well known today that Poe had no qualms about altering the truth to suit his needs. One of the greatest mistakes he ever made in his life was telling John Allan at this time that he had indeed paid the fifty dollars he owed to Sergeant Graves. It was an understandable mistake, however. What little money he had was barely enough to subsist on, and it was sheer need to survive that motivated the lie.

14. Mrs. Clemm eventually assumed the role of mother to Poe, and mother-in-law as well. There is a great deal of controversy about her, but one thing is certain: as his health and financial woes worsened, without her he might never have survived as long as he did.

15. He was so accustomed to calling her by the pet name "Muddy," which he picked up from Virginia, that he probably slipped and used the familiar term here while writing; then, thinking better of it afterward, crossed it out. This is how the handwritten line appeared.

16. There has been controversy as to Poe's exact whereabouts during this period. If we can rely on the veracity of the narrative, then he was

in Mrs. Clemm's house during the time prior to his appointment to West Point.

17. Neal wrote: "If E.A.P. of Baltimore—whose lines about 'Heaven' though he professes to regard them as altogether superior to anything in the whole range of American poetry, save two or three trifles referred to, are, though nonsense, rather exquisite nonsense—would but do himself justice [he] might make a beautiful and perhaps a magnificent poem. There is a good deal here to justify such hope." (Quinn, Chap. VII, f.n. 21, pg. 152.)

18. By "minor" Poe did not mean of lesser importance, but of shorter length. *Al Aaraaf*, for example, ran in the neighborhood of three hundred lines, and *Tamerlane* approximately four hundred.

19. These "advantageous" terms meant that the publisher paid the costs of printing and marketing, and gave Poe 250 copies to distribute as he pleased. There is no record of any royalties being paid.

20. In his preface, Neal said, "The following passages are from the manuscript—works of a young author, about to be published in Baltimore. He is entirely a stranger to us, but with all their faults, if the remainder of 'Al Aaraaf' and 'Tamerlane' are as good as the body of the extracts here given—to say nothing of the more extraordinary parts, he will deserve to stand high—very high—in the estimation of the shining brotherhood. Whether he *will* do so, however, must depend, not so much upon his worth now in mere poetry, as upon his worth hereafter in something yet loftier and more generous—we allude to the stronger properties of the mind, to the magnanimous determination that enables a youth to endure the present, whatever the present may be, in the hope or rather the belief, the fixed, unwavering belief, that in the future he will find his reward . . ." (Quinn, Chap. VII, pg. 153). Such advance notice of the book in so prestigious a literary periodical assured a substantial sale of the poems once they appeared. Such matters have not changed radically in American publishing.

21. One of the most fascinating sidelights of the Poe-Allan relationship is the fact that Allan once openly admitted that he wished he possessed the ability to write. In a letter to James Nimmo, a cousin of his wife's, Allan wrote on October 14, 1814, in part, "Now, my dear sir, these things called privations—starvations—taxations—and, lastly, vexations, show the very age and figure of the times—their form and pre-sure, as Shakespeare says,—and he was a tolerable judge. *Gods! what I would give, if I had his talent for writing! and what use would I not make of the raw material at my command!*" (Italics mine.) Under the circumstances, one would imagine that he would have encouraged his ward's literary aspirations. On the other hand, was he so envious of Poe's talent—a talent he knew that he would never have—that he did all within his power to discourage it? Unfortunately, we can only guess.

CHAPTER 17

1. These tales included accounts of traveling about England, France, Russia, and South America. One story in particular involved Poe's having been arrested in St. Petersburg and rescued by the American minister to the Imperial Russian Court, Henry Middleton. This story was given such wide circulation that at least one version of it turned up in a Russian encyclopedia years later. Some biographers have speculated on how Poe could have known the identity of that official without actually having been to Russia. The most logical explanation would seem to be that he read it in the City Directory of Charleston, South Carolina. In the front of that book is a comprehensive list of every U.S. government official from the President down. Middleton's name is included.

2. The Mackenzies were friends of the Allans, and the family who adopted Poe's sister, Rosalie, at the time he was taken in by the Allans.

3. This is either pure supposition, or biased opinion. It is more likely the latter. Poe's deep attachment to Frances Allan was such that the thought of anyone—especially her sister—taking her place would have been unthinkable to him. Thus, even the most formal and decorous sort of courting on Allan's part would have appeared thoroughly indecent to Poe.

4. Allan wrote his formal letter of permission consenting to his ward's entering West Point on March 31, 1830 as follows:

Sir: As the guardian of Edgar Allan Poe, I hereby assent to his signing articles by which he shall bind himself to Serve the United States for Five Years, unless sooner discharged, as stipulated in your official letter appointing him cadet.

Respectfully,

The Hon. Sec'y of War
Washington

Your obt. servant
John Allan

5. There is something strange about this entire description. Tradition has it that what actually took place was far more acrimonious, that it was another of the old shouting matches in which Allan went back to his usual habit of attacking Poe for his idleness and casting aspersions on his ancestry. Further indications that this alleged interchange between the two is less than true is borne out in a letter Poe wrote to Allan more than six months later, when the fateful letter he wrote to his old army comrade came back to haunt him. Poe wrote in part: "As regards Sergt. Graves—I *did* write him that letter. As to the truth of the contents, I leave it to God and your own conscience.—The time in which I wrote it was within a half hour after you had embittered every feeling of my heart against you by your abuse of my *family* and myself under your own roof—and at a time when you knew my heart was almost breaking . . ." (Ostrom, Vol. I, pp. 39-43, Letter #28 dated January 3, 1831). Allan may have been drunk during that confrontation. He had good reason. Not only was he in poor health, but his mistress, Mrs. Wills, gave birth to twins on July 1, 1830. Since Poe makes no specific reference to any accusations or

reproaches relating to his family, we can only assume that whatever took place, he had strong personal reasons to alter the facts for the sake of posterity—reasons he chose to keep hidden.

CHAPTER 18

1. Some accounts state that Poe arrived at West Point on June 25, 1830. Apparently he did not.

2. This statement typifies Poe's feelings of elitism and intellectual snobbery. Clearly his concept of illiteracy embraced those without much learning in addition to those who could not read at all.

3. He is obviously referring to Shakespeare's line in *Julius Caesar*, when Caesar refers to Cassius as having "a lean and hungry look" (Act I, Scene 2).

4. Benny Haven's was a tavern immortalized in song and West Point lore. A hangout where cadets indulged in clandestine drinking and carousing, it was also an illicit trading post. It was with Benny they exchanged blankets and other personal possessions for food, drink, and sometimes cash.

5. According to one of Poe's former barracks mates, Col. Timothy Pickering Jones (*New York Sun*, May 10, 1903 and May 29, 1904): "Poe would form a dislike to a man and his hatred was deep and unreconcilable. There was one of the teachers there, Professor Locke, who hated Poe, and the spirit of uncongeniality was mutual. It was Locke whom Poe on one occasion attempted to throw down a sixty-foot embankment in the dead hours of the night into the Hudson River. This was when he was returning from Old Benny's late one night, thoroughly intoxicated and imbued with the idea that Locke had done him some injustice. It was one of the most trying efforts of my life to prevent Poe from doing this terrible deed." Although Colonel Jones's statement is undoubtedly accurate insofar as its description of Poe's feelings about Joseph Locke is concerned, it is typical of the apocryphal tales spread by others. It is highly unlikely that Poe ever attempted to do anything of the sort to the unpopular lieutenant. If he had, we can be sure that his court martial would have come much earlier, and been of a serious nature. He probably once mentioned to Jones that he would have liked to throw Locke into the river. It is also worth speculating on another point. If Jones was seventeen at the time he was Poe's barracks mate, he would have been ninety when the article appeared in the *New York Sun*. It is conceivable that some of his facts might have gotten fuzzy by then.

6. An account of a typical one of these pranks (if true) comes from the pen of another Poe barracks mate, Thomas W. Gibson, quartered in the notorious room 28, South Barracks (*Harper's Magazine*, Nov. 1867). According to this account, the three roommates drew straws one night to see who would sneak out to Benny Haven's and do a little trading. The short straw went to Gibson, who

succeeded in exchanging some candles and blankets for a bottle of brandy and a live gander. It was such a noisy old bird that Gibson had Benny chop off its head before he returned to the barracks. The night was dark, wet, and cold. Nipping at the bottle as he trudged through the mud, Gibson flung the dead bird first over one shoulder, then over the other, observing afterwards that, as a consequence, "not only my shirt front, but my face and hands were as bloody as the entire contents of the old gander's veins and arteries could make them." By prearrangement, when Gibson returned (there was also a visitor from North Barracks in their room) he and Poe tied the bird up into a tight bundle to disguise its true nature. Gibson continues: "Poe had taken his seat, and pretended to be absorbed in the mysteries of *Leçons Française*. Laying the gander down outside the door, I walked, or rather staggered, into the room, pretending to be very drunk, and exhibiting in clothes and face a spectacle not often seen off stage. 'My God, what has happened?' exclaimed Poe, with well-acted horror.

"'Old K*____, old K____!' I repeated several times, and with gestures intended to be savage.

"'Well, what of him?' asked Poe.

"'He won't stop me on the road any more!'—and I produced a large knife that we had stained with the few drops of blood that remained in the gander. 'I have killed him.'

"'Nonsense,' said Poe. 'you are only trying one of your tricks on us.'

"'I didn't suppose you would believe me,' I replied, 'so I cut off his head and brought it into the barracks. Here it is!'—and walking out the door, I caught the gander by the legs, and giving it one fearful swing about my head, dashed it at the only candle in the room, and left them all in the darkness with what two of them believed to be the head of one of the professors. The visitor leaped through the window and alighted in the slop tub, and made fast time for his own room in the North Barracks, spreading as he went the report that I had killed old K____, and that his head was there in Number 28. The story gained credence, and for a time the excitement in the barracks ran high. When we lit the candle again, 'Old P,' [Pickering Jones] was sitting in the corner, a blank picture of horror, and it was some time before we could restore him to reason."

7. The rumors were, of course, accounts of his "foreign travels" and his supposed descent from Benedict Arnold.

8. Poe's anguished letter to John Allan of January 3, 1831 speaks for itself. Poe wrote in part:

Did I, when an infant sollicit [sic] your charity and protection, or was it of your own free will that you volunteered your services on my behalf? It is well known to respectable individuals in Baltimore, and elsewhere, that my grandfather (my natural protector at the

---

*An unpopular professor.

time you interposed) was wealthy, and that I was his favorite
grandchild—but the promises of adoption, and liberal education
which you held forth to him in a letter which is now in possession
of my family, induced him to resign all care of me into your hands.
Under such circumstances, can it be said that I have no *right* to
expect anything at your hands?
You may probably urge that you have given me a liberal education. I
will leave the decision of that question to those who know how far
liberal educations can be obtained in 8 months at the University of Va.
Here you will say that it was my own fault that I did not return. You
would not let me return because bills were presented to you for payment
which I never wished nor desired you to pay. Had you let me return, my
reformation had been sure—as my conduct the last 3 months gave every
reason to believe. You would never have heard more of my
extravagances. But I am not about to proclaim myself guilty of all that
has been alledged [sic] against me, and which I have hitherto endured,
simply because I was too proud to reply. I will boldly say that it was
wholly and entirely your own mistaken parsimony that caused all the
difficulties in which I was involved while at Charlotte[s]ville .... If I
had been the vilest wretch on earth you could not have been more
abusive than you were because I could not contrive to pay $150 with
$110.... But books must be had, if I intended to remain at the
institution—and they were bought accordingly *upon credit*. In this
manner debts were accumulated ... for I was obliged to hire a servant,
to pay for wood, for washing, and a thousand other services. It was then
I became dissolute, for how could it be otherwise? I could associate with
no students, except those who were in a similar situation with myself—
altho' from different causes—they from drunkenness, and extravagance,
I, because it was my crime to have no one on Earth who cared for me,
or loved me. I call to God to witness that I have never loved dissipation.
Those who know me know that my pursuits and habits are very far from
anything of the kind. But I was drawn into it by my companions[.] Even
their professions of Friendship—hollow as they were—were a relief. ... I
then became desperate, and gambled—until I finally i[n]volved myself
irretrievably. If I have been to blame in all this, place yourself in my
situation, and tell me if you would not have been equally so. ... You
promised to forgive all—but you soon forgot your promise. You sent me
to W. Point l[ike a beggar]. The same difficulties are threatening me as
before at [Charlottesville]—and I must resign. As to your injunction not
to trouble you with further communication rest assured, Sir, that I will
most religiously observe it. (For complete letter and notes, see Ostrom,
Vol. I, pp. 39-43, letter #28.)

A meticulous record keeper, John Allan wrote the following endorsement on
Poe's letter when he received it:

"I rec'd this on the 10th and did not from its conclusion deem it necessary to reply. I made this note on the 13th and can see no good reason to alter my opinion. I do not think the boy has one good quality. He may do or act as he pleases, tho' I would have saved him but on his own terms and conditions since I cannot believe a word he writes. His letter is the most bare-faced one-sided statement."

John Allan's syntax is confusing to the modern reader. What he means is that he would have supported Poe, but not on Poe's terms.

CHAPTER 19

1. The date mentioned here was clearly February 21, 1831, the day he wrote the letter in question to John Allan (Ostrom, letter #29, p. 43).

2. *Bios Theoreticus* is best described by the late Czech critic and literary historian, F. X. Salda, who wrote in *The Alchemy of Modern Poetry*: "*Bios Theoreticus*, the life of contemplation, is the realm of poetry, and its main principle is the human quest for transcendental beauty." (F.X.S. Zapisnik #3, 1930-31, Prague, translated by Vladimir R. Piskacek.)

3. According to the *Baltimore American* of Tuesday, August 2, 1831, Henry Poe died on August 1. Whatever is the correct date of his death, his funeral was on August 2.

4. Henry Herring, who had married Poe's aunt Eliza Poe, was a well-to-do Baltimore lumber merchant. His house was a gathering place for a local literati, and Poe spent a fair amount of time there himself, where he enjoyed a mild flirtation with his cousin Elizabeth.

5. This is a fascinating statement, referring to opium as "heroic." Many years later, when medical researchers at the Bayer pharmaceutical company in Germany first synthesized diacetylmorphine hydrochloride, they were so impressed with its analgesic, anti-tussive, and euphoric qualities, they pronounced it to be *"heroische"* or heroic, and promptly named it heroin, under the misapprehension that it was not habit-forming as was its first cousin, morphine.

6. Although there is ample external proof that Poe never became addicted to opium, there is at the same time unassailable evidence that he used it occasionally, and was well acquainted with its effects. Frances Winwar wote: "Poe's visions, sublimated into his works, from now on revealed the unmistakable characteristics of the opium dream. As such they were recognized in Poe's day by Dr. John Carter, later by that connoisseur of the drug, Charles Baudelaire, and admitted with reluctant yet admirable candor by the poet's biographer, George F. Woodberry, who concluded his findings: 'No candid mind can exclude the suggestion . . . of its share in the morbid

side of Poe's life.' " (Frances Winwar, *The Haunted Palace*, Chap. XIV, p. 165.)

CHAPTER 20

1. So vicious were Poe's literary diatribes, his publishers often printed disclaimers when they felt the need to fend off potential lawsuits. As a result, a number of his victims would cheerfully have strangled him. Few had the ability to match his verbal whiplash. The older he became, the more mercurial and irascible was his temperament.

2. He refers here to *The Gold Bug, The Raven*, and *The Murders in the Rue Morgue*.

3. This sounds like the rationalization of an alcoholic with paranoid tendencies. This statement is also a contradiction of one he made in a more lucid moment, the well-known admission that his drinking stemmed from his own insanity rather than the reverse.

4. Here is an interesting sidelight on the persuasive manner in which Maria Clemm managed to extract money, food, fuel, old clothes, and other necessities of life from all those to whom she applied for aid.

5. (Letter to John Allan, dated Baltimore, April 12, 1833)

It has been more than two years since you have assisted me, and more than three since you have spoken to me. I feel little hope that you will pay any regard to this letter, but still I cannot refrain from making one more attempt to interest you on my behalf. If you will only consider in what a situation I am placed you will surely pity me—without friends, without any means, consequently, of obtaining employment, I am perishing—absolutely perishing for want of aid. And yet, I am not idle—not addicted to any vice—nor have I committed any offence against society which would render me deserving of so hard a fate. For God's sake pity me and save me from destruction.

(signed) E.A. Poe

(Ostrom, Vol. 1, letter #36, p. 49.)

6. Of John Pendleton Kennedy, whose first novel, *Swallow Barn*, was quite popular in Poe's day, Arthur Hobson Quinn says, "The most important result of the contest was the friendship with John Pendleton Kennedy. Kennedy, then thirty-eight years of age, was one of the most respected men in Baltimore, and a prominent member of the bar. . . . It was not only his material help, but more particularly in the sympathy and understanding which only one writer can give to another that Kennedy helped Poe."

CHAPTER 21

1. Poe may have contracted malaria when he was in the army, stationed at Fort Moultrie. Most biographers, however, seem to agree that most of his sickness was the result of overwork and excessive drinking. We know today about the pernicious effects of anxiety on the mind and body, and certainly Poe was suffering from severe anxiety during most of his adult life.

2. Poe's grandmother received a pension from the federal government of $240 per annum in recognition of her husband's services to George Washington and the Continental Army.

3. We must never forget that as often as Poe used the word "passion" his definition of it was far different from that of ordinary men; it did not necessarily imply sexual content.

4. Is he rationalizing here, because he knows that they take such good care of him? It is hard to tell. He contradicts himself and exaggerates again and again.

5. It is the theory of Marie Bonaparte that Poe became terrified whenever he experienced even the remotest beginnings of sexual arousal under so-called normal conditions. If this is so, then perhaps he was beginning to have feelings of desire for Virginia which not only terrified him for their own sake, but complicated matters with implications of incest.

6. This is an interesting choice of words, probably a coincidence. But in psychoanalytic jargon, an imago is an infantile conception of a parent that is retained in the subconscious.

7. Poe was actually hired as an assistant to T. W. White, though the duties he performed made him the de facto editor.

8. About this letter Quinn says in part: "We seem to be looking into a naked soul, pouring out his passion, his craving for sympathy, his weakness of will, his willingness to sacrifice, his appeal that Mrs. Clamm will decide for him and Virginia" (Chapter X, p. 224). Poe wrote in part in his letter: ". . . My bitterest enemy would pity me now could he but read my heart— My last my last my only hold on life is cruelly torn away—I have not desire to live and *will not* . . . . Adieu my dear Aunty, I *cannot advise you.* Ask Virginia. Leave it to her. Let me have, under her own hand, a letter bidding me *good bye*—forever—and I may die—my heart will break—but I will say no more . . . . FOR VIRGINIA, My love, my own sweetest Sissy, my darling little wifey, think well before you break the heart of your cousin Eddy." (Ostrom, Vol. 1, letter 48, dated Richmond, Aug. 29, 1835, pp. 69-71.)

9. This clearly indicates that they would not share a bedroom.

CHAPTER 22

1. When Poe first assumed editorship of the *Southern Literary Messenger* it had a relatively small circulation of approximately 700 local subscriptions. During his short association with the magazine he more than quadrupled its readership, and in so doing established himself as the most discerning critic in America. His reviews attracted attention even in England. His editorial instincts were uncanny.

2. Aristocractic gentlemen of the South were known to challenge editors to duels and perforate their bodies with bullets, after having their fragile egos wounded by literary darts.

3. Not only does this statement clearly indicate the nature of Poe's love for Virginia, it also gives evidence of John Allan's influence. He was, in effect, displaying an attitude toward her exactly like that of his foster father's toward him: that Poe should do Virginia's thinking for her and make major life decisions for her.

4. *Blackwood's Edinburgh Review* was a prestigious British magazine which Poe regarded very highly.

5. Although congressional debate over the matter prevented Americans from getting there first, Jeremiah N. Reynolds' arguments were directly responsible for the first American Antarctic expedition.

6. Poe gave Burton more than his money's worth. While in his employ, supposedly as a writer only, he found himself eased into editorial duties. His name on the masthead of the magazine meant something. Billy Burton knew perfectly well that Poe's name lent prestige to his otherwise second-rate magazine. While working for *Burton's Gentleman's Magazine*, Poe wrote and published in its pages *The Man that Was Used Up, The Fall of the House of Usher, William Wilson, Morella, Conversation of Eiros and Charmion* [an intriguing science-fiction/fantasy piece about the destruction of the earth after the collision with a comet], the poems *To Ianthe in Heaven* and *Spirits of the Dead*. He also wrote reviews, articles, and essays, such as his curious *Philosophy of Furniture* in which he coined the popular phrase, "an aristocracy of dollars." His reviews are little read today because most of the works he wrote about were so bad that they justifiably faded into oblivion.

7. Scholars would disagree with this point. Roderick Usher was far more of a psychological self-portrait than a physical one.

8. A contract for *Tales of the Grotesque and Arabesque* was signed with the firm of Lea & Blanchard at the end of September 1839. The book was published in December. Poe was to receive no royalties unless the book made a profit.

9. Henry B. Hirst was a hard-drinking lawyer and poet, John Sartain a transplanted English engraver with a fondness for absinthe. Both had the reputation of being convivial carousers.

10. This is probably a bit of an exaggeration, due largely to Poe's state of mind when he wrote the lines. It is a fact that after he left *Burton's* his output declined. Yet it was during this period that he produced his tale, *The Man of the Crowd*, described by Hervey Allen as "... a curious combination of a 'hero' under the effect of remorse for a crime, and the scenes of London which Poe recollected from his sojourn there with the Allans now grotesquely recalled through the cloud and pall of a dream." (*Israfel*, Vol. 2, pp. 478-9.)

CHAPTER 23

1. It is ironic to think that Poe should have regarded the thirty-second year of his life as one of "his older years," but it proved to be true.

2. At that time tuberculosis was a paradox. A known killer, it was feared as cancer would be in the twentieth century, and as unmentionable as venereal disease. Yet its victims, with their waxen complexions, unnaturally glistening eyes, and flushed cheeks, were looked upon as romantic ideals as they languidly wasted away. And certainly the popular, nineteenth-century theme of the consumptive heroine gives us ample evidence of that attitude.

3. This description almost seems as if Poe were "recalling" the eyes of the mother he never really knew.

4. This is an intriguing paragraph, because it clearly describes the awakening of sexual desire in Poe. If the theories put forth by Marie Bonaparte are even partly correct, this would tend to validate them. In other words, Virginia was now doomed to die of her consumption; therefore it was safe to have sexual relations with her without endangering her life by so doing. Whether he actually consummated his marriage is unclear.

5. Actually, after this Poe did fifty pieces for *Graham's Magazine* including *The Masque of the Red Death*, which is quite significant, for it was during this period that Virginia was frequently hemorrhaging and succumbing to a kind of terrifying Red Death. Perhaps, as he mentioned earlier, he was also inspired by an old Scottish legend, but there can be no denying the influence exerted by Virginia's declining health.

CHAPTER 24

1. This is not a misprint. During the last seven or eight years of his life he referred to Maria Clemm as his mother, since she had become his de facto mother.

2. Sydney Smith, original editor of the prestigious *Edinburgh Review*, wrote in the year 1803: "In the four quarters of the globe, who reads an American book, or goes to an American play, or looks at an American picture or statue?"

332

3. Louis A. Godey was editor of *Godey's Lady's Book*, a popular magazine of the mid-nineteenth century best known for its art reproductions and hand-colored fashion plates. The magazine was later merged with Sarah Josepha Hale's *Ladies' Magazine*. Mrs. Hale, who also published a number of Poe's writings, was an early feminist activist, an early advocate of the movement to establish a national day of Thanksgiving, and author of "Mary Had a Little Lamb."

4. "Groundling" is a term that goes back to Elizabethan England. It referred then to the lowest class of theater audiences, and developed into a pejorative, meaning individuals of inferior taste.

5. The "Laura Matilda School" was a contemptuous term among mid-nineteenth-century editors and critics used to denote a certain type of syrupy romance that was quite popular in the cheap fiction of the day.

CHAPTER 25

1. Maria Clemm kept careful track of all the money when it came in. She also cooked, cleaned, mended, and took in sewing to help keep the pot boiling. In addition to this she wrote query letters on Poe's behalf to editors, and when time permitted called on them in person. So, in effect, she was also his literary agent. When times were especially hard, she actually went out and foraged for whatever food she could find, even to the point of digging up edible roots and picking wild berries, fruits, and vegetables.

2. A characteristic symptom of tuberculosis is copious sweating at night.

3. To fully understand his increasing reference to Maria Clemm as "mother," his sonnet "To My Mother," written after Virginia's death, should be read. The first six lines are especially significant.
Because I feel that, in the heavens above,
  The angels, whispering to one another,
Can find, among their burning terms of love,
  None so devotional as that of "Mother,"
Therefore by that dear name I long have called you,
  You who are more than mother to me.

4. Richard Adams Locke, an earlier editor of *The New York Sun*, perpetrated a sensational hoax alleging that a super-telescope had been built which enabled scientists to see all sorts of flora and fauna on the surface of the moon. For full details, see Poe's essay on Locke, *Works* by Stedman & Woodberry, Vol. 8, pp. 136-146.

5. In Poe's day the term "shilling" was still commonly used to denote twenty-five cents. The expression "two bits" did not appear on the scene until much later.

6. There is evidence which indicates that Poe might have had bachelor quarters on Ann Street at this time, because the apartment at 130 Greenwich Street was too small for the three of them. If this is so, he probably used the Ann Street room strictly as sleeping quarters.

7. Bloomingdale Road has long since become Broadway, and the Brennan farmhouse referred to below was located at what is West 84th Street between Broadway and Amsterdam Avenue, on New York's Upper West Side.

8. It was said that this weeping willow tree grew from a sprig taken from the tomb of Napoleon Bonaparte.

9. In the jargon of the day a "mechanical paragrapher" was a kind of all-around columnist and general assistant editor. It was a come-down for Poe, having been such a powerful editor in the past. But he needed money desperately and he took the job without complaint.

10. The "someone" was probably John Augustus Shea, a former commissary clerk at West Point who became a friend of Poe. Shea made a slight name for himself in the literary world, and often helped Poe to place his writings. (See *Israfel*, Vol. 2, p. 631, f.n. #702.)

11. Willis's introduction to *The Raven* reads as follows:

We are permitted to copy (in advance of publication) from the 2nd No. of *The American Review*, the following remarkable poem by EDGAR POE. In our opinion, it is the most effective single example of "fugitive poetry" ever published in this country; and unsurpassed in English poetry for subtle conception, masterly ingenuity of versification, and consistent, sustaining an imaginative lift and "pokerishness." It is one of these "dainties bred in a book" which we *feed* on. It will stick to the memory of everybody who reads it.

CHAPTER 26

1. The colleague was actually Charles F. Briggs, co-founder, with John Bisco, of *The Broadway Journal*. Strictly speaking he was Poe's employer. They eventually became bitter enemies, which would explain why Poe does not mention his name here, even though his ego couldn't resist the quote.

2. It is not hard to understand how he felt. Imagine his reaction upon receiving the following praise from Elizabeth Barrett after she learned that he had dedicated *The Raven and Other Poems* to her, calling her "the noblest of your sex.":

... may I thank you as another reader would—thank you for this vivid writing, this power, which is felt? Your "Raven" has produced a sensation—a "fit horror"—here in England. Some of my friends are taken by the fear of it, & some by the music—I hear of persons haunted by the "Nevermore"—and one acquaintance of mine who has the misfortune of possessing a "bust of Pallas," never can bear to look at it in the twilight. I think you will like to know that our great poet, Mr. Browning, the author of "Paracelsus" & the "Bells and Pomegranates," was struck much by the rhythm of that poem. . . .

3. This refers to Auguste Dupin, the fictional detective-hero of *The Murders in the Rue Morgue* and *The Mystery of Marie Roget*.

4. In *Eiros and Charmion* a comet collides with the earth. All the nitrogen in the atmosphere is consumed. In the ensuing conflagration all life on the planet is destroyed.

5. The Poes now lived at 195 Broadway, a short distance from the office of *The Broadway Journal*.

6. This is the period during which Poe began drinking more heavily than ever before. It was the beginning of his final decline. When drunk he was unstable, hostile, and surly; all of his frustrations, anger, and bitterness overflowed. Many who had been subject to his stinging literary assaults took advantage of his inclinations to retaliate on a personal level.

7. The sickness was usually due to excessive drinking.

8. Many of the physical characteristics of the women who attracted Poe were shared by the mother he scarcely knew. Was it a coincidence that Frances Osgood also suffered from tuberculosis?

9. This is Poe's projection. Frances Osgood was a coquette and a flirt. When she saw how much he apparently loved her she became alarmed and fled. She was, however, in the long run a loyal friend, not only to Poe, but to Virginia and Maria Clemm.

10. The scandal reached such proportions that the well-known feminist, Margaret Fuller, appointed herself head of a committee, called upon Poe, and firmly but courteously demanded that he return all of Frances Osgood's letters. He was hurt and angry, but he complied.

11. Thomas Holley Chivers was a wealthy poet, mystic, and physician from Georgia. A strange, peripatetic character, he was once referred to by Poe as "one of the best and worst poets in America." After Poe died, Chivers wrote a worshipful memoir of his friend.

12. On Valentine's Day, 1846, Virginia wrote the following verse to Edgar. In the fashion of the time, note the first letter of each line.
Ever with thee I wish to roam—
Dearest my life is thine.
Give me a cottage for my home,
And a rich old cypress vine,
Removed from the world with its sin and care
And the tattling of many tongues.
Love alone shall guise us when we are there—

Love shall heal my weakened lungs;
And Oh, the tranquil hours we'll spend,
Never wishing that others may see!
Perfect ease we'll enjoy, without thinking to lend
Ourselves to the world and its glee—
Ever peaceful and blissful we'll be.

13. Thomas Dunn English was an editor, a friend who became a bitter enemy, and whose allegations of plagiarism against Poe triggered off a literary feud. It culminated in Poe's libel suit against the *Mirror* in which English's attack appeared, and in which Poe won damages and costs of $492.

14. The facts have been obscured by time.

15. See note 13.

16. Mary Gove, a mesmerist, phrenologist, and dear friend of the Poes, did a great deal to help them materially during this bitter and tragic winter. Mary Louise Shew was a nurse and friend of the Poes, who similarly brought them money, food, and other necessities while caring for Poe and Virginia.